I0788165

defiance and DEDICATION

Untouchable

For Sara, because fuck Brad.

Series so Far

Rules and Roses
Changes and Chocolate
Keys and Kisses
Whispers and Wishes
Hangovers and Holidays
Brazen and Breathless
Trials and Tiaras
Graduation and Gifts
Defiance and Dedication
Songs and Sweethearts
Legacy and Lovers
Farewells and Forever

Foreword

Dear Reader,

Welcome to book nine of the Untouchable series. Nine books. It hardly seems possible that we've had that many and yet, there are only so few left after this book.

When I first started the series, as I've often said, I imagined a trilogy. That quickly grew to ten books before I'd even finished the first one. Not all that long ago, I added two more books. Two more because I wanted to do the tale of Frankie, Archie, Jake, Coop, and Ian justice. I didn't want to rush past moments that were so important. Just to be clear—that means we're on book nine of twelve.

For the majority of seven books, we traveled with these five best friends as they became lovers over the course of their senior year. In turn, they became a real family unit and eventually graduated high school. They hit a lot of challenges along the way, faced some terrible truths, and eventually overcame even the worst of their obstacles. In the last book, we got a huge summer hurrah for them after meeting Frankie's dad for the first time.

It was both a glorious coming of age and bittersweet, because the real world was out there waiting for them and they were ready to conquer it.

College is not high school. You're not living at home anymore. They may not be in a dorm, but they also have so many other challenges facing them beginning with the accident that occurred at the end of the last book.

I can honestly say that this was hands down my most challenging Frankie book to write. The kids are growing up. Growth and change are not always easy, nor is it pain-free. I have loved every moment of their journey and this one is no different despite how difficult the journey became.

On the home front, I had surgery to repair a herniated disc in my spine and I've been in rehab coming off months of bedrest and rebuilding atrophied muscles. I'm also prepping to move my kid across the pond so he can go to school in Wales for his college years. Talk about challenges and changes.

Through all of this, a very dear friend of mine has gone through a health crisis of her own. We joked in some ways we were twinning, and yet, we got the best news possible following her surgeries.

I've referred to my #girlgang before, but I truly believe I have one of the best ever. They always have my back and they're more than willing to listen to me whine and complain as they are to cheer me on and I'm very much the same for them.

Being a writer can be a lonely existence, but building worlds that other people come to love as much as you do? That's priceless. If I could list every single person I want to thank right now, we'd be here for days and you're not here for that, you're here to find out what happens next.

Just know if you're reading this right now, thank you for reading, for reviewing, for reveling, and cheering. Thanks for swearing, laughing, crying, and hopefully *not* breaking your kindle. This series wouldn't be the same without any of you.

I rather doubt we need these housekeeping notes anymore, but I'd rather be safe than sorry.

For those of you who have never read a reverse harem before, first let me thank you for picking this up and giving it a shot. Second, a reverse harem means the heroine will not make a choice in this book or any other between the guys in her life. It may take her a while to reach that conclusion, but it's the journey that drives it. There are many ways to frame this kind of relationship, currently reverse harem fits it very well.

Also, this is the ninth book in a series. If you haven't read the first eight, I encourage you to pause here and go grab them. While there may be no specific happy endings at the end of each of these books, there will be one to the whole series, that I promise you. Some of these books will have cliffhangers, largely due to the size of the story, but the happy ending has to be earned as part of the journey.

Again, thank you for reading and being on this journey with Frankie and the boys. I can't believe I can say this again, but you really haven't seen anything yet.

xoxo

Heather

Chapter One
SHIT HAPPENS

Frankie

My head hurt. It really, really hurt. The smell of antiseptic burned my nostrils. Worse, the beeping of machines seemed to add to the dull thud hammering inside my skull. I debated rolling over but my stomach revolted, so I stayed put. I had zero interest in puking.

The air was cold and warm. Weird. It took a minute for the fact my eyes were closed to even register. Where did I get this damn headache? Ugh, I started to stretch out a hand. There was always someone curled up nearby, maybe they could grab me some aspirin, but I didn't find anyone.

Suppressing a groan of frustration, I peeled my eyes open. The door knocker banging away in my brain got considerably heavier and louder. The smell of antiseptic seemed to increase and I swore I could taste it in the back of my throat.

I hated hospitals.

Hated them.

I hadn't been a fan of them before Homecoming, and after... a shudder raced through me. Waking up there, groggy and out of it, all of that helplessness and shock bled from fresh wounds. I squeezed my eyes shut.

Maybe if I refused it, pushed past, it would go away.

I'd survived Mitch. That was in the past. The guys and I... oh the guys. I frowned and forced my eyes open again. Why was I in the hospital? I tried to reach for the reason, but the fog in my brain swept the information away. Like it was right there on the tip of my tongue. The IV in the back of my hand stung when I gripped the rail.

The cold metal grounded me and I licked my dry lips. Too dry. Even my throat hurt. It took me a minute to focus my eyes. I was in a room. That was something. The beeping machines were really annoying. Didn't they turn those off? At least the sound? Also, why was...

A grunt of sound in the corner and I turned my head. A smile stretched my sore mouth and I ignored the headache. Coop. He was sprawled back in the chair like someone had dropped him in it bonelessly.

It was one of those that would stretch out for sleep. He kind of hung off the end with one of his legs straight out and the other bent, the foot on the floor like he was ready to go somewhere. He looked—great, if tired.

"Coop." Oh my voice came out a solid croak and I coughed. I glanced around, but there wasn't even a cup within reach. "Coop..."

At my second call, his eyes fluttered open, and his head lifted a fraction from the fist he'd braced it on. Those gray-green eyes I loved so much were as unfocused as I felt. I probably shouldn't laugh at him, not when there was an indentation mark on his face from his own knuckles. I definitely shouldn't laugh when he frowned so fiercely the sleepiness fled from his expression.

"Frankie?"

If I thought I was croaky, I had nothing on him. His normally deep voice seemed rougher and far more raw. There was an ache in the word that made me want to fumble off the bed and pull him in for a hug. I had cables and wires and tubes sticking out of me for some reason.

Even a quick sweep around me didn't reveal any quick way to ditch them and climb out of the bed. I had to settle for thrusting out my free hand, the one without the IV sticking in the back of it. Coop shot to his feet and his hand clasped mine in a grip so tight, it actually hurt.

"Hey," I whispered as I tugged him closer. It took no effort on my part at all, I went from holding his hand to enveloped in his hug.

"Holy shit," he whispered. "You're really here."

"Of course, I'm here." Yeah, I was a few marbles loose at the moment, I swore the fog was eating away at my thoughts. The damn marching band playing in my head didn't help either.

My eyes drifted closed though as he buried his face in my hair. The scent of him filled my lungs. Coffee. Chocolate. Coop. All together it was home. He was home.

We sat like that forever. His hand trembled as he stroked my hair. It was that single thing that kept me from demanding what was going on. Well, that and the softness of his shirt, the warmth of his hug, and the smell of coffee tickling my nose. I probably shouldn't push it, considering I'd wanted to throw up just a few minutes ago. Still, I might legit kill for coffee.

His shoulders shook, this time with laughter, and he finally loosened his grip to lean back. Letting go of my hand, he dropped the rail so he could sit on the edge and then he gathered my hand back in his.

I met his gaze and looked at him. Really looked.

"What's wrong?" Before he could call me on the stupidity of that question, I gave a small shake of my head. Small, because the first shake just increased the slam of the drumbeat against my temples. A droplet hit my lap and I glanced down. Runny noses were—oh, I was bleeding.

Coop pressed a cloth gently to my nose. "Easy," he murmured. "We got this."

It was sweet but.. "Coop, what happened?"

"What's the last thing you remember?" The guarded tone and the careful expression set off warning bells. The cacophony joined the rest of the rock band that had taken over for the marching one to hammer away at my brain.

"Um..." I frowned, focusing on him as I tried to get my thoughts sorted. The foggy feeling hadn't gone away, if anything, it intensified. "I... what is the last thing I remember?"

The corners of his mouth quirked a bit higher. "I asked first."

"Ha ha." I would have smacked his chest, but he still had hold of one of my hands and the other had the IV in it. Each time I flexed my fingers, it hurt. Why did I not notice it and then when did it begin to throb?

"Frankie?"

Right. Last thing I remembered. I snapped my focus back up to him and frowned. "We—we drove out to see my grandparents." That filtered through the fog, a single piece of information like it got lost and wandered out on its own. "Right, we went to the Hamptons."

It was like putting together the pieces of a clear puzzle where the colors and images only filled in as I snapped the disparate sections together. The more I thought about it all, the more it hurt.

"We were spending the weekend out there." An image of that first night after we'd arrived when Patience asked us to get dressed flitted across my mind like an exotic bird bursting out of the mist. It really did fall into the category of one of these things was not like the other. "We had to get dressed up for dinner, so strange. They change clothes three times a day and that's only cause they're on vacation. In the city or in more formal settings it might be five times."

Insane. Absolutely insane. Archie's amusement at my quiet rant about it while I looked in the closet of dresses they just *happened* to have on hand since I hadn't packed *anything* remotely this fancy had been the only thing keeping me from actually getting mad.

"It was absurd. Like a theatre of it. Why did we have to get into fancy clothes to eat dinner at home? I thought at first we were going out, but nope... just dinner in a formal dining room. Archie was in a nice tux and so was his grandfather. So was mine."

I shook my head again. The dull thump had quieted some. Coop's small smile had a kind of sad glimmer to it, but he didn't interrupt me.

"Anyway, it was just weird. But I refused to change for lunch the following day and my grandfather harrumphed his way through the meal." Then he did something really sweet. He hadn't changed for lunch the following day and when Patience glared at both of us, he just lifted his glass to me. It was probably the most warmth we'd ever shared.

Grandpa Ted could get him to smile. The two of them could ramble on for hours about various subjects. But whenever I offered something, Ted would respond and my grandfather would frown into his glass. It stung, more than a little. Patience begged me to—well, have more patience and what stunned me more was that Archie said the same thing that first night.

Coop's frown deepened as I relayed that. "Maybe they both saw something I didn't, but at lunch on Sunday, when he didn't change and instead just sat at the table with me. It was like—we finally had something in common we could share." Not that we were going to be holding hands and sharing life stories, but some of the chasm between us closed. A little.

I'd take it.

More, the look on Patience's face had been its own reward and Archie...

"What next?" Coop asked, prompting me as though I'd gone quiet. Maybe I had.

"Um," I said as I searched my memory. The moment he asked, the fog rolled in and swarmed the thoughts until it was just me, alone and drifting. "I don't know, Coop. My head hurts. My mouth is dry...I swear every muscle in my body is sore. What's going on?"

He scrubbed a hand over his face. Interlocking our fingers, he gave my hand a squeeze and I gripped him tighter. For as long as I could remember, when something bad happened, he held my hand. Good things, too, but it was when I needed steadiness, he shared it with me.

Fear crawled through me. "Coop?"

"No easy way to say this," he began, then paused for a breath. The tension ratcheting up my spine pulled taut. Finally, he continued, "You're in the hospital."

I glared at him. "No shit." Only the fact the faint movement of his lips could barely be called a smile kept me from pushing it. "Talk to me," I begged him. Because the playfulness had long since drained out of the moment. "What happened?" I had to bite off the question of why was I here? If he were going to supply that easily, he would have already.

"It's been a few months," he admitted and my stomach bottomed out even as cold raced over my skin. Goosebumps prickled my flesh. I dug my nails into his hand, waiting for the punchline. "We've been here every damn day. At least one of us, often all of us."

"That isn't funny," I whispered, and his expression turned so tragic tears spilled out of my eyes.

"I'm not joking, Beautiful," he whispered in a voice that held so much apology, I swore my heart cracked. "It's been months. We've been waiting and waiting for you to wake up."

Wake up.

"From what?"

Indecision rippled across his expression. "The doctors warned us..."

I exhaled slowly. "Cooper." I never called him by his full name. He winced. "Just tell me. Because right now, you're scaring the hell out of me."

"You've been here for months." Here. As in the hospital? Before I could ask though, he added, "Unconscious for months."

Disbelief flashed through me like a summer storm, fierce and loud. Even my headache seemed to take a backseat to the horror unfolding within me. "What do you mean months?"

"Exactly what I said, Beautiful." He cupped my cheek and the absolute candor in his eyes coupled with a complete absence of humor threatened to crush me. How could I have been in a hospital for months? "There was an accident..."

The scream of metal sheering and the explosive crash as glass gave way. Horns. Shouting. Maybe me and—

"...and all we've been able to do is wait for you to wake up." I missed some of what he said and at the same time, the disjointed thoughts pushed at the fog.

Wrenching the wheel.

Horns blaring.

I licked at my lips again. I needed water. I needed... "Can you get me water?" I whispered.

"Of course," he said and gave my hand a squeeze before he stood. I lifted my hand to touch my forehead. The bleeding from my nose had stopped at some point. The taste of it was still in my mouth. It didn't help with how dry my mouth was on top of it.

Months?

I'd been in the hospital for months.

I fell back against the pillows.

But what about school? What about my grandparents? What about...?

"Yeah, I don't want to hear that," Jake shouted from somewhere beyond the room. He had to be pretty upset if he was that loud. "Find someone who knows."

My heart sped up. "Coop..."

"Yeah?" he glanced at me from the little bathroom where he was filling the pitcher with water.

Orange metal buckling.

"Where's..."

The blast of an eighteen-wheeler's horn.

"...Archie?"

We'd gone to my grandparents together. The accident.

Coop glanced away as he shut off the water.

"I mean it," Jake yelled and I glanced at the closed door. Who was he yelling at? Coop didn't seem concerned. So maybe this was normal behavior? But still...I kept waiting for the door to open.

"Did you tell them I'm awake?" I asked and Coop shot me a guilty smile.

"I should have, but I was kind of caught up in the fact you were talking to me again. The silent treatment doesn't work for us, you gotta promise to never do that again."

Guilt swarmed me. "I promise it wasn't on purpose."

"I know, Sweetheart," he said with the saddest smile. "But I'm boring as fuck on my own and you didn't laugh at a single joke and I swear, I was going for my best material."

A weak laugh escaped me, but his eyes didn't brighten at all. If anything, I swore he looked sadder.

"Coop, you're scaring me."

He crossed back to me and held out the ugly little peach, plastic cup. "I don't mean to scare you, Babe."

Babe? "Where's Archie?" At his distressed look and glance toward the door, I focused on it, too. Were they all three going to walk inside? Jake's voice climbed, his tone agitated but I couldn't quite make out the words. Whatever answer someone gave him, he was *not* happy about it. I half-expected Coop to go and see what was wrong but he didn't move.

I'd been in the Ferrari. On the way back from the Hamptons.

Flashes exploded out of the fog. Zooming past cars as the Ferrari raced faster and faster. Zipping around big rigs. Keeping an eye on the odometer... where was a cop when...

The crash of metal and the screaming—me screaming—as the vehicle flipped ripped through me. For the longest moment, I hung there, suspended by my seat belt and I couldn't breathe.

Where was Archie?

Chapter Two

REPORT A PROBLEM OR AN EMERGENCY

Frankie

I snapped my eyes open and sat up abruptly. The world swam sickeningly. The smell was the same antiseptic of the hospital. The beeping noises were there. I had an IV, there was a monitor hooked to my finger. I wasn't in a room though and Coop had vanished.

Fuck, my head hurt.

"Frankie Curtis and Archie Standish?" Jake said. "They were brought here?" The sound of his voice was like a gift from beyond the curtain.

"We're the next of kin and emergency contacts." The crispness of Jeremy's tone brooked zero arguments.

"She's in bay seven," a woman answered them and I glanced around the cubicle I was in. I guessed this was bay seven. The curtain got yanked back and relief swarmed through me at Jake and Coop both standing there, concern rolling off them in waves.

A dream.

It had been a damn dream or maybe a nightmare. Jake slowed only long enough to sweep a look at me from head to toe. "Baby Girl," he muttered and then he scooped me up into a hug. The monitor started beeping faster as Jake crushed me to him, albeit gently. The moment my arms were around his neck, I swore I felt every damn bump and bruise on my body.

I didn't care.

The throb in my head gave me a bit of pause, but I didn't let go of Jake. A light hand on mine and I opened my eyes to find Coop right there and he pressed his lips to my forehead. "You look like shit," he murmured.

"I look better than you," I retorted, and a smile replaced some of the worry in his eyes. My appearance must really be cause for concern though, because Ian frowned when he saw me. I swore he traced his gaze over every inch of my face, closing in to almost complete the circle as Jake kept me close to him.

"Ease up on her," Ian ordered and Jake grumbled.

"I'm not hurting her, asshole," he muttered but he said it with a smile as he moved me back to sitting on the bed. Like Coop and Ian though, Jake paused as he ran his gaze over my face. I was pretty sure I'd hit my head when I'd taken out that guardrail.

Panic flashed through me, and I straightened in the seat. "The other car..."

"In a moment, Miss Frankie," Jeremy said firmly as he appeared with a young physician. "Let this doctor look you over and if you would be so kind as to tell me where Mr. Archie is."

"He wasn't in the accident." My head hurt. My body hurt. But my memory was fine.

"But he went with you," Coop said slowly and shot a look at Jeremy.

"The service called about the Ferrari. Indicated it had been in an accident and all passengers had been brought here." Jeremy's frown deepened.

The doctor he'd brought with him cleared his throat. "Miss Curtis?"

I nodded to him. "I know, I was unconscious and I probably have a concussion." That had already occurred to me, but at the same time...

"Jeremy, Archie had to leave with..."

"Me," Edward announced as he and Archie arrived from the other side of the curtain, and I ignored him but let out a sigh when I locked eyes with Archie. Seriously, even though I knew he hadn't been in the car. Even though it had been *me* driving, it was still a relief to see him. "Archie and I had some business..."

Circling Jeremy and giving his shoulder a quick squeeze, Archie moved to where the doctor was standing. "Babe, don't you ever scare the hell out of me again."

Tears welled up in my eyes, but the doctor's entire demeanor shifted. "That's enough, all of you. Miss Curtis just woke up, let's not crowd the room, at least four of you need to leave."

"Not moving," Archie and Jake said in the exact same tone.

Rolling his eyes, Coop said, "I spotted a coffee shop across the street. You want something?"

Even with my rolling stomach, I did. "Please. And maybe a burger or something?" I was suddenly starving. Jeremy gave Archie another once over and then nodded.

"We'll bring you coffee, Miss Frankie and something small to eat depending on what the doctors say. Once we get you home, I'll fix a proper meal."

With that, he ushered everyone not named Jake and Archie out. Jake's hand was locked on mine and Archie pivoted to face the doctor. Honestly, I wouldn't want to have been him as they stared at him for the length of the exam. A nurse came in. Then there were more reports. A police officer stuck his head in to check on me.

There would have to be an accident report.

All at once the tears flooded my eyes again and I looked at Archie. "I killed your car."

"I don't care about the car," he told me. "I care about you."

That wasn't true. "You love that car."

"It's a car, Babe," he said, narrowing his eyes at me. "I can replace the car."

But it was a classic, and before I could go on, the doctor had a light in my eyes and they wanted to look at the x-rays they'd done. Apparently, I'd also gotten a CT scan. When had they had time for all of this?

"Well, you definitely have a concussion," he said, then went over the x-rays on the screen. Nothing broken, but I'd definitely bruised the hell out of myself. Soft tissue damage. The aftermarket airbag had done its job. I half tuned out of the conversation until the doctor said something about me staying overnight.

"No."

Mutiny filled Archie's expression and I pointed a finger at him then looked at the doctor. "I'd much rather go home."

"You lost consciousness," the doctor said with a firm tone. "We're going to need a few more tests and I'm not comfortable sending you home this soon."

I hated this, but Jake linked our fingers again. "We'll stay with you. Watch Archie upgrade you to some premium suite."

"I'll do it, too." Archie already had his phone out and the doctor gave us all a look. I had a feeling we were irritating him. But no sooner did he and the nurse leave with word they'd have me moved up to a room shortly, than Jake rounded on Archie.

"Why the fuck was she driving back alone?"

"Jake," I said as Archie glanced up, eyebrows raised.

"Because I had to be somewhere else, and Frankie wanted to drive the car."

I winced.

"It's fine, Babe," Archie repeated and leaned over to cup my face. "Seriously, I don't care about the car. I care that they had to cut you out of it. I care that you were in a wreck in the first place."

"I care that she was alone," Jake said, but when I squeezed his hand some of the tension bled from him. He glanced at me, "I care."

"I know," I whispered. "But Archie and Edward had some things to do, and I didn't want to cut my visit short."

"You wanted to give us time to talk without you there," Archie said lightly as if my reticence hadn't been a clear ploy. "And you wanted more time with your grandparents."

And I'd wanted to drive his car. He'd left with Edward on a helicopter after he'd tucked the keys into my hand and kissed me soundly. Not even a word about being good to his car or not scratching it. Nothing. He'd trusted me to get it back to the city.

"Stop it," he and Jake said in the same tone, and I groaned but kept silent this time. Coop, Ian, and Jeremy returned, along with Edward, before they moved me to a room. I had no idea why Edward had come back, unless he and Archie weren't done.

When he found out I was staying the night, he headed out of the curtained area with his phone and Archie in hot pursuit. If my head hadn't hurt so bad, I might have laughed. The longer I was awake though, the more it hurt. Maybe I should stay the night.

The hospital room—if you could call it that—was a great deal more like a hotel room at a five-star hotel. Four-star if you asked Archie, but I caught the hint of a smile. Jeremy got us all settled, then made arrangements for fold out cots for the guys.

I wasn't allowed any pain medication, but they gave me something for the nausea. I finally got to drink my coffee. Not much, but some. Jake slid right up onto the bed with me, and I curled up against him. My face hurt, but his shirt was comfy. I was out before the thought fully registered.

The next time I roused, food was there, and the guys were playing some game on their phones. We ate—burgers, bless Jeremy cause no way this was hospital food—and drank. The nurse came in and checked my vitals. They also checked my responsiveness and how my headache was doing.

I only managed about half the food, before my stomach revolted. That was fine, I was back to sleep before long. As much as my head hurt, I was surprised I could sleep. It was well into the evening when the police officers came to see me.

They had questions, but assured me I didn't have to answer tonight.

"I appreciate that," I told them. "Honestly, I don't understand what happened. It was a great drive, then there was a car that cut me off and I nearly hit them but when I tapped my brakes—nothing happened." It had freaked me out a little.

Archie frowned.

"I thought maybe I'd done something wrong, so I just switched lanes to keep from hitting the other car..." That just seemed to cause a domino effect. I couldn't even place the exact sequence of events. Some of it was sketchy.

"The brakes didn't work?" Archie repeated and I tried to smile at him. I'd shifted gears, and I'd used the clutch, but something... something had been off.

"Maybe I did something wrong, but they got more and more sluggish about responding, and I tried to slow down, but there's a slight downhill incline." Nothing I did slowed me down. I'd moved around cars, but it had taken all of my concentration and then I'd had to make a choice, hit the slow traffic in front of me or take the Ferrari off road.

"I want the car looked at," Edward said from the doorway, and it was the first time I'd realized he was still here. He and Jeremy both stood there, along with Grandpa Ted.

When had he gotten there? Oh crap, I hoped he hadn't called my grandparents. The cops stated the investigation would continue, but no one had been hurt except me. I'd smashed the Ferrari into a guardrail, using that to slow my momentum down.

The screaming along the side of the car might haunt me for a while. If not, forever. Still, there was something unsettling about the cops and the fact they'd asked me three times if I was certain about the brakes.

I wasn't an idiot.

They weren't even gone a full minute before Jake pivoted to face us. "I don't like them."

"Me neither," Ian said. Like the other guys, he had a taut worried look on his face. "Is there a way to get the car from them?"

"I'll take care of it," Edward said before Archie could, and Archie cut him a look.

"I don't recall inviting you into this conversation, much less asking you for an assist."

"You should never have to ask me for that," Edward told him and I glanced at Coop who just shook his head at me. Archie's dad had been making an effort. That whole, he might or might not be my sperm donor had been traumatizing enough, but the one semi-decent thing to come out of it was the wakeup call for "Eddie."

So far, I hadn't seen him with my mother and hopefully I never would. The fact he'd shown up while we were visiting my grandparents had rang a few warning bells, but Grandpa Ted was also there, so it made a certain amount of sense. Or were they staying at Grandpa Ted's house? That whole thing was kind of fuzzy.

I'd loved being there with Archie. It might be fun to go back the following summer with all of us.

"Wait for me," Archie was saying before he glanced down at me. "You okay if I go work on this, Babe?"

"I'm just going to be boring and sleep," I told him and then smiled when he pressed a kiss very gently to my forehead.

"You're not boring, even when you're asleep. Take care of that beautiful brain of yours and that great big heart."

"My heart is just fine, it has four guardian angels to protect it." It was kind of sappy, but after everything that happened, I needed sappy.

"Take care of our girl," Archie said as he gave me another kiss. "I'll be back soon. I promise."

Then he was out the door with his father. Jeremy left soon after with Grandpa Ted. Jake surrendered his spot in the bed to Coop and I glanced over at Ian.

"You okay?"

"I'm fine, Angel. I'm too wound up to sleep. Let Coop hold you for a while. I'll take my turn at home."

"Well, that wasn't what I meant," I said as Coop settled in behind me to spoon and wrapped himself against my back. The steady thump of his heart settled my own. "I just..."

"I'm fine, Angel," Ian promised as he leaned forward and brushed a finger down my cheek. "You gave us a scare. Accidents are bad enough, we don't need anything happening to you.'"

"I totally did it for the attention," I told him, determined to see those eyes smile. Jake hadn't stopped worrying and there was just this low-level hum of aggravation to him. He'd been like that over his dad, too. Coop seemed the most relaxed, but he also tended to bury his responses until everything was fine and then he'd probably lose it a little.

We were alike that way.

But Ian, he and Archie both tore everything apart, looked at all the angles and they wouldn't let it go. I needed his smile right now, almost as much as I needed air. That bizarre dream still kind of hovered there, like a phantom memory of what could have been, and I'd prefer to skip that experience.

"Did you now?" Ian raised his brows. "Because we all know how much you love when we gang up on you."

I didn't roll my eyes, instead I batted them and ignored the way it irritated my headache. "I love when you all bang me, yes."

Surprise widened his eyes and laughter suddenly sparked as his mouth spread wide and he chuckled. Coop huffed behind me and a soft snicker from the far side of the room added a little more lightness to my day.

"You know," Jake began, but Ian shook his head.

"No, we're not banging her in the hospital, I don't care how nice this room is."

I couldn't help it, maybe I was a glutton for punishment, but I bit my lip. "Well, sex does release a lot of endorphins and those are nature's pain relievers."

"Good to know," Ian said, his tone firming. "We'll test that out after I spank you for that suggestion when you're feeling better."

A delighted shiver went through me at both the promise and his smile. That was better. I kind of ruined it by yawning, but all three of the guys chuckled and relaxed.

"Go to sleep, Angel," Ian ordered before kissing me. "Feel better. We'll be right here."

The tension in the room began to leak out and it helped. A lot. Almost as much as Coop nuzzling a gentle kiss to the back of my neck stroking his fingers through my hair. I swore it was the barest touch and I was out before he'd done it four times.

Chapter Three

THE COMPANY WE KEEP

Archie

They ended up keeping Frankie for two nights, rather than just one. Despite the VIP room Edward arranged for her before I could and the fact that one of us, if not all of us, stayed right there with her—she was pretty pissed. I couldn't blame her, she had developed a particular dislike for hospitals after senior homecoming.

Fucking Mitch.

Still, with her reticence, I didn't score any points by backing the doctor. Of course, I wasn't alone in that support, which landed all four of us in the dog house. At least she was still talking to us because we didn't call Hank. Mitigating factors are a good thing. I didn't admit that the thought of calling him hadn't even crossed my mind.

I like the guy. We all do, but he's not cemented in that spot if he needs to know anything. Still, I'd seen the Ferrari. It was a damn miracle of engineering she was alive, much less only had a few bumps and bruises. Every time I pulled up the accident photos on my phone, fury blew through me like a hot wind.

In addition to the professionals that went over the car for transport, I had serviced the Ferrari regularly for the last two years. I'd had an expert and a guy who used to work for them building the damn things train me. The brakes shouldn't have failed. Anything could have gone wrong, but I needed the wreckage back to know.

The cops had asked if maybe Frankie just hadn't been able to handle the car, but that was bullshit. She was the safest driver I knew. In fact, knowing Frankie, she'd been under the speed limit because it was my car. The fact she kept trying to apologize fucking killed me.

A part of me wanted to shake her and another part of me just wanted to gather her up close and wrap her up in so much security nothing could touch her again.

Ever.

Ian was as bad as I was so I had no idea how he controlled his urges. Jake didn't pretend he was going to try. Instead, he focused on being right there with Frankie every step of the way. If Coop hadn't made him take a shower there in the hospital room and change, I doubt he would have. I didn't want to leave her either, but I also wanted to deal with this situation.

Deal with it so it never happened again. Failing brakes was problem enough. Failing brakes that endangered her? Unacceptable on all levels. It would have hurt her regardless of whether I'd been there. It didn't help that Jake remained pissed that I hadn't been there and that I hadn't let them know she'd be driving back on her own.

To be fair, I hadn't intended for that. But that fight would just have to wait for another day. As it was, I'd made the trip down to the police impound where they'd taken the wreckage of my car. Seeing the photos had been gut wrenching. Standing in front of it was nauseating.

"As you can see..." The accident investigator and the crime scene technical specialist spoke at length about their findings. Granted, it had only been four days since the accident and Frankie had been home for two. Flexing Standish weight got things done fast in the big city, too.

Maybe faster.

Edward standing right there engaged in discussion with the men kept them busy while I inspected the crushed remains of the vehicle. She wasn't wrong, I loved the Ferrari and seeing it in so many shattered pieces, metal sheered away, paint stripped—it was a sucker punch. Losing Frankie would have been a hundred thousand percent worse.

The call from the service to my phone asking me if I was all right sent fear bleeding through me. I'd walked out of the meeting with the lawyers and headed straight for the elevators. I hadn't even realized Edward had followed me until we reached the lobby.

All I got was the name of a hospital and the EMTs and fire department were on scene.

That had been the longest drive of my life, as we fought our way through traffic. I hadn't even realized the guys had been trying to get ahold of me until we'd arrived at the hospital.

"How long before this is released to our people?" Edward asked as I jerked my mind away from the destruction and the dangerously littered path of *what ifs* I'd been wandering down.

"I don't see why you can't have it by the end of the week. Our techs want a few more days to go over it and make sure they've documented everything. The insurance company has requested a full report as well."

Fuck the insurance company, but I got it. They needed to verify in triplicate before they paid out the car's value.

Assholes.

"I'd like it sooner rather than later," I informed them and stepped into the conversation Edward had been having on my behalf. Since his appearance in the Hamptons, he'd all but made himself available to me for everything. I hadn't even realized he was still at the hospital until I went to make arrangements for a car to take us home.

He'd done that.

Jeremy had set up everything so she could be comfortable. Minimal screen time, don't use her eyes, keep her comfortable. This wasn't her first concussion in the last twelve months, so the doctors wanted us to err on the side of caution. The airbag had bruised her face and left it burned but that didn't compare to the bruise across her chest from the seat belt strap.

Both were far preferable to the alternatives.

Edward, however, had not only arranged for our ride home. He'd stopped by two days running, both times bringing flowers for Frankie, as well as chocolate treats, as his excuse. He never stayed longer than a cup of coffee and a quick conversation with me, because both times she'd been asleep when he arrived.

I'd glanced at Jeremy after that first visit and raised a brow. "Any idea what he's up to?"

"None at all, Mr. Archie, but he bears watching."

Agreed. On all counts.

The investigator who'd joined us on the visit to the expired Ferrari, inclined his head toward me. "Understood, Mr. Standish, but we need to make sure we do a full and complete investigation. You'll have the wreckage back as soon as we're able to release it."

"Very well," Edward said as he dusted off his suit like being close to all these ruined cars had gotten it dirty by association. "If we haven't received word to retrieve it on Friday, expect our lawyers to be in touch. This accident has been a very unfortunate episode that we would all like to put behind us."

"I'm sure the young woman driving would like that, too," the investigator said and it wasn't my imagination, he gave me a measuring look. "Considering she's your son's girlfriend, maybe she really was in the wrong place at the wrong time."

"What's that supposed to mean?" I demanded, focusing on him.

"Archie..."

"Didn't ask you, Edward," I said, shutting him down. "I asked the investigator here. What exactly are you fishing for with that implication?"

"It wouldn't be the first time a wealthy young man tried to rid himself of a clingy girlfriend." The guy gave a shrug. "Not that I'm implying you did, but it could be construed that way, so you're better off letting us do our jobs."

What.

The.

Fuck.

"No," Edward said in a chill, arctic tone. "You straight out said it. No implication required. If you are looking for a way to charge my son, Officer, you'll be sorely disappointed."

"Detective," the man corrected but Edward barely spared him a look. He'd already dismissed him as ineffectual. Someone beneath our notice. It was a tactic I'd used myself, and often to great advantage, when dealing with a road block to what I wanted.

"As I said earlier, our attorneys will be in touch," Edward continued, catching my eye then nodding toward the gate we'd entered via. "Today, I think. I wouldn't want you to strain yourself or your credibility looking for something to fill out the fiction you've been constructing."

As much as I wanted to punch the guy, fuck it, I let Edward handle it and strode toward the gate. He was right. We weren't going to get anything here and they quite clearly had an agenda they were exploring. Next time, it would only be our attorneys they spoke to.

Well, *my* attorneys, not that I corrected Edward on that supposition. He'd been replaced on the board and in the day to day primary decision-making for Standish, but he was still employed.

He'd been working overtime to get Grandpa Ted and I to at least keep him involved in an active role. One where he would report to Grandpa Ted, not me. Not sure why he insisted on meeting with me so often. In fact, his visit in the Hamptons had not been about Standish at all, but finalizing all the paperwork transferring the house in Texas to me, as well as going over the properties in the city.

Apparently, we'd hurt his feelings by not asking to stay in one of his properties, but since he and Muriel had to divide several key real estate holdings, I was being given first dibs. It would almost be funny if it weren't so sad. At least the one thing Edward had stressed was he didn't want to put the properties in my name to hide them from Muriel.

He'd even offered to put them in Frankie's name, if I would feel better about it. I didn't, but I appreciated the sentiment. Once we were in the car, Edward looked at me. "Where to?"

"Back to the brownstone," I told him as I leaned back in my seat. I had a headache after that bullshit. The sun felt almost too bright, even with the sunglasses on and the tinted windows.

"Drink?"

"No," I told him as I rubbed the side of my head.

"Here," Edward stated crisply and passed me a bottle of water, despite my refusal, along with a small bottle of pills. "That's ibuprofen. Take it for the headache before it digs in. Then don't worry about this. I'll speak to the attorneys. They'll get it all sorted out then contact you about where you want it taken. You want a chance to pull the whole thing apart yourself, don't you?"

I stared at him a beat. Who the hell was he and what had he done with the man who donated my sperm? Granted, he'd made some rather bold statements at graduation, but this seemed really out of character for him.

Tossing some ideas around, I gave myself a moment to take a couple of the ibuprofen and wash it down with water before responding.

"That bad, huh?" Edward asked as he loosened his tie and sat back. He'd already unbuttoned his suit jacket before he slid in and sat down. I was dressed in a dress shirt and jeans, having not opted for a suit for this visit. My dress shirt also had the cuffs unbuttoned and the sleeves rolled up. Casual as fuck. Not Edward.

Then again, it was rare to see him in casual mode. Even at home.

"Depends," I said, finally. "What's the game we're playing?" Because

I seriously couldn't figure it out. I wasn't blocking him at the company. Honestly, he could sink or swim on his own as long as he didn't have the power to make sweeping decisions. He didn't. Grandpa had seen to that.

The real estate he could keep or sell, that was the reason I'd bought our own place, so our past didn't taint or touch our future. That Maddy and Edward were still out there was more than enough. Edward wanting to pursue this agenda of his didn't help, but I'd get a damn restraining order if I had to in order to keep Maddy away.

The brownstone was about the five of us. Us and no one else.

Edward sighed, "I suppose I deserve that."

No argument here.

"I can tell you this isn't a game, but you won't believe me. You have no reason to, and I accept that your suspicion and doubt are something I am going to have to deal with until I earn your trust."

Not snorting took every ounce of willpower I possessed. I wasn't sure it would be possible for him to earn my trust. I could tolerate him better now than I had at any point in the last decade, and that was about it.

"That said," Edward continued. "You have my support in this and anything else."

"As long as I keep supporting your involvement at Standish?" I took another swallow of water. At least that seemed to be helping with the tension banding my skull.

"You can support me or not as you see fit," Edward told me bluntly. "I have to prove myself to my father as much as I have to prove myself to you. I would like it, but I'm not asking for it or am I making my support conditional. You could have just as easily been in that car with her, Archie. I'm not prepared to lose my son, not when I have so much to make up for."

"You realize it's a little too late for us to have whatever this father/son bond is you're looking for?"

"Perhaps," he conceded. "But maybe it isn't too late to become friends."

Lowering the water bottle, I stared at him.

"Or at the very least, family you do more than tolerate."

No sense in denying that so I shrugged. "I can't make you any promises."

"I'm truly not asking for any," he assured me. "But believe me when I say if you need help for anything, I'm right here. You or Frankie—or I suppose any of the boys really." The near grudging part of that admission actually made me smile.

"Words get stuck in there, old man? "

"Perhaps, a tad," he admitted. "Not entirely certain what I think of this relationship the five of you have or that you're apparently sharing your girlfriend with others." Before I could say a word, he raised his hand as if to placate me. "And I clearly do not need to understand it to respect it. Jeremy has also made his feelings clear on this issue."

That did surprise me, and Edward actually chuckled.

"Of course, he has your back," Edward chastised me. "He likes you far better than the rest of us and he's terribly fond of your friends, and of Frankie."

That I knew. "All you have to know is they are my family. They are the family I chose and the family I want."

"And I will respect that," Edward assured me and after that, there was nothing else to say. Not really. I watched the flow of traffic pass as we made our way down through Queens and over the Queensboro Bridge back into Manhattan proper. Edward maintained his silence until we pulled up in front of the brownstone. "One last thing?"

I glanced at him.

"Don't speak to the police again without an attorney."

"Oh, I got that part," I assured him. The fact they even gave me an ounce of side eye like I could hurt Frankie in any way pissed me off. "I'll call them today."

"So will I."

The driver opened the rear door for me, and I slid out, bottle of water in hand, and made my way up the steps. Jeremy already had the door open as I got to the top. He stared past me down at the car after giving me a once over. His nod amused me.

"I'm fine, Jere," I told him. "Nothing Edward can do would hurt me anyway."

"Hmm," was Jeremy's only comment. "I was about to take Miss Frankie's breakfast up to her. She has showered and had coffee. Mister Jake and Mister Coop went to the gym because she was quite cross with them, and Mister Ian is downstairs working on music, allowing her some time to 'cool off,' I believe."

Fuck. "What did they do?"

"I'm sure the word 'allowed' entered the conversation, but only because the volume at which she repeated it carried down the stairs." His clear disapproval registered in both his delivery and his expression.

So did the unspoken 'fix it.'

"Would you bring me some coffee with her food and make arrangements for a car to be here in..." I checked my phone. "Two hours? I'm going to try and get us all out of trouble."

"That would be an excellent idea. You might take Mister Edward's flowers up with you."

Well, he wasn't wrong about that. "Good idea."

"Of course," Jeremy said. "I'll give you ten minutes before I bring up the coffee and the food, do try to stay dressed for that long. I promised Miss Frankie I wouldn't walk in on her again."

I didn't laugh. Oh hell no. No matter how fucking funny that had been. Neither of us had expected Jeremy to bring lunch up so fast and we'd gotten carried away. I'd never seen her dive off me and a bed so fast to land on the other side. Thankfully, Jeremy had just left the tray and exited, *after* he made a point of locking the door and given me a pointed look.

Oh yeah, Frankie was the favorite and Jeremy didn't care what I did with my dick, but we weren't allowed to embarrass her in any way.

"Pretty sure that keeping them on won't be a problem." As long as she was on *rest,* her penis tunnel was closed. The direct quote had Rachel written all over it. I liked a challenge though and if it took a little tongue work to get access again, well, hot damn, I'd totally take it for the team.

"Ten minutes," I repeated as I headed up the stairs.

"Yes, Mister Archie," he called after me. "Ten. Not a moment longer. Clothes. On."

Chapter Four

SORRY NOT SORRY

Frankie

I was curled up in the window seat with my phone, half listening to an audio book, since reading was officially off limits for another couple of days. The curtains were drawn, dimming the light. And the room was half in shadow. Even the bulbs in the lights next to the bed had been changed to a much lower wattage.

Brain rest they called it.

Boring as fuck, was my word for it. I understood why, but I didn't have to like it. The concussion wasn't as bad as it could be. Just like my injuries could have been far worse. But the fact I'd had a second concussion in the last twelve months meant they wanted me to take every precaution with this one.

Worse, the guys were raging pains in the ass about it. I wasn't a child, I understood the rules. But no, it didn't matter how capable I was of making a decision. All four of them agreed with the doctor, and turned into the roadblocks from hell, and I got stuck for a second night in the hospital. Didn't matter how nice the room was, it was still a hospital.

I blew out a breath and tried to let some of my aggravation go. Everything ached, but brain rest also meant not getting upset. So, I'd kicked them all out of my room. They could sleep in their own. It didn't matter that I missed them when I was in bed alone, I was still mad at them.

Not that it had much effect, Coop was in my bed the first night I'd been home. He must have snuck in the minute I went to sleep. The next, it had been Jake and he tried to pretend all was well this morning.

Ugh. I hated being mad at them, but they didn't get to do this.

"Knock knock," Archie said in a soft voice and I sighed. Turning off the book, I clearly wasn't even listening to, I glanced at the door. He stood there with a bouquet of flowers in hand and a small smile on his lips. If he had any remorse for his actions and choices in leading the charge to keep me in the hospital, he didn't show it. "Permission to enter?"

Stretching my legs out along the window seat, I raised my brows. "You're kind of already in here," considering my room and bathroom took up the entirety of the top floor. It accommodated the huge bed where we could all sleep and play to our hearts content. Made it that much lonelier when I was the only one in it. Tiddles actually had the center of the bed right now and he was working on cleaning one of his legs like he had all the time in the world.

"True, but I can leave these and go if you're really sick of our faces at the moment."

I snorted. "You'd just find another reason to come in to see if I'd changed my mind in fifteen minutes or something."

"Well, I might give it a whole half hour," he teased before setting the vase with the profusion of flowers, some I couldn't even name, onto the desk I wasn't using. It would probably look better over here at the window but as lovely as they were, they were just a pass to get up here and see me.

The real reason was he wanted to see me.

"I miss you," he said softly and I swore everything in me sighed. "And I know you miss us." He wasn't wrong. I totally missed them, even when I was mad.

He crossed the room to stand a couple of feet from me, then paused and snagged the chair from the desk to pull over. Rather than asking to sit on the window seat, he straddled the chair and leaned on the back of it to study me.

"I miss you and I wanted to see you, but I also want to find out what I can do to make this better." I swore his brown eyes softened to the point of painfully cute. Puppies had nothing on him.

I lifted my shoulders. "I don't think you can. This isn't something we fix, this is just something I have to stop being mad about."

"Fair," he murmured. "But maybe there's something I can do to help alleviate your anger faster?"

"Don't take sides against me again," I countered, and the corners of his mouth dipped.

"When it comes to your safety, I'll always put you first, even if it means you get mad at me. The crash scared me, Babe." He'd said as much before, but this was the first time he let the rawness out. "You were—so fucking lucky, and so were we. I saw the car...I know how bad it was."

I glanced down at my phone. The screen was dark and I didn't attempt to turn it on. "I did everything I could think of and nothing was slowing me down. Then I tried to use the guard rail to do it and that made it worse."

"Tell me about it?" The offer came in such a gentle voice and my resolve just evaporated.

Dammit, it was impossible to stay angry with him. With any of them, really.

"I was driving, she moved like a dream," I admitted. Driving his car had been something I'd kind of wanted to do forever. Archie never let anyone drive his car. After this, he'd probably never let me again. Lifting my gaze, I met his. "Do you really want to hear this?"

"Babe, I think I need to hear it and I think you need to tell me. You feel so damn guilty about the car, but I meant what I said at the hospital. I don't care about it, except that she endangered you. At the same time, I wish like hell I'd been the one in the driver's seat making those choices and maybe—I don't know if I could have done anything, but maybe I could have done something. If nothing else, you wouldn't have been alone."

Tears filled my eyes, and I tugged the earbuds out and stood. I didn't have to say a word, Archie abandoned the chair and swept me up in a hug. I buried my face against his neck and took a deep breath. Pulling as much of him into me as I could.

"I was scared," I admitted. "After. Not during. During, I just focused on trying to not hurt anyone else. It wasn't so bad when there wasn't a lot of traffic, but I was already going seventy when I realized the brakes weren't responding anymore." They had responded when I was leaving the house and driving through Montauk. The brakes had totally responded.

Archie picked me up and settled onto the window seat with me in his lap. I tucked my head against his shoulder, and he ran his fingers over my hair in a light, soothing gesture.

"Why didn't you try to call anyone?" he asked.

"At the time, I didn't want to take my hands off the wheel. My phone was in my backpack, and it was on the floor of the car. I know there's a handsfree system in the car, but I forgot to pair my phone before I got on the road."

I felt more than saw him nod. "And the emergency service?"

Guilt struck me like a brick. "I completely forgot it was there. The last time we talked about it was in junior year right after you got the car."

"Fair," he murmured. "And it's fine, Babe. No one's angry, I just want you to tell me so you can get it out."

Closing my eyes, I tried to remember the craziness of those fifteen minutes. That it had only been fifteen minutes from the moment I discovered the brakes no longer responded to the time of the actual crash itself seemed surreal. It had gone on forever.

I told him about shoving the brake pedal all the way to the floor, then pumping it to no avail. I debated dropping the car out of gear so I could just coast to a stop and I'd done that, but there was just enough incline that inertia kept me going too fast.

That and the presence of other cars meant I had to be frenetic in changing lanes and when I realized I'd have to accelerate...

"I had no choice then, it was accelerate and risk a bigger accident or try to use the rail to force the car to slow. I mean, if I was grazing it—then in theory it would pull force from dispersing it..."

"Do you have any idea how sexy it is when you talk about physics?" Archie asked and the fact his dick was hard beneath my ass confirmed his words. Though, I was pretty sure he'd been hard about three seconds after I sat in his lap. I know I'd already soaked my panties.

Our bodies were too in sync. Wanting them all was something I thrived on.

Before I could respond though, Jeremy cleared his throat about fifteen seconds before he appeared in the doorway.

"You're safe, Jere. We're not naked and there's no fucking going on, yet."

Oh my god. My face flamed and I jerked back to look up at Archie who gave me the sexiest, most sinful smile as he winked.

"Don't be so rude to Miss Frankie," Jeremy chided. "She's supposed to be taking it easy, not satisfying your prurient desires."

I snorted. It escaped me before I could clap a hand over my mouth.

"Who said my desires are prurient?" Archie challenged. "Maybe I just want to encourage her to feel better. Orgasms release endorphins—" I slapped my hand over his mouth to shut him up and Archie's eyes positively gleamed with mischief. My face burned so much he could probably feel the heat.

"I will order you a gag for him," Jeremy offered as he set up the table with my breakfast and a fresh carafe of coffee and two large mugs. I've prepared all of your favorites. I know you've been a bit off food the last couple of days because the young men of the house forgot how to persuade a woman rather than order her around." The last he offered with a firm look at Archie, before looking at me again. "But I would prefer that you eat."

"I will," I promised him. "Don't worry, there will be no sex after breakfast."

"You may have sex whenever you wish Miss Frankie, I just think we both agree that we don't need to share any more on the subject."

"Oh, we're very agreed." I did my best to ignore the trace of Archie's tongue as he wrote 'I love you and I want you' over and over against my palm. I swore my pussy clenched so tight it resonated through me as all of my muscles went taut. "Thank you, Jeremy."

"Quite welcome, now I have some errands to run so you'll have the house to yourselves, though Mr. Ian is downstairs in the studio. Try not to have too much fun and do keep the lights low for at least another day."

I was dying, over and over again, as Archie kept up his sensual assault and Jeremy gave us both a knowing look, before he vanished down the stairs. I whipped to look at Archie and pulled my hand down. But the moment I opened my mouth to scold him, he pulled me forward until I fell into him, and our lips fused together.

Liquid heat spilled out to ignite in my blood, as Archie took masterful control of the kiss. His fingers were in my hair and he tilted my head gently, as his tongue sought entrance and then stroked mine. All I could taste on him was a hint of coffee, a touch of sweetness. The rest was Archie. The very gorgeous masculine scent of him filled my nostrils and I surrendered any pretense of not wanting this, or being angry.

Still... "Archie," I told him between kisses as I began to unbutton his shirt. He nipped at my lips and helped me turn so I was straddling his lap. All I had on were sleep shorts and a tank top.

"Yes, Babe?" He found his way under the hem of my shirt and began to massage my breasts, careful as hell of the bruise the seatbelt strap left across my chest. My already taut nipples ached for him as I spread his shirt wide to run my hands all over his chest.

"I'm still angry at you," I whispered in between sucking kisses and gentle scrapes of his teeth over my lower lip. A groan slipped out as he kissed a path along my jaw to my throat and he had a hand in my shorts, fingers sliding along the slick wetness of my labia so he could part them. Fuck I wanted to ride that hand.

"Okay, Babe," he whispered before biting down on my earlobe and spearing two fingers inside of me. "You can be angry all you want. You're still coming on my hand, then my lips and after I've eaten my fill of this perfect pussy, I'm going to fuck into you so deep, you forget your name."

I arched, rising up to ride his hand and he thrust up to meet my downward push, fingers curling to stroke a spot deep inside, that left me chasing sparks.

"This doesn't fix anything," I reminded him, desperate to hold onto some semblance of the conversation as he urged me to lean back, and then he was sucking my nipple through my shirt. "Not everything," I amended. Then as he bit down and his thumb found my clit, I chased my orgasm with fervor. "Fuck it," I admitted, and Archie chuckled against me before giving me the exact pressure I wanted, and I splintered.

Still shaking, I rested my forehead against his. "You're such an ass, sometimes."

"I know, Babe," he promised, giving me a sweet kiss as he eased his fingers out of my spasming pussy. "I really am, and I promise to make it up to you over and over again." He stood and carried me over to the bed.

The minute he set me down, he stripped down my shorts and panties then tugged my tank up and off. The heat in his eyes didn't diminish as he raked his gaze over me. For a long, breathless moment, he stared at my chest, at the diagonal mottling of bruising where the strap had kept me suspended and done its job. With a wordless kiss to his fingers, he then touched the bruise lightly. I blinked back tears while he shed his shirt, and his shoes went flying, before I reached for his jeans. He interrupted my efforts by sliding his hands under my thighs and tilting me backward.

"You can have my cock," he promised. "You're going to get it as hard and deep as I can make it—but first, I want my treat. Because I've missed you and I've missed this beautiful pink pussy. Hello, my gorgeous girl, let me make it up to you." His mouth locked over my clit with a powerful suction and this close to having come, I orgasmed again without much effort. "There she is," he crooned, and I fucking died as he seduced me and my pussy. Not that he needed to do much.

We were totally a sure thing for him. When he speared his tongue inside me and went to work playing with my ass, I closed my eyes and tilted my hips back. I didn't need my brain for this at all. It was just an ocean of sensation and need with Archie right at the heart of it.

By the time he thrust into me, I was crying from coming and I dug my fingers into his back as he pounded into me, hard, deep and fast. His kisses were equally urgent and his fingers biting where they locked with mine.

"Love you," I confessed as I danced right on the edge, but I needed Archie to come with me this time. Desperately wanted it. "Love you, so much."

His deep groan and shudder were my only warning before his hips stuttered and he came. The rush of him filling me sent me sliding over the edge and I floated on that feeling as I spasmed around him. We lay like that for a while, just holding each other and shaking.

"Still mad at me, Babe?" he asked against my ear.

"A little," I admitted. We needed to talk about the siding against me and not letting me make my own choices.

"Okay," he murmured and began kissing his way down my sweat-dampened torso toward my aching pussy. "Let's talk again, Beautiful girl and see if we can work this out." He dove into eating me out with such gusto I did forget my name and how many times I came.

Dammit.

That did it.

Chapter Five

TEARS FOR FEARS

Jake

Every blow delivered to the heavy bag just seemed to make my temper worse, not better. Coop's steady stare against my back wasn't helping either. He wanted me to talk about it. Talk about my dad. Talk about Frankie. Talk about the fucking *accident*. The last thing I wanted to do was dig deep while he played armchair psychologist.

I got it. I had *feelings* that needed to be worked out. That was what I was doing. Working it out. Three days in a row now, I'd left first thing in the morning to hit the gym. I needed to vent it out here so I could avoid kneejerk reactions when Frankie insisted she could do something whether I *allowed* it or not. That, and hopefully not earn another glare of rage from her.

The fact she'd focused on that single word hadn't been lost on me. Probably not my brightest moment, but goddammit. Inside the gloves, my wrapped knuckles were going numb from the pounding I delivered in a flurry of blows to the bag. Sweat stung my eyes, but I didn't let up.

I didn't slow until the burn in my back and shoulders matched the tread marks the accident burned across my heart. Dad was fine. Frankie was fine. They were both fine.

It didn't matter how much I kept repeating the thought or how many times I hit the heavy bag, the sentiment wasn't going away.

"How long has he been at it?" Then there was that fucker. I kept my focus on the bag and not him.

"About an hour," Coop said with a sigh. "This has got to stop."

"I'll tag in for a while, go get your own workout in, and we'll catch up with you later." Would he really? Well, wasn't he just a special fucking asshole.

"Arch..." Coop's voice held a warning and I paused to face them as I sucked in deeper breaths. Sweat soaked my shirt. It didn't seem to matter how hard I hit the damn thing. I caught the towel Coop flung at me and tugged a hand out of the glove so I could wipe my face.

"Let him, Coop, if he thinks he can go a few rounds with me." Only I wasn't looking at Coop, I stared at Archie. He dressed for the gym and he had a pair of sparring gloves with him. We'd gone a few rounds in the ring before. He wasn't bad.

"I can handle you, Benton," Archie said in that smug asshole tone he usually reserved for dicks who fucked with us. "Particularly, if you can't get a grip on your own."

A snort escaped me. "Right, and if you can't you'll just hire someone to take on the fight."

Coop groaned but Archie just smiled. "Don't hate, you benefit from it as much as I do."

"Do I now?" I downed a few gulps of water on my way to the ring. There was a free one at the end. No doubt paid for with Archie's money, because money meant he could allow or not as he saw fit. Then he could literally talk his way out of the shit with Frankie over it.

The fact it was his fucking car and his fucking fault she was in it alone, started throttling up in my brain. I ducked under the rope and slid inside. Archie followed at a more leisurely pace. Coop stared at both of us, arms folded.

"You fuck up each other's faces and you're on your own explaining this shit to Frankie."

"We're big boys, Coop," Archie said easily. "We can handle it."

"Is that what you told her when you took her to fucking campus the other day?" We'd gotten back from the gym to find out that not only was Frankie not resting the way she was supposed to be, but that she and Archie had also *left* the fucking brownstone.

We didn't find out until they got back three hours later that he'd taken her to campus to look at the bookstore and pick up things for her classes. Things she wasn't supposed to be reading or doing, much less running around. Archie tried to blow it off that she pointed, and he would pick it up and read it for her, he also carried everything—but it wasn't the fucking point.

The longer I stared at his smug face, the more I wanted to put my fist through it.

"Actually, what I did was listen, Jake," Archie corrected me as he held up his mouth guard. "And I'd put this in, because I'm not telling her why I knocked out one of your teeth."

A laugh shook me, but it had nothing to do with humor. I wanted to tell him to go fuck himself, but Coop pinned me with a look as he held up my mouth guard. The one I almost never wore.

You know what, fuck it. I let him slide it in and once I had it clenched in my teeth, he said, "Do us both a favor and remember Archie is also our friend? And whatever else is eating at you, he wants her safe and happy every bit as much as you do."

I glared at him.

"And he just might be feeling more than a little guilt."

Good. He should feel guilty. Probably not what Coop meant, but I didn't care right now. I rolled my head around to loosen up my neck. The warmup had left me angrier than when I'd started, so hopefully this would do something with all that suppressed rage.

Well, maybe not so suppressed.

"Rules?" Coop reminded us, but either Archie didn't hear or he didn't care, because he knocked his gloves together and headed straight for me. Adrenaline coursed through me, alongside excitement. The urge to punch him had been there since the moment I realized Frankie had been alone in that car.

I took the first blow to my jaw and slammed my own into his. Archie was not bad. But I was a whole lot better. Still, he avoided my next hit and I took one to the shoulder.

"Oh, for fuck's sake," Coop muttered from where he stood, glaring at both of us, but Archie didn't pay him any more attention than I did. The sweat on my face ran toward my eyes but I shook it off as Archie dodged left. Fast on his feet. Fast to run his mouth. Fast with his fucking choice in cars.

I was ready for his next dodge and nailed with a right-left-right jab combo. That would get his ears ringing. He shook his head as he danced backwards. He'd gone for my jaw, so as far I was concerned, this wasn't about rules. This was a chance to beat the crap out of him.

Two breaths and then I was after him again. He did a little dance around the ring before switching tactics and coming straight at me. Gloves up, I blocked a number of his hits from landing. Pushing him to wear himself out, as he battered my gloved fists and arms, then I went for another jab-punch-uppercut combo. The jab got him in the gut he wasn't protecting, the punch in his shoulder, but he managed to avoid the uppercut, barely.

Fury filled his eyes. Oh, there was an emotion I empathized with. It echoed the anger bouncing around inside of me.

We collided in a fury of blows and locked there. Rules said we should back off, but neither of us did. Finally, Archie had to wrench away, blood spotted his nose and my breathing was coming hard and fast. The ache in my jaw redoubled and the sweat stung my eyes.

Undeterred, Archie lifted his chin and did a come at me motion like he was freaking Morpheus from the Matrix. Dick. I rained blows down on him as we collided together, he didn't hold back as he pummeled me. At one point, one of us grabbed the other by the back of the neck and when he tried to sweep my legs, I headbutted him.

Fuck.

Stars exploded in front of my eyes and Archie staggered back to hit the ropes as he blinked. He looked as dazed as I felt. A piercing whistle split the air and one of the guys who worked at the gym walked up to the ropes.

"You two," he said in a booming voice that took me back to my first days at high school with the coach. "You're done. Check the attitudes, hit the showers, cool off, then get out of here."

Archie turned slowly to the face the guy, then spit out his mouth guard. "Or what?"

"Or you're both banned for life. There are rules here and this isn't a place for the two of you to make each other bleed."

Bleed?

Archie's nose was barely bloody. And I was... a drop of blood landed on my arm and I tugged a glove off to touch my forehead. Oh. Well, all right, bleeding.

Didn't hurt.

The big dude just glared at us, arms folded over a massive chest. He could probably bench press 350 and hit like a freight train. I raised my hands in surrender and backed off.

Coop wasn't waiting for either of us outside of the ring. I stripped off my gloves and stuffed them in my bag, then used the towel to mop at my face. Blood got all over it, I'd be stealing a towel I guessed, and then I headed for the locker room.

What I liked about this place when we'd first come here was the layout as much as the set up. The gym itself was a pretty big space. There were machines on one end and rooms for classes. Then there were the strict weight machines in the middle. And down here, we had a couple of rings, some heavy bags and a few speed bags.

It was a fighter's gym. The place was located in an affluent neighborhood, but it had a real earthy feel to it. This wasn't a place to just pretend to work out. The people who came here, came to train. It was good for getting Frankie to work on her uppercuts and left hooks. Or it would be after she healed up—again.

My mood soured as I stalked inside the locker room. I rarely showered here, usually just rinsed the sweat off and threw on fresh clothes before heading back to the brownstone. That said, we'd all been getting in the habit of bringing clean clothes and travel toiletries.

In the shower, I yanked the water on and hissed as it hit me with a blast of ice cold. My muscles trembled with the adrenaline still dancing through my system. Pink rivulets ran down my arms to fall to the tile beneath my feet and get washed down the drain.

As the water warmed up, I sluiced off the sweat and washed up. The cut on my forehead wasn't deep, but it fucking stung *now*.

"You done being pissed at me?" Archie asked from the vicinity of the shower next to mine.

"Nope," I admitted. Didn't matter how fucking unreasonable my anger was, not when it involved her. "You should have been there."

"Agreed," Archie said and then offered nothing more. Once I shut off the water, I took the time to towel off in there and pull on boxer briefs before I exited. I wanted to give him time to leave.

Maybe a break was what we needed. That was why Frankie booted us out of her room. Or had, until Archie pulled whatever fast one he had to get back in her good graces.

Unfortunately, he was still getting dressed when I finally walked out of the showers with a towel around my neck. He held a pair of socks in his hands, looking at them like they held the answer to the quandary. A dull throb settled in behind my eyes.

"Arch, I don't want to do this."

"Clearly," he said, cutting a look up at me and there was a faint puffiness around his eye and jaw. I'd gotten him good, gloves or not. "That's not going to make it comfortable at home."

"Well, that was why you made sure we all had our own rooms. We don't have to deal with each other if we don't want to." I ran the towel of my hair, and then my beard, probably a lot harder than I should have and it just increased the ache in my head. Instead of agreeing or quipping, Archie just waited for me to get dressed.

When we were both ready, he tracked me outside and we walked side by side on the route back to the brownstone. Coop was still AWOL. I guessed he washed his hands of the both of us and took his well-adjusted ass back home.

"I'd give anything for it to have been me in the car," he said in a harsh tone. "If you think anything else, then you're a bigger ass than I thought possible."

I opened my mouth, but he sliced a hand through the air.

"Save it. I get why you're pissed at me and what you're thinking. If I'd been there, maybe it wouldn't have happened. Or if it had to happen, I'd have been with her and she wouldn't be alone. Trust me, I've gone over this in triplicate in my head. But the truth is...I wasn't there. And I have to live with that. So, if you can stick your opinion up your judgmental ass, I'd appreciate it. Because no amount of you blowing fire in my direction is making me leave."

Leave? "Who the fuck said anything about you leaving?"

"Your attitude," he said when we reached the steps to the brownstone. "Until you stop blaming me for the accident, that's probably going to make things uncomfortable for everyone."

"I can play nice," I told him. "You're not the only one who can sell an act when he needs to."

His eyes narrowed. "You think Frankie's gonna buy that? Or Coop?"

"You leave her out of it. You're already on thin ice taking her up to the campus and letting her run around when she's supposed to be resting."

"What did you want me to do, go all Caveman Jake on her and make her stay put?" He raised his eyebrows and his sunglasses. "How's that working out for you? Oh right..." He snapped his fingers. "You're still not welcome in her bedroom. Whereas... I am."

It was a low blow.

"You're a real dick."

"Takes one to know one." He gave me the most insincere smile. "I gave you the freebie to get your aggression out. Keep spoiling for a fight and I'll give you a real one next time. Now get your act together, school starts in a few days and we've still got to balance these schedules out."

Yeah.

We did.

And I was about to change mine. Archie and I had way too many fucking classes together. "Fine," I told him through gritted teeth then made the effort to stop grinding them. "We'll be just fine."

He studied me for a long moment, then shook his head before he ascended the steps to the door. I took a minute to stuff my temper down before jogging up the steps. Jeremy paused with a basket of laundry in his hands and gave both Archie and I a critical look.

Not interested in having him join Archie's side on this one, I just lifted my chin toward him and headed up the stairs. The quiet murmur of his voice and Archie's followed me. No one was in the second floor entertainment room and I headed up to the third where my room was.

Coop's door was open and I paused to glance inside. He sprawled on the bed a tablet in front of him with some book on it.

"We're back," I told him and he spared me a look.

"You need to fix the cut on your forehead."

"I will."

"You feel better?"

I sighed, bracing my shoulder against the doorframe as I shook my head. "Not really. Is Frankie upstairs?" Maybe I could get cleaned up and go talk to her. Make up for pissing her off the other day. Maybe I could...

"No, she went to see Rach, Bubba was going to drop her off on his way to meeting his music advisor."

"Since when did he have an advisor appointment?"

Coop just shrugged. "Since Frankie wanted to see Rach. And before you lose your shit, she needed to get out and she's doing much better. She's not even light sensitive anymore."

"They said a few days of brain rest," I reminded him.

"It's been a few days," Archie said from behind me and I spared him a look. Right. He wouldn't see the problem with it. Probably wouldn't until he realized you couldn't always throw money at something to fix it.

"I've got some work to do," I told Coop, turning my back on Arch. "Let me know when she gets back."

I'd text her too, just to be on the safe side.

"Yep," Coop said, but my tone and my question hadn't fooled him in the slightest. If anything, he looked even more disapproving. I continued down the hall to my room and did my best not to listen if Coop and Archie started talking.

Inside, I shut the door and dropped my bag in the corner before moving over to fall on the bed and stare up the ceiling. Dragging my phone out of my pocket, I scrolled to her name and opened the message.

Couldn't hurt to ask.

While she didn't answer right away, I was okay with that. She needed Rachel time, too. For now, I rolled over and went for my laptop. I needed to make some adjustments to my schedule.

Chapter Six

TEA FOR TWO

Frankie

"**S**o, just to clarify that I understand everything... the boys are freaking out because you were in a car *crash* that *totaled* the Ferrari," Rachel said, ticking off the items as she snapped clothing out and then straightened it before folding. I'd caught her in the middle of washing and rearranging everything in her dorm apartment.

The place was nicer than she detailed. She had an entire room and her own ensuite bathroom, though the common area and little kitchenette was shared with a roommate. It was also super colorful in her bedroom with a sunrise bedspread and multi-colored pillows decorating the full-sized bed she'd wedged into a corner and set up almost like a sofa.

"A Ferrari *you* were driving alone because rich boy took off with one half of bad meatloaf..." She paused and made a face. "Does that make him the actual meat or the loaf? You know, let's put a pin in that." She snagged another shirt and snapped it neatly. It was like she shook the wrinkles out and it worked. "Okay, so rich boy is off with the meat-head."

Her wicked grin almost made me laugh, but I bit the inside of my lip. Not because it wasn't funny, but more because I really wanted this to work out for Archie and his dad. Edward had truly fucked his son over, but maybe—*just maybe*—he could finally let go of Mad Maddy and make a go of it with his son.

Fingers crossed.

"You drive on your own and get in a crazy, insane accident—yes, I saw the fucking pictures." The last came out a sharp reprimand and I winced.

"Rach..."

"Nope, it's fine that no one called to tell me at the time. I understand the general freakout. It's the fact *you* didn't call me for three days after."

My wince became a real grimace.

"However, I love you and will eventually forgive you, so we'll set that aside for now. Maybe I'll get you to do some nudes for me to photograph with good light and that will be your penance." She gave me a wink and no matter how she played it off, I got it. I'd fucked up.

"I'm sorry."

Shirt folded, she hugged it to her chest. "Apology accepted. Don't do it again."

"I won't."

"Good." Then she moved right along. That was Rachel, plowing through the bullshit to get right to the heart of it.

"I love you."

"I know." The smugness just made me grin. "Still, we're back to your dilemma here. The boys are being overprotective, overbearing, and generally a pain in the ass..."

"Jake told me what I was and wasn't allowed to do."

"Well, I always did say it was a good thing he was pretty, because that dick of his would get him in trouble."

"Rach, be serious," I scolded as she settled the last of her shirts into a drawer before turning to her jeans.

"I am being serious. He beat the shit out of guys who looked at you sideways for years, you don't think he isn't a little Captain Caveman?" She pinned me with a look. "See, you can't deny it. You probably love it, except when he goes too far."

I flopped back against the pillows. I still ached in places. The bruise on my chest was going to be there a while. It wasn't quite the livid purple and black thing it had been. Now, it had some bluish edges. Rachel had already decorated the walls in her place, there were pictures from her time in Paris. I caught sight of Mathieu and his girl—Claudette? Was that her name? Ugh, I was the worst friend. Though, Rachel spent more time talking about Mathieu than she had Claudette, so... yeah.

He looked good. Happy. It seemed a million years ago he'd been in my kitchen while I attempted to make that French dessert and I sucked so epically at flirting. Though he had tried to give me a kiss, or had I tried to give it to him?

Who could remember? It wasn't important.

"What are the others doing? Or is it just Jake?"

"No, it's all of them. Actually, Ian's being great about it. I can tell he *wants* to step in and wrap me up in silk and lace..."

"I'm going to pause you there because that's a pretty erotic image, but I don't need to know more about that kink than I already do." The teasing note made me laugh.

"Ha." I rolled over onto my side because lying on my stomach sucked. "You're such a liar."

"And you're a twunt, but we're not debating our merits." She winked.

"A *what?*"

"Somewhere between a twat and a cunt resides Frankie, Queen of the Twunts, because she lives to tease me and make me appreciate my existence at the same time."

I gagged and Rachel laughed for real.

"*Anyway,*" I said, stressing the two syllables. "I can't blame them, not really. They were scared. But smothering me is not something I'm willing to go back to." Not when...

She didn't pressure or push, she just waited. She folded the rest of her jeans. I'd offered a couple of times when I first got here to help, but she waved me off. It was just easier for her to do it herself.

A door closing pulled my attention to the open bedroom door. A girl wandered past with dark hair, dark eyes, and a nose piercing. She was pretty, though she went with really bold colors for her cosmetics and I didn't think they were doing her any favors.

"Your roommate?" I asked, figuring it would be more rhetorical than anything else.

"Yep," Rachel said as she swept toward the door. "Roommate, Frankie. Frankie, Roommate." Then she closed the door with a thud and leaned back against it, arms folded.

Wow.

"So," she continued like she hadn't just shut her roommate out. "Tell them to back off."

"I have, that just made it worse. Then we ended up in a fight and I finally kicked them out of my room."

"Ouch, sucks to be them," she said with a mirthless chuckle. Well, maybe not entirely mirthless. "However, it's not like you to get so dug in. You're usually the one who finds a way to work it out and to balance those neanderthal tendencies of theirs. Tendencies I would be forced to admit they earned the hard way."

I met her stare for stare.

"Homecoming," she said, ticking the items off. "Your car, bitchy girls, Halloween, then let's not get started on your mother..."

"You're not wrong," I said. "I get *why*, but I also get that I need them to stop, too. I need them to trust me with me. It was an accident. Mostly."

Eyebrows raised, she just stared at me. When I didn't say anything, I swore she began to tap her left foot.

"I don't know anything for sure," I told her. "And I can't discuss this with them, not until I am sure, because frankly they will lose their fucking minds if I tell them, I think Maddy had something to do with it."

Thinking about it for days was one thing. Saying it aloud seemed to just make it so much more real. My stomach rippled as agitation burned the inside of it, and I had to swallow back the nauseating sensation cascading through me.

"You think I'm going to be *less* agitated than them?" Rachel stared at me like I'd sprouted a second head. "Don't be a dumb blonde joke, Frankie. You know better. What the fuck are you talking about?"

"I don't have any proof. I know the police are investigating, but Archie's car was *fine*. We drove it up to the Hamptons. She handled as smoothly as she ever did. And it's *Archie*? You think he doesn't diddle that car as much as he does me?"

"Not sure that's the mental image I would have gone for," Rachel said slowly. "But I agree. Archie would also never leave you with a vehicle he thought could be defective in any way."

"Exactly. And he's been driving that Ferrari since the day he got his license. He *loved* that car." My heart ached for it all over again. Nothing would replace that first car, that classic Ferrari he adored so damn much. Even if I could find one exactly like it, it wouldn't be the same. "I know him. I know his car. So why did it suddenly lose all brakes while I was on the L.I.E.?"

That was the one thing *no one* had answered yet. Archie was fighting to get the remains of his vehicle back from the police. Edward was even helping him, a fact that left Archie more than a little suspicious. More because, why was Edward trying to help him now? Not just with that, but with everything at the hospital and more.

"How do you go from that, to thinking your mother had something to do with it?" Rachel asked as she crossed the room to sink down on the bed next to me. She snagged one of the pillows to hug and I lifted my shoulders.

"Because that's what my gut is saying."

"You think Maddy is trying to kill you?" Yeah, the thought deserved a healthy amount of skepticism.

Except... "I don't think it was me," I said slowly and met Rachel's gaze. "I think she was trying to hurt Archie." Because that crash hadn't killed me, I'd known a way to handle not having brakes. There wasn't a single doubt within me that Archie would have handled it exactly the same way I had.

Frowning, Rachel reached over to catch my hand. "You think she's trying to hurt Archie to hurt you? Or to hurt meat-head?"

I licked my lips as I gripped her fingers. "I think she's trying to hurt both of us. But I don't think it matters as much if we're hurt—I think she blames Archie."

"For...what? Her being a wreck of a parent? A total cuntasaurus? I mean rich boy is talented, but what could he have possibly done?"

I smiled as pain slid through me. I'd had a lot of time to think about this over the last few days, and the more I tried not to obsess about it, the more it wouldn't leave me alone. I knew Maddy. I knew her moods. I knew how she would lash out when she felt threatened, how she always turned everything into an attack on her.

I'd spent a lot of time working on those feelings with Erin in therapy, exploring them and examining them. I'd separated fact from fiction and sometimes—sometimes I'd just had to accept that Maddy's issues weren't mine.

"She can blame him for being born," I said slowly. She'd more or less said that during one of her rants. Edward getting Muriel pregnant had destroyed their future. "She can blame him for turning me against her."

"Frankie's not for sale, Edward. You two have a lovely dinner. You really do seem well-suited to each other."

I couldn't even get the words out as Archie hustled me out of the restaurant. The valet went to get the car, but not fast enough. My mother was outside and she caught my arm. The bite of her fingers hurt. "Frankie, we need to talk."

"Not here, Mom," I told her as Archie moved to get between us. "Please...I don't want to have this fight."

"Why are you doing this? Do you want me to be unhappy?"

"No, but I also don't think this is what you think it is. It's not just about you. You want to change everything in my life, get rid of my cats, and expect me to just stand here and say yay? Why? Because he has money? I don't want his money."

"Let her go, Ms. Curtis." The warning in Archie's voice seemed to give Mom pause, and she let me go. The fact we also had something of an audience in the other valets who were present also sank in.

"Archie," my mom turned to him, from furious to imploring in a heartbeat. "If you would just be more open to it, you and Frankie are close. You surely can't object to having her around more."

"Not even in the slightest, but Ms. Curtis, I know my dad. This is not going to end well for you. I wish I could make you see it. Frankie's worried about you, and she doesn't want you hurt. But all you can see is what you want, and that's pretty normal for the people in Edward's world. You don't get to hurt Frankie in the process, we are close and I am going to protect her, even if you won't."

"You're ruining everything."

Those words echoed in my head as I told Rachel about that dinner. We'd talked about it before, but never in this detail and never through the lens of what we knew now.

"They were going to tell you meat-head was your dad that night," Rachel said slowly and I nodded.

"Looking back, the set up of it. The dress, the new car, the fancy dinner at the really exclusive place and the fact she'd wanted me to come alone—yeah. That's exactly what they wanted to tell me." And it would have fucking killed me if I'd been there alone and they dropped that bombshell on me.

In all honesty, Edward had completely believed her lies. Worse, he'd *wanted* to be my father, when he had an amazing child he'd ignored. A child he'd blamed, whether he could admit it aloud or not.

"Maddy blames Archie's existence for why she is where is." I licked my lips. "I won't let her hurt him."

"No shit, but what do you plan to do about it?"

This was the thing... "I need to find her. To know what she's doing. To prove she messed with the car. If she did and Archie figures it out, he'll be out for blood."

"Girl, we'd all be out for blood. She damn near killed *you* if she was responsible. And you know what, I don't give a flying fuck what her *intentions* were. The fact you survived is still a damn miracle."

"And she meant that for Archie," I said slowly. "Rach, she blames him for everything." I let go of her hand to scrub at my face. It itched in places where the airbag burns still healed. I had to know if she did it. If I could prove it, I wanted her to go to jail. I wanted her far away from Archie and the others...they wanted me safe. I needed them the same way. "Will you help me?"

She let out an aggrieved sigh. "When do you want to start?"

My phone buzzed.

I swore my heart sighed at the words. They were right there and I missed them. Fighting with them sucked.

"Soon," I told her. "I made a call to see if I could get the accident report and the final analysis of the vehicle before Archie does."

Rachel raised her eyebrows. "How did you do that?"

"Apparently, having money gets you access." Wittaker knew people and he'd put me in touch with a firm here, and resources.

The corner of Rachel's mouth curved upward. "Look at you getting to be all badass. You're gonna to try to out 'rich boy,' rich boy."

"Maybe not that far, but he is an excellent teacher."

She laughed and I thumbed open the message.

His answer was immediate.

I answered his kiss emoji with one of my own. Then looked at Rachel. "We need a plan."

"Yes," she said as she rolled off the bed and grabbed her laptop. "First things first—where do you think Cuntasaurus is?"

Chapter Seven

KILLING ME SOFTLY WITH HER SONG

Ian

I gave Frankie three days. Three days from when she'd all but tossed all of us out on our asses. Her biting comments at Jake and Archie weren't directed at me or Coop, not really. Still, I gave her the space anyway. Respecting her needs, particularly when she vocalized it so clearly, was not something I could ignore.

Even if I did want to wrap her up and keep her safe from the bruises the world inflicted. From the moment Jeremy told us about the call, to seeing her in the hospital, I'd been on a knife's edge. Seeing her smile. Hearing her laugh. Touching her fingers. Tasting her kiss. Holding her close. Every single one of those sensations had played on repeat through my head.

Finding her alive and *mostly* unharmed helped, but I couldn't fight the need to protect her and take care of her. Not for long. Especially with the rising tensions in the house. I wasn't sure who Jake and Archie thought they were fooling, but the absolute *lack* of conversation between them coupled with the fresh bruises on both of their faces spoke volumes.

That in mind, I made my way up the stairs and knocked quietly on her door.

A sleepy, "I'm awake."

Smiling, I pushed the door open. The sun was barely up outside and it was early. Jake and Archie had already left to run, going in opposite directions. Frankie sprawled in the bed, looking far too fragile against the dark sheets and comforter, with her hair all spread out on the pillow.

Everything inside of me tightened at the view. The last few days had seemed ridiculously long, considering the month she and Jake spent in Germany. I stood there, drinking in the sight of her with the early morning light spilling over her. Classes kicked off soon and we'd be back to running on chaos, cuss words, and coffee.

Not just yet though.

When she stretched out her hand to me, I went straight to her and slid onto the bed. Frankie melted right into me, fitting my arms like she'd been made to be there, a split second before she arched to kiss me.

The tension holding me rigid relaxed and I slid my fingers into her hair, careful not to pull, but only to cradle. Giving her control of the kiss, I let her tell me when she wanted more. The soft gasp as she parted her lips had me swooping in to stroke her tongue.

With a groan, she pulled back a little and I paused. Those sleepy eyes opened slowly revealing the deep green waiting for me. "You taste of peppermint and coffee, and I have morning breath."

A chuckle escaped me. "You taste like you, Angel," I informed her, before I rolled her over and kept my weight on my elbows. I wanted to blanket her with everything, but not while she was still so sore. This time when I kissed her, she let out a true moan. I meant it when I said she tasted like Frankie, she tasted like heat and passion and home. Her fingers dug into my shoulders, then skated up over my hair as I took my time reacquainting myself with her lips and her reactions.

She shivered beneath the sheets and wiggled a little, then she had a leg wrapped around my waist and I chuckled against her mouth. "As tempting as this is, Angel, I had another idea in mind."

My dick wasn't all the way on board with the plan, but he would be fine. Frankie and I deserved a day.

"What did you have in mind?" With her lips puffy from kissing and her sleepy expression softening more, it proved a challenge to hold to the plan I'd already made.

"Run away with me?" I asked. "Just—you and me. We'll go up to grab my bike and just get out of here for the day."

Absolute gentleness marked her fingers as she stroked them down my cheek and then she stiffened. "Oh shit."

"Shh..." I caught her hand and kissed it.

"Ian." The plea in her tone threatened to undo me. "We..."

"Shh...no worries, Angel. You're here and you're safe. Best birthday present, ever."

The wealth of apology in her eyes sliced at me. "I'm a terrible girlfriend."

I bit the tip of her finger lightly. The gesture wouldn't break the skin, but she would definitely feel my teeth. "No one talks bad about you, Angel. Not even you. While I might not be spanking you at the moment, I am keeping count."

She shivered once, then wound her arms around my neck. "I love you, Sir Ian. But I should have done something for you for your birthday."

A chuckle escaped me. She would beat herself up about this for days. The thing was, we had made plans—then the accident. That accident and the aftermath had kind of erased all our plans and shifted all our focus. I was nineteen. No big deal as far as I was concerned. The bigger deal nuzzled at my chin.

"I'm sorry," she whispered when she got to my ear.

"We have years to do it over and over again," I reminded her. "This birthday is already a thousand percent better than the last one. I've got my girl—my beautiful Angel, and what does the birthday boy also get?"

Her smile grew. "Whatever he wants."

"Get dressed and run away with me?"

I didn't have to ask again, she met my kiss with the kind of fierceness I'd been craving. We'd definitely get back to this later, but for now, I had to satisfy my need with the long, lingering kiss before I dragged us both out of the bed. Once I had her on her feet, I gazed down at her.

One of her breasts had tried to escape the tank top, so I took a moment to suck the nipple against my teeth and lave it with my tongue. Her soft little gasps a reward all their own. When I slid my hand into her panties, she was already slick and warm. Glancing up, I began to massage her clit. Slow, teasing circles. Not enough to get her off or even to really begin ramping her up.

It would, however, leave her wanting more. She sank her teeth into her lower lip as she fought her own desires. The muscles in her legs flexed and twice she started up on her toes, then she forced herself to be still. If she tried to ride my hand without permission, I'd stop and she knew it.

"You really are perfect, Angel," I murmured as I gave her one last lazy stroke then pulled my fingers free to lick them clean. "Go shower. Let me know if you need anything."

"What should I wear?" The dilated pupils and breathlessness just added to my enjoyment of her pleasure.

"Jeans and a comfortable T, grab your motorcycle boots and your jacket." I'd gotten her gear all set up. Safety had never mattered to me more.

"Wanna watch me shower?" she asked from the doorway to the bathroom, stripping off the tank top. The bruise from the seat belt was still livid across her torso. I studied the way the mottled colors shifted as you got to the edges of it. Still dark and painful though.

"Always." Following her into the bathroom, I leaned back against the counter. I already had a small bag packed. It would fit in the saddlebags on the bike. I waited until she stripped all the way down and stepped under the water before I pulled out my phone. Surprise flickered across her expression, and I chuckled. "Not taking pictures, Angel. Just letting the guys know I'm stealing you away for a day or two."

That got her attention, but instead of scolding me, she just grinned wider. "Birthday boy gets what the birthday boy wants." With that, she tilted her head back into the water and some of the tension weighing on me over the last few days drifted away. The only thing I wanted for my birthday was right there.

Drinking in the sight of her for a moment, I let out a slow breath before I fired off the text.

Frankie's phone was in the bedroom, but I'd also only used the group text the four of us used, rather than the family text we used with Frankie. One, she didn't need to deal with their reactions, particularly if any were negative. Two, because I'd stayed out of it and not interfered. I'd let her handle everything.

But birthday boy got what the birthday boy wanted, and what I wanted was for her to enjoy herself for the next day or two, however long we decided to be.

I gave it a beat, then Coop came through.

The dead silence in the messages pulled a grin from me. They hadn't "forgotten," but everything else going on drowned out the birthday. That was fine. If their guilt kept them from making a big deal of this, even better.

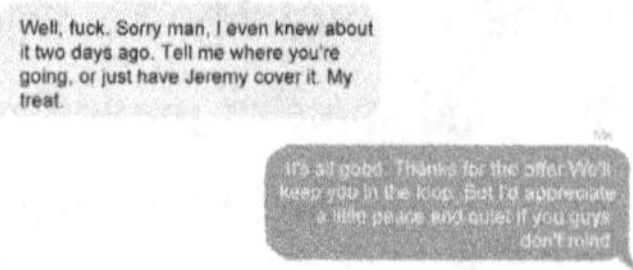

I would never keep her from talking to them at all. That would be serious bullshit, but I also wanted our focus to be on each other, not the guys. Not for the next twenty-four to forty-eight hours.

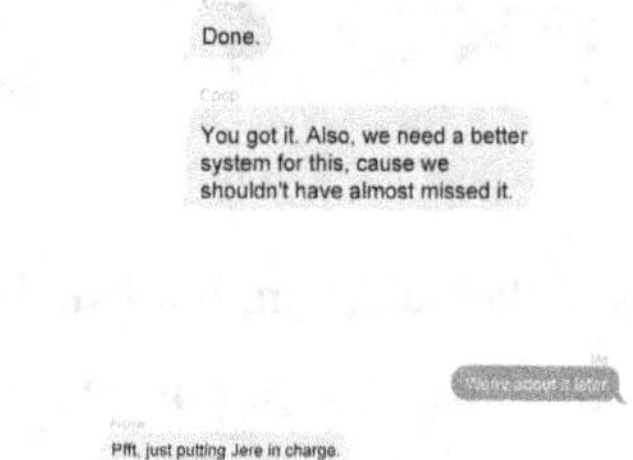

I laughed.

The only one who hadn't answered yet was Jake and I gave him time. He'd been marinating in a lot of—

"The guys aren't pissed are they?" Frankie asked as she rinsed the conditioner from her hair. The glistening skin, still golden tanned from our summer, had my palms itching to just run them all over her. As it was, I waited. The slow build and anticipation would be well worth it, for both of us.

"Maybe a little salty," I told her. No sense sugar-coating that. "We're all a bit selfish about our time with you, Angel. We wanted all of your time before the accident. That just highlighted how much we all had to lose."

It wasn't a scold, but her sigh carried the weight of the world. "I wish there was a way to go back and make sure you guys knew I was okay."

"Me too," I admitted. "You're safe now, but no one wants to take their eyes off you because we're afraid you won't be there when we open them again."

She shut off the water and I put the phone down to snag one of the oversized fluffy towels from the rack warmer. They really had thought of everything with this place. I wrapped her up in the towel and tugged her to me.

"Ian," she whispered and I grinned. I really fucking loved how she said my name. This time, however, when I kissed her, I let out some of the pent up emotion from the last few weeks.

The towel kept her arms trapped and I gripped the front as she stepped into me, keeping her in place. Her mouth softened and opened to mine without hesitation, and I groaned. Sometimes, I didn't think there were enough words, songs, or touches to convey how much I loved her. Yet, in that one perfect kiss, not only had I poured all my feelings into it, but she also welcomed it in kind.

Her trust and the warmth stole through me, settling another agitated piece that had been eager to take care of her from the beginning. Lifting my head, I smiled down at her. "Get dressed, Angel," I whispered then brushed a kiss to one corner of her mouth then the other. "It's still warm enough you can probably just braid your hair to wear under the helmet."

"Would you like my hair braided?" The counter question made me grin.

"I love your hair all ways, but yes, I think braided today."

"One braid or two?" The image of wrapping her braid around my fist as I sank into her was provocative, but two of them?

We might not make it to where I wanted to go.

"One would be good." One last kiss and I let her go before I forgot my good intentions and just locked her door and started our celebration here. My cock was not impressed with this plan and strained against my jeans, but I ignored the demand.

I needed a lot more than just a fuck. Though with Frankie—it was never just a fuck.

It never would be.

She took her time drying off, then blow drying her hair while standing there utterly nude and giving me and my dick every reason in the world to blow off my plans and just sink into her right there.

The rub of her thighs together told me she was as affected as I was. That settled me and I reached for my phone. Yes, I was denying us both. It would make it that much sweeter later.

A message from Jake waited for me.

He followed that up with a cheesy grin emoji. It had taken him a hot minute to get his temper under control, but I could respect that.

While I wouldn't normally make that offer, right now Jake and Archie needed that measure of control so I'd allow for it. Coop seemed a lot more relaxed about it, but he just wanted the assurance she was okay.

It was something we'd discussed while Jake and Frankie had still been in Germany. We didn't *have* to see her every single day, but we wanted to see her. We didn't *have* to talk to her each day, but fuck it ached when we didn't. Jake needed her and that was more than enough, but we'd grown to crave every second or morsel of contact.

Three of the four of us were still dealing with that when the accident happened, and now I was stealing her away. So, I got it and I'd do them the courtesy so they wouldn't worry.

As soon as Frankie finished lacing up her boots, she glanced at me with a grin. "Ready?"

I held out my hand for her. On our way down, I snagged the bag I'd left for us down the landing and she eyed it, but didn't ask.

Jeremy waited for us in the front hall with two disposable cups of coffee in hand.

"You are so my favorite person," Frankie said by way of good morning, and she gave him a kiss on the cheek that he accepted with a kind of quiet serenity I found myself envying.

Unsurprisingly, the coffee was perfect, and I took an appreciative drink before I nodded. "We'll be back sometime tomorrow, though it could be the day after. If anything changes, we'll let you know."

Jeremy gave me a firm nod. I'd have given him the full itinerary anyway, but since he'd actually used some magic to make the reservation I'd wanted for us, he already knew. "Have a safe..." He gave me and then Frankie a meaningful look before glancing back to me. "And fun trip. We'll see you both in a couple of days."

Frankie flashed him another smile, but she was still cuddling her coffee like she hadn't seen it in years. It was freaking adorable. "Thanks Jeremy."

He held the door for us and with the duffle over one shoulder, I caught Frankie's free hand in mine after she'd slipped on her sunglasses and her smile grew. "Thanks for coming with me."

"Always," she promised and leaned into me before taking another sip of coffee. "Especially because this trip apparently comes with treats, as well as you."

The impish grin was the cherry on top and I laughed.

It was already two thousand percent better than my last birthday and we were just getting started.

Chapter Eight

I CAN'T HELP FALLING IN LOVE

Frankie

The leather jacket with its inserts of gold against the red was one of my favorites. It matched Ian's black jacket with red inserts. Something different from the older ones we'd used. Our helmets had been customized to match the jackets. It was cute bordering on painful, at least according to Rachel. I, on the other hand, just loved it.

We'd finished our coffees in the time it took to get to the garage, and Ian swiped his keycard and showed the attendant his ID. We owned our parking slots for some ridiculous amount of money. The place also had an elevator that took cars up and brought them down.

It was like one of those claw machines, but for cars.

My snicker got Ian's attention and when I shared the observation, he laughed. Weirdly, it took me a minute once the bike was in front of us. Apprehension wrapped around me like a suffocating blanket of scratchy wool sweaters. The agitation on my skin seemed to increase and while the heat wasn't altogether comfortable, I hadn't been sweating that much.

Until now.

The ride from the hospital back to the brownstone was a bit of a blur. Jake had walked me back from the university. We'd taken the long way just like Ian and I had on the way there. It had been nice. Even if Jake had only said he and Archie got carried away in boxing.

Carried away.

The bruises Archie had were just as bad. The cold war brewing between them had definitely made for a chilly dinner, and when Coop asked if I wanted to watch a movie, I'd chickened out and escaped with him. Still...

"We don't have to go, Angel," Ian said and I blinked slowly as sound rushed back in. The bike was right there and he sat astride it, but I hadn't budged from my spot. The weight of his worried gaze settled on me, and I blew out a breath.

Rubbing a hand against my chest, I shook my head. "I'm fine." The accident hadn't been on the bike. "I can't afford to be scared of cars. I *refuse* to be scared of your bike."

His smile softened and his eyes held only encouragement. I pulled my helmet on and buckled it before I climbed on the back of the bike and settled my hands against his hips where I could grip his belt loops. The urge to hold on for dear life was there, absolutely.

Not going to be afraid.

Fuck Maddy.

That thought did more to dislodge the unease and apprehension than anything else. Maddy didn't get to take anything else from me. Not happening.

I closed my eyes as I gave Ian's waist a squeeze.

"You good?" he asked over his shoulder and I grinned, even if he couldn't see me fully.

"Absolutely! Let's get your party started."

His laughter rumbled through him, and the bike's vibrations were giving me a little grief. Not my bruises. Nope. The needy state he'd left me in almost had me wanting to rub myself back and forth on the bike.

That was not something I'd considered, but before I could even comment, he pulled out of the garage and into traffic. A thrill skated through me side by side with the apprehension, but within the first thirty minutes of the drive, most of that had been blown away as we weaved through traffic.

Had I been here long enough to already think the traffic wasn't that bad? As it was, we headed north through Manhattan and into the Bronx. The changes in architecture and shopfronts made me wish we had time to explore, but I was also just enjoying being with Ian.

It wasn't all that long before we were leaving the city behind and heading north. The abundance of trees along the corridor we drove grew more plentiful. I swore the air had cooled, some. The sun kept me more than warm in my jacket, but the breeze as we whipped along kept me from overheating.

My muscles began their protest at about ninety minutes into the ride and Ian found a rest stop for us to use and I got to stretch. After we both hit the restrooms and came out, I asked, "Do I get to know where we're going yet?"

Dropping a kiss on my lips, then the tip of my nose he chuckled. "We're almost there, Angel."

"I'm supposed to be surprising *you* for your birthday," I pointed out and that earned me an arm around my waist and being dragged right up to him.

"You're my present, Frankie," he whispered then delivered a searing kiss that did more to ease the ache in my muscles and joints than the walk around. When he lifted his head, I just leaned against his arm and trusted him to keep me on my feet. "That's all I need," he murmured and I grinned.

I might even have been floating a little by the time I pulled my helmet back on and we mounted the bike once more. This time I slid a little closer and wrapped my arms around his middle.

He rubbed my hands with his once before he got the bike rumbling again and we were off. A part of me wished I didn't have to wear the helmet so I could lean against his back, but the rest of me knew better. Not to mention, Ian would probably spank me at the suggestion.

I swore my smile grew at the thought. It had been a while since it had been just the two of us, and I ached for time with him both in and out of the bedroom. It wasn't long before we were off the highway, and he navigated his way through the most charming of towns. It was hard to believe Manhattan and the rest of New York City wasn't that far away and yet we were in a totally different world.

We passed village shops and the most adorable main street. Probably not something I should ever describe it as for the locals. The winding road plunged us back into the trees and the shade dappled the road.

Since Ian had throttled the speed down, it gave me ample opportunity to gawk. There were mansions visible through the trees, some more than others. Half of me was dying to explore and the other half rioted with craziness at the idea of where we were going.

I wasn't ready for him to turn at a stone sign that read something Inn, I didn't catch the first name. The winding drive took us up through another gallery of trees lining the drive, until they spread apart again to reveal a huge mansion that looked like some had taken a fairy tale cottage, right down to the stonework, and just expanded it into something huge.

The wings jutting off to either side had cobblestone walks in front of them along with patios. The upper floors had balconies. Huge windows decorated the whole building along with porticos and breezeways between the wings of the building and the center. Rather than pull up at the front, Ian continued around the building to a parking area hidden rather neatly in the back.

Once there, he pulled us into a narrow little slot reserved for motorcycles and then dropped the kickstand. It wasn't until we were off the bike and he'd stowed our helmets on it that I turned to face him. Yes, my body still vibrated from riding the bike and I was pretty sure my legs would hate me in the morning, but right now...

"Ian?"

"Hmmm?" The pure pleasure in his smile sent a shudder through me. Without another word, he pulled the duffel bag out from where he'd stowed it in the saddle bags and then held out his hand to me.

"You're pretty awesome."

"Glad you noticed," he said with an uncharacteristic smugness that had me laughing even as he winked. The air out here was cooler, I swore. Definitely a little more humid, but cooler than the city. All I could smell was pine, and forest green. Good god the pine though. It was like the air had been freshened a thousand times over.

Once inside, we passed through a gallery with artwork and little placards attached to each. Curiosity ate away at me, but I saved that for later. The lady at the desk greeted us warmly and took Ian's credit card and driver's license. Then she said our room wasn't quite ready as we'd been bumped up to one of the private bungalows.

I bit the inside of my lip. Jeremy or Archie.

My money was on Archie getting Jeremy to do it.

Ian let out a soft sigh. "Can we leave the bag with you here then, while we grab some lunch and take a walk?"

"Absolutely," she said. "I'll send you a text as soon as it's ready. Everything else you requested will be in place."

"Thank you." We stored our helmets, jackets and overnight bag with the bell staff.

Then we wandered into the restaurant. It was open seating and the wide doors at the end were open to the air with the ceiling fans all turning to give us a breeze.

We talked about everything and nothing over our lunches. Both of us went for lighter fare, though the size of the burgers they brought and the chocolate shake we split was hilarious.

I finished all of mine and Ian fed me fries from his plate after. Sleepiness invaded me, but I was having far too much fun to just want to nap. Besides, we didn't have a room yet. After lunch, we went for a lazy hike around the property—that turned out to be two hundred and fifty acres. Ian indulged me with a brochure he'd nicked from the desk when I hadn't been paying attention.

David Thoreau and Ralph Waldo Emerson had once been guests at the establishment. Other historical figures who spent notable time at Trebeck Inn included the Roosevelts, and a Kennedy or three. The property had been modernized over the years, but it still focused on service, comfort, and luxury. They even had bicycles you could borrow, and they'd pack you a picnic lunch.

"We can do that tomorrow if you want," Ian offered as if this was the most natural thing in the world. The place was incredible. I kind of wanted to go everywhere. The hike felt good. We found babbling brooks, downed trees, and a place where a stone bridge created a walkway over a ravine. One that I'd bet filled with water in heavy rain.

Everything was so cozy and distant. It was like we were forever and a day away from anything that could remotely give us trouble. At one point, I paused to gaze up at the trees and I just breathed in the fresh air, the scent of the earth, the trees, and honeysuckle.

Somewhere the lazy buzz of a bee hummed past and birds called to one another. There were no cars. No people. It was like it was just me and Ian and no one else.

So caught up in my thoughts, I jumped a little when Ian wrapped his arms around me. I relaxed back into him and tilted my head to rest against his shoulder as I kept looking up. Even the way the sunlight played on the earth through the trees was somehow magical.

"Not going to press," Ian said softly. "But I need to know how you're doing, Angel."

It was his birthday, and this wasn't a fun topic. I closed my eyes for a moment and took a deeper breath. "Better," I admitted. "Still sore in places. Pretty sure I'm going to have that bruise forever. Working on getting past being mad. I miss all of us being us." It hadn't been all that long, yet it seemed like forever. "Not as freaked out about moving vehicles. I hadn't realized how nervous I'd be until we got to the bike."

"Hence, why I offered to skip this."

"Oh fuck, I'm so glad we didn't." I glanced up as he pressed his lips to my temple. "I love that you wanted to do this for your birthday."

"Angel, we could stay in a broken down and smelly hotel on the side of the highway and it would be paradise because you were there."

I wrinkled my nose. "Ewww."

His laughter was rich and free. "Fine, a respectable and clean hotel on the side of the highway."

"Much better." I shot him a look. "Also, if we're ever touring and that's our only option, I'm sleeping in the car."

His eyes danced with merriment. "If we're doing that kind of a tour, maybe we'll have a bus or at the very least a van. Pretty sure I can rig the back of a van to tie you up quite nicely."

Liquid heat bloomed in my belly at the image and I licked my lips. "Yes, please, may I have some more?"

After turning me around, Ian cupped my face. "You know you can have whatever you want."

"I hope so," I whispered as I pushed up on my toes to wrap my arms around his neck. I wanted Maddy in jail. I wanted my guys safe. I wanted them happy. I wanted to get back to our lives before a car wreck turned us upside down again.

Ian slid his hands under my ass and lifted me. I locked my tired thighs against his hips to hold myself there. My little groan earned an arched eyebrow or two. "That turned on, Angel?"

"That sore," I admitted. "Though, I'm definitely turned on enough I don't care about sore."

He rubbed one of my thighs gently as he nuzzled my lips with these light little kisses that were tempting as hell, but offered no satisfaction.

"Does my angel need a massage?"

"If it involves your hands on my naked body, I need everything you got." The words just slipped right out, and my face heated for a split second before I grinned. Ian's own smile just grew wider.

"There she is, getting stronger, more confident, and very capable of asking for what she wants."

I carded my fingers through his hair. It was soft, even after being smashed under a helmet. "I learned a lot about myself this last year," I told him. "Learned a lot about you guys, too."

"What did you learn about me?" The curiosity in his voice just made me want to swoon. It didn't help that his gaze was like a velvet stroke on my skin.

"That you're always going to want to take care of me, even when I tell you not to. You'll find a way to do it that doesn't involve being pushy or overbearing." Because there was no doubt in my mind that this trip was for me, too.

"Not even a little sorry, Angel. You are always going to be my priority. But I will listen. You asked for space, and I gave it."

"And now?" Honestly, it didn't bother me that he wasn't sorry. Look at what I was already willing to do to protect them and all they'd done to protect me.

"Now, I'm asking for you," he said simply. "Just us. Together. And to know you're really okay. If you still need time to sort some things out, fine, but I'd rather close the gaps between us then let them get any wider."

I didn't have the words to express the depth of feeling his declaration aroused so I settled for kissing him. "Same," I whispered. "Are you okay? After everything?"

"I am now," he promised, then fisted my braid before dragging me in for a soul branding kiss that had me forgetting we were still in the woods, until his phone vibrated. Ian's groan resonated through me as he shifted his grip so he could get his phone out and keep me plastered to him. I nipped and sucked at his neck on my way to his earlobe. I didn't get to play with him that often. "Oh, thank fuck," he whispered and then held his phone up for me to see.

Our room was ready, and they'd already taken our stuff to it. We were free to go there whenever we wanted.

Oh, we wanted.

It took me half the walk back to convince Ian to put me down, because walking a few steps and pausing for long make out sessions wasn't going to get us there very fast.

And we *definitely* wanted. Right now.

Chapter Nine

WHITE LACE AND SILK

Frankie

Our room upgrade proved to be a shift in location to a private bungalow on the other side of the building. It was connected by another of those breezeways, but there was no one nearby. Even more, the exterior cottage gave way to a place with an interior garden. It was gorgeous. From the modern appointments of thick comfortable sofa and chairs to the rustic looking fireplace to the rich wood floors covered in the softest rugs. There was a loft bedroom above and a bathroom with a skylight that let you see the stars. The light pollution here was significantly lower than in the cities.

It had everything we could possibly want and then some. A huge bouquet of roses waited on the coffee table and there were a pair of notes—one on the flowers addressed to me and a second on the table addressed to Ian.

"Archie," we both said in the same breath and Ian shook his head. "I swear, he's always got to try and one up everyone."

"It's not that," I scolded him. "He just wants to fix it so everything is great. I know it seems like a competition, but I don't think it is—well at least not anymore." Archie wanted us all happy and safe. "It's his love language."

"I thought that was dirty talk and making you come," Ian teased me and I grinned.

"That too." I bumped him with my hip. While I was still aching for him, our little cottage getaway was a hell of a lot more than I was expecting. Ian, too. I passed him his note and then opened mine.

Babe,

We all feel like assholes because our plans for Bubba's birthday kind of fell apart after the accident. Don't even start blaming yourself or feeling bad. We're the dumbasses who failed. That said, he's got the right idea in stealing away with you. The whole weekend is covered if you want to stay.

The flowers are for you as are the chocolate strawberries that will come with dinner. I had Jeremy arrange catering service for your meals so you can stay inside if you want, or not—just let them know your plans. Miss you like hell, but want you guys to have a great weekend. Give him a blowjob or three for me.

Yes, that sounds really fucking weird, doesn't it? Tell you what, give him one for each of us. Fuck it. Brother boyfriends should mean something, right?

Love you, babe. Rock his world.

Archie (Coop and Jake, too)

I burst out laughing reading the note and when I glanced over Ian wore the most peculiar expression as he read the single sheet of paper. "You know," he murmured. "Just when I think I've got the guy pegged, he pulls something like this."

My stomach bottomed out, but Ian's eyes held nothing but a smile when he glanced up at me.

"It's not bad, Angel, here." He held the note out and I glanced at mine and then we traded because seriously, nothing in there I was worried about him reading.

Bubba,

Okay, so, as penalties for being the worst brother boyfriends in history, the three of us are voluntarily giving you the right to take a date night each from us when you need it. Doesn't matter what plans we've made, or anything, our present to you is three nights with Frankie at your discretion.

Coop has also suggested that you get at least one night a week between now and Christmas to declare as yours and no one else will join you. That means Coop won't sneak up there when it's your date night with her. I'd make the same promise, except we both know that sometimes she likes both of us there, so we'll call that at your discretion.

As for Jake, he said he'd clear it with you later. The place is paid through the weekend, all the upgrades are on me. I thought I'd share a secret with you about a certain way Frankie likes me to curl my tongue, then I thought that you have your own moves and I'll keep mine. It works better that way.

Sorry again, man. We'll do better. Expect at least a family party when you two are back.

Arch (Yeah yeah and Coop and Jake)

I was giggling by the time I reached the end and Ian grinned. "You're supposed to give me blowjobs for them."

"Apparently, they are giving you the right to veto their dates or take their places," I said with a shake of my head. "Not sure where I get the veto on that."

"You always have veto rights, Angel," he whispered as he cupped my cheek. "Also, you're the only one giving me blowjobs and it's never for them, no matter what they think."

Another string of giggles escaped me even as he kissed me, and our teeth clacked more than once because he was grinning. It was probably one of our most awkward and yet fun kisses at the same time. Resting his forehead against mine, Ian smiled so wide it stretched across my heart.

I didn't write music, but I'd have to tell him that line later, maybe he could work it into a song. With his thumbs, he caressed my cheeks. It took me a moment to even realize we'd begun swaying, dancing without any music.

After a moment, he pulled out his phone while we still swayed, and he chose a song. The soft determined strings of his guitar accompanied the familiar piano melody. I opened my eyes and glanced up to find him watching me a beat before his voice joined the instruments in a sweet, savage song of love lost before it had even begun.

Even though I knew the song, this wasn't how it opened. In fact, this was one of the songs that KC had pointed to as an example of where we needed to feature his voice more. The love and longing carried in each note held me captive. As his last note hung there, my part began and holy shit...

I sounded so damn haunted, isolated, betrayed, and hurting. When I would have said something, Ian pressed a finger to my lips and kept us swaying to the almost tragic melody. He cut in again, picking up where I left off. Only now there was determination and desire in the song and punctuating our kiss.

All I could feel was him as the song played and our voices twined together. I had no idea when he'd had time to do the music mixing and remaster that demo, but it ripped all the emotions out of me.

Panting, I broke the kiss as the last note faded and stared up at him. "That was beautiful."

"You like it?" I swore a faint red touched his ears and there was an eagerness to him that only appeared when we discussed his music. My fierce, strong, utterly proud lover and the man with so much control waffled only in his confidence in his own music. Me singing? He was a thousand percent supportive. Him? He worried that he sucked.

Cupping his face in my hands, I smiled at him and let the tears fall. No hiding anything. "Your music always affects me. I love it so much. I love the changes. I love the way you tied your story into mine, because it's not just my love story, it's yours too."

"It's ours, Angel," he said in a ragged voice. "Not sure I can send that to anyone else though."

A shuddery breath escaped and I studied him. "Then we don't. It's our song and no one else's." I loved the music. I loved singing with Ian. But the music was inextricably linked to him, and I wanted him happy. If he didn't want to expose himself that way, then I got it.

"Just like that?" Mirth flickered in his eyes as he began swaying and slid his arms down to my hips. The gentle grinding as he pressed me closer had me sighing and I traced my fingers up his face to his hair.

"Just like that," I promised. "Ian, Bound Hearts is us. That means if you don't want something then I don't. That's what you told me, right?"

He chuckled. "That was in part to encourage you to take the risks."

"I'll take any risk with you. Any single one." The words came out a vow and I meant every syllable. I swore his eyes darkened at the declaration.

"Any one?"

"Yes."

He gripped my ass and began to massage it. "Strip, Angel. All of it. Off."

One last kiss, more a nip and sip before he pulled away from me and went to lean against the sofa. Arms folded, he studied me as if we were just hanging out and he'd asked for a demonstration.

My shoes came off, then my socks and I stripped down my jeans and soaked panties. Both clung to my skin a little and required me to peel them down. I did a little wiggle to finish stepping out of them. It wasn't my sexiest move and to be honest, I didn't think I'd ever be the one seducing them.

And maybe that was something I should work on. Filing that thought away, I tugged my shirt up and off. The air inside was cooler thanks to the air conditioning, but my nipples were pebbled long before I stripped off my bra.

Finished, I faced him hands on my hips and then slid my hands to my thighs as I knelt. Eyes closed, I tilted my head down to show obedience. Ian never asked me for this, yet he loved it when I submitted so willingly, and I adored the elated feeling flooding me along with the sense of absolute safety.

Ian would protect me, I was his to do with as he pleased and fuck me, did he please.

"I love you, Angel, but we're not doing that tonight—well not fully." Surprise flickered through me, but I stole a look up as he moved around and knelt behind me. When he loosened my braid, I let out a little sigh. The light scrape of his fingers against my scalp was heaven.

The lividity of my bruise remained a physical reminder of the crash. I had other cuts and scrapes, but nothing so vicious as that strap bruise. As my hair loosened and spilled down my back, Ian continued his slow sensual assault with his fingertips. The petting motion lulled me. When he ceased, I floated, bereft, then the music started again.

It was the song from the studio—the day he and Coop shared me and pushed me until I could hit those smokey notes. He'd played it on a loop then and I had a feeling... Ian ran his hands down my arms and helped me stand then pulled me back against him.

He was still wearing clothes and I would have pouted, but he kissed a path along my neck as he ran his hand over my stomach and gently pressed me back into him as he began to roll his hips. The grind of his jeans against my ass was a teasing friction, but I rolled my hips in time with his.

A groan escaped me as his kisses reached my jaw and he began to cup my breasts with his hands. They were so damn warm, they bordered on hot. With care, he pinched my nipples, teasing them and then I turned my head, fusing our mouths together.

The stretch, the rolling hips, and the contact was everything, but I wanted more. If we weren't playing tonight, then I could demand what I wanted. If it made me a brat, then I'd take my punishment gleefully. I reached behind me to run my hands over his thighs and back. It was awkward but the press of his hips to mine ground his erection against my ass.

The beat of the music thrummed through me as I unsnapped his jeans and tugged down the zipper the heavy weight of his cock brushed against my fingers...

"Ian Rhys," I whispered, both awed and delighted. "Are you going commando?"

"I wanted as few barriers between us as possible, Angel, and believe me when I tell you that my jeans were choking my dick just fine, briefs would have killed me." He bit down on my lower lip, sucking it out as I stroked him. The hot heat of his cock and the silky soft skin filled my palm with decadent temptation.

He left my breasts aching as he slid one hand up to my throat, gentle as hell. There was still a bruise along my neck, and he traced it with his lips and tongue. I shuddered at the assault. "Hands on your ass, Angel." He bit down right over my pulse point and I swore my pussy spasmed and my thighs clenched.

I let go of his cock, reluctant, but I obeyed and I pressed my hands to my ass. Every grind of his hips rubbed his dick against the crack of my ass, and I had to wonder if we were going straight for anal tonight. Then he was urging me to bend slightly, and I let out a happy little sigh as he ran his cock against my clit before bumping the head to my entrance. It was like he needed to slick himself up with me and the image had me clenching again.

He let out a strangled "*fuck*" as I squeezed his cock with my thighs even as we kept moving. "Do that again." So I did, tightening my thighs as I rolled and rotated my hips. It mimicked the thrusting motion, and I swore a trickle of dampness slid against my thighs as I teased him.

"You're so fucking perfect, Angel." The passion in his voice was another tease to my senses. Then he pushed forward. The relentless thrust a perfect counterpoint to the deep beat of the next song. I didn't recognize this one, but it had a hard bass line and fuck...I couldn't breathe as he filled me and then we were moving, still grinding and rolling our hips together.

He had to be crouching a little to keep the connection, but he pushed in and out fluidly, teasing me with every stroke and then he was cupping my breasts and he nipped at my earlobe. "Ready, Angel?"

"Yes."

I didn't need to ask for what. I was ready for whatever he wanted, and the bass line beat gave way to a rhythm so fierce it stole my breath as Ian began to piston into me. His arms around me kept me securely against him and I met his pounding rhythm. The slap of his hips to mine had my hands actually spanking me slightly and I let out a throaty laugh.

Oh, I was going to..."Ian, I need to come." Oh, fuck did I need to.

"Grip the sofa, Angel." At his order, I half bent and put my hands on the back of the sofa, for all our dancing and grinding we hadn't moved far, and hell, Ian still had his clothes on. Those thoughts drifted away as he settled his hands on my hips, one of them anyway. The other continued downward and he added his fingers to my clit, stroking and teasing until I splintered.

The cry I let out matched the ragged notes in the song, and still Ian drove into me, and I answered the press and twist of his hips and then I came again, this time I nearly collapsed under the quaking in my system. My vision whited out and all I could feel was Ian.

The hot rush of his release as he came and the harsh shout above me was like paradise. I could feel him everywhere, touching me, kissing me, filling me and when I opened my eyes, I had my head on the back of the sofa with my breath coming in swift pants while sweat slicked my skin.

His shirt clung to me. He traced my earlobe with his tongue as he softened, but not much. I swore he was half-hard and still deep inside of me.

"More?" It was both a question and a promise.

"Birthday boy," he began with a grin.

"Gets what he wants," I answered with a sigh as he pulled away and I went to my knees again. This time I reached for his cock and Ian let me have it. When I guided him to my lips, he slid his hands into my hair.

"Take everything you can," he ordered, and I swallowed around his dick. It took him almost no time to recover, as I stroked him with my hand, mouth, and tongue. When he was thick enough I was choking on him, he fucked into my mouth with care and I delighted at his shout as he came.

I was still licking my lips when he picked me up. I swore his legs were quaking.

"Ian," I told him as he carried me up to the loft where a bed waited covered in rose petals and I had to laugh. "You still have clothes on."

"Give me two seconds, Angel and I'll fix that, I promise."

I don't think we left that bed the rest of the night—except when Ian went down to grab the food and water. Then we played, we laughed, we talked, and he made love to me until I couldn't see straight.

It might have been his birthday, but I swore I got the presents. Or at least, he shared them with me. Perfect, from start to finish. My only real regret was we never did get back out to hike and see the sites.

Oh well. Maybe next time.

Or not.

Chapter Ten
THE DAY EVERYTHING CHANGED

Frankie

Words and ideas can change the world. People tended to forget that. Hell, I forgot that. But the morning of our first full day at university dawned and I wasn't racing downstairs to grab my coffee and head to the campus three hours before my first class. To be fair, I had three alarms set.

The first was to wake up. The second to get dressed and if I hadn't already, to grab a shower and then get dressed. We'd already planned to pick up food on the way to our first classes. We didn't actually have classes together today. Somehow, we'd managed to get all our joint classes on the same Tuesday/Thursday rotation while everything else fell Monday/Wednesday/Friday.

Except me, I didn't have classes on Friday. Lucky little happenstance. The guys all did though, so Rachel and I were waiting for Friday to drive out and meet the Long Island police detective assigned to investigate the accident. I also had put in a call to the insurance company. They had investigators, too, right? I'd had a message from one asking me to be in touch when I was up to discussing it. They needed a report.

Instead of lounging in bed, I'd crept up the stairs to the roof, to watch the sun rise. The city was an entirely different kind of heat than I was used to at home. The buildings could trap it or sometimes they provided wind tunnels that offered cooling. It was—weird and fascinating. But the sunrise never bored. I had the perfect angle on the roof to watch it come to life and flood light between the buildings, elongating the shadows—painting the city in contrasts.

"Hey," Coop murmured as he slid up behind me and wrapped his arms around my middle. The kiss he pressed to the side of my neck made me smile. "I thought we agreed you worrying before coffee was not a good plan?"

I laughed and leaned back into him, folding my arms over his where they rested against my middle. "I'm not worrying...well, not much."

"First day at a new school, I'd be more worried if you weren't worried."

"You bet me I'd be ready to go before sun-up." My smile turned fleeting. It hadn't even been a real bet. The truth was... "I'm a little scared."

"It's going to be different," Coop reminded me. "But we walked into the halls of that high school every year and you spent all of last year dealing with a bunch of nosy bitches and people trying to make you feel bad about who you are and what you wanted. You kick ass, Frankie. This is a different school..."

"With different cliques, requirements, politics, and expectations."

He nuzzled a kiss to my hair. "You're going to blow them all away."

I made a face. "Stop getting all your encouragement and pep all over my pity party, table for one."

"Oh, sorry," Coop retorted. "You're right. It's going to suck. Let's change your schedule so we share all the same classes and are never, ever apart."

While he might be teasing me, I had to admit. "That sounds kind of good right now."

Honestly, being nervous about it all hadn't really hit until five, when I woke up to pee. I hadn't been able to go back to sleep. Even with Coop and Ian right there, I'd ended up watching them sleep before I dragged myself up here.

"Hey," Coop whispered as he turned me around to look at him. Hands cupping my face, he locked his gray-green eyed gaze on mine. "Talk to me. What's wrong?"

"I think it all just hit me. We're not in Kansas anymore, Toto."

"Toto was Bubba," Coop teased, but his whole expression gentled as he brushed some of the hair away from my face to tuck behind my ears. "I'm the Tin Man, remember? He was Toto."

A laugh escaped me again. "You guys looked so good that night."

"I look good every night." The wink was perfect, and I rose up on my tiptoes to wrap my arms around his neck.

"Not as good as me," I replied with the familiar comeback and his grin widened.

"That right there is just plain facts and nothing but facts." The teasing expression vanished behind a far more serious one. "Frankie, it's okay to be scared. We're in brand new territory. But it's still school. You're still an academic badass who over-plans everything and prepares so much you make the rest of us look like untutored slackers."

Lips twisting, I squinted at him. "I am not that bad."

"No, you're far worse. It's definitely one of your truly adorable traits."

"That doesn't make it sound much better."

Coop kissed me as he walked me backward away from the half-wall I'd been leaning on and over to where we'd set up a table and chairs. By the time he sat and pulled me into his lap, I had to admit, I felt a bit better.

Okay, I felt a lot better. "I should go get some coffee."

"Nope," Coop murmured. "Bubba's bringing it up. He just took a shower first to give us some time to let me check on you."

I frowned. "You both knew something was wrong." It wasn't a

question.

"Well, I kind of have the inside track on how one Frankie Curtis operates," Coop teased, rubbing his hand against my thigh and I sighed. "I also know you've been distracted."

"A little," I admitted, trying to ignore the guilt twisting inside of me. A part of me wanted to tell Coop everything. What I suspected regarding Maddy, and why. But he would tell the guys. They would close ranks and I'd have a harder time protecting them.

"Talk to me." The soft plea threatened to break me. "I can't help if you won't tell me."

Tracing my fingers up his bare chest, I sighed. "Honestly? It's a little bit of everything. The accident, my grandparents—Hank."

"I thought things were good with Hank."

"They are," I said, lifting my gaze to his. "But I talked to him for an hour last night and never found a place to tell him about the accident. I mean—if I tell him now, it's going to hurt his feelings that I didn't trust him enough to tell him when it happened."

"Blame us," Coop offered up. "We're the assholes who didn't call him right away."

The ease of the suggestion coupled with the faint curl of a smile touching the corners of his mouth made me smile. "I'm not about to throw my boyfriends under the bus." Before he could respond, I pressed a finger to his lips. "You guys not calling him that first day or two, fine. You were focused on what happened to me. But every day since then is on me." Just like it had been with Rachel.

"You were planning to go to his place for a weekend soon, right?"

We'd talked about it for Labor Day. That wasn't that far away. Still...

"Tell you what," Coop said. "How about when you tell him, one of us is there. We can take the heat for the initial oops. He'll be mad at us and then forgive you when you tell him you wanted to tell him face to face so he can see with his own eyes that you're fine."

"That sounds like an excuse," I admitted even as I turned it over in my head.

"It's not a lie though," he said. "Now that we've figured out a plan for those two issues, is something else is bothering you?"

I sighed. "Yes, but nothing I want to talk about yet."

"Will you talk to me when you're ready?"

I could have kissed him for not pushing. Archie would have tried to sweet talk it out of me. Jake would have been a barnacle on my ass until I admitted it, even if he had to piss me off to get me to do it. Ian? He'd let me get away with it as long as he didn't think it was hurting me. But Coop? Coop trusted me with me.

"I don't know if I'll ever be ready for this particular conversation," I told him. "But before you ask, I'm talking to Rachel."

"Good." He stroked this thumb over my lower lip. "Anything else I can do to make your morning better?"

Biting down on his thumb, I held it captive for a brief moment. "Tell me you're at least a little nervous about all of this too?"

"Not a huge fan of not having any first day classes together," Coop said before tugging me down into a kiss. The slow rock of his tongue along the seam of my lips had me opening to him instantly and I swore we both sighed in the same moment. "But that just means we get to say hello again after classes."

"That's not being nervous," I teased.

He grinned. "Ask me again later. I'm feeling pretty invincible at the moment."

"Yeah?"

"Yeah," he said, tugging the neck of my top to the side in order to press a kiss to my collarbone. "See, my girl needs me to be calm and steady so she can quietly freak out, without unsettling all the alpha dicks around her."

"Is that so?"

"Yep." The playfulness in his eyes beckoned to me. "Not that I won't beat up the bad things driving you crazy, but I accept Rachel as a good confidante. As the first bff to the new bff, she has my approval, ten out of ten."

"You're only saying that because she's meaner than you."

Coop considered me for a long moment, then shrugged. "Not going to argue facts, Sweetheart. If Rachel thinks she needs to take it out, she'll do it and with great glee. Just remind me to *never* get on her bad side."

He ended that sentence by blowing a raspberry against the side of my neck and I giggled. Of course, that set me off squirming and he teased his fingers along my ribs as his dick woke up all healthy and interested beneath my ass.

"No naked shenanigans on the roof," Ian called as he pushed open the door and carried out three huge mugs of coffee. "You know Jeremy's rules."

"That's not Jeremy's rules," Coop argued cheerfully as he cuddled me closer and honestly, the hug and the holding was doing so much to settle my anxiety I wasn't going anywhere. That and I loved just being cradled against him. "Those are yours."

"I guarantee if you asked Jeremy, he'd say the same thing." Ian set the coffee mugs down on the table then swooped in to cradle my face and kiss me. He tasted of peppermint toothpaste and hot fresh coffee. Freshly showered, he also smelled sinful. Maybe I shouldn't have snuck out of bed early. This would have been a much better way to wake up.

As if reading my mind, Ian winked.

"Don't get all frisky, Angel. Bad girls who sneak away don't get prizes."

I made a face.

"But they do get coffee."

"You know," I admitted as he pressed it into my hands, and I cradled it to me before taking a first prized sip. "This is still winning."

He chuckled and took the chair nearest ours and lifted my feet to his lap. He was dressed casually, cargo shorts and a t-shirt, but like me and Coop, his feet were bare. His hair was damp and his face freshly shaven.

Definitely need to rethink how I get cuddles to get rid of what's bothering me.

"Did she tell you?" Ian asked Coop before taking a swallow of his own coffee. This stuff was heavenly, and it had just a hint of nuttiness to it that told me it was the good stuff and Jeremy had brewed the pot that morning. The guys all made it just a bit differently. Not that I complained. Just like them, I loved the unique ways they prepped the coffee.

"Enough," Coop said. "She's fine." He punctuated that with a kiss to my head. "We're going to have an amazing first day."

"Good." That settled that. It really was that easy. Ian and Coop had definitely talked then, or they'd both picked up on something. I'd never been more grateful for how my brother boyfriends communicated than I was right now. I didn't want to lie to any of them, but I also didn't feel comfortable admitting anything aloud until I had something concrete.

I could have kissed them both for how easily they transitioned to just talking our plans as we all figured out where we would be. Our schedules were pretty staggered. Ian had music classes today, he'd also be getting studio time. Something, he reminded me with a gentle tap to my ankle, we both needed to take advantage of and put together the rest of our demo.

At the rate we were going, we were gonna have a full album.

Coop's classes were almost all intro to psych, statistical models, and a straight introduction to analysis course.

Me? I had introduction to business, intro to economics, and basic ethics course.

Core classes began on Tuesday when we all had humanities and history courses. The fact my AP credits got me out of a lot of them, didn't mean I didn't want to take them. In fact, I'd seen at least a dozen history courses I wanted to take.

"Come back to us, Angel," Ian teased and I blinked over at him. More than half my coffee was gone, and I glanced from him to Coop and back again. They were both grinning at me. "If only you swooned over us the way you do over an academic catalog of classes."

Yeah, they laughed but I just lifted my coffee mug to toast them. "Love me, love my weirdness."

"Oh, we do," Coop promised. "We love every quirky inch of you."

I snickered. "At least we're all together tomorrow, right?" The general education credits we'd managed to schedule together since every degree required them.

"That's the plan," Ian said as he gave my foot a squeeze. "Just remember, you have time to get your feet wet here and don't think you have to have it all locked down the first week."

"Hey," I argued. "It's me."

"We know," they said in the same aggrieved tone.

Well then. I drained my coffee and twisted to give Coop a kiss before leaning over to give another to Ian. "Just for that. I'm showering alone."

Their laughter followed me all the way to the door, and I didn't even mind. Of course, when I got to my shower, Archie was already standing inside it, water sluicing over him, and I let out a little sigh.

"Good intentions and all that," I murmured to myself before shutting the door and stripping. Archie turned to face me as I slid into the shower with him, and he grinned.

"Morning, Babe."

Oh yeah. Good intentions.

Just, his intentions seemed way better than mine at the moment.

Chapter Eleven

ARE YOU KIDDING ME?

Coop

Four days.

I gave the assholes four days after classes started to get their shit together. Not that either of them seemed to deserve it. If anything, they'd drifted further apart. I blamed Archie, who made a point of getting in Jake's face every chance he got to prove to him he couldn't be pushed way. I blamed Jake for letting his temper make his decisions.

In my defense, I'd told them both they were being idiots from the moment they went for that boxing match at the gym. That hadn't been a match. That had been a brawl. It had been a long time since I'd seen the two of them pitted against each other. I thought we'd settled this shit in our sophomore year, after Archie had stopped trying to date Frankie and relaxed into the same friendship we had with her.

Now?

Fuck, this was worse.

The icy wall between them seemed to be climbing higher. If Archie was in her room, Jake wouldn't go anywhere near it. If Jake was up there, you could almost see the wheels turning in Archie's head, but he resisted the temptation to butt in and push him.

Detente seemed to be found only at shared meals and usually they both just focused on Frankie. Bubba watched them as closely as I did. But this was escalating in a way that was going to get seriously old if they didn't find a way to resolve it. Frankie and I joined in on the morning runs on Tuesdays and Thursdays right now. While Jake and Archie might leave every morning to run, they weren't running together.

Tuesday, however, Jake dropped the bomb that he'd had a schedule shift. He tried to make it sound casual, but it wasn't just one class. It was all of them. Friday was the first day the four of us were alone because Frankie left at the crack of dawn to head over to Rachel's.

I'd just finished lacing my shoes up when Bubba knocked on the door. I glanced up to see him shaking his head. "I'm just going to tell you right now, this is not going to go well if neither of them is willing to compromise."

"I know," I said, before stretching. "But I don't have to be on campus until ten. So, who do you want? Stubborn jackass one or stubborn jackass two?"

Bubba laughed. "I'll handle Jake. You deal with Archie."

I debated that, then nodded. Jake and I went way back, we got each other. The wake up call might come better from Bubba. "Just try to avoid the beating the crap out of each other aspect of the fight."

He snorted, but he'd known Jake for years and fighting wasn't new for any of us. The stakes were a lot different right now. Frankie might not have noticed the tension because school had her distracted, but she had picked up on something being wrong. I'd bet every dollar in my wallet. Well, I'd bet all the dollars in Archie's wallet.

"Coop," Bubba said, his tone taking a more serious note. "We can't fix this for them. Those two have to solve it for themselves. They're both angry."

"And they are taking it out on each other," I reminded him as I stood and snagged a sweatshirt to pull on. "The fact Jake changed his fucking schedule then told Frankie it was because his focus had shifted slightly and the new one would work out better for him..."

Teeth clenching on that last part, I couldn't finish the thought. He'd delivered it with a straight face and she'd frowned. Her disappointment at Jake's absence from most of our shared classes had been profound. The only one he'd kept was the history class they shared. The one the rest of us weren't in.

Asshole.

"Technically," Bubba said, arms folded. "He didn't lie."

I stared at him. "Are you for fucking real, right now?" Cause that was the last thing I expected from Bubba. Had he lost his damn mind?

"Just listen," he cautioned, raising his hand. Then stepping further into the room, he closed the door and leaned back against it. "What got me into trouble with Frankie before was deciding I knew what was best and assuming that everyone was moving too fast for her. In some ways—I still think I was right. However..."

Yeah, that however saved him. 'Cause I had listened then, I'd understood what he'd been trying to do.

"However," Bubba continued. "We only know some of the surface of what these two are fighting about. The parts you've heard. They are *not* having these fights in front of me."

"Probably because they don't want to kickstart your protect Frankie at all costs genes." It was a dry observation, but an accurate one. Archie fixed things. Jake took out threats. I tried to smooth the waters. But Bubba? He put her in front of all of us, and that meant if he thought they were a problem for her, he'd deal with it.

"Maybe." He shrugged. "Maybe not. The point is—this matter is really between them."

Tilting my head back, I stared at the ceiling. "I would agree, except it's affecting everyone. She may not have said anything to us." I used 'us' because I presumed she hadn't said anything to him either. Not that he had to tell me and I wasn't asking. "We all respect that our personal relationships with Frankie are personal. But what Jake and Archie are doing..."

"...is going to make this all of our problems, I know," Bubba said with a sigh. "Like I said, I'll take Jake. You take Archie. If that doesn't work, we confront them together."

If that didn't work, there wasn't a snowball's chance in Hell of keeping this from Frankie.

"Maybe we should let her deal with them," I mused aloud. "Fuck knows she put us all in our place after the hospital."

Bubba laughed. Actually laughed, and I raised my brows. "I'm not disagreeing with you, but since we know there's an issue and *have* known, we'd be just as guilty. Not that I won't do or give her what she needs. Right now, I'd prefer if this *never* became her problem. We're going to have fights. That's a foregone conclusion. But we're adults, we should be ready to resolve them without her having to play referee every single time."

Fine. He had a point. Except... "You're only saying that 'cause you're not the favorite." I smirked as he actually flipped me off. There we go. That was better. "I can pretty much tell her anything. Cradle to grave has its privileges."

"Well, go ahead. Call her." No matter how he deadpanned it, I got it. Neither of us wanted to be the bearer of bad news. "Right, that's what I thought." He checked his watch. "Archie should be downstairs."

I nodded and shoved off the bed. Jake wouldn't emerge until Archie was out of the house. Fuck this was old and it hadn't even been that long. I didn't think my nerves could take a few more days of this, much less weeks.

With a bump to my shoulder, Bubba opened my door and let me out of my own room. I didn't waste time, because I found Archie in the foyer just putting his earbuds in when I appeared. The look he shot me shouldn't have made me laugh, but he lowered one of the ear buds with a sigh.

"Can we save the soul sharing until we finish the run?"

I dug my own earbuds out of my pocket and held them up. "Just as long as you know that you can run but you can't hide."

He nodded and stuffed his earbud in before he pulled the door open, I was a half-step behind him, but a sound on the step made me glance back. Jake stood there, a frown tightening his whole expression. I lifted my chin at him and kept my expression open, if neutral. We weren't picking sides in this fight.

The route Archie followed took us away from the gym and toward Central Park. We had four or five different ones mapped out. It was still early, but the city was already waking up as traffic picked up on both the sideways and the street. As much as I hated running, I matched Archie stride for stride as the music filled my ears with motivation.

I'd tried listening to Frankie and Bubba once, at least the recordings I'd been able to talk them out of and that proved way too distracting. All I could think about when I heard her sing was the day in the recording studio, and then I was just horny as hell. So in deference to my dick, I saved listening to those tracks when I was alone or with Frankie.

As soon as we hit the park, Archie turned west for the outer loop he liked to follow and I just stuck it with him. If he did a ten mile run, I might have to kill him. That would totally solve the problem. As it was, my sides burned as we finished what was apparently the first circuit and he switched paths. Sweat soaked through my shirt and like Archie, I stripped it off and secured it through a loop on my shorts. If I'd realized he planned to run to Hell and back, I'd have ambushed him after with an ice coffee.

Drowning didn't leave marks, right?

When we neared the lake closest to Strawberry Fields, he finally slowed his pace and I fell into step with him as we walked. Dehydration might actually be an issue as the mugginess around us seemed to climb the longer the sun was up.

After pulling his earbuds out, Archie pocketed them and then loosened the thermos he was carrying. He drowned about half of it before he passed it to me. The water was cold and more than welcome. Like him, I shut off the music and we walked in near companionable silence before he said, "Fine, you kept up with me and you didn't have to. So let me have it. Shrink me, Doc-to-be."

I was still trying to get my lungs to stop hating me, so I just flipped him off. "I'm not here to shrink you."

"Yeah? Why are you here? You hate running and the only times we get you out here with us is if Frankie is coming along." He didn't need to add that she was absent.

"You." I took the last of his water and dumped it over my face before handing him back the empty thermos.

"Ass."

I grinned and wiped my face on my shirt. "And Jake."

"Fuck Jake."

I sighed. "No, thanks. He's still not my type, no matter how much we share."

Archie shot me a dirty look. "You know what I meant."

"Actually, I'm not going to assume." We moved further over on the path to get out the way of the other runners. At least there was a hint of a breeze pushing through the trees. I needed gale force to cool down and I had a feeling a cold shower was in my future to avoid heatstroke. No wonder they were a bunch of surly bastards sometimes. They did this regularly. I'd be a shit, too.

"Then spit it out," Archie invited and despite his expression, his tone carried more than a hint of grating annoyance. "I'd rather not play twenty questions."

"You and Jake need to settle this shit between the two of you."

"I tried. He's not interested."

"Then try harder. He's got his issues and so do you," I reminded him. "But this isn't about issues. This is about the fact you're rubbing your relationship in his face."

The look Archie gave me this time held nothing friendly in it. "Don't start that with me. This isn't about my money or who I am. That hasn't changed. The one with the issue is Jake. He's pissed I wasn't in the car, which if you care to know, so am I. I'd have swapped places with her in a heartbeat."

With a long sigh I stopped, and Archie continued another couple of steps before he paused to look back at me. "I know that. That's never been a question for me. I know how much you love her."

"Good," he said, not quite sounding mollified. "I gave him some free shots to work off his aggravation with me."

"And it just made it worse," I reminded him.

"No shit." Archie spread his hands. "But I'm not fucking leaving, no matter how much he tries to shut me out. It's not his call."

"No," I agreed with him. "It's not. But how much longer before Frankie recognizes the tension between the two of you. She's distracted right now, but..."

He shook his head. "Coop, stay out of it. This isn't about Frankie, not yet. Jake's mad at me because of what happened with his dad and now something being wrong with my car. He'll get over it or he won't. I'm giving him his space."

"Making a point of sitting right next to her every time he's there or snagging her as soon as she gets back from somewhere?" I raised my brows. "You call that giving him his space."

"I call that being who I've always been." Not an ounce of rancor marred his tone. "You tell me, honestly, you think I'm behaving any differently? Or that I'm taking some joy out of his distancing himself?"

Fuck my life.

I turned my gaze up to the sky and then shook my head. "No."

"Thank you." The absolute quiet sentiment in his voice sent a wash of guilt through me. "I'm not a fan of being on the outs with him. I fucking hate he decided to change his classes. He dropped anything we had together—he also managed to lose the one class he really wanted this semester because the others were probably full."

Introduction to Robotics.

"Arch, we gotta fix this."

"I can't force him to forgive me for being alive and unhurt when she was injured so badly."

Despite the fact we hadn't really discussed it between us, the litter of bruises all over her and the rush to the hospital took us all back to another night when we hadn't been there when Mitch had tried to hurt her. Even if Bubba had broken the fucker's jaw, it hadn't changed the loss Frankie went through afterward or the hurt.

"He was scared. He's lashing out. Right now—I'm an easy target. So let him take it out on me." Archie shrugged. "Better me than Frankie anyway."

"He'd *never* lash out at her." Let's just nip that shit right in the bud.

"I know that. You know that. Pretty sure he isn't so certain." The analysis gave me pause. "He has to work through this. I'll see what I can do about making it a little easier for him, but she's my everything Coop. I'm not going to be squeezed out because he's having a tantrum."

"And I wouldn't ask that of you."

"Then why are you here?" It was a simple challenge but a real one.

"Because you're my friend too, jackass."

The corners of his mouth twitched and he nodded. "Well, in that case... coffee's on me. But only if you can keep up. Cause your slow ass needs some work."

He didn't even wait for my response before he took off like we hadn't just run a fucking marathon.

Archie Standish was a dick.

I took off after him.

But he was our dick, so we'd keep him.

Nassau County Police Report

Case Number: VA-2021-4-20-1140-NK

Incident: Vehicle accident

Reporting Officer: Nolan Kilby

At approximately 1140 hours on 15 August, I arrived on the scene of a single vehicle accident located on the west bound side of I-495 between Exit 425 and Exit 422-B. The vehicle, a 1987 Ferrari F 40 had suffered severe damage along the driver's side and to the tail section as the result of collision along a concrete barrier. [See Attached Photographs]

The driver and only passenger, Francesca Curtis, age 18, was found unconscious and unresponsive. Fire Department, also on scene, needed to cut the driver out of damaged vehicle. She was then transported to the local hospital. A cursory search of the vehicle found no illegal substances or alcohol. Detectives contacted with information on the hospital transport so they can proceed to interview the driver.

Vehicle was loaded onto a flatbed as it was in no condition to be towed and taken to impound for further examination. Upon surveying the scene of the accident, scattered remnants of the vehicle along a three-quarters of a mile stretch from the final position of the vehicle. Orange paint found on several sections of concrete barrier.

Noteworthy: No sign of tread marks to indicate brakes were engaged.

Witnesses interviewed. [See attached for statements].

The accident has been logged into the station database and all notes turned over to the detectives of record. A secondary search of the area found no evidence of any other vehicles involved in the collision.

Addendum: Malfunctioning brakes appear to be the cause of the accident. Interference or general failure remain undetermined.

Second Addendum: Insurance investigator has requested and received copies of all accident scene photographs.

Third Addendum: Blood work and tox screens released by driver via patient authorization. No evidence of alcohol or other illegal substances found. Driver was not impaired while operating the vehicle. [See interview with Curtis, Francesca also attached.]

Chapter Twelve
THE RACHEL MANNING FILES

Frankie

The drive from Manhattan out to Long Island seemed to take twice as long as it had when Archie and I had made the drive just a few weeks earlier. Then again, we'd been in the Ferrari—I sighed at just the thought of that beautiful car—and we'd left midday rather than early morning. Traffic within Manhattan proper sucked.

I'd told the guys I was off to meet Rachel, which was true. I hadn't told them that I was meeting her at the garage where we parked our cars. I also got there well before Rachel so I could get any freakout from climbing behind the wheel out of the way.

As it was, my racing heart and sweaty palms stuck with me until we reached the Queens Midtown Tunnel. Maybe it was the comfort of being behind the wheel of my own car, even if I wasn't totally used to driving her yet. Maybe it was the fact Rachel pretended not to notice me freaking out while keeping up a patter of observations about her first week of classes.

The professors were nowhere near as hot as she'd been led to believe. How was she supposed to have some taboo seduction with a naughty age-gap when they were either married or way not her type or both. Even the ones swinging for both teams...they were too easy. She wanted that elusive instructor—male or female... "Like I said, I'm not picky, except I refuse to be a notch on their headboard when I want them for a notch on mine."

"Rachel! That's...wrong on so many levels."

"But so wrong, it's right. I mean, I should have at least one terribly bad decision relationship while I'm in college and why shouldn't it be with some sexy TA or better, full on professor. I mean—I can definitely go for the librarian with her hair all tight-rolled up and I'll get it all disheveled while her glasses are fogged. Then again—there's stealing his boxers after a hot little quickie right before class so the whole time he's teaching, he has to know I can still feel him between my thighs."

The wistful sigh she released at the end left me torn between laughter and shock.

"Oh, don't even play that with me, Frankie. I guarantee you've gotten enough dick in the last year, there's probably a permanent imprint for all four of them between your thighs and you can imagine them with just a thought."

I absolutely did not give her the satisfaction of squeezing my thighs at the reminder, because I had zero issue picturing each and every one of them and the wild way they made me feel. "So, you seriously want to seduce a teacher this year?"

"Call it a fuck-it list," Rachel said as she leaned back in the passenger seat. She saluted me with her iced coffee and took a long drink. "I learned a lot about myself in Paris. Like guys who know how to use their dicks are worth it."

Laughter bubbled out of me and some of the tension knotting my stomach let go. "Well, I could have told you that."

"You don't count," Rachel snarked, lips quirking into a wider grin. "You literally hit the lotto with your first, your second, your third, and your fourth dicks at bat. Even if number four sat on the bench longer than necessary."

Heat flooded my face. "You do this on purpose, don't you?"

"Hell yes, I do it on purpose," she said, laughter edging every syllable. "You're also not on the verge of hyperventilating anymore."

Well, she wasn't wrong about that.

"And as much as I like giving you shit about them, I envy what you guys have together, not that I want *that* much dick in my life. I just like how tight all five of you are and yet—you still make room for little ol' me."

"Nothing little about you," I reminded her. "You have personality for days."

"I accept that description." Head back against the seat and with sunglasses shielding her eyes, Rachel continued, "Have you set yourself up with mental health services on campus? Found yourself a new psychologist?"

Grimacing, I just said, "I haven't had time."

"Bullshit." From anyone else that might come across hostile, but Rachel's love language fell into two categories. Vicious teasing and haranguing. We were definitely in the haranguing portion of the day. "Make time. The accident had to fuck you up some if the way you were sweating when we started this ride is anything to go by. You're still balancing four relationships, moving to a new city, starting a new school, getting to know your bio-dad and you'll soon be meeting step-mommy and the new siblings..." With every item she ticked them off on her fingers. "Oh, what else? Right, the psycho cuntasaurus who served as your womb with a view for nine months, probably the one and only unselfish thing she ever did for you and even then I question it."

"Well, when you put it like that....I'm a model of mental health and stability."

"Yes, you are," Rachel agreed with me. "And I intend for you to stay that way. So, move getting a psychologist up your priority list. Call Erin if you have no other options or at least until you find one you like."

"You don't want me to just confide in you?"

"Always, but you need someone unbiased as a counselor and I am very much biased."

"I love you, too," I murmured before letting out a long breath. "And I do feel better. Thank you."

"You're very welcome. Now—let's check out the stereo on this bad boy."

The music offered a respite because not everything at home was as harmonious as I might like. Jake had changed all his classes. Instead of the two we'd had with everyone else, there was only one class I had with him. He said it was going to work better for his degree and focus, that the change up meant he got a better position in one of his labs and better access.

The problem was, the schedule meant he was gone most evenings and I'd barely seen him this week. The other problem was the guys hadn't said anything at all about his absence. They plowed on through like it was perfectly natural.

No shock. No questions. Not even teasing remarks. If anything, Coop had shifted the subject to jokes and picking on me and Ian. Archie's silence though, spoke even louder. They all knew something was going on and no one was saying a word to me about it. So, did I confront them? Or Jake?

It wasn't unrealistic to think Jake had discussed it with all of them before he changed his schedule, even if he hadn't mentioned it to me beforehand. Considering where I was headed right now, I couldn't even fault him for not telling me.

It just sucked that instead of three classes together, we only had one. I had two with the other guys. Monday and Wednesday classes would keep me busy enough, but I didn't like the idea that Jake's schedule meant he'd be at home when we weren't and not home when we were.

"You're gonna miss your exit," Rachel murmured even as the GPS informed me to take the next exit in Jeremy's easy voice. "Also, that's kind of creepy."

"It's not creepy. Jeremy sounds relaxed. He also gives great directions."

"Right." She elongated the word. "Whatever you say." Still her lips were twitching. Bitch.

I checked my phone after we parked. The guys knew I was with Rachel. They all had classes today. A twinge of guilt hit me because I'd somehow managed to score Fridays off and I wasn't complaining.

The police station was actually kind of nice on the inside. It lacked the institutional feel of the only other one I'd been in and there was a decent sitting area. I checked in at the window and precisely five minutes after we'd sat down to wait, my lawyer walked in the front door.

"Dominic Walsh," he said, introducing himself. Mr. Walsh was a lot younger than I'd been expecting. Dark hair with dark eyes and a tan like he'd just come in from the beach. Despite all that, he was dressed in a suit, though his tie wasn't quite precise and his hair had the disheveled look of having raked his hand through it too many times.

"Frankie Curtis," I said as I accepted the hand he offered. It was a perfunctory shake, firm, but not overlong. "And this is…"

"Rachel Manning," Rachel took over her own introduction and shook his hand, only she didn't let his go. "Best friend and mean sister. Here looking after my BFF's interests. Are you a helper or a hinderer?"

His eyebrows rose a fraction, but instead of being shocked, he seemed far more intrigued. "I'm a helper when it's required of me and a hinderer when necessary. For example, I'm Ms. Curtis' attorney, Miss Manning, aka bff and mean sister. That means either you're helpful to her or I'll definitely be a hindrance."

"I'd like to see you try," Rachel countered, throwing down the challenge like a gauntlet. "Been here long before you and will definitely outlast you, and she doesn't have to pay me by the hour."

"You also can't guarantee her attorney client privilege. Anything she says to you can be subpoenaed." The chill in his voice razored into a pure dare.

"As if I'd admit shit." The air practically crackled at Rachel flinging his taunt right back at him.

"They call that perjury," he clarified.

They were still holding hands.

"Only if I lie. I do not have to answer questions. I can refuse. I have the right to remain silent and I can easily exercise that."

The corners of his mouth curved and dimples appeared in his cheek. "You can only exercise the right to refuse in a courtroom by pleading the fifth."

"Then it's your job to make sure I'm never called into court." The warmth in Rachel's tone had me staring, but it was nothing compared to the gleam in Mr. Walsh's eye.

Well, then...

Clearing my throat, I rubbed the back of my neck and the pair of them finally tore their attention off each other to look at me. "If you're done with the verbal throw down, can we get back to why we're here?"

"Absolutely." Abandoning the more jocular tone he'd been favoring with Rachel, he withdrew a step, then opened his case and pulled out an iPad. "I just need your thumb print and a couple of signatures Ms. Curtis. As you know, Mr. Wittaker has retained our firm on your behalf and we will be representing all your interests here in the state of New York."

"How are you supposed to replace Wittaker?" Rachel asked. "You look like you're still in graduate school."

"I was a clever boy," Walsh retorted without missing a beat as he turned the screen toward me. Habit kept me from just signing anything, I sat down to read the pages. Scrolling through each one without leaving my initials or thumbprint until I'd reached the end.

Wittaker had schooled me on contracts. The key phrases I should look for and never sign. Also, if I had any issues with one, I was free to run it by him. While I read, the air around me seemed to surge with pressure. One glance showed Rachel and Dominic staring at each other.

His expression was patient and amused, but hers?

Hers was defiant and—dare I say playful? I gave Mr. Walsh another thorough once over. If anything went down between these two, I needed to know more about him. Pulling my phone out of my pocket, I fired off an email to Wittaker with a couple of screenshots of the contract.

Apparently, he'd been waiting for my email because he explained the passages and told me it was safe to sign. That was all I needed to know. I went through and marked my initials and then signed it at the bottom with my thumbprint. I was almost loathe to interrupt them. But we had an appointment.

"Excellent," he said, transferring his attention to me. "It's good to have you as a client, Ms. Curtis. Mr. Wittaker has already taken care of the retainer. I'm an associate at the law firm, but my father is the senior partner. He will also oversee everything to do with your business, financial, and legal matters or concerns. But I'm generally going to be the boots on the ground."

Yeah, as much as he was telling me, I was pretty sure he was showing off for Rachel.

"So, he just graduated law school," Rachel said. "Great. Well if he messes up, we can always throw him back into the pond. I'm not big on shrimps."

"Don't worry," Dominic assured me. "I'm more than capable of getting the job done and with satisfaction guaranteed."

I was still searching for a response when the door opened next to the reception desk and a detective called my name.

"Oh, thank God," I muttered as I turned to the detective. I'd never looked forward to answering questions more or trying to get copies of everything. Mr. Walsh was right at my side as I shook the detective's hand. Then he and the detective exchanged pleasantries.

When it was time to go back to a room, Rachel had to wait. She was neither a witness nor an involved party. The detective had questions regarding the accident. What happened. When it happened. What I noticed. How I responded. Mr. Walsh was right there, he only intervened twice, telling me I didn't have to answer a question when it involved something to do with my relationships and whether there were any bad feelings between me and Archie.

The third time, he scolded the detective. "It was an accident," he reminded the man. "Not sure what direction you're taking this case, but we stand by the initial report, Ms. Curtis gave at the hospital and again here. She has no reason to believe that Mr. Standish was in any way involved in the accident itself."

"According to your client," the detective said, addressing my attorney but his gaze was on me. "Mr. Standish handled all of his own maintenance and he had to leave rather suddenly for her to drive back to Manhattan on her own."

"Your point?" Walsh asked.

"My point is the brake lines were severed in two places. Not enough to break them all the way, but under the stress of acceleration and road debris, they broke. That stopped the brakes from working at all."

I swore I went flush and then ice cold as my stomach bottomed out. It was one thing to think Maddy had something to do with this. It was something else entirely to hear it confirmed there had been sabotage. I swallowed, or tried to at least, but I didn't have any spit in my mouth.

"Then you're treating this as attempted homicide?" I swore my head pounded at that idea. That was even worse.

"We are. Mr. Standish requested we return his vehicle as soon as possible, but you'll have to understand that we can't do that as it is evidence in an ongoing investigation."

"I'll want all the copies of the accident and the survey of the vehicle," Walsh said. "As well as any witness statements with relation to the accident."

I was still back at the idea the brakes had been deliberately cut.

"I'll get you what I can," the detective said before he looked at me again. "I would like to ask you some more questions, Ms. Curtis. Because if your boyfriend isn't behind the brake failure either through negligence or intent, then one or both of you was the target."

Yeah. I'd gotten there a while ago.

"So, can you tell me if there's anyone out there who would like to see you hurt?"

I hesitated for only a micro-second. "My mother."

Even my attorney shot me a look at that one.

"Your mother?" the detective repeated.

I nodded once. "Madeleine Curtis, she goes by Maddy. She was born Madeleine Grayson."

Still puzzled, the detective leaned forward and studied me. "Are you certain?"

"That she's threatened me and Archie before?" I said as composed as I could manage. "Oh yeah. She definitely blames Archie for her failed relationship with his father—well maybe just hiccups in the road of that relationship. I don't actually know what the status of that relationship is. But she blamed me for putting a kink in her plans, too." I licked my lips. I wasn't going to bring my grandparents into it yet. But I would if I had to.

"Maybe we should start at the beginning," the detective said, and I blew out a breath.

It took two hours, and he questioned every fact I presented and challenged any assumptions I'd made. But he wrote it all down and I didn't get the feeling that he was humoring me. The only problem was, I wasn't even sure where Maddy was right now. She could still be in Texas for all I knew. I hadn't seen or heard from her since graduation.

Not that I'd reached out either, or had any intentions of doing so. The detective promised to look into it, and he'd be in touch if he had more questions. Walsh sent me out to where Rachel waited while he stayed behind to talk to the detective.

I was as limp as a wet noodle as I dropped into the chair next to her.

"You okay?" she asked.

"Nope."

"What do you need?"

"No idea. But give me a few and maybe I'll figure it out."

Because I'd just involved my mother in a potential attempted homicide investigation. One way or another, our next step was finding her.

Walsh said as much when we left the precinct station and walked out to the lot. We needed to know where Maddy was and when. He'd get their PIs on it.

Look at that. Their investigators.

"Well, it looks like you may not be useless after all," Rachel told him.

"That seems awfully fickle for you Miss Manning, to reach that decision so quickly."

"I said it looks like—the jury is still out because we haven't seen enough evidence. You just made it past your opening argument, counselor." With that, she slid into the passenger side of my car and I glanced at Walsh who stared after her speculatively.

"It was good to meet you, Ms. Curtis," he said, shaking my hand again. "I'm undecided on your friend, but..."

"She's an acquired taste."

He laughed. "Well, maybe I'll acquire it then. But I'll be in touch soon and I'll have a courier bring you copies of the reports as soon as I have them."

I nodded, still breathing a little shallow. "That's it?"

"That's it. They aren't filing charges against you, it's clear you did everything possible to avoid involving anyone else in the accident. The majority of the damage was done to Mr. Standish's car and we have a detailed accounting of your own injuries. Go back to Manhattan. Focus on school and let us do the work now. Once I have information on your mother's whereabouts, I'll make sure you know too."

I couldn't ask for more.

"Thank you," I said. "For everything—including Rachel."

He chuckled. "Thank you for bringing her. If we do this again, bring her along. The sparring is good for me."

With that, he walked away and I slid my sunglasses on before slipping into the car.

"He's full of himself," Rachel commented as soon as I got the car running and the air conditioning on. It was definitely hot in there. "Arrogant. Probably raised chewing on law books with Big Daddy right there to bail him out."

"That's a lot to discern from a simple interaction," I said, and it was really the last word I got on the subject, Rachel gave me chapter and verse on what she liked and didn't like about Dominic Walsh.

Including the fact he didn't look like a Dom to her. He looked more like a Nick.

And apparently that was important.

Who knew?

Chapter Thirteen

HONEYMOON'S OVER

Frankie

Three weeks.

Three weeks at our new school, living in this fabulous place that Archie had found, diving into new classes that excited me and challenged me, even if I was horrifically distracted trying to figure out where Maddy was. I'd done a little sleuthing on where Edward was staying—here in the city apparently—but Maddy wasn't there.

Dominic had been in touch and said they had also put their firm PI on it. While he never mentioned Rachel by name, he circled the topic enough for me to get a feel for what he was looking for. And sorry, buddy, I might be dense about flirting, but if he wanted her number—well, he'd need to earn it and ask for it.

Still...

"Miss Frankie," Jeremy said as he stepped out onto the deck where I'd gone to do homework. It was the third Friday, and all of the guys were at classes and I was here. I didn't have anywhere to duck off to today. Though Rachel had texted twice about the sorority rush that was coming up and how she wanted to give it a shot.

"Hey," I greeted him and then glanced at the food he'd brought me an hour earlier. The plate was still covered, and I hadn't touched any of it. I had drained the coffee though. Tiddles was my only other companion out there, sprawling on the sun-warmed patch like a god awaiting his tribute. He probably was. The last few nights had been so strange and the guys weren't sharing my room so much as taking turns and if that wasn't bizarre, I didn't know what was. "Sorry, I guess I don't have as much appetite as I thought."

"That's understandable, however, I expect you to eat something at supper or I shall be cross with you."

I smiled at him. "I promise, I'll do better then." But that didn't seem to allay his concern one whit. If anything, his brow furrowed deeper. "I could go for another coffee. If you don't mind?" It was warm out today but there was a decent enough breeze out here.

Jeremy nodded slowly. "Give me a moment, Miss Frankie." He took my uneaten food and empty mug with him and I grimaced. I didn't want Jeremy waiting on me, but he'd come down a few mornings earlier this week and found me getting a bowl of cereal and starting the coffee pot and I swore he was going to have a stroke.

While he didn't comment, there was this little vein in his forehead that seemed to throb the whole time I was in his kitchen doing things. Archie told me later that Jeremy *liked* to wait on us and make sure we were well looked after. Me in particular, though I was pretty sure he was stretching that one.

Then again—maybe he wasn't so far off the mark. I sighed and glanced back at the textbook I'd been in the middle of reading. I'd read the same chapters over and over. My phone buzzed with an invitation from Rachel.

Rush events were starting this weekend. She really needed a wingwoman. No excuses allowed. She expected me there or she was coming hunting.

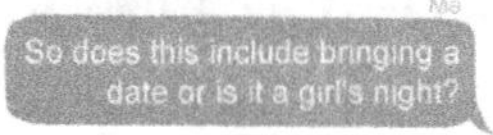

I knew the answer. Particularly when she sent me a rolling eyes emoji.

Nothing for a solid five minutes and then I got a middle finger followed by the words: *girls only*. I laughed. Okay, I wouldn't normally pick away at her but there had been something going on there with "Nick" as she put it and maybe she was into doms, that may just be a me thing but still...

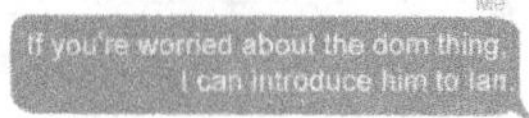

Not only did that earn me a middle finger emoji. It earned me a slew of them followed by...

Snickering to myself, I typed in, *Rachel and Nick, sitting in a tree...*

Wow the speed of the middle finger emojis threatened to blow up my phone.

I hugged it to myself and laughed. It was the best chuckle I'd had in days. With that realization, my smile faded and my humor sobered. We weren't really laughing or playing as much. School was busy, but it was more than that. I had nights out with Archie. Evenings with Ian, sometimes hours in the studio downstairs. Coop and I could curl up or Jake would invite me down to his room rather than come up to mine.

But we were all doing it separately.

Rubbing the edge of the phone against my lower lip, I was still turning that idea over in my head when Jeremy returned with a tray, cookies, coffee and envelope. He took a seat at the table with me, much to my delight, and after he poured the coffees, he gave me a studious look.

"Why do I feel like I'm in trouble?" Not that he'd ever scolded *me*, generally he saved that for the boys.

"Because I am weighing how appropriate it would be for me to speak to you on matters that are not necessarily my business."

Since I wasn't really reading the textbook anyway, I flipped it closed and set my phone face down on it and then cradled my coffee mug. No one made coffee like Jeremy. Archie was getting damn good at it, but Jeremy just seemed to have a gift.

"It must be something if you're troubled by it," I said slowly, giving him my full attention.

Instead of answering me immediately, he prepared his own coffee, then set a small dish of milk down that had Tiddles rising from his lounge and walking over to take a drink from the saucer. I bit back a smile behind my mug.

"It is," Jeremy said. "Largely because I feel like one of your young men, particularly Mr. Archie or Mr. Bubba would have said something by now, but they have been rather preoccupied."

"Well, we're just getting into the rhythm at school, there was bound to be some bumps along the way." I don't know who I was trying to reassure, but Jeremy gave me a flinty eyed look, so I mimed zipping my lips. That earned me a frown and a sigh. Unwilling to hurt his feelings even unintentionally, I said, "Jeremy, whatever it is—you're family. You can say it to me. I'm a big girl. I can handle it."

"Of that, I have no doubt," Jeremy said before taking a sip of his coffee. Once he set it down though, he picked up the letter. "This came for you earlier this week while you were at classes. I debated having Mr. Archie give it to you, but he is less than clear headed on the subject. Mr. Bubba can be, but he and Mr. Jake have become far more protective since your accident."

Oh, I knew that.

"And Mr. Coop should not have to bear the burden of everyone's problems no matter how well-suited he is to listen. Not to mention he has his own issues with this."

Setting my coffee cup down, I frowned. "There are problems between the boys."

"That is not for me to say, Miss Frankie." Not even a twitch of a muscle or a flicker of his eyelids. Jeremy was a vault. "Nor would I reveal to them that you seem to have engaged the services of a new law firm and two private investigative services with regard to the accident involving Mr. Archie's Ferrari."

"Point taken. Thank you."

He nodded and then handed me the letter. I didn't recognize the handwriting but the name and return address were painfully clear.

Muriel Standish.

I stared at it and then at Jeremy. "She sent this to me?"

"By courier," Jeremy said with a nod. "I apologize for not delivering it sooner, but I have my own reservations on why she would be reaching out to you as well."

"Thank you for caring, Jeremy." Still, I didn't slit it right open. Muriel Standish was not on my list of favorite people. At the same time, she was Archie's mother and no matter how terrible a job she'd done, she was always going to be his mother. Just like Maddy would always be mine.

We were not our parents.

"You have also delayed going to your follow up appointments," Jeremy said. "If the issue is the drive to the physician, I would be more than happy to take you."

I winced. "I feel fine. Really, I do. Most of the bruising has faded and my chest doesn't even hurt that much."

Clearly unimpressed, Jeremy gave me a look. "When they were unable to reach you by cell phone, they called here. I took the message. If you'd like, I can call them back and make arrangements. Then we'll take you to the appointment and back without worrying the young men."

Without worrying...

I'd missed a doctor's appointment or two actually since I'd changed it the first time and just outright canceled it the second. Something was going on with the guys. "I know you can't tell me, but do I need to be paying closer attention here?"

"Perhaps," Jeremy said. "Though as likely as not, it is not your lack of attention that is keeping you in the dark."

So, they weren't telling me stuff. I'd kind of figured that part out. What the hell had happened between them? Or was it my accident? Were they mad at each other over that?

Goddamn Maddy.

The anger rushing through me seemed almost irrational but so much blame could and *should* be laid at her feet. "I know you're not going to be the model of discretion," I began slowly and met Jeremy's gaze. "But if it goes too far, I need you to let me know if I should step in." A part of me already wanted to. But if the boys didn't want me to know and this was an issue between them then—I needed to respect that right?

"I believe I can agree with that, Miss Frankie, as long as you allow me to exercise that same discretion to alert Mr. Archie and the others if I believe you have gone too far and require assistance."

He maneuvered me so neatly, I couldn't do more than nod. "That's fair. I promise, I'm being careful. And I have gotten assistance but..."

"You wish to handle this yourself and protect them. I do understand. Much as they wish to handle things themselves and protect you."

"Are we being stupid?"

Jeremy favored me with a kind smile. "That is not for me to say. You have all weathered your fair share of storms over the past year. But relationships require constant effort and communication. They also rely on trust. I will trust you to do what you believe is right in your heart and them to do the same. Just remember—some actions cannot be taken back and some withheld truths can leave a lasting mark."

Noted.

I glanced down at the letter in my hand. "Like this one."

"Precisely. I weighed my options and now I have given the burden to you. Open it. Discard it. Burn it if you wish. But the letter was sent to you, and it should be your decision about what is to be done about it." Rising, he set his finished coffee on the tray and retrieved Tiddles' now empty saucer. "But I would advise that you proceed with caution where Miss Muriel is concerned."

Oh, he didn't have to tell me that twice.

"Thanks, Jeremy."

He nodded.

"I mean it, thank you for everything."

Another nod, but he hadn't left yet and I sighed.

"I don't have classes in the afternoon on Tuesday."

"I'll ring your physician and set up your appointment. Would you like me to pick you up on campus?"

Did I really have a choice? "That would be great."

Still, he waited.

"Something else?"

"Were I the one in this circumstance, I would think now would be the time to notify Mr. Jackson of the incident. If the investigation continues, there's every chance it will appear in the news. If the Standish name is linked as it very well may be as well as your grandparents..."

Oh.

Shit.

"I'll call him."

"Very good. Enjoy the cookies." He refilled my coffee and then he vanished back inside the house. I shook my head and stared at the letter for a long time as I nibbled on one of the cookies. It was macadamia nut with white chocolate, and it practically melted in my mouth but my stomach twisted the longer I stared at the letter.

Well, I didn't have x-ray vision, so I slit it open and slowly and pulled out a single sheet of paper.

Francesca,

I grimaced at the first line, instantly irritated. Why that woman insisted on using my full name, I had no idea.

I would imagine I am the last person you would expect to hear from. To be frank, I resisted sending this note for a few months now. However, after the incident I witnessed after the graduation ceremony, I feel this might be the time for hard truths.

Newsflash, Muriel Standish hated Maddy. Also, water was wet.

I have my differences with Maddy as I am sure you can imagine, not the least of which has been her on-again, off-again affair with Edward all these years.

I stared at Tiddles. "You know, I don't care how they phrase it, I don't want to think about them having sex. Ever."

He gave me a baleful look then resumed cleaning his own ass. Well, at least we were of like minds on this subject.

However, I believe these differences have gone well beyond the various infidelities and half-truths we have all deluded ourselves with. I have known Madeline Grayson for many years, longer than perhaps she ever alluded. We attended the same schools. I was there as she and Edward began their courtship and twisted it into something painful and ugly.

I am not saying I didn't make my own choices and that I haven't been burned by them, but I know things about Maddy that she would likely not want anyone else to know. If your war with her is genuine, I will be your ally. The enemy of my enemy does not have to be my friend, but you are the one my son wants to marry and that will make him a target for her madness.

Consider this an invitation. If you choose to decline, then so be it.

Muriel

I read, then re-read the letter another half-dozen times.

Leaning back in the chair, I stared up at the sky and what little appetite the cookies had aroused in me died. I guess I was going to make an appointment to see Muriel Standish. But how much of what she told me could I even trust as truth?

Still, if she could help me take Maddy down once and for all—I'd wear a damn dress and Sunday hat to the get-together if I had to.

Only one problem. I couldn't go see his mother and not tell him.

Archie was going to go through the roof.

Chapter Fourteen

WE'RE NOT IN TEXAS ANYMORE

Jake

Double-checking my watch, I waited just outside of the hall where Frankie's introduction economics lecture was about to get out. I didn't have classes for another two hours. She was done for the day after this one. Right on schedule, the doors pushed open and the students began to flood out. It was stupid, we'd curled up together last night in my room with popcorn and movies. It had been so much like the old days. I swore I'd half-forgotten the tension in the rest of the house.

But she didn't stay, as soon as her alarm went off that morning, she'd groaned but given me a kiss before heading back up to her own room and a shower. Archie had early classes too and she'd left with him. Which meant he'd been down there for breakfast, so I'd waited until the last minute to go down and kiss her bye.

Bubba had pretty much called me a jackass and I'd *tried* to be more present, but then Archie would smirk or crack a joke and all I wanted to do was punch him in his smug face. Instead of distance easing my anger, it just seemed to make it worse.

"I'm not going anywhere, Jake. So, you can keep ignoring me or we can work this out." Archie had said to me three days earlier. But I was not in the head space to discuss it with him. Hell, I wasn't in the head space to discuss it with Coop and he even seemed to sense it.

Frankie was one of the last to leave the lecture hall, laughing at the guy following her as she said, "Then do the reading next time. If you haven't noticed, he assigns reading but his lectures are always different."

"Maybe we could make it a study date," the guy offered with what looked way too much like a flirty smile and when his gaze swept down to her ass, I pushed away from the wall.

"And maybe you can learn to manage your own study time," I told him. "Instead of leering at her ass like a perv."

"Jake," Frankie said, but the jackass standing behind her was a good two inches shorter than me and I had him beat by at least fifty pounds. He retreated immediately.

"Sorry man, didn't realize she was taken." He raised his hands. "No harm, no foul. See you later, Frankie."

"Kurt," she said, but her tone was terse and then she was glaring at me.

"Hey, Baby Girl," I said closing the distance and she avoided my arm like a pro and managed to elbow me in the side at the same time.

"Don't you 'baby girl' me." Her temper flashed in her eyes as she glared at me. She stared after the loser who'd been flirting with her and then back at me for a minute. "What are you doing here, anyway? You don't have classes this early."

"No, but this is your last lecture of the day and I thought I could come by and steal my girl for some coffee or maybe a late lunch." Really late considering it was after three.

She sighed and I couldn't tell if it was impatience with me or what. "Sometimes you can be such a jerk."

"But only to people who deserve it," I offered with a faint smile, because she seemed to be wavering and the last thing I'd wanted to do when planning to hook up with her was to piss her off. "Let me buy you some coffee, or maybe go exploring what options we can find in the library here?"

Her snort couldn't quite hide her smile. "No, I think there are rumors about others making out in the stacks and while I think that could be a thrill, I'm not in the mood to flash my ass at someone else."

Nope. "Definitely not," I agreed with far more of a growl than I intended. Frankie's real smile came out then and she rose up on her tip toes.

"Hey, Jake?"

"Yes, Baby girl?"

She fisted my shirt and tugged me toward her. Now this I needed no more guidance in. Wrapping an arm around her waist, I lifted her up and fused my lips to hers. The flood of relief through my system at her nearness only increased as she hooked her arms around my neck and I picked her up and held her to me. The soft brushes of her lips were the balm I hadn't even realized I needed.

So lost in the taste and feel of her, it rocked me when I realized how tightly I was holding onto her. But when I would have loosened my grip, she actually fisted my hair and bit my lower lip. Startled, I leaned my head back to find her grinning.

"I'm not gonna break if you hug me. And I've *missed* this." Missed being in my arms. Missed me wrapped around her. Fuck, I'd missed this too.

"Your ribs?"

"Are fine. So are my bruises. I am scheduled to see the doctor tomorrow afternoon, but I am more than capable of saying what I'm up for and what I'm not up for."

My cock stood right up at that implication.

Fuck classes.

"Let me take you out," I murmured. "Just you and me. We'll get coffee or food or those terrible hot dogs you like so much."

"They aren't terrible," she scolded and swatted me on the shoulder.

"Besides, it's all your fault. You insisted we had to have hot dogs at the very first baseball game we went to."

"Oh, how could I forget."

The tension melted away, loosening my muscles and the stiffness in my spine as I set her down, snagging her backpack before she could put it on and slung it over my free shoulder. Her eyes gleamed when she smiled up at me and I hooked an arm around her shoulder. Leaning into me, she fit against the curve of my side like a phantom limb had somehow reattached itself. Weird, considering we'd been snuggled up in my bed the night before. Then again, I'd been aware of the other guys in the house. Not that it ever used to bother me and now...

Fuck.

I shoved all of that to the back of my mind because Frankie was right here, right now and she needed to be my focus. It might have looked like we were wandering aimlessly, but as we headed downstairs and then out of the building to the street, I knew right where I wanted to take her.

After the air conditioning, the air on the street was muggy and the smell of exhaust from the cars didn't quite mesh with where we'd spent so many years back in Texas, but I almost didn't care. Just like when we'd been in Germany, as long as we were together, I could handle it anywhere. In a way, I kind of missed Germany. No competition for her attention, no worries about what dumbass shit...

"Jake," she said, pulling me right back to the present. "Where are we going?"

"It's a surprise," I teased. "I found it last week and I thought of you as soon as I saw it."

It didn't take us long. It was only a couple of blocks away. There was a lot of foot traffic in the area this time of day, but I kept Frankie tucked close and no one jostled her. When we arrived at the Corner Creamery, I knew I'd made the right call. Her eyes lit up. Inside it was just as old-fashioned as the exterior promised.

The soda counter with its stools, booths like the old ice cream place back at home, and decor that looked like someone threw up all the colors in here and just went for sparkle and cheerfulness and somehow it worked. Frankie half-bounced and the fist around my heart eased for the first time in weeks.

"I love it," she declared and pressed a kiss to my cheek before hurrying ahead and snagging my hand so I'd go with her. As if I'd be anywhere else. Frankie ordered one of the largest sundaes they offered with bananas, three scoops of ice cream, fudge and caramel, whip cream and nuts. I settled for a hot fudge sundae. We claimed a booth in the corner so we could see the door and the windows and at the same time we had some privacy.

The guy who took our order was in a red and white striped shirt, an apron, and one of those jaunty little paper hats. Frankie propped her chin on her hand and said, "This kind of reminds me a little bit of Mason's."

"Yeah? Don't even know if they make burgers."

With a careless little shrug, she transferred her attention to me. "Thank you."

"For what?"

"This." A wistful smile settled on her face and I frowned. "I've been kind of homesick. I didn't even realize it until the other day. Everything is just so different, and we haven't had a lot of time..."

I sighed. "I know. But I'm working on that."

"I just...I know you said that you were shifting your focus and the new classes would be better for it, I just hate that it seems you're on campus when I'm home or I'm on campus when you are. We barely see each other. Or you're working on something in your room even when everyone else is there."

Internally, I winced. Lying to Frankie hadn't been my plan. What I told her wasn't a total lie, if I still wanted the degree, and I did, but I didn't want to be in classes with Archie then the shift in schedule had to happen.

"I'm sorry, Baby Girl, I'll work harder. Maybe we need to set date nights again. Lock down time that's just ours." I stroked a finger down her cheek. The last thing I wanted was to lie to her. "I'll do better."

Even though they delivered our desserts, Frankie didn't look away from me. Instead, she caught my finger and pressed it to her cheek. "Tell me what's wrong."

I opened my mouth to say 'nothing' but I couldn't bring myself to deny it. Especially when she looked at me with all that trust in her beautiful green eyes. I never wanted to see anything else in them. Not hurt. Not sadness. Not...

"It's nothing you should worry about," was what I said instead. "Just—working out some issues with the guys."

"All of them?" The barest tilt of her head and a faint narrowing of her eyes warned me she wanted the truth. I sighed. "Jake," she continued squeezing my hand and then leaning forward. "I'm worried about you. I'm worried about all of you. I've been distracted but that's no excuse. If something's going on and I can help..."

"Baby Girl, you're perfect. This—this isn't something you can fix. It's something we have to fix ourselves."

Her frown razored right through me. "Jake, do you know what I love most about you?"

That question caught me off guard and cooled some of the irritation flaming through my system. "My winning personality and ability to make you smile?"

Frankie laughed, exactly like I'd hoped. She kissed my fingers before letting go of my hand and picking up her spoon. Digging into her crazy ass sundae though, she watched me from beneath her lashes. "Those are definitely in the plus column. But what I love most, is your ability to call bullshit even when it's uncomfortable. Even when I want to avoid something or someone...like say, the guys I'm in love with, because they hurt my feelings and I didn't know how to cope with it."

I grimaced.

"You were right to do that. You were right. So was Coop and Ian and Archie. You guys gave me space then you were done with it, you were all determined to bring me back into the circle and that was just when we were friends."

"Baby Girl, you've always been more than just our friend. If we had to settle for friendship, fine but...never mistake that you've always been more." A memory from the cabin we'd spent the holidays in and the conversation we'd had on my birthday. "I'll always find you—just like you said you would have found me."

Something shifted in my chest. Something that had fractured when we got the call about the accident. It burned, but it felt like relief too.

"I promise," she said before stuffing the largest bite of ice cream, whipped cream, fudge, and nuts into her mouth. For just a split-second, her eyes closed, and an orgasm face appeared and every ounce of blood in my body pounded southward. This was what I'd been missing. How the fuck had we let intimacy go the last few weeks I had no idea. But...

When her lashes fluttered up, I was a deer caught in the headlights of those deep green eyes. She licked her lips, but I couldn't tear my gaze away.

"I promise, I will always find you. But I'm worried about you. You're spending more time alone. You're avoiding me—or maybe it's..." The second her eyes narrowed, I wanted to curse.

"Baby Girl..."

"You're pissed at Archie." She lowered the spoon and the crinkle between her brows deepened. "Jake, the accident wasn't his fault."

"Baby Girl, I don't want to argue with you." And I sure as shit didn't want her to defend him.

"It *wasn't* his fault," she insisted. Swirling the dessert in the bowl, she scowled at the dessert like it was the ice cream's fault. "The brake lines didn't malfunction."

What? "Excuse me?"

"They didn't malfunction. Rachel and I went to meet with the detective investigating the accident."

That was news to me, and I sat back and stared at her.

"I had to know. Because I was worried about Archie."

"He wasn't even in the fucking accident." I couldn't quite keep the snarl out of my voice. "You were. You were the one who was hurt. For almost two hours we had no idea if you were okay or not. If he was—just like my dad and then that asshole waltzed in there without a scratch on him and you were..."

"Fine."

No, fine was a paltry word and I glared at her, but she met me glare for glare. "You were not fine. You had a concussion and bruises. There are still some fading over your chest from the seatbelt."

"And I'm still a little freaked out about driving, but I did it. Ian's motorcycle scared me a little, but I did it."

Fuck. I ran a hand over my face. "I'm sorry." The words tasted like ash on my tongue. "I should have paid closer attention."

"Hard to notice when I'm fighting to make sure it doesn't upset you guys any more than it already has. Jake, I was there when we were on the train to see your dad. I remember how scared you were. I hate the idea that my accident scared you, too."

Understatement, but I didn't want to examine the sense of loss too closely or how angry it still made me.

"But more than that, it pissed me off that someone did that to the car because they wanted to hurt Archie."

I frowned.

"It was his car, Jake. There was no reason to assume I'd be driving."

"But a hell of a lot to assume you would be in the car," I argued and then froze. "That fucking bitch."

Her mother.

Frankie looked down at the ice cream and then scooped up another bite. But she didn't deny it.

That cunt actually tried to kill her own daughter.

The rest of Frankie's statement registered then.

She'd tried to kill Archie, too.

Goddammit.

Chapter Fifteen
WHEN IT RAINS...

Frankie

The talk with Jake seemed to have helped. If nothing else, the guys seemed a little more normal. Jake wasn't hiding in his room as much when they were around. Of course, there was the additional problem of his schedule being so radically different from ours. I hated it. Worse, I hated the way it felt like we were always passing each other on the way in or the way out. Some nights I'd wait up for him, but lab work and a partner he didn't care for made him later and later.

"Hey," Coop murmured, wrapping an arm around me and tugging me back against him. It was another Friday. They had classes and I didn't. "Why are you awake and thinking so hard over there?"

Tipping my face up, I tried to find a smile. What seemed impossible suddenly blossomed as I looked into his eyes. Coop had been and always would be my best friend. I adored Rachel and she was great, but Coop just... "Do you have to go soon?"

"No," he murmured. "What's up?"

"I need to talk to you as my friend, not my boyfriend."

His eyebrows did a comical little jig as he stared at me. I didn't shy away from the searching look, but right now I needed Coop. I needed his steadiness and his clarity. Most of all, I needed him to tell me I wasn't crazy.

"I'm always your friend," he said slowly. "Always going to be the guy who loves you, too. So, if you need me to dial down possessive boyfriend so I don't go beat up some schmuck who upset you, I will."

Rolling over, I sprawled against his chest. We were naked and his cock was definitely awake and interested, but his focus was on my face and not my body. My head was almost too full. I'd talked to Jeremy, to Rachel, to Jake, and to each of the guys, but not the whole thing. Jake was the closest.

I'd asked him to not tell Archie about Maddy yet and he'd disagreed with me and I got it, but until I was certain...no I had to be certain. That was all there was to it. But I also needed to talk to Muriel and I wouldn't go behind Archie's back to do that. Which meant...

"Hey." Coop stroked the hair away from my face. "Talk to me." A knock on the door silenced the words on my tongue, but not his. "Thanks Jere, but just leave it outside for us? I'll grab it in a second."

"Very good. Mr. Archie and the others have gone running. You should have at least an hour of privacy."

My face burned and I hid it against Coop's neck. I swore I could have kissed him for not laughing or sounding anything other than genuine when he replied with, "Thanks, Jeremy. We'll be down for breakfast in a little while."

It wasn't until I was certain the gentle thump of his feet descending the stairs meant he'd gone that I threw myself off Coop and hid my face in the pillows. He chuckled as he slapped my ass.

"Don't be such a drama queen, Jeremy knows exactly what we're up to. It's why *he* knocks."

Yes. I was aware. "But it's so..."

"What?" Coop asked as he strolled across the room naked and I rolled onto my side to watch him. He pulled open the door without an ounce of shame and retrieved the full tray with the carafe of fresh brewed coffee, creamers and sugars. There were even a couple of blueberry muffins on there and from the smell of them—they were fresh. "Natural?"

"Awkward."

Tray in hand, he nudged the door shut with his foot, but not before Tory strolled in and leapt up to settle on the window seat. I hadn't had a single morning to worry about feeding the cats since we'd gotten back from our summer trip. Nor evening for their supper. Jeremy provided for them even better than I could. I suspected they loved him better now, but they still came to see me.

Coop set the tray on the chest at the end of the bed then poured coffee for both of us. "It's only awkward if you let it be awkward."

"You're only saying that because it wasn't your naked ass up in the air when he came in with something Archie requested. I've never ducked and covered so fast in my life." To his credit, Jeremy never mentioned the incident to me and Archie had apologized profusely in between bouts of laughter.

"You're right," he said, passing me my coffee before taking a seat on the bed. "Absolutely right. Next time it happens, I'll make sure it's my ass in the air, but you better be on bottom, cause Archie's not my type."

I snickered. "You would, too."

"If it made you feel better? And less embarrassed? Hell yes. Now, talk to me. My dick and I had different plans for waking you up this morning, but you wanted to talk. So, the boyfriend down there is gonna just suck it up while we talk."

"You mean he's forgiven you for waxing your balls?" When Coop admitted that to me, I hadn't been able to contain my humor or my horror. His poor balls. Having just had my first Brazilian this last summer, I could honestly say that I was not a fan. Archie pointed out laser treatments would probably be more comfortable.

And since the guys didn't seem to mind the smoother look, I might do that. There I went off the rails again. Huffing out a sigh, I lifted the mug and then took a long sip. It was perfect. Closing my eyes, I tried to soak up the caffeine to make sense of the chaos.

"Jake changed all of his classes," I began slowly. "I'm pretty sure he did it to get away from Archie. There's been a lot of tension and I tried to talk to Jake the other day. I think I got through to him, but now he's angry for an entirely different reason."

Mostly because I'd asked him to let me tell the others about my suspicions where Maddy was concerned. While things had been better, he and Archie still seemed too distant, too chilly, too polite.

It was enough to make me scream.

"Okay." The non-committal non-answer didn't help, but somehow Coop's neutral expression and warm eyes did. He was being my BFF and not my boyfriend right now.

I didn't think I could love him more. "Things have felt very different since we got home from the summer vacation. I mean, I know that was special and we can't expect to be in each other's pockets all the time. But even when Jake and I were in Germany, I still felt close to you guys, we talked all the time and now I feel like we're all going in different directions." I sucked on my lower lip, I had a thousand words vying to get out and I needed to stay focused. "Maybe it's not fair because we knew school would be hard. Especially when we have so many different classes."

Then Jake changed all the ones where it would have been the five of us together. He hadn't admitted it was because of Archie, but he also hadn't denied it. To his credit, whatever the fight was, Archie hadn't brought it to me either. It made me think about their bruised faces a while back and the 'sparring' they'd done at the gym.

"But it really changed with the accident."

"That's to be expected," Coop said gently. "It scared the hell out of us, Frankie. We didn't have enough information and then when we got there, you looked like crap."

"You always know how to make me feel good about myself."

He chuckled. "You were bruised, battered, and still the most beautiful girl in the whole wide world. But you're our girl, and you were hurt and *none* of us was there. Jake's not the only one who was angry about that."

"It wasn't Archie's fault," I began, but Coop pressed two fingers to my lips.

"Never said it was. I was angry that you were alone. I was angry that once again the world seems intent on hurting you. I wanted to sweep in there and kiss every bruise and scratch and make them go away. Did we all get a little intense? Yes. You were right to yell at us to back off."

I winced. "I didn't have to be so harsh."

"Eh," Coop said, his expression still easy. "We're thickheaded and stubborn. Also, we know you. Honestly, if we can't take you at your worst, we don't deserve you at your best."

A little offended, I straightened up and glared. "That was not me at my worst."

"No, you're worst was when you hit shark week at the same time as finals and had a cold while refusing to listen to anyone. Trust me. I've seen your worst. This? This was barely a speed bump. But it was a speed bump we needed to hit. This isn't what's bothering you though."

I sighed. "Coop, I don't deserve you."

"Bullshit. Next."

This was what made us best friends and always had. It didn't matter that we were sitting in this huge brownstone that probably cost millions of dollars, and the less I thought about that the better, in the middle of New York City, naked, drinking expensive coffee and talking about these amazing lives we had. Even with the speed bumps as he called them.

Big girl panties time, Frankie. Big girl panties time.

"It wasn't an accident." Why those three words were so impossible to say, I couldn't understand. Then again, even with a mother like mine, who wanted to believe their parent was capable of something as heinous as trying to kill the man you loved? "Everything that happened with the Ferrari. It wasn't an accident. I spoke with the detective and got a look at the report. It's why they won't release the car back to Archie or his family yet. The brake lines were cut."

A muscle ticked in his jaw.

"A couple of weeks ago, Rachel and I went to Long Island, talked to the detective and I had an attorney meet us there. Who knew, money really can move things..." I licked my lips because Coop's whole expression seemed frozen save for that single muscle ticking in his cheek. His gaze held mine captive, but there was no missing the way his knuckles whitened on the mug. "They are looking into Maddy as a person of interest. Because she's the only one I can think of who would have an axe to grind with Archie."

"And you." I swore he ground those words out between his teeth.

"Yes. But she couldn't have known I would be driving..."

"Could she have known you were with your grandparents?"

I spread my hands, I didn't know. "I don't want to ask them."

"Because you're afraid they'll say yes," Coop said with a deep sigh and with care he took my nearly empty coffee mug from my hands and set it with his on the nightstand, and then enfolded me into a crushing hug. "Fuck me, Frankie, you should have said something sooner, why are you carrying all of this on your own?"

"Cause I want to protect you—to protect Archie and Jake and Ian..."

I swore I could feel his sigh even if he didn't let one out and he pulled back long enough to cup my face. "BFF still here, but boyfriend wants back out. Tell me the rest of it. Tell me what you need."

Oh hell, I was going to cry. The open ease in that offer. Was there any doubt they would do this? None. In fact, that was what held me back. "We're trying to figure out where Maddy is and after I told Jake the other day, because I didn't want him blaming Archie, I know I need to tell Archie and Ian."

Coop blew out a breath. "You want me to smooth the way?"

"Well, maybe just kind of stand in front of me when they get mad at me for *not* telling them in the first place." I worried my lower lip, then shook my head. "For not telling any of you. But I couldn't. Not until I was sure. Maddy's always been so many things, but this—this goes past any of the horrible things she's ever done."

"She neglected you. She made you feel small. She denied you even the smallest measure of affection and isolated you from an extended family that could have and *would* have loved you. She's done worse."

"To me," I said and leaned my head back, but he tightened his grip and then pulled me all the way into his lap. I wound my arms around him. "Coop, I can't stand the idea that she could go so far as to hurt any of you. I know she blames Archie. Blames him for me rejecting the idea that his father is mine. Blames him for the confrontations and maybe even blames him because she's lost Edward again. I don't know."

I licked my lips.

"Patience told me that the reason they never came round was because she threatened to kill me if they did try to take me from her." Even repeating it didn't seem real.

"You're struggling to believe your mother could be capable of this, even if you know she is." Coop summed it up so easily. "And that's okay," he continued. "No matter whatever else she is, she's your mother. You're the most loyal and loving person I know. Jake calls it your big ass heart, but we know. Fuck me, Frankie, you don't have to carry this on your own."

"You guys were already upset about me being hurt, but I don't think it's me she was trying to hurt."

"You think it was Archie."

I nodded.

"And you think not telling him is going to protect him?"

"I think not telling him keeps him from racing headlong after her and throwing everything he has at it to fix the problem." Which was the bigger fear. "Archie..."

"Probably already suspects." Coop stroked my hair. "But I get it. I don't *like* it. But I get it."

Relief sagged through me. "I hate keeping this from all of you, I wanted to be wrong but now...now I have to find her. I have to know if she was involved. I can't stand the thought of her hurting any of you."

"Okay—as your best friend, I got your back. I'll be right there with you when you tell them, and I'll even keep Bubba from spanking your ass for holding this back."

I almost laughed, but the way he tightened his hand in my hair held the sound at bay.

"Anything else you need from your best friend right now?"

"I'd say a hug but since you're already holding me, I'm good."

"Excellent." Then his mouth crashed down on mine, and I couldn't breathe for the way he swept his tongue inside. One moment we were up sitting upright and the next I was on my back and gazing up at him. His fierce expression sent a wave of wild tingles through my whole body. "Boyfriend time."

Oh, that sounded like a warning.

"Don't you ever keep stuff like this from us. You want to protect me. Fine. But I get to protect you, too." The growl underscoring the words registered in all the right places. "I hope like fuck for your sake, that bitch Maddy had nothing to do with this. But if she did? Then you aren't facing her alone and you have all of us at your back."

"What if she...."

"Comes after one of us again?" He shook his head. "We'll figure this out. I promise. But this only works if we're all talking. I get it, I told you. I understand *why* you held back and all of that tangled emotion because your heart is one of the best things about you. But I *need* you to remember to trust us, too, even when we're being stubborn, neanderthals who want to thump our chests and say our woman, no touchy."

I opened my mouth and then closed it. Then opened it again. "Our woman, no touchy?" Finally escaped on a squeak.

"Hmm-hmm," he said and pushed up and flipped me over with such ease, I could have sworn he practiced. "My woman," he whispered right against my ear, one hand curling my hair around his fist and then he nudged my legs apart and I swore I shuddered at the first brush of his cock. Relentless and claiming, he thrust into me without giving me time for the stretch. It didn't hurt, but fuck I could feel him all the way to my bones. "No touchy."

"This feels like a lot of touchy," I managed to exhale, and he bit down against my neck.

"You haven't felt anything yet." That was his only warning as he began to rock into me at a furious, almost punishing pace. I ached for more and he slid his hand around to tease my clit even as he used my hair to hold on to. It was easy to forget that Coop knew what he wanted when he wanted it and I let go.

Fuck, I needed this.

I needed him.

I hit my first orgasm and he didn't slow, the rocking force of him kept me riding that edge of lightning, the pleasure spiraling out only to coil, pull taut, and then burst again. I shook under the force of it.

His shout of release seemed to hold us suspended there. I was almost too sensitive, the feeling of him pulsing inside of me was too much and not enough. We collapsed together, and he stayed with me, locked inside me as if he had every intention of picking up where he left off.

Not that I had any complaints about that, even as I couldn't catch my breath. "Coop," I whispered.

"Hmm?"

"I love boyfriend you."

He chuckled. "Yeah?" He eased up and delivered a stinging slap to my ass that had me clenching around him and we shuddered together. "Oh fuck," he swore. "Still love boyfriend me?"

"Oh yeah."

"Good." Another slap followed the first. This time to my other ass cheek and I was clenching around his softening cock, though it didn't seem to be softening that much. Fuck, that was hot. "I promised to keep Bubba from spanking you." Another swat. This time he massaged the heat into my aching butt cheek. "But your BFF and your boyfriend are in complete agreement." Another swat, then another. When we hit ten, he slowed and massaged my ass and I was a damn puddle and he was hard as a stone inside of me.

"Yes, sir," I whispered, and he shuddered all over again.

"You don't have to sir me, Frankie," he whispered, biting down on my ear. "Remember, I already told you I'd get on my knees for you."

I lifted my gaze to his. "And I can't get on mine for you?"

Surrender was easy when you already belonged to each other and honestly, I adored this side of Coop. He let it out so rarely. I loved all sides of him. "Do you want to get on your knees for me?"

Showing was better than telling, I pushed up to my knees and he rocked within me, shifting his weight as I pressed my hands down and then I looked over my shoulder at him. "Player 3 has leveled up."

His laughter eddied out of him and I swore tickled me, but he rocked forward and we both groaned. Too sensitive by far, we took a longer, lazier route to chasing our pleasure and we were still shaking from it all when the guys got home.

We still had to tell them, but right now, wrapped up in him....I was okay with it. We'd get through it.

They were going to be mad, but we'd had fights before, right?

Chapter Sixteen

FIGHT NIGHT

Frankie

"What the *hell* were you thinking?" Archie demanded.

"Yeah, that thing I said about having fights before.

"Don't," Jake snapped.

"Don't what?" Archie snarled. "You can't possibly be okay with her having gone off on her own and not telling us what she suspected."

"You're right," Jake fired back closing the gap between them. "She should have told us and she's trying to tell us now, so maybe stop acting like an entitled dick for once and just fucking listen to her."

"Fuck you, Jake, you knew. You figured it out or she told you before she told us, otherwise you'd have gone through the roof. If anyone here has an anger management issue, it's definitely not me. Entitled? Hardly." The disdain in Archie's voice hurt nearly as much as the razor wire in Jake's.

I pinched the bridge of my nose. So far, Coop had done exactly what he promised, planted himself right at my side when we got everyone together. I'd managed to get less than a third of the way through the story, getting so far as to reveal that the accident really hadn't been an accident when Archie flipped.

The cats scattered. I hadn't even realized they were in the room with us. The second floor living area and game room seemed like an ideal spot to have the conversation. We'd not used it all that much and there was plenty of seating to sprawl about on. But Archie wasn't sprawling, no he was pacing.

Jake opened and closed his fists, the knuckles on his hands whitening, but he didn't lunge and the only anger in his eyes seemed to be directed at Archie instead of me. Yes, I had told Jake and to his credit, he'd been just as pissed as Archie. I felt like an asshole for ambushing Archie this way.

"Please don't take this out on each other."

"We're not," Archie and Jake snapped in the exact same irritated tone of voice.

"Oh, but you are," Ian interrupted, hands braced on the back of the sofa. So far, he was the only one who hadn't yelled at me. "Right now, Angel is trying to tell us. So shut up and save your comments for the end." I could have kissed him. "I know I am."

Or not.

I sighed. Dropping to sit on the edge of the sofa, I said, "I'm sorry I didn't tell you all right away. I had my reasons. Doesn't make them good reasons, but I had them." Ian nodded his head once as if accepting that answer. Swallowing, I looked at Archie. "It was *your* car that was sabotaged. I was pretty sure whoever did it wanted to hurt you."

"Babe, then that's an even *bigger* reason for you to tell us."

"Maybe," I said, not totally disagreeing. "But I also think it was Maddy who did it. And I couldn't tell you until I was sure. I'm still not altogether certain. Rachel and I have been trying to find her and Dominic has one of their investigators working on it."

"Who the fuck is Dominic?" Jake demanded.

"The attorney," Coop supplied.

"Oh." Jake scrubbed a hand over his face and then dropped onto the sectional so he was opposite me. Ian and Archie were both still standing, but they were looking at each other, not at us. Coop exhaled and sat down next to me, pressing his thigh to mine in a show of solidarity.

"Tell them the rest," he encouraged me quietly.

"It was a lot easier when they weren't so pissed at me. You know when I imagined this in my head." It was lame but Jake actually chuckled, and Archie shook his head. Neither said anything, so I looked to Ian. The encouragement was back in his eyes. So I told them the rest, about the report, the cut brake lines and maybe that I had been running interference to get the report on all of that before Archie did.

The anger and irritation in Archie's expression transformed to pride. "Sneaky. I like it. Just not when you use it against me."

"I learned from the best," I pointed out and for the first time since this conversation started, he smiled.

"Babe," he exhaled. "You learned too well. I want that report."

"I know, it's up in my room. I'll get it when we're done. The point of all this is that they've officially ruled this a criminal investigation and whether it will be for tampering or..."

"Attempted murder?" Ian supplied. "Because that's what it was. You could have died."

I nodded because there was zero point in denying it. "The trouble is proving that it was Maddy. I don't know where she is." I glanced at Archie, but he already had his phone out and he was typing rapidly.

"Checking with Edward. If that psycho bitch is with him, I know where to send the cops."

"Archie," Coop snapped and Archie paused then winced.

"Sorry, Babe."

"Psycho bitch sounds about right." I spread my hands. "Archie, I don't know if she did it. But I know what she threatened before and I know how much she blamed you..."

His phone buzzed. "She can blame me all she wants. Let her take a swing at me...no, she's not with Edward. He hasn't seen her in over a month. I'd take that with a grain of salt, though he does seem to be trying to honor his word these days."

The bitterness in his words tasted like ash on my tongue.

"Wait," Archie said abruptly then glanced at me. "If the car was sabotaged, then it happened while we were at your grandparents."

That was the part that I'd been chasing around in my head. I covered my face with my hands, cupping them over my nose and mouth as if it would help me slow down the sudden hammering of my heart. "We were there most of the weekend." The words were muffled but Archie nodded. "I never saw her, and I don't think she's in touch with them. Things were pretty...hostile, I suppose is the best word."

"Babe, your grandparents can't stand up to your mother. Where she's concerned the depth of their ability to fend her off is less than a teaspoon."

Harsh. But then, Patience had been the one to try before. I don't think my grandfather had any interest. Then again, her threats against me kept them away. This was all such a mess.

"Hey," Ian said, having circled the sofa to where I was seated. He held out a hand and I took it then he settled back into my spot and pulled me into his lap. Arms tight around me, he kissed my temple. "It's going to be all right, Angel. Five heads are better than one. Let's start with the most basic questions, have you spoken to your grandparents?"

I shook my head. "No. I'm terrified of what their answer will be and before you ask, no I haven't told Hank about the accident. I don't want her to decide to take this out on him. He's got a family and little kids..."

"Your family," Coop interrupted.

"And he's *your* father," Jake tacked on. "A job he really seemed enthusiastic about."

"Babe, we can't protect you when we don't know that there is a threat. He needs to know." Archie groaned as he perched on the coffee table not far from me and Ian. Jake shifted to sitting on the other side of Ian, the four of them boxing me in neatly. "Babe—I love you for wanting to protect me, but not when it risks you. Nothing is worth risking you."

"Nothing is worth risking any of you," I argued. Ian's arms tightened around me, and I leaned into him. I needed the strength more than he realized or maybe he did realize it and that was why he moved. "I get to protect you, too."

Jake let out an aggravated sigh, Coop swept in. "Yes, you do. But I think the not sharing of potential problems should end now."

Archie and Jake both glared at Coop who met their expressions with a bland one of his own.

"Secrets have a habit of coming back to bite us all in the ass. If Maddy really has had a break with reality enough to actively try and hurt both of you, then we don't need issues chewing on us behind the scenes and breaking down the trust we've built." He was still staring at Jake and Archie.

"Coop's right." Ian rubbed his chin against my shoulder. "As aggravating as it is that Frankie took this on herself, she had the forethought to involve Rachel and the attorneys. Then she came and told us. It might not be the kind of news any of us wanted to hear, but Frankie faced all of us. You two just have to face her."

I shifted in his lap then focused on Archie and Jake. Neither looked happy. With Coop and Ian or with each other.

"Fine, fuck it. I'll go first," Jake said and he locked his gaze on me. "I told you I changed my schedule because it would be better for my focus. I let you think it was because I'd shifted my discipline, but the truth was I needed a break from Archie."

My stomach bottomed out.

"Right, wrong, or indifferent," Jake continued. "He should never have left you alone at your grandparents' to drive back. I'm not saying I wanted him hurt in the accident, but you shouldn't have been alone. His car. He should have been there."

"I was trying to settle this between us," Archie said after a long pause.

"But even boxing didn't help."

All those bruises. I frowned.

"He's not wrong, Babe, I should have been there, that said, he doesn't get to decide who stays or who goes."

"And you could learn to give a guy some space," Jake bit out each word as though he were literally holding back his anger. To be honest, the two of them were closer right now than they'd been in the last few weeks. "But no, you have to be right there *all the fucking time*."

"Did it occur to you that we're always all here?" Archie retaliated, only his tone iced. "You got a problem, you deal with it. But we're not punishing Frankie with some metaphorical tug of war."

"Metaphorical my ass, you just have to do everything your way and the consequences be damned."

So much of what Jeremy had gracefully danced around became clear. I'd gotten that there was tension. But this was more than that.

"Enough." I pushed out of Ian's lap as Archie and Jake both hit their feet. I was right between them and I'd be damned if they were going to keep this up. "Seriously, that's enough."

I glanced from one to the other. Pivoting, I faced Archie and I swore he damn near smirked and my blood heated. Not the time, Archie. Not the time. "You should know better than to keep shoving at Jake when he's already dug his heels in. It just makes him angrier and more bull-headed. You can't force people to like you and forgive you just because you wear them down and talk them into it."

"Babe..."

"Don't you babe me."

"You tell him, Baby Girl."

At that, I whirled and poked a finger into Jake's chest. "Don't you start. You are not without fault here. Archie didn't cause the accident. And I'm all right. You need someone to blame because it scared you. It scared all of you. Blaming Archie isn't helping anyone right now. Add to all of that you changed your entire schedule so now we barely see each other and you thought *that* was the way to handle it?"

Jake's expression fell and I threw up my hands before retreating from all of them and folding my arms.

"You're all right, I should have told you about the Maddy thing right up front. But I get a say in protecting you as much as you get a say in protecting me. You hover, you make decisions, and you surround me like I'm fragile and I'll break. But the one thing all of you forget is that I lived with Maddy my whole life. I know her better than all of you and I'm not wearing my willful blinders anymore."

Ian frowned. "Then what do you think she's doing?"

"Blaming Archie for losing me or maybe for losing Edward. Maybe both. She's going to lash out. Archie is an easy target."

"Excuse you." Archie almost sounded offended, but Coop swatted him on the shoulder.

"She means you're an easy target for Maddy's rage."

"I know what she meant," Archie threw back at Coop. "But I'll be fine. Frankie's the one she's always hurt."

"But I'm also the one she wants." Me and Edward apparently. Not something I'd ever think I'd have in common with Archie's father.

"If she really is the narcissistic personality she seems to be, with psychopathic tendencies—then yeah. She won't stand for being supplanted in your life. Archie's the one who has been standing up to her the most." Coop slid his hands into his pockets, and I swore my stomach dropped again.

It was bad enough to consider all the possibilities. "We need to talk to Edward. He might know what resources she has."

"I'll take care of it," Archie said. "You don't have to talk to him at all."

I sighed. "Muriel also invited me over to discuss Maddy and to offer me assistance. Enemy of my enemy and all that."

If I thought our earlier argument had been bad. This one was worse.

"I forbid it." Three words. Three words and the whole room went quiet. I just stared at Archie.

"You what now?"

"I forbid it. My mother is functional alcoholic and interested in very little outside of herself. You do not need to be exposed to her. In fact, I think we're going to make sure you have company wherever you go. It'll be a little bit like high school again..."

I tuned out and stared up at the ceiling.

"Arch," Coop said. "We're not in high school."

'And you don't get to make fucking decisions for everyone," Jake said, jumping in and I swore my head hurt. All I had to do was agree. Agree to what they all seemed to want and the argument would probably stop.

But I didn't agree. Maddy was my mother. I had to know.

Muriel—she wasn't a friend and I wasn't so blind to her faults as to think she would be.

"Angel," Ian said softly as he moved away from where Jake and Archie were verbally tearing into each other. "They're fighting because they don't want to be helpless."

I got that.

"But this isn't helping either."

"I know. They'll settle it, sooner or later. We always do. It's a little different now. The last time we had a falling out like this..."

"It was you and Jake."

The corner of Ian's mouth kicked a little higher. "That was different. Believe it or not, the four of us don't always get along and we don't always agree."

"No, really?" I rolled my eyes. "I've seen you guys fight before." Just not like this. I couldn't think of another time where they'd verbally attacked each other like this. There was real malice in their tones and I swore Jake was about to take a swing when Coop shoved them apart. "I can't stand that you are all fighting over me like this."

"It's not *over* you, Angel," Ian promised, then wrapped an arm around me. "C'mon, let Coop talk them down. At least they're talking, even if it's at a higher volume. That's more than Jake's been willing to do in days." As reluctant as I was to leave them, on the off chance I could prevent the violence, I really didn't want to see them fighting like this.

Instead of going upstairs, Ian guided me down and then down to the studio. Inside, the moment the door closed all the other sounds cut off. It didn't mean the guys weren't fighting, but the rough timbre of their voices didn't carry, and I didn't have to worry about what they were saying.

"Have they really been fighting this whole time?" How the hell had I missed that tension? First it had been the accident and hurting. Then getting ticked with them all crowding around me and making decisions. I stopped talking to them for a couple of days.

"Not the whole time," Ian said as he gave my shoulders a squeeze and then he moved over to the piano. As he took a seat, I smiled. I couldn't help it. Heat swept through me whenever I saw a piano bench now and this wasn't even the same one. "Fear hits us all differently. I think—I think I have the most intimate knowledge of what it is to lose you."

He played a few keys, they were sad, almost. The tones low and thoughtful.

"The day you broke up with me, it gutted me, Angel. I deserved it because I couldn't seem to get the words to work to tell you what I was thinking and feeling."

I licked my lips. "I hated doing it, but—Maddy..."

"I know," he soothed in a gentle voice as he danced his fingers over the keys. I didn't know the melody he was playing but it helped with the headache pounding behind my eyes. "I do. But the thing is—for a few weeks there, I lost you. You were still my friend, but it wasn't the same and it wasn't all I wanted. There was this Frankie-shaped hole in my life."

I walked over to lean against the piano as he shifted by quarter notes.

"We spent a whole summer without you and I swear, we fought more than you might think. Jake and Archie even tried to beat the shit out of each other."

Wait.

"What?"

"It's true," Ian told me. "Bro code and all, they can share the details with you when they are up to it, or not. They may not mention it because it's over and done with. Resolved. Coop and Jake got into it, too."

"And you?"

"Archie," he admitted with a careless little shrug. "But here's the thing I can tell you. Those guys love you every bit as much as I do. When they thought I was causing you pain, they staged an intervention and got right in my face about it. They weren't going to let me hurt you and if they had to set me straight, they were going to do it."

For a moment, he ran his fingers up and down the scales. It was a little Looney Tunes, but it made me smile.

"That's the thing, Angel. That's how we fight. How we resolve things. Sometimes, we need to get the aggression out. Then we can listen."

"That's not how you guys fight with me."

He paused mid-keystroke and gave me a patient look. "You backed Jake up a step up there and you tore a strip off Archie's hide. You don't need your fists."

I sighed and moved to sit next to him.

"We're not messing this all up, are we?"

He didn't answer me right away, instead he played another melody I didn't know but it was bittersweet and thoughtful.

"I think life is messy sometimes," Ian said after a long pause but never stopped playing. "I think we're supposed to fight. To push each other. To grow. Sometimes we have to make mistakes because we're not perfect."

"Are you sure about that?" I teased. "You're pretty damn perfect for me."

"Well, you're pretty damn perfect for all of us, too. It's only been a year for them." That gave me pause.

Oh shit.

He chuckled softly. "Forgot that did you? Anniversaries and such?"

I grimaced. "Worst. Girlfriend. Ever."

"Not even," he whispered. "You remember the important things. Anniversaries are dates and we'll celebrate them sometimes and sometimes we'll forget. But as long as we remember each other and figure things out, then we'll be okay."

"You sound like Coop."

He really did.

"Coop's going to be a great psychologist. He's got the patient listening thing down." That he did. "And he gives pretty good advice." That, too. "But the thing is, he cares and unlike some of us, he doesn't need anger to motivate him to show it or fear."

Fear. Archie.

Anger. Jake.

I studied Ian.

"What motivates you?"

"Need," he told me simply. "The need to take care of you. Oh, don't worry that it's the only thing driving me. But that need nearly cost me you, so I've learned to temper it. They'll temper theirs."

They had for a while. Then the accident.

"Ian, if Maddy really tried to kill Archie..."

He stopped playing and faced me. "That's not your fault, Angel. None of this is your fault. It's not Archie's fault. It's not your fault. It's not your grandparents' fault. It's the work of a madwoman. If she did it—and that's still an if at the moment, then lay the blame where it belongs."

"With Maddy." I let out a long breath. "If she did it."

Ian settled his hand over my heart. "You were right up there when you said you knew her. You've lived with her your whole life, and you made excuses, but that didn't mean you didn't know."

I wanted to deny it even as shame crawled through me, but Ian held my gaze and I lifted my chin. I'd never had the choice when I was younger. I did now.

"What does this big heart of yours tell you?"

I swallowed.

"She did it."

"Then we find the proof and we send your mother to jail or have her committed. Whatever it takes. She doesn't get to hurt you..."

"Or *any* of you," I insisted, and Ian favored me with a featherlight kiss.

"Angel, if something happened to one of us that would also hurt you."

It would gut me.

"But we'll protect each other. Just give those hard heads some time to work it out."

He moved back to position and started playing as I leaned my head against his shoulder. "If they don't, I guess I'll just have to kick their butts until they behave."

"You'd do it, too," Ian said without an ounce of irony. "But make sure you have gloves on before you punch Jake. I swear he's got lead in that jaw of his."

It shouldn't have been funny.

It really shouldn't, but I laughed even as tears slipped out and I wiped them away while Ian continued to play.

We would figure this out.

Even if boys were dumb sometimes.

I could almost hear Rachel's eye roll from here.

Dumb or not, I loved my boys and I needed them to work this out. Their friendships were important. All of our friendships were.

Chapter Seventeen

HANK AND ME

Frankie

Resolutions did not come over night. Ian and I stayed in the studio for as long as we could, but hunger eventually sent us out. The smell of spaghetti sauce and garlic bread had me racing up the stairs with a chuckling Ian in my wake. Coop was in the kitchen, an ice pack on his right hand and fork in his left. Jeremy nodded us toward the table. If he thought anything amiss it never showed in his expression.

No sooner had the spaghetti been put in front of me than I dove in. I glanced at Coop after the first several mouthfuls and finally asked, "Do I want to know?"

"I may or may not have punched Jake," Coop said with a shrug. "He deserved it."

Ian shot me a look that said 'see?' but I just shook my head. "Are Archie and Jake not eating?"

It was Jeremy who answered. "No, they will both spend some time working on their manners and communication skills before they can rejoin us at a dinner table. I expect a peaceful evening."

Uncertain of what that meant, I decided to let it go. I could go find them individually later. All of this started because I'd come clean about what I'd been doing. No sooner did that thought take root then I shook my head. No, all of this started because of the accident. It stripped us back to basics. Relationships took work, Erin said that to me constantly.

And I needed a new therapist. Rachel was right. If I got too lost in my own head over all of this again, I couldn't afford to mess things up. Maybe we did need date nights again. The summer spoiled us. We were always together, all of us, we found time easily.

Now?

Now, we needed to make it work.

Making it work proved even more challenging than I was ready for. In fact, Archie and Jake now both seemed to be avoiding me. Or maybe I was imagining it. I had given Archie the reports and he'd nodded, picked up his phone and stalked away.

Yep. Work. They needed time to forgive me for not telling them stuff, just like I'd needed time when they were hovering. Ugh, I hated the distance between us. I hated having to take my own advice. Coop kept me sane though. Oddly when I asked why wasn't he angrier? His answer surprised me.

"Because you're you," he told me with a shrug. "You always try to do everything yourself. You don't like leaning on others or having to be dependent and I blame that bitch of your mother for that. She taught you not to trust."

I'd never thought of it that way. "But I do trust you."

"I know you do and so do they. But you also have something to lose now and that makes you even fiercer than you were before."

"How do you know me better than I know myself sometimes?"

"Perks of being me," he said with a grin. "Not everyone can handle perfection."

I thwapped him with a pillow, but he was right. It was the perk of being him. So, when Hank called to invite me to the twins' birthday party the coming weekend, I was trapped. I'd held my hand out and Coop grasped it easily then tugged me onto his lap where he could hear Hank as clearly as I did.

"Not putting pressure on you and I promised to be patient. But you canceled on Labor Day and I know the first few weeks of school are tough. But Chloe's dying to meet you and it's the only thing she asked for her birthday."

Guilt swamped me. I'd canceled Labor Day because I'd been so bruised and I still hadn't told Hank about the accident. I'd had an extended family for all of five minutes and I was a terrible daughter and sister.

I looked at Coop and raised my brows. Would he go with me? This was a lot of family to meet at once. Hank had been overwhelming and I'd had all of my guys there. Meeting all of them at the same time? *And* on Chloe's birthday? Well Craig *and* Chloe's birthdays. They were going to be eight.

No excuse on the planet would be worth disappointing a little girl on her birthday. Birthday boys and girls got what they wanted. As if aware of my panic, Coop rubbed my back in slow circles and let me grip his free hand as tightly as I needed to.

"Is Craig okay with me coming up on their birthday too?" It came out more a squeak than I was proud to admit, but I cleared my throat. "It's not that I don't want to come." I really did want to meet them. "But their birthday should be about them and not the new girl."

"First of all," Hank said in a stern voice. "You're not some random *new* girl. You're their sister. Secondly, Craig would probably pay you his birthday money if you'll show up and make Chloe stop asking me every day when you can make it."

I winced and Coop pressed his mouth to my shoulder, but his shaking gave away the laughter he was trying to suppress.

"Alec, on the other hand, will probably be testy and I don't want you to take offense in any way." The fact Hank felt the need to tell me that gave me pause. "He's used to being the oldest. He's been reticent on committing to feelings one way or the other." A pause and then he spoke as if away from the phone, "Yes, dear, I'm getting to that part." The deep well of affection he had for his kids seemed to double when he spoke to his wife.

She sounded like a neat person. I was glad my siblings had a good mom.

"Kelly wants to meet you, she has since that first phone call and she feels that she's been very patient and promises she won't smother you." He dropped his voice almost confidentially. "But she's a hugger and she's offered to hold off until you're comfortable. That's *huge*...ow." But the last bit carried so much laughter, I couldn't help but grin.

"Do you mind if Coop comes with me? I know you wanted to hold off on all the boys but..."

"We don't mind in the slightest," Kelly answered for him. She even sounded warm on the phone. "I do want to meet all of these boys at some point, but we've got the room. So that's a yes, you'll come?"

I blew out a breath. "I wouldn't miss it. Could someone please text me birthday wish lists for them?"

"You don't have to buy them presents."

"Yes, I do," I said in the same breath as Coop said, "Yes, she does."

I elbowed him and he grinned.

"I have one birthday rule," I admitted. "Birthday boys and girls get what they want."

There was a pause on the phone and then Hank said, "I can respect that, but—don't tell the kids yet. They'll take you to the cleaners on that one. Give them an inch and they'll take the whole marathon."

I laughed. I couldn't help it. "Deal."

"See you this weekend, sweetheart," Hank said.

"Yep, see you then."

The call disconnected and I stared at the phone in my hands for a long time.

"It's going to be a blast," Coop whispered against my ear. "And you tell every negative Nancy talking in your head right now that your kid sister and brothers are going to love the hell out of you."

"Alec might not," I pointed out.

"Ha," Coop declared. "Just let him meet you. He'll come around."

Oh hell.

We were going to see the whole family.

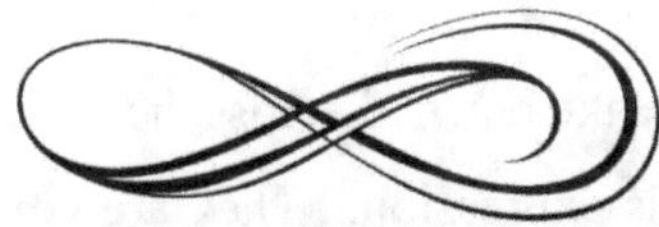

Anxiety about the weekend went from a steady forty to a hundred and sixty when the road trip came up with the other guys. Ian went quiet. Jake's scowl deepened the bruising around his eye to the point it made me want to wince. Coop hadn't been kidding about belting him one. Archie, however, was the one who startled me the most.

Everything emptied out of his expression before he rose and slammed out of the room without a word. Putting a hand over my mouth, I stared after him, then back to the guys still here torn between where to go.

"Stay," Coop murmured, kissing the top of my head. "I'll go make sure he doesn't do anything insane like buy a building so he can blow it up."

Was that even something he'd do? But Coop left to go after him, leaving me with Jake and Ian. Exhaling, I faced them and sucked it up. "I didn't think that saying we were going to drive up would be a big deal. It's only three hours or so and..." Well, I kind of wanted to stop in at a couple of places in Connecticut but I had a feeling saying I wanted to see the towns that inspired Stars Hollow wouldn't go over right now.

"Angel," Ian said. "We know and we all knew you'd want to go up and visit your dad and his family."

"Could you maybe take a train?" The question came from Jake.

I mean I supposed I could...

"No," Ian said. "She has to deal with her own fear of driving and being in vehicles, we can't let ours take over hers."

"Fuck," Jake swore as he leaned back in the chair. We were outside, sitting in the sunshine on the deck. It was cooler today, at home—well in Texas—we'd still be sweating our asses off, but it was nice out here. "Coop is going with you and staying with you the whole time?"

"I sure as hell hope so," I admitted. "I'm terrified of meeting all of them and the kids decide they hate me and his wife is just being nice because it's polite."

"Hey." All at once, Jake reached across the table to cover my hand and the anger drained from his expression. "They are going to love you. Come on, Frankie. My sisters like you better than they like me."

"That's cause you're a boy," I reminded him, and he chuckled. The rakish smile lightened the dark expression his bruise created. "And that's different...I've known them forever. Just like Trina. Chloe is...she's always talking like I'm the best thing ever, what if she meets me and is just flat out disappointed?"

"Then you'll win her over because she's probably worried you won't like her either," Ian offered and I gaped. "Angel, she texts you regularly, she wants to make sure you don't forget her."

"That's true," Jake agreed. "The girls have talked to me more since I moved out than they ever did when I was at home." His smile turned almost indulgent. "I almost miss them."

A laugh escaped me. "You adore them."

"From miles away, they are way more adorable," Jake agreed, but he glanced at Ian then at me. "Frankie, if you want to drive up there, I'm not going to forbid it or anything."

Which was good cause that word needed to vanish from our vocabulary.

"And I'm glad you looped us in," Ian added on to it.

"But," Jake interjected and my fingers twitched in his hold, but he threaded his fingers with mine. "Check in with us? Make Coop text us stupid updates or something? Send pictures? Have the car inspected by a licensed mechanic to make sure no one has tampered with it?"

My heart fisted. Most of those weren't unreasonable requests. "You and Archie know my car better than I do. Can the two of you do it for me?" I really didn't know where they stood with each other. It hadn't really been all that long since the other day, but there seemed to be something of an armistice in the house.

He paused, his expression thoughtful. "Yeah, I mean—we can just have him do it. He tends to like to take things over."

"Or you can be less of a dick," Ian offered. "And just work with him. Who knows, maybe the two of you can deal with your issues like mature adults."

The look Jake sent Ian had me groaning. "Don't you two start. You already tried to beat the hell out of each other and Jake nearly ended up arrested."

For his part, Jake had the grace to grimace. "No, he's right, Baby Girl. We can act like adults. And—for what it's worth, I'm sorry I fucked up our plans for classes this semester. I should have just—sucked it up."

"You did what you needed to do for you," I suggested. "I just wish it didn't leave you so isolated."

He kissed my hand. "We'll make up for it on my birthday. I have plans."

"Your birthday isn't for another two months."

He grinned. "Trust me, they're good plans." Then his smile faded as he let go of my hand and stood. "Excuse me, I'm going to go find my mature adult pants and put them on then talk to Archie."

I almost wanted to say don't kill each other, but I was pretty sure that was implied. After he left us alone, I laid my head against my arms and stared over at Ian. "I changed my mind."

"About?"

"Being an adult."

He chuckled. "It's not that bad, Angel. They need a project to work on together. They can snark at each other and pick apart each other's work, but in the end they share the same goal. Just give them time to figure it out."

"If that doesn't work?"

With a shrug, Ian raised his brows. "Walk around naked. They'll stop arguing."

I cracked up and he grinned.

"Angel, for real, they will figure it out. But if you need me to pound one of them, just say the word."

"I thought that was Jake's job."

"Sometimes," Ian said, then matched my pose and crossed his arms on the table and laid his head down so we were eye-to-eye. "Sometimes we have to fill in for each other. It's how families work. Families fight. They pick on each other. They disagree. In the end—not a doubt in my mind that Jake and Archie won't back each other up if push came to shove, even if they want to kick each other's asses."

That made me feel better. "Do you think we'll ever get to the part where we're not having to deal with things like my mother?"

"Yes," Ian said with absolute certainty. "But I think there's always going to be challenges. Whether it's writing and performing music, passing our classes, picking career paths, and trying to make five lives work in harmony. It's not the challenges that are the problem."

"It's how we face them."

"Bingo. So far, I think we've done okay," Ian said. "Not that we haven't had our fair share of hard knocks and setbacks."

"I love you," I said.

His eyes crinkled. "Love you too, Angel. Want to go work on some more music? Or do you need to work on that economics paper?"

Oh shit. Economics paper. I was gonna do that over the weekend. "Crap. Crap. Crap." I'd have to stay up and get it all done tonight.

Ian was still chuckling as I jumped up and then kissed him.

"Raincheck on the music?"

"Absolutely. That demo is ready to go back to KC if you want, or we can bite the bullet and send it out."

My stomach dropped about fifteen stories. I didn't care if that meant it landed somewhere in the subway.

"Or, we can discuss this after you finish that paper and get back from meeting the rest of your family." He said it so easily like it was the most natural thing in the world. "Go on, Angel, you're not going to be able to think of anything else until that paper is done anyway."

He wasn't wrong about that, but I jumped up to wrap my arms around him and he caught me easily. "I love you, Sir Ian and I love you, Brother Boyfriend Bubba, and I love you, Ian." I punctuated each declaration with a kiss. "No matter how much it terrifies me, we're gonna do this."

His eyes warmed. "Yeah?"

That right there was why we were going to do it. Music was his joy and sharing it with me just made me feel so damned loved. "Yes. Bound Hearts is happening."

We sealed the deal with a long kiss and then he set me down. "Off you go. If you need to come down from the stress, say the word, until then I trust you to look after yourself. But I will bring up food if you don't come down to eat."

Jeremy would probably do that, too, so I just nodded. I had no idea if he understood what those words meant to me. Maybe he did. Maybe of all of them, Ian really did get it, because it was the not trusting me to know my own heart and mind that had nearly driven us apart.

Inside, I found Jake, Archie, and Coop in deep conversation that paused the moment I walked inside.

"Ignore me, I have to do an econ paper before we leave so I'm going up to my room. Please send food and coffee at appropriate intervals." I waved to them and headed for the stairs. It must have been the right thing to say because their laughter drifted up to reach me by the time I hit the third floor and I grinned.

Ian was right, we would figure this out. Or maybe we could go to some paintball place, and I could shoot them over and over until they were nice again.

I paused at the door to my room. Oh, *that* had possibilities.

Chapter Eighteen

FIRE MEET GASOLINE

Archie

Muriel sent Frankie a fucking letter inviting her to talk about Maddy.

Punch.

Edward wanted in on the investigation of what happened to the car.

Punch.

Jake couldn't get his head out of his ass.

Punch.

Frankie wanted to take a road trip to see her family.

Punch.

She thought Maddy targeted me, but Frankie would have been in the car regardless.

Punch.

I could barely stand to let her out of my sight.

Punch.

And the first fucking thing she does is start an investigation into her mother? Using her resources?

Punch.

She did exactly what I would have done.

Punch.

I slowed the blows and blew out a breath as I leaned against the bag.

"You're favoring your left," Jake commented. "You don't usually."

"It's fine," I told him, rolling my arms and trying to loosen up my shoulder. I'd fucked it up in one of the engineering labs the day before setting up for a project. I shouldn't have hurried, but I was in a bad mood and stuck with the most irritating jackass for a partner since Jake decided he couldn't stand to be in my space anymore.

I went back to my jabbing practice. The blows were as much to channel my anger into something physical, without actually destroying everything, and trying to hit a headspace to figure out the best solution to this problem.

Making Maddy disappear would be ideal.

Not the worst option. Yet, every time I tried to work my brain around it, I kept coming back to the one major drawback. A lifetime away from Frankie where I would be behind bars. Probably get a nice prison, some privately-run one. Standish money could buy a lot. Might even get a lighter sentence.

But killing her mother wasn't what Frankie wanted.

Then again...no body no crime.

Jake moved around so he was in my line of sight and he braced the bag so it stopped swinging quite so much. We said nothing to each other as I kept hammering blows away against the leather. He braced the bag, leaning into it and I had to control the force more to keep from actually hurting myself.

"You're still favoring the left," Jake commented. "Shift your footing."

"I know what I'm doing," I gritted out. Sweat poured off me, but I needed this. I'd thought about going for another run, but Coop was doing that following us around until we were ready to talk thing, and the last time he ran with me, I thought he was going to drop.

The gym seemed a more equitable solution. At the moment, he was over at the free weights, but I could practically feel him watching us.

"Why don't you go spot Coop before he pulls something?" Coop and Jake got along just fine. Always had. Two peas in a pod.

"Because he wants me to talk and I'm not in the fucking mood," Jake commented and I paused after the last strike to look at him. Really look at him. His eye was still a bit swollen, but the bruising had begun to fade. Coop never seemed like he had a temper, until he did.

"Same," I said. Rolling my head from side to side, I stared down at my fists then at the bag. "You got that for another ten minutes?"

He nodded. "Watch your left and stop tightening up so much. If you already hurt the shoulder, it's gonna stiffen like a bitch tomorrow. Compensate and use the footwork."

I stared at him. I hadn't asked for advice.

"Look, if Coop sees us talking. He'll back off and let us sort it out," Jake said. "So, we can talk about bullshit or we can talk about your form. You pick."

He had a point. "He means well."

"I know he does. Been friends with him long enough to know he won't leave it the fuck alone until we sort our shit out."

I grunted and shifted my stance to deliver a series of right jabs. The burn across the back of my shoulders eased up some but it didn't go all the way away. "We might have already sorted it if you hadn't ditched classes with me like a little bitch."

"Well, if you weren't such a smug fucking asshole, maybe I'd have stuck around longer."

"Great, so you're a pussy and I'm a dick. Good talk." I slammed my fist into it.

"Right. We're talking now."

"Noticed."

Jake let out an aggrieved sigh like I'd invited him over here for this tete-a-tete. I'd been trying, he shut me down at every turn. Fine, he wanted to have blue balls and be off in the land of martyrdom, fucking so be it.

"Fine," Jake ground out. "I'm sorry I was an asshole."

"I'm sorry, what?" I slowed my strikes down again and raised my brows.

"You heard me."

"Huh." I resumed my punches.

"Now it's your turn."

I laughed. He probably didn't mean it to be funny, but seriously... "What are we five? We have to apologize to each other because one person said it? What the hell good is an apology anyway? You're gonna do the same damn thing the next time something happens. You'll blame me and then blame my money and we're back to square one like the last four fucking years didn't matter."

The bitterness swelling inside of me burned like I'd swallowed something too hot and it blazed a trail to my gut. We both loved her. That accident scared the hell out of both of us. But Jake blamed me for it. Why shouldn't he? I blamed myself.

"It wasn't your fault," Jake said slowly. "Frankie's kind of pounded that into my head. I don't know why I blamed you."

"Because you see me as a threat," I retorted. "You always have."

Jake considered me for a long moment, but I was done with hitting the bag and him. If I kept it up, I'd end up punching him in the face again.

"I used to see you as a threat," he admitted as I stripped off my gloves. He tossed me a towel and I mopped at my face. "You showed up. You wanted her. You went for it. Then...she wanted to date and you went for it again. It's like I know how much you care, and I know your life hasn't been roses, but I fucking envy you how you can just talk your way out of everything no matter what."

"Well, I was weaned on corporate negotiation and parents who argued and debated the finer points of their prenups over meals more than they did their days. I used to think it sucked that I had no siblings, now I'm grateful no one else had to deal with that shit. I envy you. You've been there nearly from the beginning. She trusts you and Coop in ways...that are all yours. You share her openly and without an ounce of fear. You've got a family. Sisters. A mother who loves you. And apparently a dad and a—look I don't know how you refer to Klara, but you have her, too."

His shoulders drooped. "I hate that she was in that car alone. Not even six weeks after my dad...and the hours of not knowing."

I gripped his shoulder and he glanced up at me in surprise. "I was with Edward when I got the call. It was the onboard diagnostic and emergency services system. It recorded the crash. It notified nine-one-one, then it called me to let me know that help was on the way."

Fear like I'd never experienced before hit me. Not when Frankie stopped talking to us. Not when we couldn't find her the night Mitch went after her. Not when we came out of that Halloween party and found her and Bubba being attacked.

"I locked up." That was hard to admit. "I froze. I didn't want to listen to the operator on the phone. Didn't want to believe it. But Frankie texted me not even an hour earlier to say she was on her way back and she'd take care of my car. My two girls, together..."

Jake let out a harsh exhale. "We got the call at the house. Jeremy took it. He was cool as a cucumber, got us moving, had a car ordered and we were out the door and on the way to the hospital."

"It took for fucking ever to get there." I almost laughed. "And you want to know how I got there?" He shot me a questioning look and I reached for the thermos of water, twisting it open to take a drink. Only after I'd swallowed about half could I say it aloud. "Edward. I froze up and Edward of all fucking people, just took over. He got us a car, got the information from the service and got us to the hospital. I don't think I even remembered how to breathe on my own until we got there and I heard her voice."

"Well, maybe he isn't a complete waste of space." Jake spread his hands. "I don't remember the drive. Just that it took forever and Jeremy and

Coop were both the epitome of calm. Bubba? Still waters run deep, but I could practically hear him bracing for the worst."

"So basically, that was the worst case scenario and we're lashing out at each other because...?"

"No, worst case would have been if she'd died in that accident." That Jake could even give voice to the words made me sick.

"Not happening," I said. "I don't care what I have to do. I'll break laws..."

"With a pep in my step and cheer in my heart," Jake agreed. "Arch...I blamed you because I didn't want her hurt and in some part of my mind...I expect whoever is with her to be the one who takes those hits for her. Maybe that doesn't make much sense..."

"No, it makes total sense. You did that on the field. You've been doing that for her since you met her." I got it. "I can't say I wouldn't have reacted the same if she was supposed to be with you."

That was the reality of it. "You know the first time I met her, she was slugging this jackass who took her book, right?" Jake asked.

I chuckled. "That sounds like her."

"Man, she was hell on wheels. Fearless. If she thought someone was being hurt, she was right there to pick that fight. I got good at getting in the way of the hits because she was so damn good at giving them." Jake scrubbed a hand over his face. "Coming together is a beginning, staying together is progress, and working together is success."

"Henry Ford?" I frowned as I looped the towel around my neck and grabbed my gear. We were done anyway, and Jake didn't seem to be in a hurry to get a workout.

"Yep," he said with a nod. "At the risk of fucking up this detente," Jake continued as he fell into step with me. "What are you going to do about your mother inviting Frankie over?"

Fuck, I'd tried to forget about that. Hell, I'd point blank asked Edward if he was still seeing Maddy and if he knew where she was. He claimed they were no longer together. This time was final. Time would tell, I supposed. Muriel?

"She can't be trusted."

"Fair," Jake agreed with me. "But Frankie's determined."

"Which means I go with her and mitigate the damage."

"Then I go with you to watch your back while you're watching hers."

That stopped me dead in my tracks. "Seriously?"

"Like I said, I can be pissed and watch your back at the same time. And I'm still angry, but not at you." Not anymore was what it sounded like.

I huffed out a laugh. "I'll take it. And the company. I'd prefer *not* to warn her we're coming. Catching her day drunk and off guard will get us somewhere faster."

"After Frankie and Coop get back?" Jake checked and I nodded.

"Yeah."

Coop chose that moment to join us. "Have you two finally kissed and made up?"

I didn't even look at Jake as I said, "Nope," and he echoed the thought.

The fact our friend looked so damn disappointed was the only reason I didn't press the joke. "We went one better."

Jake clapped Coop on the shoulder and we were all heading for the doors. We could shower and change back at the brownstone. "We're plotting," Jake told him.

"Oh, Hell. You're on the same side again." Coop let out a mocking groan. "We're doomed."

Ass. Jake held him still and I dumped the rest of the cold water over his head. But we were laughing. That was something.

Chapter Nineteen

LOVE AND WAR AND BIRTHDAYS

Frankie

The weekend got there way too soon. I had packed, unpacked, then repacked my overnight bag four times, when Coop took it away from me. "It's a birthday party for *kids*, we don't have to worry about formal dress. Your dad said to just be comfortable."

"I don't have pajamas in there." I hadn't been able to decide on sleep shorts or a shirt or something with more coverage.

"You won't need them," Coop told me firmly and I stared at him. "Nope," he continued, shaking his head. "Trust me, if you get shy you can wear my shirt, but I have a feeling you're going to need a lot of courage and comfort, I've got it all in spades. I'm even bringing the little buddy with me."

My mouth opened. Then closed. There were no words. I mean...Jake and I had sex at his dad's place. It was hardly the first time I'd have sex with one of them under someone else's roof. Hell, Ian and I had our first time with his parents right downstairs. But this was...

Coop wrapped his hand around my nape and tugged me to him and then he closed his mouth over mine. He took advantage of my gaping to stroke my tongue with his and then he slid his free hand down to my ass and gave it a squeeze. I forgot about the bag. The bags of presents. I forgot about where we were going to as he sucked on my tongue and then slowly released me. I swore I swayed for a moment.

"There, better?" He wore the most impish grin and his gray-green eyes seemed more green than usual.

"Yes," I admitted though my pulse still raced for an entirely different reason now. "Why am I freaking out like this?"

"Because you've never had a family that loved you," he whispered. "Loved you for just being you and you were taught you had to please others, to be the best, to be unobtrusive, and to be cooperative to the whims of a toxic woman in order to get even an ounce of approval."

The truth hurt. But I didn't deny any of it.

"The difference between then and now?" Coop continued, cradling my face. "Is you have us. We're your family. We love you just the way you are and every little quirk that comes with it. The other difference? Hank *wants* you there. Hank's family—your family—*wants* you there."

Every hair on my body kind of stood on end as cold rippled over me.

"It's okay to be scared of that. Because this is a new normal for you." He slid his hands down to my shoulders. "But I'm going to be there every step of the way. You're not alone. And you like Hank, yeah?"

I nodded, I did. "I still haven't told him about the accident."

"We'll cross that bridge when we come to it. Let's focus on the chaos of a big family who are all going to want your attention. You're used to that. We got that at Jake's house all the time."

I laughed. "But that feels different. I guess...maybe cause I met all of his sisters when they were really little."

"Well, can't argue with that. Once you've seen someone have their diaper changed, it kills a lot of the scary factor."

Eyes rolling, I gave him a little shove. "Fine. You're right. They're the same age Jake was when I met him. Alec's a little older. I can do this—"

Doubt kept creeping in though. What if...? So many what ifs.

"Let's go, grab your phone and your charger," Coop said as he gave me one last squeeze then snagged my bag from where he'd tossed it. His own was already downstairs. "I will not be the one getting in trouble because they couldn't get through to you on the phone."

I groaned. "I already promised to check in at all points on the trip there and back. I half-expect that Jake and Archie have programmed the car to let them know where we are at all points, too."

"Not quite," Archie said from the bottom of the stairs as I followed Coop down. "Tempting as it was, we resisted. However, there is an option for you to share your location with us via the GPS and that's up to you."

I wrapped my arms around Archie as I got to the last step and he picked me up. The squeeze of his hug told me more about how worried he was than anything else. "I'll send you lots of annoying updates," I promised him quietly. "Pictures and everything."

"I can't wait," he answered, then buried his face against my throat and whispered, "Thank you, Babe."

"I love you," was the simplest answer and he set me down and gave me a gentle kiss.

"Tempted to tell you in binary code, but that's just cause I don't want you to leave." He winked. "Love you, too."

Jake was next, like they'd lined up or something, but he stood in the doorway to his room. His hair was damp, likely he'd just gotten back from a run. "Make sure Coop takes good care of you," he instructed, then gave me a gentle kiss. I feathered my fingers over the remnants of the bruise around his eye. "Doesn't even hurt, Baby Girl. He was right, I deserved it."

I chuckled. "Not going to ask."

"Good, some things are just better settled between the brother boyfriends."

Ian's groan flowed up from downstairs and my grin widened. "Told Archie I'll be sending you guys all the updates and pictures too. You'll get sick of them.”

“Ha,” Jake snorted. But this time when he kissed me it held all the promise of what he felt for me and everything he looked forward to when we got back. “We’ll make time, Baby Girl. I promise.”

That was all I could ask for. Ugh, if I didn’t get moving soon, I’d never leave. With reluctance, I tore myself away and headed down the next flight to where Ian stood in the game room. There were books open on the sofa, which told me he was studying for something before classes. Coop was totally skipping his classes for the day to go with me.

“Have fun,” Ian told me as I wrapped my arms around him. “Take a breath when it gets overwhelming. Call if you need us. And remember, I love you.” Each one felt like an instruction and to be honest, it actually helped. “Don’t worry about Jake and Archie,” he added in a whisper to my ear. I squeezed him tighter. That was all he said and I’d take him at his word.

“Already miss you guys,” I admitted, and I felt more than heard his laugh.

“Good,” he teased, then gave me a soft kiss before letting me go. “That means we get all the welcome home sex when you get back.”

“Hell yeah,” Jake’s comment floated down from upstairs and I grinned.

“Only if I’m a good girl?” I pitched my voice a little louder, cause why the hell not.

Ian’s eyes darkened. “Be a bad girl and find out.”

Oh, that was a challenge. But he gave my ass a swat as I stepped away.

“Just paying it forward,” he said, then winked. Okay, now my panties were officially ruined thanks to the three of them.

No one had christened my car yet, but I might have to fix that by jumping Coop later. As it was, Jeremy stood with Coop at the bottom of the stairs and my face warmed. I really hoped he hadn’t heard any of that, but the sad reality was he probably had. Jeremy would never let on though and I adored him for it.

“I took the time to make some special cupcakes to take with you and they're boxed up with cooling packs to keep them fresh. Something to maybe help break the ice with your new siblings before the actual party."

Oh man, I did not deserve Jeremy. "Brace yourself, Jeremy, I'm giving you a hug."

He chuckled and accepted it graciously even if he did look a bit uncomfortable.

"We'll call when we get there and if we stop along the way. I promised updates to the guys, but I'll send them to you, too, if you'd like."

"I would very much appreciate that," Jeremy said, and not even his serene expression could hide elements of relief. "I also called a car to take you down to the garage rather than carry all your things. If you'd like, I can arrange for it to take you all the way..."

"We appreciate that Jeremy," Coop answered before I could. "But we'll be good with driving. Promise. It's good for Frankie, too."

I threw him a grateful look. Driving still made me nervous. I didn't do it a lot here in the city. Not like I had at home, and I'd been sweating bullets when I went out with Rachel. This was really only my second time behind the wheel.

"Very good then. Have a lovely weekend." Jeremy opened the door and as promised, a town car waited for us at the curb. I would never get used to this life, no matter how much I pretended otherwise.

Really, we weren't leaving with much or for very long, yet the whole farewell production and the presence of the car had me giggling. Not more than glancing up to finding all three of my guys who weren't going with us watching from different windows. I blew them kisses and then ducked into the car before I lost it laughing.

Coop was no damn help, he was snickering all the way to the garage. Not that it was a long trip, but I didn't mind not having to carry our stuff. When the car let us out, Coop was still laughing. I slapped his arm.

"Stop it."

He grinned. "I can't help it. I mean, I know I'd be just as bad if I was one of the guys waiting for you to get back. I *was* one of the guys waiting the last two times, but they were all but killing themselves to not tell me everything to do and not do.”

“They were being sweet,” I defended them. “And thoughtful.”

“Yeah,” Coop said with a smirk and held up his phone. “I know.” He snapped a picture of me and then my phone dinged as Coop kept laughing as he went to request my car from the attendant. I fished my phone out of my pocket and had to bite my lip to keep from laughing.

The string of fuck offs and middle finger emojis killed me, but I glanced over to find Coop grinning.

“You’re having too much fun with this,” I called out.

“Hell yes, I am,” he replied. “They’ve been up my ass so much this week, they can tell me what my colon looks like. This is just a healthy dose of getting what you asked for.”

I couldn’t blame him, not really. Still, all the laughter in the world couldn’t quite quell the nerves erupting in my stomach as we climbed in the car. Coop loaded our stuff and the cooler protected cupcakes into the backseat.

“I can drive,” he offered, but he was already at the passenger door. If I asked, he’d do it, but he wasn’t going to press the issue either.

“Maybe after our first break.”

“Break?” he asked as we both pulled on our seatbelts and then I took a selfie and sent it to the group chat.

I hit send then checked that the GPS had the directions in for the town, as well as Hank's address for the next destination and then pulled out into traffic. Even leaving this early it would take some time to get out of the city, but I kept it slow and steady.

Coop shook his head as he laughed. "We're stopping for coffee, right?"

"Hell yes," I told him. "Then we're gonna go do some sightseeing. I mean, I know they didn't *film* it there but it's a classical quaint New England town and I wanna see it."

"Then we'll stop and see it. Course, now I get why you wanted to leave early."

The drive turned out to be a lot prettier than I expected. What neither of us planned on were the fact that some of the trees along the route as we drove further north had already begun to change colors. They weren't just green. Some had yellow tips, others orange. No red that I could find, but we were definitely looking.

After we found our first stop for coffee, we snapped pictures of the trees and sent them to the guys. Granted they weren't fully turned yet. But it was definitely cooler and far more comfortable than in the city. "I want to come back up here," I said. "I want to see it in all the spectacular colors."

We just didn't get these colors in Texas.

"Deal," Coop agreed. And because I wanted to look, we traded spots and I let him drive for a while. My nerves had settled the longer we drove, and I was having fun trying to find the bright spots of color amidst the green foliage.

The little town in Connecticut was almost right on the way, or at least it wasn't far off the interstate. The anxiety over my family and the driving abated as Coop pulled into the little town and I swore I started bouncing. We found a place to park and I checked the time and then couldn't decide where to look first.

Stars Hollow might be fictional, but the state of mind it put you in wasn't. Catching my hand, Coop tugged me over to the town sign and had me pose for pictures. For all that he teased me about the show, he joined me in picking out what shops might have inspired Luke's Diner or Taylor's grocery or even the original Independence Inn.

"I want to come back here, too." The town seemed almost deserted, yet the shops were open and people were friendly. There was a hardware store that was definitely for hardware and another cafe that sold breakfast and coffee.

The minute I spotted the bookstore, Coop groaned but off we went. Granted, there wasn't a town troubadour, but maybe I could talk Ian into doing that on a visit. Or maybe I was just being ridiculous. Stopping here had just been this spontaneous idea I had and while there wasn't a colorful cast of characters like the show, everyone we met seemed genuinely nice. They were also used to folks stopping by looking for Stars Hollow.

We probably spent way more time in the little town of Washington than I intended, but it appealed to me. New York was great. Manhattan was great. But it was always loud and busy and there were people everywhere. This might be too slow compared to the too fast, but I loved it nonetheless.

I practically skipped back to the car with a few more presents for my siblings and some for Jake, too. I'd picked up a book on writing songs that I hid even from Coop. I still had no idea how Ian did it, but it was about time I spent some research on it. He picked up a few books, too. And we found a classic set of Dungeons and Dragons manuals. A whole set of them and we bought them on the spot. Archie would love them, and he had birthday coming up.

Course, how I would top singing him a song the year before—you know what—birthday anxiety over the twins was enough for the weekend. We stowed our treasures away and headed out again. I was much more relaxed this time.

While I drove, Coop updated the guys on our visit to the town and included some pictures. They didn't respond right away but they were probably in class. It took us another two hours to get to the exit for Newton, and another fifteen minutes of navigating through the streets to find their house.

Even when we'd come up to Harvard over spring break, I hadn't noticed just how many trees there were. There were literally trees just everywhere. We missed whole shopping centers hidden behind trees.

Thank fuck, I wasn't alone in my gawking and Coop was helping to point street signs so we could go where the GPS wanted us to. We ended up in a charming little cul-de-sac made up of three houses in front of a gable front house that had to be at least two stories and possessed an enormous front porch that extended well past the door.

If anything, it looked like Lorelei Gilmore's house and that cracked me up. Only this house was the most cheerful shade of yellow with perfect white trim. There was an actual picket fence around the yard and a huge tree from which a couple of swings suspended.

I stared at it all as we parked and I almost couldn't make myself get out of the car. It was—like the perfect house in the perfect street with the perfect family.

I swallowed.

Coop covered my hand with his. "Breathe," he murmured. "You belong here, too."

I glanced over at him and found a smile even as all the earlier nerves surged to the surface. The front door of the house opened, and Hank stepped out wearing a huge, if hopeful grin.

Too late to back out now.

Chapter Twenty

THIS ONE'S FOR THE GIRLS

Coop

For the rest of my life, this was a moment I would treasure. The moment when the hesitation and fear in her expression gave way to marvel and joy that Hank was striding down the sidewalk to greet her. He didn't wait at the door, and I swore the man was there before Frankie even made it out of the car.

I gave them a minute as he picked her up into a warm hug, then he was there offering to help me with the bags. Of course, the minute he saw all the presents he gave Frankie an affectionately scolding look. "You're going to spoil them."

"Maybe," Frankie declared. "But they just turned eight, so I have seven other birthdays to make up for."

Hank chuckled then gave her a sideways hug. A woman, most likely Kelly, waited for us on the porch. Like me, she was giving Hank and Frankie time to catch up. "Come on kids, you made good time coming up from the city."

"Well, we'd have been here earlier," she told him. "But I wanted to stop in Connecticut and look at a town."

"Just a random town?" Hank asked as he reached the steps. "Also, Frankie, this is Kelly." Hank grinned even wider. "Kelly, this is Frankie. I've been looking forward to introducing the two of you."

With her dark hair and dark eyes, she couldn't be more Maddy's polar opposite right down to the comfortable jeans, light colored shirt with a second, larger shirt layered over it. "I'm so glad you could make it," Kelly said in a warm tone with just a hint of a Bostonian accent. She held out her hands to Frankie. "And yes, I promised no hugs but ever since Hank found out about you, we've wanted to meet you and get to know you better."

My girl wasn't quite up to the hug, but she did take Kelly's hands and squeezed them. "I've been excited about meeting all of you, and well..."

"A little nervous?" Kelly suggested. "Come on inside. Don't mind the mess. The twins were in a tizzy this morning getting off to school and Chloe wanted to have the perfect outfit to be in for when she met you. I swear she had a fashion show."

"I'm sorry," Frankie apologized immediately. The living room didn't look that bad. The front door opened right up into it and it had a huge multi-sectional sofa and two recliners. The room seemed centered around the fireplace and the television mounted over it.

There was some home redecorating show on, but it was muted. Clothes were stacked somewhat haphazardly on one end of the sofa with at least four different pairs of shoes on the floor.

"Don't be," Kelly assured her. "Chloe's just been excited for so long. She loves to send you messages and that you answer her. Thank you for that, I know she can be a bit much."

"I think she's wonderful." The complete sincerity in Frankie's voice won Kelly over and the two shared a grin.

"Come on, Coop," Hank said. "Let's take this stuff up to the guest room while the girls chat then I'll introduce you, too. She won't notice, she's too busy trying to figure out how to get a hug out of Frankie."

"I heard that," Kelly called and I caught Frankie's eye and raised my brows. If she didn't want to be left alone down here, I would totally make an excuse, but her grin widened. "Men, I swear," Kelly continued and Frankie laughed.

"We'll be fine, I'm just shooting a text to the guys and Jeremy to let them know we're here safe and sound."

"Got it!" Good idea. Before we got too caught up. I followed Hank up the stairs. The walls were literally filled with photos and tons of those huge collages with pictures of all their kids. I could pick out Alec from his deep serious look and Craig younger and definitely wearing a mischievous smile. Chloe reminded me of Frankie, if Frankie had darker hair. All the kids seemed to take after their mother in that respect.

At the top of the stairs, Hank nodded to one hall. "The kids all sleep down there. Kelly and I have a master bedroom on the ground floor. The guest room is this way." He took me in the opposite direction of the kids. "Kelly keeps an office here for when she needs to work from home. I have one too, but I'd much rather just spread out downstairs." He shrugged. "I do better in chaos."

"Understood." The guest room was the very last room, and I couldn't put my finger on it, but I didn't think this had been a guest room all that long. It had a hastily put together feeling about it. A queen bed with mint green linens and a heavy quilt didn't quite match the white curtains and there were a couple of beaten up chairs near the window set up with a rickety table and then there was the dresser that I was pretty sure had probably been built before the last century.

I would not want to move it.

"Frankie surprised you by saying yes, didn't she?" I asked as I set the bags on the bed, and he put the bags with the twins' presents on the dresser. Wiping his hands against his jeans, he gave me a pained look. "That obvious?"

"Well, I know her and I know she canceled Labor Day Weekend and you were disappointed and now it's nearly the end of September and we've got mid-terms coming up soon, so it would have been natural for her to put it off maybe to the holidays."

Hank let out a deep sigh and ran a hand over his face. "The holidays are a stressful time for families that know each other," he admitted. "I don't want to pressure her. I just...I wish you guys were at least up here going to school, then I could try to see her more often."

"You didn't pressure her," I told him. Folding my arms, I considered him for a long moment. "If you don't mind taking a word of advice on this, just be yourself. That's who you were when you came to her graduation. It's who you've been in the texts and the phone calls. She's not used to parental approval and that's all I'll say on that front."

His whole expression fell. "I hate that I wasn't there."

"You're here now. You weren't given a choice then and you have that choice now and you're choosing her. That means a lot more than you may realize." Watching him tell Maddy off had been a highlight of our graduation, I wasn't gonna lie.

"Good deal. Thank you for that." He turned to the door then paused and looked at me. The intensity in that stare had me bracing for whatever came next. "This door locks. Use it. The kids aren't big on personal space and I'd rather not explain anything I don't have to. Our bedroom is on the other side of the house and the walls are sturdy and that's the last of this discussion we're ever going to have."

I did not laugh. "Yes, sir." I kind of wanted to salute, but I appreciated the heads up. If I had Frankie naked and screaming, I did not need kids interrupting. No thank you.

Course, maybe we should work on the being silent part. That gave me all kinds of ideas. Ideas I definitely kept to myself. Downstairs, I found Frankie sitting at the breakfast bar in the kitchen while Kelly worked on something at the stove. "We've been slow cooking the stew all day. It's almost the perfect time of year for it. Cooler at night, pleasant in the day."

"It's not quite so cool in the city yet," Frankie told her. "But it's definitely cooler than Texas."

The weather conversation gave way to food then to drinks and we were all going out to the living room. I noticed it before Frankie did, but I waited as she settled in next to me. The kids were due home soon.

"The party is pretty informal," Kelly was saying. "The twins can never agree on a theme, so we always go with something neutral. This year they wanted to go to the trampoline place, so we'll be driving over there and about a dozen other kids will join for some bouncing fun, cake and presents, then back here for dinner and a little more quiet time."

That sounded kind of fun. Even Frankie grinned.

"In other words, you won't be so on the spot," Hank assured her.

"I got it, I got it," Frankie murmured. "I am making this a huge deal and it's not."

"No," Kelly said. "It is a huge deal. They're your brothers and your sister. You're my step daughter. You're Hank's daughter. This is very much your family. We want you to be a part of this with us and I get that might be overwhelming for you, just understand we are campaigning for some annual holiday visits and craziness with all of your boyfriends." The last she said with a glance to me. "But thank you for also easing the kids into it."

Frankie laughed but it held a little bit of tears and when she reached for me, I clasped her hand. The fact she always did that, even unconsciously, when she needed support was something I treasured. I might not be able to solve everything, but I could be there.

"That's them," Kelly said as she stood. "Hang on a sec, the whirlwind rushing in here in a minute will be Chloe."

Hank followed her to the door and Frankie glanced at me. "I really like her," she mouthed more than said. The disbelief in her expression and wonder made me smile.

"Me too."

The calls from outside, the sound of children laughing. Kelly and

Hank's voices taking on a sterner note of parenthood all washed over me, but the second Frankie spotted the photo on the mantle her whole expression changed.

I said nothing as she stared at the picture of her and Hank from graduation. He'd had it framed and put it somewhere prominent. Lifting her hand, I kissed her fingers. Her dad loved her. Maybe now it would really sink in.

She was blinking back tears and trying to wipe them away when Hurricane Chloe arrived and thank fuck, I was inoculated against childhood cuteness, or this little doll with all of Rachel's daring and every bit of Frankie's charm would have snookered me good.

Thank Trina I was over that.

Chloe wasted no time in throwing herself at Frankie for a hug. If there was going to be even a brief moment of shyness, it didn't appear. In fact, I don't think Frankie got a word in edgewise as Chloe immediately told her everything about her day, but she was so open and unabashed in her affection. There was a ferocity to it, too. Like she was determined to make sure Frankie liked her and that was all there was to it.

Damn did that take me back to when Frankie decided to adopt Jake into our group. Then later he brought in Bubba and Frankie took to him. When Archie showed up, she saw something in him long before the rest of us.

If I had to guess, I would almost say loneliness called to loneliness. I wasn't the only one watching Frankie and Chloe, a pair of boys, one far more open and the other suspicious eyed us from the other side of the sofa. They hadn't ventured closer. Hank and Kelly lingered, but they were giving the kids time to adjust.

"Chloe," Hank said finally. "Breathe."

"I am breathing," Chloe declared with a huff. "But I suppose it's okay if Frankie wants to say something."

Frankie burst out laughing and I grinned. The younger of the boys also smiled and he marched over and with all the care and concern of a brother for his sister, gave Chloe a shove to the side before offering his hand. "I'm Craig. I'm much more polite."

"Oh, I can see that," Frankie said, humoring him as Chloe huffed and glared.

"It's two versus two now," Chloe told her twin. "And the girls win cause Frankie's lots older than either of you."

"Ahem," Frankie said in a tone that wasn't quite as playful but also wasn't quite scolding either. "There will be no picking of sides, nor will I be dragged into a battle where I have no history or understanding of the rules."

Alec snorted. "Told you she wasn't going to want to be on your side."

Frankie flicked her attention to Alec. "I didn't say that, either. Don't assume you know something when you haven't introduced yourself. I'm Frankie."

"You know who I am," Alec said his tone bored and put upon, but there was something in his eyes. His heart might be on his sleeve, but he was watchful and wary. Frankie's arrival in the family had definitely tossed a stone in and he didn't know what the changes were going to be.

"Alec," Kelly reprimanded. "Manners."

So far, they'd stayed out of it but only so far.

"Sorry, Mom," he said in a genuine tone before he walked over, feet dragging to where Frankie sat. But she stood up and I had to hide my own smile. Alec was going to be a tough nut to crack, but she was going to start it by treating him the way she wanted to be treated.

Fuck, I loved this girl so goddamn much. She did the same thing when Trina was in a rage.

The kid stuck his hand out. "I'm Alec Jackson."

"I'm Frankie Curtis. It's very nice to meet you." She shook his hand with all due solemnity. "I've never had brothers or a sister before, so this is all kind of new to me. Since you've been the oldest for a while now, do you think you could help me out? At least until I get some experience."

Alec frowned. "Help you out, how?"

"Well, I don't know yet. But Chloe said she'd teach me all about being a sister. So, I figured you can teach me all about being the oldest, though—that might still have to be your job since I don't live here."

Craig cracked up and Chloe made a face but Alec gave a grudging nod. "I'm still the oldest boy."

"Yes, you are."

Alec transferred his look from Frankie to me. "So, you're my sister's boyfriend?"

Oh, this should be delightful. "That would be me," I told him and stood up to shake his hand. He followed my progress until I kind of towered over him. I felt almost bad about it. Almost. "I'm Cooper, friends call me Coop."

"Huh." Alec eyed me. "You're too big to beat up, but as a brother, I'm supposed to threaten my sister's boyfriends."

Only years of delivering similar threats kept me from laughing aloud. Hank groaned, but Craig laughed. "Exactly," he crowed. "Dad said we can't ever let boys near Chloe."

"Wait, what?" Chloe demanded. "Boys are gross."

"Hank," Kelly scolded and I caught Frankie covering her mouth with her hands as if to try and contain the laughter.

"Tell you what Alec, one big brother to another—you're doing it right. One warning is all they get. I promise, I've got a few friends who will help you out if I cause Frankie any problems."

"Really?" Alec looked intrigued and Kelly groaned.

"Enough threats. All of you. We're enjoying a good family weekend, not learning how to beat up other people." The exasperated note in her voice was filled with rough affection.

Behind her back, Hank looked pointedly at me and then down to Alec and I just gave him a thumbs up. His expression went angelic when Kelly shot a look at him. Chloe grabbed Frankie's hand and declared she wanted to show her her room and Alec nodded then informed me, I could see his.

It was entertaining as hell. The best part was all of Frankie's fears and anxieties evaporated with the banter and the kids just being themselves. She was good with kids. I could have told her that. I'd watched her with my sister and Jake's for years. Hank tracked her going upstairs with Chloe and if there was a way to take a picture of his expression and send it to her later, I would have.

He looked so damn proud.

The evening pretty much turned into a mini party. After the stew, which was freaking delicious, we opened the cupcakes that Jeremy had sent up and the kids were definitely wowed. So was I, holy hell, he needed to make these more often. They were huge and had the perfect frosting to cake ratio. It wasn't long before the kids had to go to bed and I'd remembered to send a couple of messages to the guys about how well things were going, but Frankie would want to talk to them before sleep.

Instead, she surprised me when she murmured, "I need to go and talk to Hank. Do you mind running interference here?"

The accident. I glanced at her. "You okay on your own?"

"Yeah," she said slowly. "I am. What's more, I owe him this much." Her lips brushed mine and behind us Chloe made a gagging noise. Then Craig joined in. I couldn't help it. I pulled Frankie closer and deepened the kiss until Alec let out his own gag of complaint. "Mean," she teased.

"But fun," I retorted, then winked at her. She squeezed my arm and then headed over to Hank. He snagged a jacket from by the door and then the two of them stepped out. A part of me wanted to follow, back her up, but the more I saw of Hank the more I liked him.

"Upstairs," Kelly was ordering. "Pajamas, faces washed, teeth brushed. We have a long day tomorrow."

"Can Frankie sleep in my room?" Chloe asked, but I didn't catch the answer as Kelly shepherded them upstairs. I'd been doing dishes. Most of them were rinsed and loaded into the dishwasher, so I grabbed my drink and found a place to sit in the living room. I wasn't going up until Frankie was back in the house.

Pulling open the text I kept for just the guys, I filled them in on the day and added some pics I'd been able to snap. The relief in their responses echoed my own. We liked Hank. We liked how he cared about her.

I glanced up at the photo of Hank and Frankie at graduation again. He was the kind of dad she deserved. If he was the kind of dad I thought he was, she was about to get in trouble for keeping him in the dark about the accident, then forgiven because they were still feeling their way through this relationship.

With that in mind, I leaned back and glanced around for the remote. Hopefully, they had some good stations to watch, not that I cared much. I was just waiting for my girl, in her dad's house where her baby brothers had threatened me.

I grinned. Jake and I would have to give them some lessons for when Chloe hit dating age.

That would be fun.

Chapter Twenty-One

TRUE CONFESSIONS

Frankie

It was dark outside, but there were street lamps, and porch lights on elsewhere. The cooler air brushed against my face. It felt a little like November back in Texas instead of the end of September. Hank had snagged an extra jacket for me, and I pulled it on as we started walking. I didn't really have a destination in mind, but telling him what happened was long past due.

We saw someone out walking their dog. The cul-de-sac connected to another residential street. The houses were all different styles. And while I was delaying the inevitable, Hank was being sweet in allowing me to do it. Folding my arms, I blew out a breath.

"Whatever it is," Hank offered. "I'm sure it's not as bad as you're making it out to be."

A smile touched my lips as I glanced at him. The night softened his profile, but there was a warmth to him that I never wanted to lose. "I want to begin by apologizing," I said finally. Somewhere a nightbird let out a call and another answered it. "I—was in an accident a few weeks ago. Instead of calling you, the guys didn't think of it and after, when I should have, I didn't want to worry you."

A faint hitch in his step was the only thing that betrayed his surprise. "How bad of an accident?"

"I was driving back from Long Island where Archie and I had spent the weekend with my grandparents. Archie had left early with Edward—and before you get angry that he left me there to drive back on my own..." Because frankly I'd had enough of that from Jake. Fear and anger went hand in hand, I understood that. I just didn't want Hank to blame Archie as well. "I told Archie to go, he and Edward—well they're working on their relationship. At least I hope they are and I was going to drive Archie's Ferrari back to the city myself. I was excited, but the brakes went out and I managed to not hurt anyone else."

Hank had stopped walking and his hands were deep in his pockets. Facing him, I bit my lip. He wasn't looking at me, but upward at the sky. "How bad was the accident?"

"I cracked a couple of ribs. Burned my face from the airbag deploying. Had a concussion."

A single nod. "Hospitalized?"

"Overnight."

"Follow ups?"

"All clear now. I mean my ribs twinge a little but not my first rodeo with bad ribs." Which I probably shouldn't have said, because Hank jerked his gaze from the sky to me.

Fuck.

"It's a long story," I admitted. "But I am very sorry no one called, especially that I didn't. I'm still getting used to having a parent that even cares much less someone as cool as you for a dad."

Dragging a hand from his pocket, he ran it over his face and then looked at me. Really looked, as though he were trying to see everything despite the fact we'd stopped somewhere between two lights and shadows surrounded us. "Will you tell me? I hate the idea that you went through any of that alone. But will you tell me all of it that you can?"

I hesitated.

"Maddy didn't..."

"Hit me?" I shrugged. "Sometimes. But I wouldn't have called it abuse, others might have. Her abuses were more mental and emotional. She has manipulation and emotional blackmail down."

He grunted a sound.

"And I can tell you. Some of it isn't so pretty, but I don't want you to think it's all horrible too."

"I'd like that."

Really, it wasn't all that bad. Hank offered me his arm, and I threaded mine through it. We walked for the next hour and I trusted him to know where we were going. I told him about finding out the guys had made me untouchable at school. He seemed to find that part amusing, at least in so far as it meant guys left me alone. Ha ha. But the lonely summer in between, the fact I'd wanted to go up to Harvard on a college exploration trip but Maddy's constant absences and then expenses on my car made it impossible.

I skimmed some details, but we talked about how the guys all decided to date me and the fun. Then the not so fun break-up with Ian, but spoiler-alert, we made it through that. Then came homecoming and when I described the mum the guys had made for me, he laughed. He'd never heard of the homecoming mums like we did them in Texas. I found pictures on my phone to show him and his expression cracked me up.

We'd made it back to the house, but rather than go inside, we settled on the porch swing as I detailed the rest of homecoming. From the arrival at the dance to the roofie'd drink to Mitch's attack, not that I remembered the actual incident, only what I learned about it later. His jaw tightened and his teeth ground, but he didn't interrupt.

The guys staying with me, helping me, and looking after me earned another dour look. I was pretty sure because Maddy hadn't been around. By the time I got to the part that Maddy had basically moved out and the guys moved in, he just nodded.

The Halloween attack earned another long sigh, but I had to laugh a little at that one. Particularly because I broke Sharon's nose and while I probably shouldn't take such glee in that, no lie, I did.

It was closing in on midnight by the time we got to the part where Edward told me he was my dad because Maddy had lied to him and brought him all the way up to where we were now. At one point, Kelly had come out with coffee and mugs for us, then kissed Hank on the head before she said she was going to bed. Coop sent me a text that said he was heading up to our room and to take my time.

"I'm so used to doing things on my own," I said as I finished the last of my coffee. "That it really didn't occur to me to call you and I'm sorry about that. I want...I want this to work. I like your kids."

"You're one of my kids, too," Hank reminded me gruffly. "It's going to take you time to feel that, I know. But I do feel it already. I want you in our lives, I want to be a part of yours. So—all of you get a pass, but if anything like this happens again..."

"Hank," I murmured. "I really hope it doesn't." Mostly 'cause I hadn't gotten around to the worst part and I tossed it back and forth in my head. Finally, I couldn't leave him to be blind-sided again. So, I told him about Maddy and my suspicions. The investigation. All of it. Even the fights with the guys, because I'd been relying on my own funds and resources.

To my surprise, he laughed a little and shook his head. "You know, when you mentioned you needed to talk to me in private, I got it into my head you were going to tell me you were pregnant."

It was my turn to gape at him.

His laughter deepened. "I almost wish you had."

"Bite your tongue," I retorted. "I am eighteen, Hank. I'm not ready to be a mom yet."

"You're more ready than you think, but you don't have to be and I'm glad you don't." He leaned back and shook his head. "Hell, Frankie...I am so sorry your mother is like this. More sorry that I didn't know, so I could have fought for you all those years ago. Sorrier still that I don't know what I can do to help you now."

"Believe it or not, the fact you want me here and want me around your kids and that you care, at all?" I didn't know if I could express this to him. "That means a lot more than I can possibly ever express to you. And I love the kids. Chloe's adorable, Alec is fierce and Craig—he reminds me of Coop. Easy going and quick to tease. He doesn't have to be first, he just has to be involved."

When he opened his arms and stretched one along the back of the swing, I took the invitation and leaned into the hug. He tucked his head atop mine and held me close. "You're family, Frankie. I'll tell you that every single day until you believe it."

Closing my eyes, I gave into the urge to hug him back. The fact he had that photo of us on the mantle with all the other family pictures around meant so damn much. There'd been a lot of phone camera shots tonight. Chloe and I had even indulged in some selfies that Craig photobombed. It was hilarious.

"Normally, I would think this goes without saying, but you're welcome here," Hank told me. "Anytime. You kids might have your own plans for Thanksgiving and Christmas, but if you don't—or even if you do and can only come up for a day. Please come up."

We hadn't even talked about that yet. Sitting up, I smiled at him. "I'll tell the guys and thank you. You guys are welcome to visit us in the city too, you know. Chloe was already asking about going to see musicals and those are definitely on my list of things I want to do. "

"No doubt."

Pushing my hair back behind my ears, I exhaled. "But for now, I want to keep some distance. While I don't have absolute proof she was involved, Maddy is unpredictable. I don't want her to attack you or the kids for some perceived slight."

"And I appreciate that," he said. "I don't want my family in any danger either, but my family includes *you*. So, I want to be in the loop and if that means I take the train down to see you for a bit, then I will. Deal?"

"Deal." My jaw popped as I yawned.

"And on that note, definitely time for you to get to bed, young lady. Birthday mornings start early, and Chloe and Craig won't want you to miss anything."

"As long as it involves coffee and food, count me in." On impulse, I kissed his cheek. "Thank you."

"For what?" He stood, following me and he took my empty mug with his own.

"For being a pretty cool dad."

"Well, that's high praise, so I'll thank you as well. For being an honest daughter. You'll get cool points the next time you don't cut me out of something I need to know."

I mock gasped and clasped my hands to my chest. "He shoots. He scores."

His chuckle followed me into the darkened house, and I hesitated on the stairs as he took care to lock the door and carrying mugs into the kitchen. He had his own routines. His whole family did and as much as I'd hated disappointing him with that confession about the accident, I was glad I'd told him.

Telling him about Mitch had been difficult too, but for different reasons. At least Mitch was in jail. When I could say that about Maddy, I'd feel better. I made my way upstairs and down the hall to the room Coop and I were sharing. Inside, I found him sprawled on the bed in his boxers. There was a movie playing on his laptop but it was turned down and he had his phone to his ear.

"And here's the lovely lady now," he said. "You losers get five minutes, then I'm getting her back."

He held out his phone to me and I laughed, before switching it to speaker. Coop rolled off the bed and went to lock the bedroom door while I stripped out of my clothes. "Hi guys, sorry I didn't check in sooner, went to talk to Hank."

"How'd that go?" Jake asked.

"It went fine, I ended up telling him the whole sordid thing from the last year or so, including the shit with Mitch."

Coop pivoted and frowned.

"Babe," Archie said, concern filled that single syllable. "Are you okay?"

I smiled, because I could almost picture them. They'd been so good to me in the aftermath of all of that. Fierce, devoted—and all the crap they'd had to help me with. "I'm good, actually. It wasn't as hard to tell him about that. I mean, Mitch is in jail, he's not in my life, I don't really think about him and in the long run, the worst he did to me was break my wrist. And then Ian broke his jaw. So—I feel like we won that one."

Ian's soft chuckle echoed down the phone. "I broke his arm, too." From Ian, that wasn't malice, that was pure pleasure. "I'd happily do it again."

"Same," Archie and Jake exhaled and then they shared a laugh. Coop unhooked my bra for me and I slid it down my arms.

"But Hank is understandably not thrilled we didn't tell him about the accident, but he also understands. I told him we wouldn't keep him in the dark again."

"Understood, Angel," Ian agreed. "Are you guys having fun? Coop said you've already got your brothers and sister eating out of your hand."

I snorted, but when Coop hooked his fingers into my panties to tug them down, I eyed him. His grin grew wider and it didn't take a road map to know where we were going. He nudged me over to the bed and I sprawled out as he settled between my legs.

"You know what guys, it's getting late," I managed to squeeze out before Coop licked me from entrance to clit then back down again, all the while holding my hips still. Oh shit. "And I'll tell you all about it when we get back...pretty sure we..." Fuck. Fuck. Fuck. He had my clit between his tongue and his teeth and the vibrations had me clenching hard and fighting to buck.

"Pay up," Jake said, almost smugly. "Told you he wouldn't wait."

"Have fun, Angel. Love you."

"Yep, love you Babe."

"And Coop," Jake said. "Next time make it video."

I gasped a laugh and then Jake murmured he loved me and I managed a strangled noise before the orgasm stormed over me. I grabbed the pillow to smother the sound and Coop looked up at me, so pleased with himself. Instead of crawling up me, he stood and went over to his case, when he pulled out the custom dildo with its piercing my whole body shivered.

"We don't get as much solo time to experiment these days," Coop told me as he wandered over to the bed. His own dick was stiff and very visible against the front of his boxers. "So, all I want to know is which do you want first? Me?" He stroked himself. "Or Mini Me?" He waved the dildo and a soft laugh escaped me.

"Coop, I'll never manage to be quiet."

"You let me worry about that." His eyes were shining at me. "Truth or dare?"

I licked my lips. "Did you bring lube?"

His grin turned positively wicked. "Yes, ma'am."

"Truth, then."

Shedding his boxers, he returned to the bag and pulled out the lube and then faced me, proud cock jutting up thick and heavily veined while he held the dildo in one hand and the lube in the other. "Which do you want first?"

Still tingling from that last orgasm and nearly boneless from that relief, I grinned at Coop. "I want both."

A flash of surprise passed over his face and his eyebrows rose. "Both?" The hint of choking in his voice just made me grin wider.

"Yes," I told him as I spread my legs a little wider and slid my hand down my abdomen. I paused at my belly button piercing and traced my finger in a circle around it. I kind of half-forgot it sometimes, but the minute any of the guys fixated on it—they went a little crazy.

Coop was no exception.

"Multi-player," he murmured. Then he eyed the dildo, then me and nodded firmly. "Roll over, sweetheart and get that ass in the air."

I giggled, but possessive Coop had been peeking out more and more lately, and I was never going to complain about that. He pressed kisses along my spine to my tattoo, then traced his tongue over it. The alternating light and heavy touches had my nipples pulling taut and my thighs rubbing together.

In almost no time, he had lubed fingers up my ass and stretching me. We hadn't tried it with the piercings in my ass and I had to admit I was a little curious, but it wasn't the dildo he slid into me, but himself and we were both sweating and groaning by the time he seated himself.

I had to bite down on the pillow when he began to rock his hips. The stretch and the burn were intense, almost too intense. He rolled us onto our sides and I let out a whimper as he swirled the dildo against my clit. He'd added lube to it, too but I was already soaked.

Maybe I shouldn't have said both.

Maybe this was going to be too much.

Then he rocked the dildo into me the same way he would himself and I clasped a hand down on his hip, digging in my nails. The first time we'd played with it, I'd been so caught up in the excitement of seeing him that we really hadn't experimented as much.

The first push of it inside me was an almost agonizing counterpoint to the ease of his cock in my ass, then he'd rock both forward and back. The piercings lit me up and I was panting. When a scream crawled up my throat, Coop captured my lips in a kiss and then drove both home and I was shaking, coming apart from being too full. There was no way that both of him should fit me and yet he did.

I swore I blacked out at one point and when I came to, I tumbled right into another orgasm. Every stroke of the dildo's piercings edged me higher as he alternated and fuck I had to admire his focus to make it work because I could only hold on and kiss him like my breath depended on it. When I splintered again, he came with me and we were left in a sweaty, messy heap and he had crescent shaped marks on his hip from my nails and I'd damn near bit through the inside of my lip.

"Truth," I panted. "Or dare."

He laughed, the sound as shaky as my own. "Not up to a dare yet, so truth..."

I grinned. "How'd your piercing feel on your side of things?"

'Cause he and Jake could feel each other through me. They'd admitted it. Coop raised his eyebrows and then kissed me tenderly as he eased the dildo out. We were both shuddering by the time he was free. "I get the appeal," he whispered. "You?"

"Oh yeah," I said. "I definitely get the appeal. But I love your dick just like it is."

"Buried inside you?" he teased.

"Always."

We lingered for a while, cuddling, then Coop finally made himself move. We had a little attached bathroom, thank fuck. So we could clean up in here and we didn't have to go out in the hallway and risk running into anyone. By the time we were back in bed, I'd already accepted there was no hiding the smell of sex in here, but I didn't care.

I cuddled into Coop's arms and tucked my head against his chest. We had maybe two hours we could snatch before the twins would be up, according to my dad. I wanted every drop, because it was going to be an amazing day for the kids, and I couldn't wait to spend it with them and with Coop.

Chapter Twenty-Two

AUTUMN IN NEW YORK

Frankie

The birthday weekend with the twins was so much fun. Even low on sleep, I couldn't help but laugh at how excited Chloe and Craig were. Well, Craig tried to play it cool but Chloe had no shame. My kind of girl. It was her birthday, so she played it up and I totally catered to it. Same for Craig. But I took time for Alec and I had a feeling he was warming to me. He was the one who let me know where Chloe was the most ticklish, so when tickle wars started, I got her good.

The trampoline place was a riot. Kelly and Hank laughed when Coop and I shucked our shoes and headed out to join the kids. Coop could actually do some tricks and I'd done pep squad one year (not that it made me a cheerleader or anything) but there had been tumbling fun and I could do a tuck roll and back to my feet.

It was a long day, but a blast and I got loads of photos. Having siblings was cool. But as much as I hated saying goodbye to them on Sunday morning, Coop and I were ready to go home. I caved and gave Kelly a hug that morning and Chloe hugged us both. "Come back any time," Kelly informed me. "And keep in touch."

"I promise."

Alec shook my hand and Craig motioned for me to lower down but instead of a hug, he gave me a sweet kiss on the cheek and I ruffled his hair before pressing a kiss to the top of his head. Hank walked us out to the car and gave me the longest hug, making me promise to look after myself and to be careful. Then he looked Coop dead in the eye and said, "If you boys don't take care of her, there will be hell to pay."

"Yes, sir."

In the car, Coop let out a laugh and I glanced over at him. "You okay?"

"I think that's the first time it occurred to me that maybe your dad has your temper and your ability to get even."

Laughter flooded out of me, and we both waved at them as we pulled away. We paused at the closest charging station and Coop went for donuts and coffee while I texted with the guys. Family dinner tonight when we were all home. That made me happy

Jake and Archie texted separately to let me know that they were talking and working on things, but both asked me to be patient.

I love you both, I hate when you fight because I hate when you're hurting. But I also trust both of you. So, take care of you and I'm here if you need me.

I sent that to each of them separately and their replies were so identical it just made me smile.

Love you too, Baby Girl, and I'll always need you.

Needing you goes without saying, but I love you more.

I snorted.

The drive back was uneventful, Coop and I rambled about everything and nothing. When I mentioned I hadn't found a new psychologist yet, he offered to go with me to Student Services. The school offered assistance in finding mental health professionals. It was a place to start.

That evening at home, a lot of the tension had bled from between us and we had fun, even teasing Jeremy into joining us briefly for dinner so I could show off the photos of the kids. His cupcakes were a hit and so were the presents. After dinner, we hit the second floor and the game room and played video games for a while before one by one, we all had to peel off to do homework.

It was normal. Or as normal as we'd managed since the accident. Ian and Archie both slept with me that night. Jake followed me into the shower in the morning and maybe I had been holding my breath over the fight between them, but that seemed to be big steps forward.

The next few weeks seemed to blow past us like we were sitting still. The weather changed and grew cooler. The leaves turned in the park and the guys lured me out for runs with them because I wanted to see the colors.

Coop's birthday arrived before we knew it, and we all had classes that day, and Archie had some huge project due, while Ian had two exams. I had my own and Coop, sadly as he put it, couldn't afford to skip because they were doing group work. We postponed his birthday to the weekend then went to Coney Island.

It was all kinds of ridiculous fun and the guys made a contest out of winning stuffed animals. Not only did I end up with a couple in my room—a patchwork colored bear and panda that was too cute for words—they gave away stuffed animals to every little kid around us.

Archie's birthday was hot on its heels and he planned a night in for us, rather than out. We had dinner on the roof. It was chilly, but tons of fun and instead of it just being the two of us, he invited the guys. Maybe because classes were keeping us all busy and our schedules were so different, it was easier for us to find private time and harder to find time just for the five of us.

Though he'd tried, Jake had only managed to switch one of his classes back. But at least he and Archie were working together again. The friction still seemed present, but not as uncomfortable as before. The anniversary of Homecoming came and went without a blip on my radar, except that Rachel showed up at the house with snacks and all of us piled in for movie night.

I'd had a couple of calls from Dominic. So far, tracking Maddy down had proved fruitless. He wanted to ask me some questions about her, including possible other locations, jobs, and more. As far as I knew she didn't have any other names and then it hit me. Maybe she'd gone back to using Grayson? That was her name before she changed it to Curtis. To the best of my knowledge, she'd never been married.

He took all the notes and then said he'd be in touch. As an olive branch, I let Archie sit in on the phone call and afterward, he reached out to Edward to find out what he knew and if he'd heard anything. That meant our next step, if we took any, was to talk to Muriel. Archie's scowl said he didn't want that to be an option.

When I offered to go on my own, that earned an even darker look. To my surprise, Jake backed him up on that. "I don't trust her," was all he said. "But," he continued, glancing at Archie. "If we're both there, then we can get a read on whether she's trying to actually be helpful or just playing another game."

"I'll think about it," was as far as Archie was willing to commit and I didn't want to push him. But at the same time. The longer we went without finding her, the colder the case seemed to be. Even the detectives had nothing new on the investigation. They were holding the wreckage of the Ferrari because it was still an open case, but it didn't sound like they were putting a lot of effort into it anymore.

Halloween was right around the corner and honestly, it seemed like every single class either had a major exam or project due. We also got our first dusting of snow, early for the season, but when I woke up to it, I almost cried.

Colorful leaves. Bright lights. Falling snow. It was almost the dream. I got a note from KC—the first one since the school year started and it didn't say a lot, other than she was starting to see that she hadn't missed out on much being on the road all the time.

Oh and boys were annoying.

The last part made me laugh.

Halloween night, we headed back to campus. There were parties in some of the residential dorms and in a couple of the social centers. For fun, we made the rounds. We didn't quite coordinate our costumes this year, though the guys had joked about the Justice League, but I was not walking around in a Wonder Woman costume no matter how great she was. When I suggested Avengers, Jake nixed me in a black leather body suit much to Archie's chagrin and Jake's laughter.

We ended up putting suggestions in a jar and then letting Jeremy draw out the winning combo. Which was how we ended up going out in Roman garb. The guys looked great in their little skirts and armor. Rachel made me take all the pictures as they were getting ready. The off the shoulder garment I wore was a lot more comfortable and showed considerably less skin.

I rather liked the hair style though and the jewelry. Unfortunately, there was no way to avoid being cold. So Archie arranged for a car to take us and then had it on standby to pick us up. The flurries of a few days earlier were gone but it was still chilly. We started at one of the frat parties because the guys had zero interest in hanging out there past a certain point.

Unbeknownst to me, they'd been getting recruited by different Frats. Rachel and I had talked about trying for one of the sororities more for fun than anything else and to buy time to look for Maddy, but since the guys knew now and the first sorority event Rachel and I went to was also our last, I hadn't really thought about it.

The music was cranked, and it was definitely too warm inside where writhing bodies danced. Some of the costumes were barely legal, like the girl who had quarters over her nipples and a bikini bottom made out of pennies.

She was Bite-Me-Coin or so she announced she slid up to Jake.

I snorted and took her arm and tugged her away from him. "Hands off. Your coin isn't good here."

She made a face and then glanced at Ian and he just shook his head and Archie said, "Catch the hint, we're all together. Off you go."

"Right," Coop added, slinging an arm around Archie. "We're together."

Her eyes grew to the size of saucers then she looked around at all of us. "All of you?"

I grinned and leaned back against Jake and said, "Choo-choo. The train's all full."

Honestly, I didn't know what was funnier her expression or the little squeaking noise she made as she apologized and wandered away.

"You enjoyed that way too much," Jake teased and I glanced up at him.

"Really? Nothing at all like you clasping your hand over my butt when we came in because the Dracula-wanna-be told me I had a nice ass?"

He shot a glare in the direction of the door. "It wasn't just your ass he was checking out."

"The point is," Coop interjected. "We're allowed to stake our claim, so Frankie is allowed to stake hers."

"Oh, Babe," Archie said with a teasing grin. "I'll happily stake you any time."

It was ridiculous, but fun. We stayed long enough to have one drink and try to dance, but honestly this party turned more into a half-orgy half-stoner fest and it didn't appeal so we moved on to the next.

Turned out the guys made a list of all the parties around campus and the local student union and clubs. We managed to visit quite a few of them, and I got to dance with everyone. I did meet some of the kids in Jake's and Archie's engineering class. They were setting off bottle rockets. We managed to clear out before the cops showed up.

One of Coop's teachers was actually at one of the parties and she was hot. Tall, long-limbed, with dark hair and chestnut colored eyes. Even Jake gave Coop a look, but he just grinned. "Don't you trust me?"

"Oh, I trust you," I promised him. "I'm just glad Rachel's not in that class with you." She wanted a teacher affair, I had a feeling Rachel would take one look at this chick and it would be on.

Kurt, from my econ class, found us at one of the last parties we stopped at, last because I was dead on my feet and really, all I wanted to do was go home and soak in a bath and hang out with my guys. All four of the guys gave him assessing looks as Kurt swayed in my direction. He'd definitely had way too much to drink.

Also, thank fuck for Ian's and Jake's swift reactions cause Kurt nearly threw up on me. Ugh, no thank you. Jake got Kurt turned away while Ian pulled me to him. Between Coop and Jake, they got him wrestled into the bathroom and Archie found some friends to look after Kurt and we all called it a night. That was a wrap for Halloween.

In the car on the way back, Jake said, "I vote we either have our own Halloween party next year or we just go to some clubs."

Murmurs of agreement all the way around. Partying campus life and getting drunk until you puked just didn't do it for me. Especially since he nearly puked *on* me.

Back at the brownstone, we all got out of our costumes, showered, and changed into comfy clothes. Archie and Jake raided the kitchen for food and then everyone met back up in my room and for the first time in months, we snacked, watched movies and everyone slept in there together.

I had no idea how much I needed that until I woke very early the next morning to the soft sound of their breathing. Archie was sleeping right up against my back, with one arm around me. Coop snored softly on his other side. Jake was in front of me, one arm up over his eyes and the other was stretched down my side so he could grip my knee. On the far side of him, Ian slept with his back to Jake, but they were all still here.

We needed more nights like last night. I yawned and Jake murmured something before leaning forward and kissing my forehead, He snuggled my hand to his chest and dropped right back off again. I hadn't been able to make out the words, but the feeling was there.

The guys didn't wake up for another hour and no matter how much my bladder complained, I didn't move. This was my idea of Heaven.

And all too soon

we'd be up to our eyeballs in work again.

Chapter Twenty-Three

MY FATHER'S HOUSE

Archie

"Y ou sure you're gonna be good?" Jake asked for the fourth time, and I glanced over at him from where I was packing the overnight bag.

"Unless you know something I don't, then yes, I'll be fine." The Standish men were going to have a sit down for the next two days, hence why I was packing a single bag. I was meeting Grandpa Ted and Edward at a neutral location. Honestly, we would be close enough I could just come back to the brownstone, but I got the idea of what Grandpa wanted to do. For the next forty-eight hours, we were talking to Edward about business, about Maddy, and about the future.

As in, if Maddy was in his future then he didn't have one with us. Clearly, he'd bent to the pressure before, but that was when I was on the way. There were no small children or babies involved this time—or at least there better not be.

Ice crawled up my spine at the idea of Maddy being pregnant. Just. No. Frankie would back me and I'd do everything I could to get that kid away from her. We got lucky that she didn't destroy Frankie, I would not allow her to do more harm to another child, much less to someone who would be our sibling.

Shoving that unpleasant thought away, I glanced at Jake again. There was still tension between us. As much as I tried not to react to any criticism from him, it always sounded like everything he said had a double meaning. Erring on the side of caution, I'd stopped avoiding him, but I hadn't rushed to be in the same room either.

We had one class together again and that seemed to be going well. Better to not look a gift horse in the mouth. Anytime the subject of Maddy or the accident came up, we were both instantly on edge and I wasn't imagining that. Jake still blamed me, even if he wasn't verbally or physically, bashing me anymore.

I still blamed me. So at least we agreed on that.

"I just worry about your dad," Jake admitted.

"I can handle Edward." Frankly, he'd been much easier to deal with since discovering Frankie *wasn't* his child than he had been in my entire life. Maybe the knowledge that I was his only kid had sunk in. Maybe he had grown up. Maybe he'd developed a conscience. I didn't know and I didn't care. The next two days were about business. Business and figuring out if he knew where Maddy was.

So far, he'd sworn to me he didn't. But he could just as easily tell me that and then turn around and provide her with attorneys and cover because of some decade's long obsession. I didn't think he could lie to both me and Grandpa. Then again, I couldn't have pictured him believing that Frankie was his kid either.

What kind of blinders did he have to wear to think Maddy would have kept quiet about that for almost eighteen years?

"Jake," I said after zipping up the bag. "Look, Edward wants detente with Grandpa and with me. But we have terms for that. One of those terms is ending that relationship with Maddy. I know if I were in the same position, with them telling me it was the family business or Frankie, I'd tell them to stuff the family business."

"You don't think Edward will?"

"I think Edward's already halfway out the door, if he hasn't kicked her to the curb completely. I want to tell myself he's never seen her behave the way she did at graduation and that her lie about Frankie cost him." But I wasn't a fool. "That said, he's had decades to get over her and apparently that didn't happen, so, we'll just play it by the numbers."

"If you want backup, I can go hang out in a lobby or something."

I chuckled, because Jake meant that. Even ticked at me. "I appreciate it, man. I do. But you have an appointment to get to work on that tattoo and I'll be fine."

"Call," he said. "I mean it. Call. Even if you just need someone to get drunk with."

I nodded and then clapped him on the shoulder. "Don't do anything I wouldn't do."

"Well, hell," Jake called after me. "With latitude like that, sky's the limit."

I was still laughing as I descended the steps. Frankie and Coop left for school early, and Bubba hadn't been that far behind them. I'd already said bye to Frankie. Jeremy waited with my coat by the door and he gave me a stern look. "You should take Mr. Benton up on his offer."

"I appreciate the advice." I set my bag down and let Jeremy help me into the jacket. "But we're doing this as a family and while Jake's family to me, he isn't family to them. Better he's here to keep an eye on things with Frankie and the boys."

Also, Jake had a temper and I was going to have to keep mine in check. We still had a week to go before the Thanksgiving break and there had been some debate on whether to fly home for the holidays—or stay here. I'd just as soon stay here. We'd had more snow flurries, but no real stickage yet and it would be fun to watch the tree go up at Rockefeller Center. For that matter, we could head into the mountains up north or in Maryland to go skiing.

"Can you make plans for Thanksgiving here in case not everyone heads back down to Texas?" If Frankie elected to go down, I could have the house opened or she and I could get a hotel with the boys and we could visit all the families. But I also had a couple of projects I needed to finish up, so I didn't want to be there long.

"I can, when will you five decide on what you're doing?"

"By the weekend," I promised. "They're only hesitating because I offered the jet to fly them down if they wanted to go for a couple of days." That meant they didn't have to worry about last minute plane tickets. Jeremy gave me a firm nod.

"Be careful, Mr. Archie. Mr. Edward and Mr. Ted are both crafty businessmen and they have not achieved their success by forgiving weakness."

That I know.

"I will. Look after my girl."

"Of course."

He opened the door and I grabbed my bag. There was a car waiting for me at the curb already. Time to get this show on the road.

I sent a message to Frankie once I was in the car. The driver knew where we were going so there was no need for conversation.

Me

On my way. Miss you already.

Frankie

Love you, be safe. Tell Edward to behave or I'll kick his ass.

I chuckled. She would, too. Another reason I hated leaving, but I wouldn't be leaving her unprotected.

The next was a kiss emoji from her and she'd probably already focused back on her class again. The fact she enjoyed economic theory and introduction to business amused me. Frankie liked to know things, she liked to know how they worked and whether it was contract language or dissecting poetry, she thrilled to the challenges.

I'd bet even money she'd make it to the Fortune 500 all by herself. Well, if she didn't donate more than she banked. Then again, could one really find fault with such a generous heart?

My phone vibrated and I checked the caller ID.

Pax.

I answered before it could ring twice. "Is everything all right?" Since putting him on the job, he'd only reached out once, and that was to confirm the parameters of my expectations.

"It's fine," the man answered easily. "I'm letting you know I'm bringing in three more bodies to handle the rotations. I've got a lead and I want to follow it. Do you want the files and the background, or do you trust my judgment?"

Nice. I exhaled. I trusted Pax. I wasn't so sure about the others. "Do you trust them?"

"Yes," he said. "All of them."

"How long do you plan to be gone?"

"Depends on what I find," Pax answered in his typically enigmatic fashion. The man committed to nothing until it was an absolute certainty. "Tell me what you want me to do, Standish. I can stay on this and run the risk of the lead slipping or I can bring in these guys and let them do the job while I find your target."

My target.

Damn right she was my target.

"Do it, make sure you send me any details I need on them and remind them we want a low profile."

"Done and done." With that, he hung up. Not chatty. I couldn't even remember the first time I met Pax. It had been a while ago, even before I met Frankie. His younger brother had been at school with me and there'd been a scandal. Pax showed up and took care of it.

All of it.

He gave me his card and said if I needed anything all I had to do was call. At the time, I'd thought it was just a favor for a favor, but Pax said loyalty was for life. He'd asked me for a favor a year ago. I'd done it, no questions asked.

It was a good relationship.

The drive took us north and out of the city toward Westchester County. I expected a hotel, but apparently Grandpa had elected another destination. I should have known. Scarsdale wasn't that far and the grand ole dame of a house on old Duck Pond Way was still there. I hadn't even realized we still owned that house. My grandparents used it for entertaining when they'd enjoyed city life more. It was somewhat picturesque with a dusting of snow we hadn't seen in the city, though it was only on the grass.

A gentlemen met the car and opened the door for me. He had the look of a butler, but I didn't know him. He also took my bag, and the driver pulled away, leaving me to follow him inside.

"Mr. Standish Senior and Mr. Standish Junior are taking coffee in the solarium while they waited for you, Mr. Standish."

I rolled my eyes. If he insisted on calling us all Standish it was going to get confusing. "You are?"

"Reginald Wentworth, sir."

"Thank you, Wentworth, please call me Mr. Archie if you need to refer to me at all."

"As you wish sir, would you like me to show you to the solarium?"

"Nope, I know right where it is." Sliding my hands into the pockets of my jeans, I made my way through the house. Nana hadn't cared for this house as much as the one in Massachusetts. She liked quieter living without the pretentiousness of a huge house designed specifically around the idea of entertaining house guests or house parties.

The solarium opened off the ladies' sitting room and included the warmth of the sun without the chill of the air beyond. It wasn't quite as humid as a greenhouse, though there were a great many plants decorating the room.

"Sprout!" Grandpa Ted greeted me, standing as soon as I arrived. "There you are. I was worried you couldn't tear yourself away."

I clasped his offered hand and gave him a brief hug. "I'm sure the driver notified you the moment we pulled away from the brownstone."

He laughed, but didn't deny it. I glanced at Edward with a nod and then took a seat opposite them. We formed a loose triangle. I couldn't really remember the last time it had been the three of us in the same room together, alone with no buffers.

"How is Frankie, Archie?" Edward asked. "Fully recovered?"

"She's fine," I told him. "She appreciated your flowers, but we're not here to talk about her." And as much as he'd shown care and concern for Frankie after the accident, we had boundaries. She was firmly on my side of that line, not his.

"Of course, I just wanted to know how she was doing since the police don't seem to be any closer to an answer on what happened with your Ferrari."

"And they're being damned stubborn about letting us have it back to do our own work."

"Not that it's stopped either of you," I pointed out as I poured my own coffee. It certainly hadn't stopped me. Frankie had shared the report. The tampering with the brake lines was obvious and inexpert. They'd clearly been cut though, not severed. The damage would have weakened them, and the driving did the rest.

"Of course not," Grandpa Ted said. "But the one person we all have questions for appears to be missing and cleverly avoiding any attempts to find her." He eyed Edward on that last and I took a sip of the coffee, more than curious about Edward's reaction myself.

"I've told you both, I have no idea where Maddy is. I haven't spoken to her in months. After the incident at graduation and the fact she lied to me about Frankie, among so many other infractions...I thought it time to cut ties."

Squinting, Grandpa stared at him. "You trying to bullshit a bullshitter, Eddie?"

"Dad," Edward said with a sigh. "I understand you've never liked her. You warned me off her again and again, and I did the right thing in marrying Muriel, even if it ultimately wasn't fair to her or to you Archie. I love Maddy, I can't change my feelings on that subject, but I can change my responses."

"So, you agree with me," I said slowly. "She's probably the one who sabotaged the car."

"I don't want to agree with you. The idea of her climbing under a car and cutting brake lines is patently ridiculous. First, I can't imagine she would even know how, much less where, and second that would have put her at the Hamptons estate, and she is not at all fond of her parents."

Grandpa scrubbed a hand over his face. "You still have blinders on where she's concerned. She's a danger to your son and her daughter. What more proof do you need?"

"I need to know she did it," Edward stated in an almost cold tone. "Incontrovertible proof. That said, I have still cut her out of my life and cut off the cards I gave her. I left her the condo in Texas that I purchased."

"The place you were planning to move her and Frankie into so you could be one happy little family?" I wasn't bitter, not really. But I did take some pride in turning the knife.

"Yes," Edward said, meeting my gaze without flinching. "Maddy has a habit of landing on her feet and as angry as I am with her, I couldn't leave her homeless."

Grandpa made another derogatory snort. "She was never homeless, not from the moment she up and left school. Whether she had to work or to manipulate or both, she managed quite fine. Stop looking at her as some fragile heiress without the skills to her name. While she may not have accumulated wealth, she was far from starving and somehow managed to raise a child worth a thousand of her."

"I don't think I'd give that credit to Maddy, but she did teach Frankie fierce independence from a young age. That said, I want her found. If she wants to come after me, fine, bring it." I'd cheerfully accept any opportunity to defend myself and end the issue with self-defense. The fact I'd been thinking about it more and more of late wasn't lost on me. "I won't allow her to harm Frankie. Not anymore."

"On this, we mostly agree, Sprout," Grandpa said. "But I'll not have her gunning for you, either." He cut a look toward Edward. "I asked you once to choose your child over that woman. I'm not asking you now, I'm telling you there's a time when a man must choose who he will protect."

"Archie," Edward said without hesitation and I swore I blinked. "I may be stubborn and thickheaded, Dad, but I would never forgive her or myself if I let her harm him."

"Then we're agreed." Grandpa Ted nodded his head as if that was that.

"Except what are we agreeing to?" I asked. "Because what happens if we find her, but we have no legal proof?"

"There are always options, Sprout." Grandpa pointed to the coffee and to the croissants. "Help yourself to some more. We have a lot of business to discuss."

Chapter Twenty-Four

THERE BE DRAGONS HERE

Jake

Finding time with Frankie took a lot of planning, lately. Not because she didn't want to hang out, but more because our schedules clashed so badly, and that was my own damn fault. Throw in the workload she'd tackled and if she wasn't with one of us, she was doing homework. Rachel had even cornered me on campus to demand that we find a way to lighten her load, she was *stressing* out.

I didn't need Rachel, of all people, telling me to look after our girl better, but what the hell had I missed that sent Rachel around to chew on my tail? Speaking of which, what the hell was up with her? She'd always been in rare form in school, but she'd been particularly biting. When I asked Coop, all he'd said was that she was juggling a lot with her classes and maybe we could all make home life a little less stressful.

I thought we had. Fuck, Archie and I were talking. It was still strained, granted and the school hadn't been thrilled with my request to change classes for a second time and I'd only managed to swap back to one he and I shared. But we were lab partners for that one. As long as we focused on the work it was easier. Try as hard as I could, I still couldn't get past the fact he hadn't fucking been there when she'd been in that accident.

It was Bubba who'd looked me dead in the eye and asked was I pissed at Archie for not being there or myself? Because Bubba and Coop hadn't been there either. Yeah, that stuck. So, when Archie went off to meet with his dad and refused my offer to go with him, even after I tried twice, I switched gears.

The week had been a weird one with Thanksgiving break literally the next week and we had that whole week off. We either had projects or tests this week and for once, I'd finished early and took two of my exams at the testing center so I could free up my afternoons.

I had Frankie's schedule memorized, but I still sent her a text to hopefully catch her before she made any other plans.

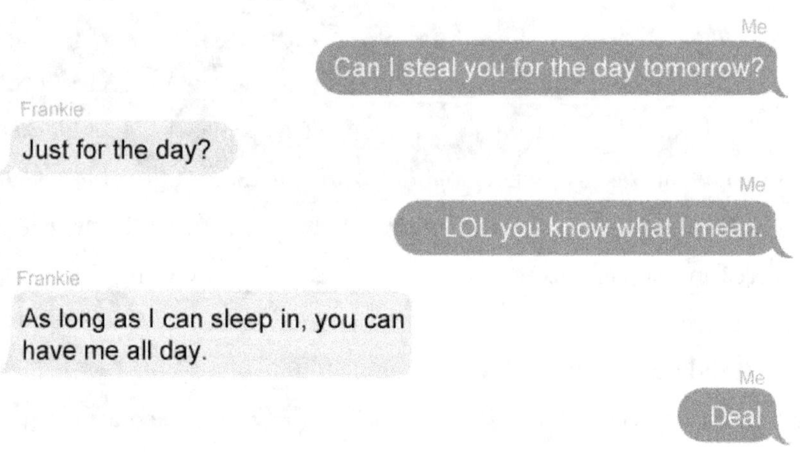

Which was why Friday morning, I dozed and skipped the run with Bubba while Frankie curled against my side. I wasn't moving until she was. My appointment wasn't until almost lunchtime anyway. No matter how much she liked to sleep in, Frankie couldn't sleep past eight if she tried. It was one of her endearing qualities. Always busy, always focused on getting things done.

Tracing my fingers against her shoulder, I followed the lines of her tattoo from memory. I knew every centimeter of it. I knew where my name was and theirs. Just like I could feel the tattoo on my shoulder that matched it, only it bore just her name. The fact we got those on my birthday last year added to the pleasure I took out of it.

When her lashes lifted, I smiled. "You can sleep longer."

The noncommittal sound she made bounced somewhere between a grunt and a groan. I caught a lock of her hair and curled it around my finger. The softness of her leg slid along mine as she burrowed closer to me, and I sighed. Outside, there was frost on the glass of the arched window that diffused the light coming in.

It didn't promise to be a sunny day, but that was all right. I had all the sunshine I needed right here. The first brush of her lips to my pec had me shifting to glance down, but she was already kissing her way across my chest. I hadn't shaved in a while, but she seemed to enjoy my beard and I chuckled as she nuzzled kisses against my neck.

"Morning breath," she warned a split-second before pressing her lips to mine.

Yeah, I didn't much care, the taste of Frankie was still the best thing there was and there was still a hint of mint on her lips. What started as just a caress, deepened the moment she stroked her tongue against my lips. Fisting her hair, I tilted her head so I could get better access. The sleepy good morning roared to life in my system. My morning wood had been stiff before she moved and now I fucking ached to just be in her.

The glide of her fingers down my sides as she shifted to straddle my lap had me moaning into her mouth. Thank fuck for sleeping naked, because she wrapped her hand around my cock and I thrust up against her grip. Her eyes were half-closed as she broke our kiss and sat up. I let go of her hair only long enough to run my palms down her chest. Her nipples peaked at first brush and then she sank down on me, and we both sighed.

The velvet slick heat of her pussy wrapping around my cock was perfection. I massaged her breasts as I thrust up to meet her rolling hips. There was no urgency, and at the same time I couldn't take my eyes off of her. The soft curve of her lips as she let out a groan. The way her hips pumped and the muscles in her legs flexed. The glitter of the piercing at her navel that attracted my eye every single time I saw it peek out from under a shirt or when she was changing.

Leaning forward, Frankie pressed her hands against my chest, curling her fingers as her hair fell in a curtain around us. I swore her inner muscles spasmed around me every time she took me deep. It was ecstasy and agony and my balls drew up tight, but I wanted this edge. I wanted her to take everything she needed. When she slid her hand toward herself, I dropped mine to knock her fingers aside and then began to tease her clit.

She sank her teeth into her bottom lip and her head tilted back as she thrust against my hand.

"You need more, Baby Girl?" My voice was rough, but I didn't give a damn. At her faint mewling sound and breathy 'yes,' I lunged forward. My mouth claimed hers as I rolled her onto her back and dragged her legs up until I nearly had her folded in half and her soft scream as I pounded into her told me I'd found the right spot.

Her fingers were in my hair and her mouth demanding as we exchanged gasps. One of her legs was up over my shoulder and hitched high. I pistoned my hips, angling for that spot that pulled those sharp, soft cries from her, and when she clamped down on me and her scream released, I let go. Fuck, my orgasm tore through me as I sank into her heat, and it was like the first time all over again.

Only better.

"Good morning," she managed after a while, stroking her fingers through my hair as I sprawled against her, unwilling to move. The crush of her breasts to my chest, the feel of her pussy still trembling in the aftermath, teased my overly sensitive cock and I still didn't care.

"I've missed you," I admitted. It was my own damn fault. But fuck had I missed her.

"Missed you too," she whispered and I finally dragged my head up to look at her and found nothing but affection and adoration in those eyes. No judgment. No anger. Not even regret.

"I don't deserve you," I told her. "I should have..."

She pressed her fingers to my lips. "We're all learning and adjusting and building and growing. It's not always going to be roses and sweet kisses. I know that. We've never been all roses and sweet kisses."

Hated to admit that she was right, but fuck she was right. "The first time I met you, you socked that kid in the face."

She grinned. "Then he hit me back and you barreled into him."

Damn right I did. "Jackass shouldn't have hit a girl." Definitely shouldn't have hit my girl. The redness on her cheeks showed the marks of my beard left and the puffiness of her lips just reminded me of her kisses.

I laughed. "You always want to fight my battles."

"Always will." And I wouldn't apologize for it. "But I'll try to be better about who I fight them with." I had blamed myself for not being there, and I took it out on Archie cause I thought he should have been.

"I know it won't always be easy and we're going to disagree," she said, cupping my face. "But maybe we both promise to not run away from the fight. Even if we're fighting with each other or the other guys. We fight for each other until we sort it out."

Huffing out a sigh, I couldn't deny that I had done exactly that. I ran away from dealing with the problem by cutting Archie out. That didn't help anyone or anything. All I'd done was fuck things up in a different way. "I may need you to remind me sometimes, Baby Girl. I can get stubborn."

"Get?" She laughed. "Pot, have you met Kettle?" When she motioned to herself, I grinned. "I think we just need to all remember we care, even when we're pissed off."

I sighed. "I'm sorry I fucked up, Baby Girl."

Cupping my face in her hands, she kissed me lightly. "I forgive you. Are you and Archie really okay now?"

I could lie, but I wouldn't. "Working on it. It's hard sometimes and might be until we have answers. Every time I think about the accident, the phone call—all of it. I feel so fucking helpless and that just makes me furious all over again." I hated that helplessness.

"I love all of you, you know. But I also love how you look after each other, your friendships, and how you've been there for Archie and he's there for you."

Pressing my forehead to hers, I whispered, "Never giving up, Baby Girl. Might take a while, but I'm all in. I meant it then, I mean it now."

The very real relief in her eyes cut at me. Note to self, never make Frankie doubt that again.

"Just remember you can smack me upside the head whenever I'm being thick." She might be the only one who could. "But I know it wasn't Archie's fault in here." I tapped my head. "It's here that's got to stop overreacting." I motioned to my heart.

"You'll get there," she whispered. "I believe in you."

That filled me with a quiet kind of elation I couldn't readily describe.

"And as much as I love you and this—I really need to pee."

That made me laugh, but I got the message. It didn't take us long once we were up to shower, brush teeth and get changed. Downstairs was quiet. Jeremy left a note that he'd gone to take care of some shopping. There was coffee waiting and fresh croissants along with some other pastries. We ate our fill, and she drank two cups of coffee while making a fuss out of the cats.

"Coats and hats," I told her as we cleaned up. Jeremy would probably scold us later, but Frankie actively did the dishes every chance she got— which wasn't often. The kitchen was most certainly his domain, but I couldn't leave dirty cups on the counter either. In the back of my head, I could hear my mother reminding me she wasn't a maid.

She had thick ugg boots, which would keep her feet warm. I liked the red knit cap she pulled over her hair, it was festive and suited her. Once we were ready, we were out the door and only remembered at the last second to arm the security system and make sure we had keys. Weird, Jeremy was always there, so we didn't often need to set the alarm on our way out. But better to make sure the house was safe.

The wind was brisk, but Frankie just grinned as we held hands. I thought about calling a car, but I wanted as much time with just her and me as possible and I'd already mapped the route the last two times I'd visited to get the art designed. We took the subway, which wasn't as glamorous as it sounded. It also didn't smell as bad as a lot of people described. Then again, I had Frankie tucked up next to me and it wasn't crowded.

We had to switch lines in Times Square and it was a lot busier, but we timed it just right. Hopping off in Greenwich Village earned me a curious look from her. When she still didn't ask, I grinned. "You aren't going to try and guess where we're going?"

"Nope," Frankie told me as we climbed the stairs. It wasn't as cold down in the subway as it was when we got to the street level.

"Huh." I frowned. "Should I be worried or complimented?"

Half-turning to face me, she walked backwards so she could meet my gaze confident that I would make sure she didn't run into anything, and she was right. "Definitely a compliment. But I figured you were going to get your tattoo started, since you've been down here a couple of times talking to different artists."

"Wow," I mouthed the word with a little exaggeration. "I'm predictable."

"Nope, you've just wanted your dragons for a long time, and I love that I'm going to get to watch you get it started. I hope I can come to every appointment." It would take a few to get what I wanted done.

Pausing in the middle of the street, I ignored the sour voices that snapped at us as I dragged her forward and kissed her soundly. "Never leave me, Frankie Curtis."

"Never gonna happen, Jake Benton. Now—let's go see what you've picked. Who knows," she continued with a laugh. "Maybe I'll get another one. Won't that be fun?"

The shop had a couple of chick artists who were excellent, so I had less issues with it than I had in Colorado, but I was curious as to what she would pick. We made it with about ten minutes to spare for my appointment. The place was called Infinity Ink, which I thought Frankie would appreciate. Her swift grin said it did.

Guy, my artist, was at the front and we shook hands and then he took us back to go over the art he'd worked out. The finished piece was even more impressive than what he'd had the last time I was here. As much as I loved it, I glanced at Frankie for her reaction.

"It's going to cover half of your chest and curl around to the back?"

I nodded.

Her eyes lit up. "Jake, it's going to be gorgeous." That was all the approval I needed. I stripped down. We were starting with the chest piece first, and in a couple of weeks, after Thanksgiving, I'd come back for the back. We'd work in stages. By Frankie's birthday, it should be all done.

Frankie sat with me and flipped through a couple of books as Guy worked the black ink into my skin. The burn was real, but it didn't bother me that much. It felt *good* to be finally adding the dragons to my skin. I'd wanted them for as long as I could remember.

"A butterfly," Frankie said. "I want to get a butterfly behind my ear."

"Yeah?" I glanced at her. "Why behind the ear?"

"Well, I still have to look at corporate work after college, but at the same time...I want it somewhere I can see it, too."

"Then get whatever you want, Baby Girl, my treat."

Guy glanced at me and then leaned out. "Hey, Tamara, you free?"

"Yep," the woman Tamara answered as she came into the room we were in. She had full sleeves and a chest full of ink. It was all jungle like with dozens of colorful animals peeking out. Frankie's eyes grew at the sight of them.

"Those are gorgeous."

"Thanks, sugar. What can I do for you?"

"Golden girl here wants a butterfly behind her ear."

"Yeah?" Tamara asked and I grinned. "Well, c'mon then. Let's go see what we can do."

Frankie glanced at me and I lifted my chin. "Go on, surprise me."

And she did. She finished faster than I did though Tamara had colored her butterfly in. It was a pale-blue butterfly, it seemed to shimmer against her skin and it was tucked neatly behind her right ear. "The best part is Tamara placed it so I could add more if I wanted."

It was perfect. It took another hour for Guy to finish my chest. Almost all afternoon had passed and I was definitely gonna be feeling this tomorrow. But we went over tattoo care for both of us and I booked my next appointment. Frankie made sure she had it in her calendar so she could come, too.

Damn, I was lucky I didn't fuck this up. Maybe I'd have Guy add that butterfly of hers to part of my dragon's pattern. Somewhere I'd know it was there. Just like she was always there for me.

Chapter Twenty-Five

DOWNTIME

Frankie

When Archie got back from his "family meeting" the five of us sat down to figure out the holiday. The girls wanted to go see their families, but they also didn't want Archie and me sitting around up here. As much as I loved the idea of going to visit everyone again, I could not eat four Thanksgiving meals again or go through all the well-meaning parenting and inquiries.

On top of that, I still had homework to do, and I could use the break to get caught up or ahead. We'd also been invited to my grandparents and to Hank and Kelly's for Thanksgiving, and I wasn't really up for any of those invitations either, to be honest. For some of the same reasons, but also because if I saw Patience and Eugene—I'd have to ask the question I didn't want to ask. I'd been reading through some of the old reports Wittaker put together and in them, their names were William and Anne, but apparently, they were Patience Anne and Eugene William. Whatever.

Everyone seemed to change their names in the family to suit their moods. It wasn't important anyway. Not compared to other things.

"Look, you guys go see your families," Archie suggested. "Let them focus on you and you focus on them. We'll figure out Christmas when it gets here, but if Frankie wants to go see her dad or..."

"I don't, actually," I said and then sighed. "Look at the risk of several I told you so's, I have a lot of classes and I'm starting to slip a little. I could use this week to get ahead and to study for finals." Which were just two weeks after the Thanksgiving break. "We already selected classes for next spring, and I think I'm going to drop two of them before they start."

That got me looks. "Yes, I realize seven was too many and everyone told me that, but...."

"You like school and you're an overachiever, Angel. We know. Would it help if we were here to work with you on different projects or quiz you?"

"Maybe, I don't know. Maybe not. I barely get to see you guys and if you're all here, all I'll want to do is hang out with you and that won't get any studying done."

Coop leaned back in the chair and folded his arms. "Okay, first things first, we don't need to be gone the whole week. Which means, we take three days? We go see our families, eat, and visit. We'll make excuses for you two. Archie, that means you have to focus on helping her study and not distracting her the whole time."

"Pretty sure I can handle it," Archie said in a wry tone. "If not me, Jeremy is more than capable."

"I am, indeed," Jeremy said as he walked into the room. "I'll take care of planning out the menu so that you will have what you need for studying, Miss Frankie. You will also make sure you allot time for sleeping and let us worry about everything else."

Before I could open my mouth to say something, Jake jumped in with, "Then you break out the subjects, we split it up and we can work on quizzing you or helping when we get back. Our research project for history is mostly done, so leave that until I'm back."

"Same with our Humanities project," Archie said. "Fortunately, that's all four of us, so you already did most of the breakdown. I can finish it with Bubba and Coop doing the proof after. That's two of your seven down, right?"

I nodded slowly. Economics was probably going to be the hardest, followed by the introduction to marketing. But if I focused my reading time, I could make up ground. "Are you guys sure you're alright with us not going?"

"Yes, we're alright with you telling us what you need," Ian told me in a stern voice. "Would we like you with us? Of course. That said, you're all right, it's our first time going home in months and they're all going to be a bit clingy, so it might be easier to divide and conquer."

"I want to do Christmas here," I said abruptly and they all looked at me. "Like we did last year. When it was just the five of us. Six, because I would never not include Jeremy, but if he has friends or family he'd rather spend the holidays with, then he should. Or we can...we can go back to the lodge in Colorado."

I just wanted it to be us.

Ian, Jake, and Coop all exchanged a look. I worried my lower lip, but Archie knocked lightly against the table. "We'll figure it out. But I think you're right, I think it should just be us. Here is fine, this is our place or I can get the lodge from Grandpa. Whatever you want."

Coop grinned. "Colorado does have edibles."

"And a hot tub," Jake pointed out.

"Lots of room for experimentation," Ian murmured and I grinned. Of all the time we'd been spending apart, Ian and I had had the least amount of time to do more than find where the local club was. We hadn't gone to more than one or two of the munches, which let us meet other members. Saying we'd have time later had gotten old.

We needed to make time.

"Then Christmas is just us, no matter where we do it?"

"Agreed," they murmured one at a time, and I abandoned my chair to climb over Coop so I could hug him and Jake at the same time. They kissed me soundly each before handing me off to Ian and he gave me a long look that I didn't need any help interpreting. We were going to have a long talk soon about how much we'd all been pulling in different directions.

I nodded then kissed him softly. A promise. Archie was next and he pressed the most careful of kisses right behind my new butterfly tattoo. "And we're all going to work on pooling our resources to figure out this thing with the accident and Maddy. Once and for all, we'll get you your answers and we'll resolve this so she can't hurt you..."

"...or any of you," I reminded him, and Archie let out a long breath as he looked beyond me. I knew he was locking gazes with the others, but he finally nodded.

"So she can't hurt any of us ever again."

For some reason, even though we had discussed it some, that had me sagging in near total relief. Archie was a fixer and Jake was a protector. Ian and Coop would do what they thought was necessary, too. I just didn't want any of them being hurt.

"Cool," Coop said. "Tonight it's beer, pizza, and Mario Kart. Top two players get Frankie. The losers can watch."

Jeremy cleared his throat.

"And we're all just going to pretend that Jeremy didn't hear that," Coop said without missing a beat.

"Indeed," Jeremy said. "I'll take care of ordering the pizzas and will bring up the chilled beer in a little while. I'm assuming after the pizza has been delivered, I should consider retiring for the evening?"

I stole a look at him, but all of his disapproval was aimed at the boys. He gave me a little wink and I grinned. "You're the best, Jeremy. Thank you."

"For you, Miss Frankie. Anything. Should you ever require me to remove these hooligans, just say the word."

"Hey," Archie protested. "When did Frankie become the favorite?"

"That you need to ask, points to why she is," Jeremy told him crisply. "Now do go begin your games."

Technically there was still homework, but the guys threw all that to the side and we headed up to the game room. I actually went all the way up to change into comfortable pajamas, thick socks and a sweater. Even with the heat on and a fireplace, New York was *cold* now. I liked being comfy. Ian pulled me into his lap and draped a blanket over our legs as Jake and Archie set up the consoles so we could play.

It was ridiculous and adorable and by the time the pizza got there and Jeremy brought up the beer, we were all yelling at each other and zooming through. I won more than once and cost guys points. I was pretty fair though, I only went after who was leading at any one time. Particularly since the four of them teamed up on me.

We played late, sneaking down to make popcorn and grab sodas after the pizza and beer was done. My tummy was full, my heart was warm, and it was probably one of the best nights we'd spent together since the accident.

We were us again.

As it was, I was yawning so hard by the time we called it, that it didn't matter who got to sleep in bed with me, I was already half asleep. I let Coop take care of the tattoo goo that had to go on my fresh tattoo while I dabbed stuff on Jake's chest and the guys admired his dedication, cause it was huge.

It would look worse when it scabbed over, but I could still see the picture Guy had drawn up and it was going to be gorgeous. All that muscle inked up and colorful. Okay, maybe I wasn't *that* tired. The yawns cracking my jaw kept making a liar out of me though. Archie and Ian had both come out with the highest scores, but Archie actually gave Jake his spot. It was a wordless act of generosity and Coop even gave me a *see* look like they were figuring it out.

More, like it was all going to be okay.

"Movie preference?" Archie asked as he reached for the remote and Ian tucked me in. I wanted to curl up against Jake, but I also wanted to be careful of the new tattoo, so I settled back against Ian and tangled my fingers with Jake's.

I had no idea what movie they ended up picking because I was out five minutes later. Morning came too soon, but no one let me sleep in. Family meeting time with all my classes, projects, and homework so we could figure out schedules.

For the first time in like ever, I seemed to be the only one behind. There was an injustice in that, but I was also the only one taking so many classes, so I accepted the faults. With Jeremy delivering breakfast and coffee, we figured out the next five days, including time for me to actually go to the gym because Jake and Archie were both of the opinion I'd been skimping, and that reminded Jake that I needed to take up my boxing lessons again. Archie was in charge of that until Jake got back.

I rolled my eyes but honestly, the exercise would probably help shake the brain cells loose, and I drew the line at running in the freezing freaking cold. I was excited about living where there would be real snow. Less excited about freezing my ass off.

Ian had homework for me as well. He'd written two new songs and he sent me the tracks to download, listen, and practice. He was pretty sure with those two we'd have the full demo and he wanted to record over Christmas.

My stomach bottomed out, but I believed in him and he believed in us. "I promise I'll practice."

"When you can, we can work on it together after finals when you aren't so stressed. But don't worry, we'll definitely take care of the stress, too."

Plan in place, the guys split up to take care of some errands to get ready for their trip, and I headed up to my room with a huge tumbler of coffee to get to work. It was quiet for the first few hours, I'd barely realized how late it had gotten, until Archie came up to get me for dinner. We had one last night, the guys were flying out first thing in the morning.

Gritty-eyed from studying all day and even tired, I was already missing them. Not enough to get up at the crack of dawn as they slid out of bed one at a time and kissed me farewell the next morning with whispered promises to call and text though.

Jake and Coop were taking home presents for their sisters for me too and I'd sent a gift with Ian for his mom. They'd done as promised and checked in with me regularly and always answered when I emailed, but as much as I would miss my guys, I was kind of glad not to go.

Instead of staying in bed with me, Archie took the guys to the airport. They offered to grab Rachel on the way, but she was spending her break doing exactly what I was. Though her reasons were more she didn't want to deal with her family.

Our last check in had us no closer to tracking down Maddy. And I was almost asleep again when it hit me.

We'd been looking for Curtis or Grayson.

We'd never looked for Standish.

Once that thought took root, I couldn't get it out. Would she change her name to hide in plain sight? I honestly wasn't even sure how she changed her name to Curtis in the first place. Maybe she bought new IDs? I'd been born Francesca Curtis. I had the birth certificate now. No Grayson in place, so legally, Curtis was my last name even if it belonged to my maternal grandmother.

So...how hard was it to change a name?

I tried to work out all the knots in the idea as I showered and then got dressed. Jeremy gave me a smile when I came downstairs. It was still early, the sun barely putting on an appearance it was so cloudy out. Hopefully, the plane wouldn't have any issues.

Jeremy insisted that I sit down for breakfast, so I did and while he cooked, I sipped my coffee and made a fuss out of Tory who climbed into the chair next to mine. In fact, Tiddles rolled around on the floor batting at my feet, but I saw no sign of Tabby. The cats loved the huge house, they rambled about in it and there were cat trees in almost every room.

They were so spoiled, and I loved it.

I did an online search for Madeleine Standish. But it only turned up a few sites and people that weren't her. Okay so Standish wasn't *that* unusual of a name. A couple of them turned up people on TikTok. Definitely not Maddy.

I barely understood TikTok.

I was halfway through my omelet and debating calling Dominic, despite the fact it was a holiday week, when Archie got back. He gave me a kiss and slid onto the chair Tory abandoned. "I figured you'd still be asleep, Babe. I was looking forward to waking you up."

The snort from Jeremy just made me laugh. Which I kind of needed. "I would have been, but I got to thinking and it occurred to me that maybe we were looking for Maddy the wrong way."

He frowned as Jeremy brought him coffee and a plate. He wasn't alone in wearing that expression, so I explained the theory. We were assuming she'd go back to Grayson or keep using Curtis. But to be honest, I didn't even know if she still had a job. Archie had told me his dad gave Maddy the new place he'd bought in Texas, but that had actually been one of the first places the investigators looked. She wasn't there.

"Then she was working for Standish in some capacity, right? Or at least her company had ties to Standish or contracts before they were bought out?"

Scrubbing a hand over his face, Archie nodded. "Edward says he's not seen or spoken to her. I tend to believe him, but Grandpa isn't so convinced, largely because of Edward's feelings. That said—after the accident, he's feeling far less generous about her."

I wasn't sure whether to be relieved or sorry that it took something like the accident for Archie's dad to get his head out of his ass where Maddy was concerned.

"Well, a phone call or two can clarify if Ms. Curtis is still employed, though I should imagine with Mr. Ted in charge..."

"Yeah," Archie said, before Jeremy could finish the thought. "No way he would let her stay, and if Grandpa already paid her off to get rid of her, he'd have said something."

I grimaced. "That's actually something he'd do?"

With a deep sigh, Archie nodded. "They did it before." Then he told me about how his grandparents figured out Maddy was pregnant and his grandmother made sure that I wasn't Edward's before they gave her a sum to stake out her new life and to stay out of Edward's life.

Wow.

"That's like stuff you hear on television." Jeremy had cleared our plates and left us with fresh coffee for the time being. "But to be perfectly clear, if he ever tries to pay me off to leave you, I'm punching your grandfather."

"Good," Archie said and there came a quiet "Bravo," from the direction of the kitchen. We grinned at each other and then I leaned my head on Archie's shoulder.

"What do we do?"

"We stick to our plan," Archie said. "You get upstairs and get to work. We'll go to the gym later to stretch and get your mind off things, come back, shower and I'll fuck you against the wall until you can't stand up anymore, then you can finish up whatever work you can focus on and if you're still stressed, well I'll eat you out until that's taken care of too."

His grin grew as he spoke.

"I almost hope your stress level requires extra TLC on my part."

"You're awful."

"No, I'm good." He winked. "Now, send a message to your Dominic." The emphasis he put on Dominic's name entertained me. It was almost like he didn't want to sneer, but had dropped him to the level of peon. Archie Standish could be such a snob when it suited him. "I'll send one to my people. We'll let them sweat the details and we'll work on getting you squared away for your classes."

"I love you," I told him.

"I know, it's my irresistible charm and magnetic personality."

I giggled. "I won't argue with any of that." I kissed him and we barely managed to sink into the kiss when Jeremy cleared his throat.

"I regret to inform you, Miss Frankie, but you are now entering study time and the canoodling will have to wait until later, after the gym, apparently."

He said it with such a straight face that I grinned at him. "Thanks, Jeremy." I rose and accepted the large tumbler of coffee he'd made me. "You're the best."

"Of course."

"Cock block," Archie muttered as I headed for the stairs.

"It's good for you to have to work for it, Mr. Archie. It builds character. Now, I believe you have your own tasks to do."

I grinned. Three pings on my phone arrived as I got to my bedroom and there were varying pics of the guys on the plane, making goofy faces.

I snapped a selfie blowing them a kiss and sent it before sending the message to Dominic, then put my phone down and Maddy out of my mind. I refused to fail. Not when we had a plan and the downtime to make it happen.

Besides, the more I got done this morning, the more time I got to play with Archie this afternoon.

Chapter Twenty-Six

BROKEN NOTES

Ian

Four days back in Texas had been surreal. Mom and Dad had been thrilled that I'd come home for Thanksgiving, but less thrilled that I hadn't brought Frankie or the guys. Apparently, the parents had all discussed the possibility of a big joint Thanksgiving. Jake and Coop heard it from their parents, too. Jake's dad even called on the day itself to throw in his thoughts on the matter.

As one could imagine, informing them that we weren't picking places for Christmas, but instead spending it together just the five of us, landed even less well. Mom didn't talk to me for nearly a whole day, but Dad persuaded her before I had to leave to meet the guys for the flight that maybe, just maybe it was time to start making different plans of their own.

I checked in with Frankie and Archie daily. The four of us had our own text message outside of the family one we shared with Frankie. Her messages seemed to gain in cheer as the week went on, despite the stress. In the meantime, Archie kept us in the loop that Jeremy was on it with food, breaks, and coffee. She was going to be fine.

The last night in Texas, she sent me a clip of her singing one of the new songs. It was only a few lines, but distraction and doubt echoed under both the clip and her message.

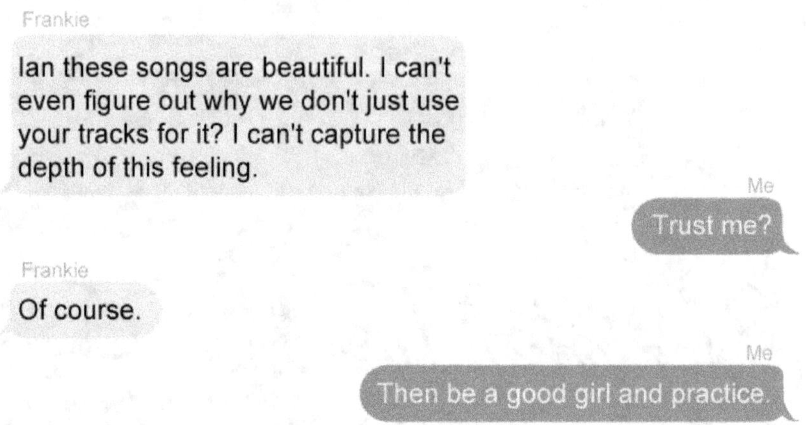

I loathed every single second of time her mother's doubting voice crept into her head. It seemed to happen less and less, which was great. But when she was tired and stressed, she retreated to the familiar. The familiar was she wasn't good enough. Bullshit on so many levels, but yelling at her wouldn't make my point. All I could do was coax, encourage, praise, and reward.

Occasionally, when she surrendered, I could pull her out of her own head. But we'd had less and less time to play. There were still clubs we hadn't visited, and it was as much my fault as hers. Differing class schedules made it a challenge to find free time at the same time they were open and available.

The last thing I wanted to do was stress her out. But there was genuine love and happiness in her eyes when we sang together. Especially when her hard work paid off. She might never be perfect in her own opinion, but in mine, there was no one else I wanted to do this with. I loved the music, I loved the notes, I loved the ebb and flow of them as we worked together.

The moment we found the right harmony, it was capturing perfection and it was worth every moment of blood, sweat, and tears.

To me.

I thought it was to her, too. But all on the flight back and our first week back at the brownstone as we were juggling exams, last-minute projects, and all-night study sessions, I began to wonder if maybe she was only doing it for me.

How many times had she gone along with things just to make us happy? I didn't want this to be something she settled for. Nor something she obligated herself to because we'd had fun over the summer. Hell, walking out on that stage when Torched let us join them had probably been the second most terrifying thing in my life.

Frankie had glowed.

Fuck, I refused to make this decision for her, no matter how much everything in me just wanted to smooth the way. The friction in the house had dramatically improved with Jake and Archie both dialing down the animosity. Frankie kept us looped in on what her attorneys and their investigators found, so did Archie's. Nothing, seemed to be the common consensus. The last bit of information on Maddy worried me.

Worried all of us. Frankie wanted us safe, but she was the one Maddy had always used, abused, and ended up hurting. One of my final projects was to compose a new piece of music based on one from a list the professor had provided. The rubric wasn't based on originality so much as being able to shift notes and harmonies to give the new piece a familiar feel, but change the tone.

Dropping a more popular, upbeat tune by a couple of octaves had taken the peppy song and given it a damn near mournful sound. That had given me an idea for the second piece I wanted to record with Frankie. It was based on one of her favorites from Torched, I'd reached out to KC and gotten permission to try it and her promise to keep it to herself until Frankie got to do it.

We were both kind of waiting for Frankie's reaction, and it was part of why I was sitting downstairs with my phone waiting for Frankie to get back from the last round of exams. If she'd managed to listen to both songs, she'd have reacted. No way she could miss it, and the lack of reaction was telling.

Worry for her ate away at me. Particularly when we woke up to fresh snow and Frankie barely reacted. Not even an ounce of her normal excitement. She'd only complained they'd have to leave earlier in case there were transit backups.

Not my angel's normal reaction at all.

When the door opened, letting her in with a brisk rush of cold air, I rose to catch her bag for her. Her cheeks were reddened from the cold and her hair that was loose beneath the knit cap was tangled. Little crystal flakes clung to her eyelashes and the red knit cap.

"Where are your gloves?" I asked because even her fingers were reddened, and I dropped her bag to take her hands in mine. Coat or no coat, she was freezing.

"I dropped them by the subway," she complained. "I was trying to get my bag on and my jacket was in the way and then I forgot to get out my card and I had to take them off to get to it..." The words came out half-stammering as her teeth clattered together. "And then they fell and there were people." I couldn't tell if it was just the cold or the anger that was breaking up her voice.

But the tears welling in her eyes were the final straw.

"Jeremy, can you get some hot chocolate made?" I stripped the damp jacket and hat off, then left them to hang before I just picked her up and headed straight up the stairs.

"What are you doing?" Frankie asked, even if every single syllable vibrated. "My stuff."

"Can wait."

Her lips weren't blue, but her face was definitely chapped. It was warmer the higher in the brownstone we went, but I didn't slow down until we were in her bathroom and I had the door shut.

I debated bath or shower. Depending on how cold she was, the bath might actually be more painful. Fuck it. I turned on the shower and stripped her clothes while she was trying to help. But her numb fingers weren't making much of a dent. I started the shower at lukewarm, because her skin was damn near frigid, even under the sweater and shirt.

"Get under the water, Angel," I directed her with a little nudge before turning up the heat in the bathroom and then shucking my own clothes to follow her in.

"It's not that warm."

"I know," I told her, ignoring how chilly the lukewarm water felt against me. One of the perks of the giant shower was we had multiple shower heads so the water could hit from different angles. "We're going to warm it up."

The prickles all over her skin betrayed her chill and I ignored how icy she felt as I wrapped around her. Bit by bit, I turned up the water until she let out a little sigh as we stood under the heated spray.

"Better?" I stroked the damp hair away from her face. I should have expected it, with all the stress and everything else, but when she lifted those damp eyes to meet my gaze and burst into tears it hit me like a brick.

I wrapped her up and just held her while she sobbed. It was too damn much. She had a habit of piling things on herself. The signs had all been there and we'd been responding, but not swiftly enough. Murmuring nonsensical words, I let her cry. As the sob gave way to hiccups, I moved her over to the stone bench to sit. She sagged there shaking her head.

"Whatever you're thinking about yourself," I informed her as I got the shampoo and began to lather it up against her scalp, carefully massaging it and being mindful of the new tattoo. It had scabbed over and the scab was starting to fall off, but better to leave it to do it on its own. "Stop right now, or I'll warm your ass right up with a spanking."

A shudder went through her and she dared a look up at me, squinting as some soap started to slide down her forehead, I caught it and pushed it back then resumed the massage.

"You had a bad day. You lost your gloves. You're cold. If you need to cry, then you damn well get to cry and that's all there is to it."

"I think I failed my test."

I paused and eased sideways so I could cock my head and catch her eyes. "Do you really think you failed your test?"

When she sank her teeth into her lower lip and shook her head slowly, I gave her a smile.

"But you're worried because you're overtired from too many all-nighters and you've been replaying the test in your head all the way back, second-guessing yourself?"

Her miserable look was all the answer I needed.

"Okay, head back," I murmured and she moved on the bench and tilted her head as I grabbed one of the sprayers and used it to wash the suds from her hair. Conditioner next. We'd all gotten the hair care routine down when she had her broken wrist. Even if I didn't get to help as much then, I got the lectures from Jake and Coop, particularly Jake who had handled most of her hair because he had the experience with his sisters.

Still, I wanted to calm her down and this was working.

"After the shower, we're getting you in warm pajamas and filling you up with hot cocoa and I bet there are brownies down there, because Jeremy was baking this morning. Then you're in bed and we're turning on rom coms so you can laugh until you cry if you need to..."

"I can't, I have to study..."

"You can," I told her sternly. "You will."

Frankie needed to be taken care of right now, particularly because she wasn't taking care of herself. She was so busy tearing herself apart to accomplish all the things while trying to protect us and worrying about her mother, she'd made herself last.

That didn't work for me.

And I told her as much.

While the conditioner was in her hair, I moved for one of the sponges she liked to use for soap and then began to work my way along her neck to her chest and then her arms. There was nothing sexual about this, but I wanted her to feel cared for and to relax. Bit by the bit, the tension ebbed from her.

"Ian, I still have a test tomorrow."

"And you'll ace it because you know the material," I told her. "You're exhausted and you'll do better if you're rested. Instead of taking time off last week, you studied and stayed up late, and even Archie said he caught you sneaking out of bed."

A guilty flush turned her pretty chest a rosy shade and I grinned as I knelt down to wash her legs.

"Apparently not even his magic tongue could knock you out. Poor guy," I said, keeping my tone light. "Lost the bet on how many times he could make you blackout from orgasming."

That pulled a laugh from her. "You guys did not."

"Oh, we did," I told her with a cheerful smile. "We always do. We like it when you come so hard you leave your body." I rinsed my fingers and then traced a line down her cheek. "I like it when you come so hard you get out of your head."

Her huff of an exhale sounded more heady than shallow and I grinned.

"Feeling a bit better?"

"A little, I'm sorry I cried all over you."

"I'm not," I promised her. "And on that note, I'm firmly putting our recording on the back burner until after the semester is done and you've had a break."

"Ian, no, I can do it, I promise, I'll get to the—"

I pressed my lips to hers and silenced the objection. The soft moan of complaint only made me smile and I tilted her head until she parted her lips and let me steal inside to stroke her tongue with mine.

"After the semester is done," I murmured against her lips. "Now be my good girl, and agree."

She shivered against me, but her expression softened. "I don't want to disappoint you."

"Never gonna happen, Angel, making music with you and recording with you is pure joy for me. But *you* are way more important. When finals are over and you've had real sleep again and you can relax. Then we'll do it all."

Licking her lips slowly, she said, "Will you tie me up again?"

"If you want," I told her. "If you need me to relax you, Angel, I'll take care of it. I'll do anything you need."

When she slipped her hand into mine, I gave it a squeeze and then I worked on rinsing her hair and the rest of her. She was warmer now, even her skin prickles had gone away and her nipples had relaxed. As tempting as it was to pin her to the wall, that wasn't what she needed right now. It also wasn't what I needed to do for her.

"Will you let me take care of you, Angel?"

"Yes please," she whispered. "For tonight, Sir Ian, I'll do exactly what you want."

I chuckled at the barest hint of a tease and my dick twitched. But no, it could wait and so could I. Tonight was about caring. A light knock on the door sounded as I shut off the water.

"It's Jake," he called. "I brought up the hot cocoa."

"Excellent, come in and help dry Frankie off and let's get her hair taken care of."

He was inside in a flash, Frankie gave me a look but she didn't argue when Jake snagged one of the towels from the heated rack and wrapped it around her. She let him dry her down, towel down her hair, then used the blow dryer to get all the damp away before he braided it. All the while she drank the hot cocoa.

I left long enough to get her clean pajamas and grabbed some clothes for myself. Jeremy said he would bring trays up for all of us when Coop and Archie were home and I thanked him. But as expected, he'd already brought up the brownies.

Once bundled in her pajamas and tucked into bed, we handed her the remote and Jake went to change before he came back up to climb in with us. He also brought up fresh mugs of hot cocoa. She was still scrolling through the movies and I didn't know if he'd heard me or Jeremy had, but her backpack stayed downstairs with her books, her laptop, and everything else.

Tonight was about her resting and sleeping. When she finally landed on a movie and began to grin, Jake groaned. "Really?" he said. "Do we have to?"

"Yes," I told him. "She wants to watch it. We're watching it."

He mock sighed like it was such a chore, but I didn't miss the hint of a grin as she hit play on *The Proposal*.

"Be nice," Frankie murmured. "And maybe we can watch Deadpool after."

"Ryan Reynolds marathon?" Jake asked and she grinned. "Sold."

I didn't say a word, cause she'd make him watch *Green Lantern* and he could never shut up about that movie when it was on. Settling in, I kept her cuddled up to me or to Jake. When Coop and Archie got there. We spread out some with trays of food and sure enough, she made Jake watch *Green Lantern* and when he wouldn't shut up, she put on *X-Men Origins: Wolverine*.

"I said maybe Deadpool," she deadpanned and something inside of me relaxed. This was exactly what we needed. What she needed.

Thankfully, she was asleep before the end of the last movie, so we all switched it over to the real *Deadpool*.

"She gonna be okay?" Archie asked, but it was Coop who answered before I could.

"Yep," he said. "Because we're going to make sure she is."

Yes, we damn well would.

Chapter Twenty-Seven
CHRISTMAS ALL OVER AGAIN

Coop

I don't know who was happier about finals being over, us or Jeremy. The first day after the last finals were taken—Jake and Frankie had their history final—we all slept in. Well, Jeremy probably didn't, but the rest of us did. Frankie was actually the last one up, which made all of us be quieter just to make sure she slept.

The deep shadows beneath her eyes were a cause for concern, but spring semester would be better. We'd managed to adjust our schedules and she'd taken only five classes instead of seven. I'd heard her on the phone arguing with Hank about five being easier than seven. Apparently, he agreed with us, but she wanted to stay focused and refused to let Maddy derail her any further.

Fortunately, when grades were posted, she not only passed all her classes, she'd done it with a 3.9. Not quite the 4.0 she wanted, but she was happy with it and thank fuck, so was I. Frankie had never failed a class in her life and this was not the time to start.

Electing to stay in New York for Christmas and not go to anyone's family also took a ton of pressure off us. We hadn't had much time to decorate. Though Jeremy had begun making some festive adjustments, he deferred to us for the tree. That was the first thing up on our schedule, after a huge meal.

We also made it over to Rockefeller Center to see the big tree and ice skating there. Not this year, but soon, we would learn how so we could go ice skating together. We did get some pictures and while we were supposed to be going to the lots to look for trees, we went shopping instead.

Three things I learned about shopping with all of us together for Christmas, we had to be extra sneaky to distract each other. The options for presents were too numerous and unreal. Either we found too much cool stuff, or it was absolutely wretched.

Frankie was a terror with a credit card that had no limit. Our frugal, cautious Frankie went a little crazy buying presents. She picked out the softest of leather coats for Rachel with a pair of matching gloves. Then she found some ridiculous shirts for her. The kids were easy to buy for, we also took advantage of the stores wrapping and sending them off to my mom, Trina, and her new siblings. Honestly, finding something for Alec proved the toughest, though she'd gotten some ideas from her dad and Kelly.

Then she mentioned that he liked trains and Archie knew just where to go, and hopefully after the massive train tracks, station, and trains arrived from Frankie, Hank and Kelly would still be talking to the rest of us. Archie kept eyeing jewelry and Frankie, but the only ring she wore with any kind of regularity was the one Jake gave her last year when we'd been at the lodge.

Our ring.

I had some ideas of what to get her, though the puppy had been nixed by the guys. She was too stressed at the moment. Maybe over the summer. Eventually, more than a little poorer, we found a Christmas tree lot and then the real debate began. Frankie loved them all, but she kept wandering from tree to tree. It had snowed recently, so it made the lot even more magical.

When it came down to a choice between a sturdy blue spruce and a fluffy fir, we were split down the middle with Archie and Jake voting for the spruce while Bubba and I liked the fir. That made it Frankie's choice, obviously. To no one's surprise, since she'd clearly been spending too much time with Archie, she picked both.

After making arrangements to get them delivered, we went in search of coffee and just wandered. Occasionally, we got a hot pretzel or candied nuts. Frankie loved vendor food and I couldn't blame her, it was amazing. We all made sure we spent as much time indoors as out, rather than let her get too cold. Eventually, Archie called for a car to pick us up, but only after the sun had gone down and she got to see the tree all lit up.

It was worth the wait in the cold, because Frankie's smile was huge. So was mine, for that matter. Maybe we'd all been more stressed than I'd realized. Time as a group had been sparse, so it was a good day just spent together.

Back at the brownstone, Jeremy had dinner ready for us and the trees had already been delivered. So that was our task after we ate. Under Jeremy's careful eye, we set up the spruce on the first floor and then took the fir up to the second floor lounge and entertainment room. We spent more time up here than down in the proper foyer.

Jeremy had ordered some ornaments, but we also had our boxes of them. So, after getting the trees fluffed, we got the trees decorated and it was kind of the perfect cap to a perfect day. The next few days went as peacefully.

Frankie's grandparents were apparently away in France for the holidays and had been since Thanksgiving. She talked to Hank and Kelly and promised she'd come up after the New Year, but that Christmas was an important anniversary of ours. She wasn't wrong, we'd all been dating her before, but Christmas was when we, as a group, became us.

For Jake's birthday, we took him to a comedy club and then went dancing. We all offered to let them go off by themselves, but Jake was good with sharing. I mean, I hadn't minded either, but then—it seemed like Jake and Archie were going out of their way to make sure that they included each other.

It might be overkill, but whatever it took to repair the relationship. If their determination kept their differences from driving them apart, then I was all for it. Though, admittedly, it was funny as hell when they both tried to give Frankie boxing lessons at the same time. Though Rachel had been invited to spend part of the holidays with us, she had already headed out to see the family she'd avoided at Thanksgiving.

Dominic Walsh stopped by a couple of days before Christmas to give Frankie an in person briefing as well as deliver a stack of papers related to her accounts and trust. To say Archie wasn't a fan was an understatement. Nor was Jake. I kind of half expected them to lift a leg and pee on her to make sure Walsh understood his place. However, the guy wasn't remotely put off. I swore the harder they glared, the more he flirted.

It was almost funny. Almost. I wasn't sure if they noticed the guy fishing for information about Rachel, but I had. So, he was interested in our cactus queen? Well, he better watch his step.

Unfortunately, we were still at a no go spot where Maddy was concerned. Archie had joked once about having someone taken out, but I don't think he'd keep it from us if he had.

At least I hoped he wouldn't. Wait, did I want to know if he'd done it or not? Hard call. No one would miss her. Except maybe the one person who'd been forced to miss her for her whole life. I shuttled that thought away, but I did actually pin Archie down when we were alone.

"If you did," I said. "Not that I'm saying you did. But if you did deal with the Maddy problem so it wasn't a problem anymore, would you be more or less likely to let us know? And I ask this out of concern as your friend because if we were to be questioned, there's no friend or brother boyfriend privilege."

Archie stared at me for a beat. "Are you asking me if I had Maddy offed?"

"Well, probably not so bluntly, but yes."

"Do you really want to know?" Archie raised his eyebrows, his poker face revealing nothing.

"If we could give her peace of mind? Then yeah, I do."

"Then no," Archie said with a wry grin. "I almost wish I could answer the alternative, but no, I haven't been able to find her either. I mean, I don't suppose we could get lucky and she could have walked in front of a bus somewhere and is currently listed as a Jane Doe."

We both pondered that and maybe it wasn't the most charitable of thoughts, but fuck would that be a relief. As it was, we both sighed and went back to business.

Christmas Day itself was fun and relaxed. Jeremy seemed surprised when we all gave him presents, though the cat cufflinks that Frankie gave him seemed to tickle him. Despite his protests, we insisted he join us for the Christmas feast he'd prepared. The cats all had catnip and were currently stoned out of their minds.

One of Archie's presents to Frankie included edibles. The state of New York had legalized recreational marijuana and Jeremy had gone to find some of the ones Frankie had enjoyed in Colorado.

"Better for your stress too," he pointed out when she laughed. Not that he was wrong, if we'd all thought about it sooner, it might have helped in the fall. We ended up with parts for new gaming computers that would keep us busy, but Frankie was the one to pull the biggest surprise.

She'd found some classic rock albums for Bubba on vinyl that he loved. For Jake, she'd gotten him a course for riding a motorcycle. He'd been talking about it forever and so she'd signed him up for one that started later in the spring. For me, she'd found a classic Millennium Falcon model set from fuck knew where, still in the box.

Archie's present, however, wasn't under the tree. It was outside and I wasn't the only one left gaping. Waiting for us on the street with a giant bow on it was a cherry red Bugatti. Archie stared at the car and then at Frankie.

"It's not his Ferrari, but I thought this might be fun. It's super rare and just barely on this side of street legal now."

"Holy shit," Jake said as he glanced from the car to Archie then back again. The Bugatti was not made for anything but speed. It was sleek, futuristic looking with smooth almost liquid lines and the red was Archie's favorite color. Granted it was only a two-seater, but the Ferrari hadn't exactly been roomy.

This car was to make Archie smile and for Archie to let go when he wanted to. It was also a three million dollar car. I wasn't even guessing, Archie had been talking about it a few weeks ago. Was *that* when she had the idea? Or had she figured it out earlier.

"Turns out, I can afford it," Frankie said with an almost sheepish smile and I wasn't the only one floored and laughing. Archie was still gaping at the car, because she'd shocked him. Well and truly. He kissed her fiercely before he and Jake descended on the vehicle.

"Nice job," I complimented her. "How much did it hurt to write that check?" Cause I had to know.

"Turns out that when you're spending that much, it's not a check." Then she grinned wider. "It's also why Dominic came by the other day. He'd finalized the paperwork to have it delivered and he wanted to make sure I had everything in order. Particularly because it had to be made street legal so he could drive it whenever he wants. Though, I'm told it's a speeding ticket waiting to happen and we should probably avoid *Fast and Furious* movies for a while."

"No shit," I said with a laugh, giving her more than a little side eye. "Archie's right, you're getting way too good at this sneaky stuff."

"You love it," she teased me and leaned into my shoulder. "Besides, you guys are always plotting to surprise me in different ways and there's only one of me."

Damn right there was only one of her and she was perfect. I kissed that butterfly behind her ear and then we went back inside to watch from the windows as Jake and Archie went over the car like two excited kids. She couldn't replace his classic Ferrari and she hadn't tried.

Instead, she'd given him a new toy, because it would remind him of today rather than the accident.

After Christmas, Bubba and Frankie locked themselves away to work on the rest of their demo. I went with Jake as he got more work done on his dragon, but Frankie promised she'd go on the next visit. I debated a second tattoo, but I really had no idea what I wanted. Honestly, watching Jake's come to life on his chest was a bit on the intimidating side and yet, it was so damn him.

"They do piercing here," Jake commented absently and I glanced around for one of the boards and then saw some books. That pretty much took the rest of my time as I checked out their work, even if it also meant looking at other guy's junk. One of the piercing artists also took some time to walk me through what the different recovery times were and what I could expect in terms of feeling.

Yeah, talking about getting my dick pierced wasn't weird at all.

Still, it was food for thought. Frankie really enjoyed the mini version and I had to admit, there was a certain appeal and curiosity. But I wasn't big on pain. Sacrifice? Sure. Pain? Not so much. Then I thought about the piercing she had in her navel and how fucking hard it made me every time I saw it.

Piercing was definitely still on the table.

We took off for New Year's and spent two days at a ski resort in Maryland. We didn't worry about anything but skiing, playing and having fun. After we got back, though, Frankie and Bubba played the demo for us in full for the first time.

More than one song took me back to the day in the studio back in Texas, but these songs weren't just good—they were excellent. One of the last tracks held so much longing and heartache in it, I wanted to cradle Frankie to my chest and keep her there forever. As soon as it finished playing through the first time, we all sat in silence, and I found Frankie staring at all of us with her hands steepled together in front of her mouth.

"Play it again," Jake said.

"Hell yes," Archie agreed and they hit repeat and the demo started all over again.

I'd tasted how powerful their music together could be that day in the studio. When they walked out on that stage last summer, their performance had blown me away. They'd been electric. But this demo? I looked over at Bubba. "Dude, you wrote all of these?"

"Most of them," he said. "There's three covers in there that we adjusted."

He said that so nonchalantly, like he hadn't been hiding all this massive talent all these years.

"What do you think?" Frankie asked and the hope in her voice had me dragging over to hug her tight.

"I think you're fucking amazing, Frankie Curtis, and I can't believe you're my girl."

"Ours," the guys all said automatically, but I ignored them.

"Listening to you sing? Hearing all that power in your voice and the songs that Bubba wrote on top of that? Fucking perfection. People would be insane not to adore you. You're not so bad either "

She'd never had the rock star dreams or the need to be in the spotlight, but they were bound to be—if they submitted this demo, there was zero doubt in my mind that they were going places. When Archie and Jake agreed even as they made copies of the demos for their own phones to listen to, I hugged her tighter. The wild beat of her heart said she was both scared and elated.

"Solid job," I told Bubba. And I meant it for more than just the music that he'd written. In a year, he'd pulled her out of the cramped box her mother stuffed her talent in by telling her how bad she was all the time, and look at her now.

At dinner, we discussed submitting the demo as a family. The vote was unanimous, Bubba said he'd also sent a copy to KC and Frankie grimaced. "She's listened to it three times and loved it. Told me if we didn't submit it, she would."

That was that. Bound Hearts officially submitted their full album demo to their entertainment attorney, who would take it from there. That just left spring semester and Maddy to deal with, not that any of us brought her up. Any time we ventured close to the topic, one of us would glance at Archie and he'd shake his head.

Her continued absence seemed to confirm her guilt more than anything else. It shouldn't have surprised me that Frankie brought her up the night before our first classes were due to start. "I think there's only one way she can be avoiding being found."

We were lying in bed and I traced lines down her naked back. Not really a topic I wanted to discuss in bed, but Frankie was relaxed enough that maybe she could.

"Do you want to talk to me about it?" I asked.

"Yes," she told me with a wry grin. "And no. I want to forget she exists and every time I seem to be right there, I remember again that she's out there and I don't know where and I don't know what. Maybe I'll never see her again. Maybe she's washed her hands of me for good."

"But you don't think so."

Frankie shook her head. "I think she's biding her time and relying on someone else's resources to keep her hidden for now, maybe she thinks this will all blow over since even the police haven't found any 'tangible' evidence that links her to the sabotage." Anger simmered in those words.

"Archie seems to think his dad is on the up and up.' For his sake, fuck I hoped Edward wasn't lying.

"I know," she murmured, then crossed her arms and lay her cheek against them as she faced me. "But my grandparents have been curiously distant, and traveling. A lot."

"You think they're hiding Maddy."

Fuck.

"Have you told your people that are looking, or Archie's?"

She sighed and I knew she hadn't.

"BFF or boyfriend?" I asked.

She smiled at me. "I know I need to tell them. My BFF and my boyfriend would say the same thing."

"Yes, we would." I stroked the hair away from her face. "And we would both like to remind you that you're not on your own. We got this."

We better have it. We weren't going to leave anything to chance. If she didn't tell Archie, fuck my life, I'd have to, and the boyfriend and BFF in me didn't care to betray that confidence.

"I'll tell them tomorrow," she whispered, then leaned over to kiss me. "I promise."

I trusted her to tell them, but it was a long time before I went to sleep. I was still awake when Jake crept in and I lifted my head.

"Sorry,' he muttered. "Couldn't sleep."

Me neither. "Worried about tomorrow when she's out of sight."

He nodded and climbed into the other side of the bed. "Don't even know how to get over this. I keep saying don't close my fist so hard, but…"

It was difficult. "I get it," I told him. "And I'm working on ideas, so when I come up with one, I'll let you know."

"Thanks."

Not long after, his breathing evened out and he was dead asleep, one hand on Frankie. We were all a little like that. Keep one hand on her. Make sure she didn't disappear. But we needed to be careful, because we were getting way too fucking close to smothering her and I for one had zero intentions of doing *that*.

Chapter Twenty-Eight

SECOND SEMESTER, BETTER THAN THE FIRST?

Frankie

Unlike first semester, I had a Friday class in spring for accounting. Weirdly, I was kind of looking forward to it. As often as I got reports for my various accounts and funds, it would probably be better if I understood it rather than having to rely on my attorneys and accountants to go over it. Archie and Jake both had a class in the exact same time slot, except theirs was a lab that would run longer than my class.

Basically, we could all share a car or ride the subway together there, but I was on my own leaving. Mondays, I'd head over to Rachel's place because we had an afternoon class together and it was an excuse to see her. My cagey best friend had been even more cagey of late. I couldn't lay the blame totally on her, we both had busy schedules.

Even with only five classes, I was still busy enough to not think about Maddy, the open investigation, or the thing that actually made me kind of ill—the submission of our demo. I hadn't been this nervous in years. Ian was a champion and seemed confident that we were on the right track. I, on the other hand, wanted this for him so bad I could spit.

We had made going to the gym together a regular thing, too. Way too early in the mornings on Monday, Wednesday, and Friday, the boys dragged me out of bed and to the gym. Twice a week I worked on my punches and dodges. The other day, I just got to hit a treadmill and run. I had to run on the days with punches and hits, but whatever. Usually, my brain wasn't all the way awake then.

Coop complained, but he always came to run with me. The best part of it all was that Archie and Jake worked together, even when they snarked at each other over what they were teaching me or working on. A big guy who worked at the gym, named Anton, actually interrupted our second week to point out that I was smaller than both of them, and had a shorter reach. He offered pointers for me to use those 'weaknesses' to my advantage and that was how we all got Anton as a coach.

"I like Anton," I told Rachel from where I lounged on her bed with one of my books open. I'd been filling her in on the winter break. "He's treating me just like the guys. Corrects my form, but doesn't flirt."

"Oh, I bet the guys love that," Rachel snarked.

"Yeah, probably. It helps that he's like 6'4 and towers over them, too." Not that my guys were short, but Anton looked like he could snap me in half with his pinky. At the same time, he showed me every weak point to aim for. He wasn't teaching me how to fight and win, he was teaching me how to fight and get away, while hopefully crippling the person attacking me.

Since I didn't particularly see, or have any desire to see, a future in MMA fighting for me, that was more than enough. The guys boxed more for fitness and stress relief. The fact they went for face shots hadn't been lost on anyone, so now they both had to wear padded head gear, which made me happy.

"Okay, so check this out," Rachel said, pivoting her desk chair so I could see her screen. It was a shot of a woman from behind in stark black and white. Her dark hair contrasted against the railing she leaned against and while she seemed the focal point of the image—it was the city spread out beyond her that drew the eye. I wasn't even sure how she'd done that. The cityscape seemed huge. "What do you think?"

"It's gorgeous," I murmured and squinted. "Why does it look like she is and isn't the focus of the shot?"

"Because," Rachel told me with a smug smile, "the whole concept is 'experience,' not person. The instructor has been really on us to develop our eye for composition. I had the same guy last semester so since this was our first assignment, I was going through some of my shots to find one that matched."

I guess that was it. It wasn't about the woman or the city, it was about the way she saw it or maybe her view of it. "That's so cool."

"Thank you. I'm rather proud of this one. We get to spend a lot of time in museums and going to galleries this semester, too. It's about learning the different styles while we find our own. There's a way to tell a story in a single photograph versus a series. Both have value and we're working with more than just digital medium."

"You're having fun," I pointed out and Rachel shrugged as she leaned back in the chair and put her feet up on the bed.

"I am. If you start comparing it to the microeconomics course of yours, you'll make me cry."

I snorted. "You take care of the art, I'll take care of the books when your photographs start selling worldwide and you're the most in demand photographer there is."

Her derisive snort as she shook her head called bullshit even if all she said was, "Name one 'famous' photographer that you know of."

"Annie Leibovitz," I said, then stuck my tongue out at her and she cracked up.

"Fine, bitch, fine, so you know photographers."

"There's Ansel Adams, too," I ticked off and tried to think of a third. "There was the lady that took the pictures of Gandhi, you were crazy about her, and I think she got to go to Russia to..."

"Margaret Bourke-White," Rachel supplied. "Fine, fine, fine. You know your photographers."

"I do, so that means when Rachel Manning is on the tip of everyone's tongue, I'll be able to say I knew her when."

"Bitch, you better still know me then or we're really gonna have problems."

I laughed. "Deal."

Head tilted, she studied me. "Any news on cuntasaurus?"

I shook my head. "Nope. The police are still considering the accident an open investigation, but the longer it goes, the more I think they aren't going to find anything. I haven't heard from Maddy, and the investigators that are working with Dominic haven't turned up anything. I thought I had a good idea with her changing her name to Standish or something, but no dice."

Nose wrinkling, she leaned her head back and stared at the ceiling. "Have you asked your grandparents yet? I know you don't want to, but..."

"They were in Paris for a while, I think they're coming back soon, or at least that's what it said in the Christmas card I got a couple of days ago." Nearly three weeks past Christmas and it had arrived, along with a check inside it for way too much money. They missed me. They loved me. They would let me know when they were back.

"How long have they been in Paris?"

I shrugged. "Since before Thanksgiving. I hadn't really seen them after our weekend there before school started. I actually don't even know if they know about the accident, unless Archie's grandfather told them." I hadn't. For the same reason, I hadn't wanted to tell Hank—initially. Now, I didn't want to tell them because I was worried they were helping Maddy somehow.

"Well, soon as you know they're back, I'll go with you if you want. Be your wing-girl and I'll even ask the hard questions." The offer wasn't an empty one. "I'll feel a lot better when that crazy bitch is locked up."

"Yeah," I said slowly. "Me too. I'm glad I haven't heard from her, and she hasn't done something to the guys but at the same time..." It was like there was this low-key dread in my stomach that never went away.

"When's your next class?" Rachel asked as she grabbed her boots and stuffed her feet into them.

I checked my phone. No messages from the guys, but it was early yet. They also knew I was heading to Rachel's. "About two hours. What's up?"

"Perfect, grab your coat, leave your stuff. We'll come back and get it before we head back to campus 'cause I have class then too."

Not arguing, I pulled my coat on and repacked up my stuff so it was together then tugged my hat down over my braided hair. The wind loved to leave my hair snarled, so it was just easier to braid it. Rachel studied me a beat.

"You know, I want to do another photoshoot with you if you're up for it at some point."

"Always," I said. "Just can it be on a warmer day if we're gonna do the nude shots and if they are nudes, you can't use them for class. Or at least don't let me be recognizable, then the guys won't have a cow."

She snorted. "Deal. Come on, let's go get coffee."

Now she was speaking my language. She locked her bedroom on our way out. It was so weird that she had locks on the bedroom door, but so did her roommate. The shared area of their dorm room was pretty sparse, even their kitchenette, like neither of them ever hung out here. "Do you even see her?"

"Eh," Rachel said with a shrug. "She does her thing, I do mine. And no, we don't. She has a boyfriend and she goes to his place a lot. I think. Either that or she's *super* quiet and stealthy like a ninja." The bland tone suggested Rachel didn't care either way. By the time we made it outside though, the wind was slicing through us like razor wire.

"Why did I think it would be fun to live somewhere it snows?" I asked for the umpteenth time. I did love the fall colors and I loved that some days the snow just came down and it was so pretty. Then there were days like today when I swore the wind was freezing my breath before it could leave my lungs.

"Because you have four bed warmers to keep you nice and cozy," Rachel teased as she linked arms with me. At the coffee shop, a guy paused and opened the door for us. I tossed him a smile and said a quick thanks. It was habit. Not everyone did it, but whatever. He followed us inside but there were a lot of people in the shop, and it was warm so I stayed huddled with Rachel as we made our way up the line.

Once we'd ordered we had to wait. Most of the tables were occupied so we'd be taking the coffee out of the shop. I had ordered a couple of pastries, and they were up first and heated. I swore I swallowed the first one whole while Rachel laughed at me.

"Score," she said and nudged me toward a table that a couple of kids were leaving, and I landed in the seat before the other guy was fully out of it.

"Sorry!"

He just laughed and winked at me. "Never apologize. I like pretty girls who are that eager to get in my lap."

Rachel made gagging noises and I rolled my eyes. Cause, really? Anyway, Rachel snagged our coffees and we sat there in the hum of the noisy shop and talked about everything and nothing. There was a karaoke night coming up soon and I let Rachel talk me into it. I did remember to send Ian a warning and I got back a kiss emoji with a thumbs up.

Our door guy wasn't so lucky, but he settled in to lean against one of those window ledge tables to drink his coffee. Rachel and I lingered so long, we actually had to double-time it back to her dorm to grab our things, and then we split up going to class. That set the pattern for the next couple of weeks. I kept running into the same guy from the coffee shop. Twice at the library. Once at the open mic night when we went to hang out and listen to aspiring comedians. He was even there when we did karaoke.

It was just weird. Or maybe I was getting used to seeing people around campus. There was a girl I saw from time to time, too. Not someone who was in any of my classes, but she always seemed to be in the same buildings as me. Usually arriving at the same time.

Worry about Maddy was making me paranoid. When I mentioned it to Coop, he spent a week tagging along and shifting his schedule just to see, but I couldn't spot the guy anywhere and then I just decided it was me. I also caved and went to Mental Health Services because they were right, I missed having Erin to talk too and while I was okay with driving and stuff, the accident had left other scars that I'd prefer healed over.

Coffee with Rachel on Monday was one of my favorite times. Ian snagged me after class on Tuesdays for lunch and then usually some studio time for fun. Jake met me on Wednesdays in between classes upstairs at the library. We'd come awfully close in the stacks, but so far, I'd resisted, besides he was constantly in the middle of getting work on his tattoo and I really didn't want to hurt him.

Archie and I took Thursdays for date nights and bit by bit, we were falling into a pattern. We had more family time with all five of us, but we made time individually, too. It eased a lot of the tension from the fall. Bit by bit, I'd have to say the second semester was way better than the first. Then the snow wouldn't stop and I was pretty sure I was gonna turn into a snowsicle, but at least it was pretty.

Hank called weekly, if I didn't call him. While he still didn't like my five class schedule, he did concede that I seemed to have the work-life-study balance down. It helped that I didn't have to get a job. It was the first time in years I hadn't had one. It was weird. I also had fewer chores because Jeremy was a magic man, he'd do laundry and run the vacuum and basically looked after the cats, not to mention shopped and cooked.

Jake had actually scored a part time job at an auto body shop and Coop was working as a tutor. Ian had found another part time spot as a music teacher. If I added a job to my class schedule, it would be harder to see the guys, but having everything done for me was apparently bugging me more than I realized.

Something I learned in my first session with Jeni, my new therapist. We hit it off and during the ninety minute assessment I also realized I'd been kind of letting life make the decisions for me and valiantly not rocking the boat. She complimented me on putting myself first like I had over Thanksgiving, needing that break, but if I really wanted to take charge in more areas, then I should start with one and go from there.

That led to the most uncomfortable conversation of my life, but Jeremy was a dear. Sunday dinners would be prepared by me. I'd also make sure we cleaned up the kitchen and I would love it if he wanted to join us, but if he also wanted to go out, then obviously that was cool. No lie, I sweated the whole conversation because the kitchen really was his domain. Eventually, I persuaded him on the condition that if I wanted to experiment with new recipes, I'd ask him for help when I needed it.

The guys cracked me up though, because Coop's only comment was, "*You* want to do more so *we* end up having to do dishes? How is that fair?" Not that he didn't do them. It was weird that such a little thing like 'cooking dinner' helped, but it did. Baby steps and all, but I'd been independent for so long and I loved that Jeremy and the guys wanted to look after me. The point was, I could also look after them.

Course, then Archie decided we should sign up for a gourmet cooking class together and I was game, but Jeremy stared at us askance until I promised him pictures. It was funny, but the fact Archie kept trying to learn how to cook just endeared him even more to me.

The first response we got to our demo tape came. Ian waited for me to be there to open the email. Breath held, I crossed my fingers for him and even though I kind of expected the rejection, it didn't make it sting any less. At least the notes the producer sent back seemed like they meant well, even if we didn't agree with them.

"That's just one person," I murmured and Ian nuzzled a kiss to my cheek.

"That's right, Angel, just one. We'll find the right fit for us and we're not changing for them. I don't care how long it takes."

I did, but only because I wanted this for Ian so badly.

And, in my quieter moments where no one else could hear me, I wanted it for me too. I wanted it to be us, even if it terrified me. Maybe because it did. Some of the best things that happened in my life had been because I did the scary thing, took the scary step.

These were definitely scary steps.

Chapter Twenty-Nine

ENEMIES OR LOVERS?

Frankie

Archie woke me up Monday before it was even time to go to the gym, with his face buried between my thighs and my body already taut with an impending orgasm. I squirmed under the sensual assault, but he didn't let up. From the faint scrape of his teeth to the thrum of his tongue, I couldn't have stopped myself from coming if I tried. Even as the first cry escaped my mouth, however, Coop swallowed it with a hard kiss.

Oh fuck, I'd forgotten Coop had gone to bed with us. His tongue swept in against mine even as he cupped one of my breasts and flicked the taut nipple. It was just too much. The orgasm crashed down on me as pleasure rolled out in waves. I was torn between reaching for Coop or reaching for Archie. One moment, I was kissing Coop and then Archie dragged me upward and I was kissing the taste of myself off his lips.

I dug my nails into his shoulders as he continued kissing his way down my neck and I shuddered when he sucked what was sure to be a hickey over my pulse point. There was a kind of urgent need to him today and I didn't know where it was coming from, but I was there for it. The bristle from his unshaven jaw scraped against me and I ran my hands down his side.

The heat of Coop's presence was right there against my back as Archie kissed back to my lips and then I caught his face against one palm while I slid the other down to cup his dick. It was hard, hot, and pulsing against my fingertips. I teased the moisture around the head in a lazy circle as he began to thrust against my hand.

"What do you want?" I asked him in a breathy whisper. The pleasurable quakes from my earlier orgasm continued to roll through my system. Every kiss and touch magnified it, like a drug that promised more and more.

"Suck Coop off," Archie told me as he slid his hand down to my ass and squeezed. "And roll over so I can fuck you so deep, you never forget I'm always there."

My pussy clenched at the instruction and not just because Archie planned to fuck me from behind. It was one of his favorite positions. Though to be honest, Archie loved all the different positions and got creative too. No, this was because he was inviting me to bring Coop into it. Well, telling me to bring Coop into it.

Since the day Coop watched us fuck against the wall of the apartment when we'd gotten back from shopping, Archie hadn't minded Coop watching. Save for my birthday, he'd never invited him in to play before, even when he was right there in the bed with us.

I leaned back, my hesitation only in making sure Archie was really okay with this. He'd shared me with Ian, but not Jake or Coop. Not like this. I swore, he and Ian were determined to destroy my vagina, the fact they both got off on it just made it that much hotter. The feeling of them stretching me as they pushed against each other was also hot as hell. No lie.

"Go ahead, Babe," Archie said, drawing a line over my lips with his thumb before thrusting it against my tongue. "Take him as deep as you can,

I want you gagging on his cock while I fill you up." The corners of his lips tilted up as I sucked against his thumb. "You good with that, Coop?"

"Fuck yeah, I am," Coop agreed readily and I tilted my head to find him palming his own cock and stroking it. It was so damn big, the first time together I'd worried he wouldn't fit, but he always did, even if it stretched me to hell and back. I'd been getting better at giving him head. It helped that between the four of them, I got lots of practice.

Releasing Archie's thumb, I licked my lips and twisted to roll over and spread my legs on either side of Archie so I half-straddled his lap while I angled my mouth over Coop's dick. "And it's not even my birthday," I teased before licking him from base to tip. His hand tightened against himself as I traced my tongue around him and then up. I swirled the tip, like he was my favorite kind of ice cream, and his breath came in shallower pants. I swore the vein along the underside of his cock seemed even thicker than normal.

Behind me, Archie rubbed his hands up and down my back, pausing to trace my tattoo or to squeeze my ass. It shouldn't have turned me on so much to realize he was watching me as I began to swallow Coop's dick and I kept going until the head bumped against my throat.

His breathing hitched along with Coop's. The slow thrust of my head up and then down as I swallowed past that gag reflex took Coop deeper and for a moment, I couldn't breathe. It was like Archie waited for that exact moment to line himself up and thrust into my eager pussy. If I hadn't already been wet, I would have been drenched by now.

I moaned around Coop's cock and he fisted my hair as he began to swear in a litany. He gave the gentlest of tugs and I lifted my eyes to meet his gaze. He wanted to control the thrusting and I was losing pace with the hard push of Archie beginning to rock into me. He twisted his hips with every shove into me like he couldn't get deep enough, and his words replayed in my head as I relaxed my jaw and gave a nod to Coop.

That was all the encouragement he needed. Every plunge seemed to push him farther into my throat and Archie deeper into my pussy. They were striking sparks in my system. My eyes watered from the gagging, but I kept swallowing around it, sucking in noisy breaths of air each time Coop allowed me.

I wished I could see Archie's face, but I could feel the bite of his fingers on my hips and hear the soft, dirty praise he heaped on me. "That's it, Babe, take every inch into this luscious body of yours. Fuck it's like you're sucking me off even as your pussy clamps down on me, like you never want me to leave. Harder, Babe, harder...so fucking beautiful when you're like this."

All I could smell was Coop, all I could feel was them, the world splintered right down the middle and I swore my vision went white as I came. Coop let out a shout and eased back some and as he released and I had to remember to breathe as I swallowed. Thank fuck Archie wasn't far behind him, because I was a messy, cum-soaked mess when I collapsed between them.

"Now that," Archie said after a while, rubbing my ass, "is how you start a Monday right." Then he gave me a light smack. Let's get this gorgeous ass into a quick shower. We still have to go to the gym."

I groaned. "I changed my mind," I told him. "I hate you."

They were both laughing at me, but no one commented on my slightly off gait walk or the fact that I was definitely moving slower than normal.

I was still basking in the afterglow of those orgasms hours later when I headed to Rachel's after class. The door to her dorm room was open when I got there and I hesitated until a raised voice drifted out from her bedroom door which was also open.

"No one fucking invited you," Rachel snarled. "Nor do I care if you think we could have a good time. How did you pass law school if you struggle to understand the concept of 'no'?"

"Because no is just an invitation to present a new argument." The voice that answered her had my jaw dropping. Dominic Walsh had definitely been interested in Rachel, but I'd been unaware that he'd actually tracked her down. "So, you don't like this case, I'll bring you another."

"Oh please, no means no you arrogant, overstuffed peacock. You strut around in your five hundred dollar suits like you're someone important. But you're the errand boy, you run errands for the partners at your law firm. Your job is to kiss up so they notice you." The hostility in Rachel's voice was jagged as hell.

"They're a little over a thousand for the suit, but thank you for noticing," Dominic continued all cocky charm. I had to clap a hand over my mouth because he reminded me of Archie. If she'd insulted him, it wasn't evident in his voice at all. "In fact, I think that's the problem, you keep noticing me and you don't want to, so you have to convince yourself you don't."

"Well, Captain Freud, maybe you should go back to school for a different degree, because psychology is not your thing."

"Go out to dinner with me," Dominic invited. "What do you have to lose?"

"Time, mine is valuable. In fact," Rachel continued. "I'd appreciate it if you quit wasting mine. I have a date due here any moment and trust me when I say, that five minutes with her is far more valuable to me than any overpriced meal you have to offer."

"You really didn't seem to mind what I had to offer night before last."

"Everyone makes mistakes," Rachel retorted. "Besides, haven't you ever heard of try before you buy. I tried. Definitely not buying."

"Who hurt you?" Dominic asked in an almost gentle voice.

Her laughter was not friendly. "There's the door, Nicky Boy, please let it hit you in the ass on the way out."

"So that's a no for dinner tonight," Dominic confirmed.

"Ding, ding, ding. Give the man a cookie."

"So, what about tomorrow?" he continued absolutely undeterred. I didn't know whether to applaud his bravery or clock him with a book for being stupid.

However, the time for me eavesdropping was over. I knocked on the door to the open suite and called, "Hey Rach, sorry, I'm late."

Something fell in the bedroom and Dominic appeared one step ahead of Rachel, though she was giving him a little shove to get him moving. "No worries, I just have to show the pest out."

'Actually," Dominic said with a sudden smile at me. "You were next on my list to reach out to, Frankie."

I suddenly regretted not having him call me Miss Curtis. Raising my eyebrows, I said, "Really? You thought you'd find me here?"

"Well, no this was a personal visit," he continued, shooting Rachel a look so heated I had to resist the urge to fan myself. "My business with you is purely professional."

"Too bad," Rachel interrupted. "Call and make an appointment. This is my time. We have our coffee date and you're not invited."

"Very well," he said as though that were perfectly reasonable, but pulled out his phone as he studied me. "When would be a good time? I have some information on Ms. Curtis and her current whereabouts as well as an update from the detective working on your case."

"Since Friday?" I asked. Because we'd spoken two days earlier and it had been more of the same. Rachel folded her arms, her expression doubtful and challenging as she glared at Dominic.

"Don't you drag Frankie into your manipulative plans. Trust me, you won't like my response to it," Rachel declared. "Or the boys if I tell Archie and the others what you're up to."

"What I'm up to is seeing to the needs of one of my firm's more important clients," Dominic assured her. "Also, this is between Frankie and me, Rachel. It's not personal at all."

Rachel rolled her eyes. "Send her an email. But do it from somewhere else."

"Maybe you should go," I said quietly. "I'll check my calendar when I get home tonight."

"Of course," he said, all easy smiles before he glanced at Rachel again. "I'll call you tomorrow."

"Call whenever you like," Rachel yelled after him as he headed out. "I'm not going to answer."

"Thanks for the invitation," he said over her second part. "I'll call you later this evening."

Rachel let out a little screaming noise and all but slammed the outer door before she looked at me.

Holy shit.

"You had sex with him." It wasn't a question.

"I'm not talking about it," Rachel gritted out. "Let's dump our shit and go get coffee. I could use a shot of vodka or two in it."

"I don't think they sell that at the coffee shop," I told her, but I dumped the stuff on her—messy bed and that was when it hit me. Her whole room was messy. Messier than normal. The boxer shorts sitting on her chair were definitely not hers.

Rachel slammed drawers and dragged out her coat, before raking her hands through her disheveled hair. The faint puffiness to her lips and a very visible hickey were just more confirmation.

"Are you okay?" I asked as I set my book bag down. I hadn't tugged off my cap or my gloves.

"I don't want to talk about it," Rachel said. "Or him."

"Okay." I followed her out of the room and paused when she didn't close the door behind her. "Do you have your keys?"

She paused mid-step, swore and spun around to charge back into her room. I barely dodged in time. "I really, really don't want to talk about it," she said when she returned with her keys and closed the door. This time, she met my gaze.

"Only if you promise me he didn't hurt you." Because if he really didn't know that no meant no, this was going to turn into an entirely different conversation involving bone breakage. Jake was on campus right now.

She blew out a breath and stared upward for a minute. "No," she said. "He didn't hurt me or force me or in any way coerce me. He literally charmed my pants off and I enjoyed every second of it."

Well. Okay.

"And that's why it's over and done with, because nothing *that* good happens a second time. But he's thickheaded and pushy and seems to think if he keeps it up, he'll make it into my pants again."

She led the way out of her apartment and I followed her.

"But you don't want to talk about it."

"No," Rachel said as we headed downstairs. "I don't want to talk about him or his pierced dick or the fact that he has a tongue piercing."

Wait... "He has a tongue piercing?"

"I said I wasn't talking about it," Rachel snapped. "He was a glorious one-night stand and that's where he needs to stay. You're going to have to hire a new law firm, I think that will just make it easier on everyone."

Uh huh.

"Smooth talking jerk," she muttered as we reached the doors to the street. Dominic's wasn't the only familiar face out there. The guy from the other day caught the door as Rachel slammed it open. She jerked to a halt when Dominic straightened from where he leaned against the car.

"Can I offer you lovely ladies a ride?"

"Hell no," Rachel snapped and flipped him off before grabbing my arm. I didn't know whether to laugh or yell at him for being a dick. But he was so clearly under her skin. Best friend rules meant if she hated him, then I had to, too.

Only I didn't think she hated him.

While Rachel never looked back, I did. Dominic wasn't there. So maybe he had taken the hint. But the same guy I'd seen everywhere was. It was weird. Like he wasn't there the day Coop went with me everywhere, but he was now? Was he just sick that week? It was hardly like there weren't hundreds of people around. NYU was huge and the student population filled the streets around us, not to mention people like Dominic who were working.

At the coffee shop, Rachel had finally stopped muttering as we stood in line and she glared at the boards with the coffee offerings like they'd done her a personal affront. When we placed our orders though, we had another surprise. The barista didn't charge us because the gentleman in the corner had already paid for our drinks.

I knew who would be there before I even looked and so did Rachel. She let out a growl. An actual growl, before she stomped over to the corner where Dominic was seated sipping his own coffee and I thanked the barista before moving around to wait for our drinks. I caught the big guy who'd been following me watching Rachel, too and I was still looking at him when he turned our gazes clashed.

He gave me a faint smile like you would acknowledge someone you caught staring then seemed to steadily focus ahead. When our drinks came up, I moved to look for a table and it was either stand there holding the drinks or head over to where Rachel and Dominic were engaged in a heated, if hushed debate. The delight in his eyes was hard to miss.

Rachel was so fucked, and I wasn't sure she'd recognized it yet. Dominic's interest wasn't going away anytime soon unless...

Well fuck, maybe I would have to get a new attorney. I slid over to the table and set Rachel's coffee down and murmured something about giving them a minute.

"We won't need a minute," Rachel snapped even as Dominic grinned. "Thank you, Frankie."

Right.

I retreated to the window ledge that served as a table for people standing. My friend was still in the store, still didn't have a table and this time set himself up against the other end of the same window table ledge I was leaning against. Eventually, Rachel tore herself away but only after we'd been there an hour. She gave me an apology that I didn't need, and we headed back for her dorm.

After my second class, I told her I'd be at the coffee shop for a bit if she wanted to talk but she said she'd text me. Once there, it was a little quieter than earlier and I managed to get a table. I'd pulled out my phone to check messages from the guys when I spotted my friend again.

He was at the counter ordering a drink. Like he'd just arrived.

Five minutes after I did.

Call me paranoid but that was just weird.

I managed to snap a pic of the guy, then I sent a message to Jake. He had a late lab on Mondays in the engineering building.

Me: *My friend is back and I'm by myself. Can you meet me at the coffee shop?*

Jake: *On my way, Baby Girl.*

The swiftness of his answer said maybe I wasn't paranoid, but I thought about all the "boxing" lessons I'd been having and kept watch while not staring at the guy. Jake arrived not ten minutes later, a little breathless, like he'd run. No sooner had Jake walked in then my friend tossed his coffee and went out another door.

Yeah. That wasn't suspicious at all. Jake took off after him, but he returned a few minutes later jaw clenched. "I lost him. Are you sure it's the same guy?"

"Yes." I'd taken a picture earlier in the day when I'd been there with Rachel and I showed him both pics. Jake's expression darkened. "I'm not imagining this."

"No, Baby Girl," he said, hugging me to his side as he called for a car to come pick us up. "You are not."

Chapter Thirty

W.T.A.F.

Frankie

It didn't take long for everyone to get home after the incident at the coffee shop. If not for the fact that I had a photo of the guy at separate times, I'd have almost been embarrassed by my reaction. Still, Jake seemed to be taking it seriously. Jeremy fixed coffee for us as soon as we were in and I paced the sitting room, torn between going upstairs and wanting to be right there as they came in.

Coop and Ian were the first two home and Archie wasn't that far behind them. Jeremy brought out more coffee and snacks as I related what happened and showed them the photos. Jake said he'd seen the guy, but only from the back. While he couldn't confirm it, he also believed me. I could ask Rachel or Dominic if they had seen him earlier, but they'd also been pretty focused on each other.

"But none of you have seen him?" Maybe I was making too much of this? Once or twice, maybe even three times could be a coincidence, but this had been going on for weeks. I couldn't swear to it, but I was pretty sure he'd been around before the holidays, too. But I'd been so distracted then.

"Babe," Archie said, catching my hand to keep me from pacing past him again. "It's okay."

"No, it's not. If this guy is following me, maybe he has something to do with Maddy." The fact that I even said it aloud made it seem even crazier to me. Suddenly, Maddy who'd been a neglectful, terrible mother seemed to have achieved super villain status. "Maybe she's watching all of us, trying to find a way to hurt you again."

Instead of letting me go, Archie slid his fingers through mine and gave my hand a squeeze. "Babe, breathe. I promise you. This guy isn't going to hurt you and he's not going to hurt us."

Any other time, the arrogant confidence would probably make me at least smile, but had Archie forgotten what she'd done to his car? Before I could say that there was a ring of the doorbell. Jeremy moved to answer it and I frowned as the man was shown inside.

It was my stalker.

Well, fine, the guy from the coffee shop.

"Miss Frankie, Mr. Archie, a Dustin Shay is here to see you."

Archie exhaled as I glanced at the guy then to him. Jake was already moving to step in front of me. "Well, not every day a stalker comes knocking on the door. Thanks for giving me a face to break."

Before Jake could hit the guy though, Archie got the way. "Wait—guys—Frankie. Wait. Dustin Shay works for Pax Security."

Security.

He shot the man a look. "They've been providing escort and surveillance back up for Frankie whenever she's not with one of us."

I swore my jaw dropped.

Archie met my gaze. "They were supposed to be discreet. But I'm guessing between the weather and the fact you love your coffee...I'm sorry,

Babe, the intention wasn't to scare you."

The man in question inclined his head. "My apologies, Miss Curtis. I really was there just for your security. When Mr. Benton arrived, I left because usually when one of them meets you, they bring you home."

Security.

"And exactly how long have you been following me?"

Mr. Shay glanced at Archie who said, "Pretty much since we found out the brakes had been cut."

That was months.

Months of people following me.

"There's a team of four, we rotate. But one of ours got pulled off the last couple of weeks and I've been covering for him." Mr. Shay sounded apologetic. "I'll keep a better distance going forward, but I'd rather be at hand in case something happens."

There was a kind of roaring in my ears as Ian and Coop asked questions. How did they decide shifts? Oh, of course they got my schedule from Archie. When I updated the group chat with changes, he let them know.

No one else had guards. Jake had asked that question and I kind of latched onto that fact. The guys could look after themselves. But... "We don't even know if I was the target," I pointed out. "It could be you. So why don't you have security too?"

Jeremy made a sound of disapproval and Mr. Shay excused himself, saying he should probably go and he once again apologized for scaring me.

Yeah. Scaring me.

I stared at Archie after the door closed behind my new—well not so new—bodyguard and waited. Jeremy stepped out, clearly not any more comfortable with the tension in the room than I was.

"Well?" I demanded. Blowing out a breath, Archie raked a hand through his hair, and I could almost hear the thought process. "You didn't want security. You wanted to be the easier target. If it was really Maddy trying to hurt you to hurt me or your father, you wanted to give her a free shot."

"I don't think Archie's that foolish," Coop tried, but Jake shook his head.

"No, it's fucking brilliant when you think about it." Of all the people to agree with Archie, I shifted my attention to Jake. "Baby Girl, security on you means we know you're safe, Arch knows you're safe. He also knows that if it's your mother and since no one else can find her, the best way to flush her out is to give her another opportunity."

I swore I could feel Ian's sigh all the way to my bones as he pinched his brow. "When were you planning on telling us this was the plan?"

"Hopefully, it wouldn't have been necessary," Archie said. "At the time, Jake and I weren't exactly getting along and you and Coop were doing your best to play peacemaker. Rather than make this another point of contention, I made an executive decision."

"I get it,' Jake said, agreeing with him. "Protecting Frankie comes first."

"But the guy scared the hell out of her," Coop argued. "How the hell is that protecting her?"

I still hadn't found the words as they batted this back and forth between them. The security had been on me for months, following me to and from class. To the coffee shop. To outings with Rachel. The only times they backed off was if I was with one of the guys.

That meant for most of the holiday season, when I'd spent all my time at home or with them, they'd been out of the picture. But it also meant that Archie had been out there with a big neon target painted on him and this was *not* okay.

"Babe," Archie said and reached out for my hand but I yanked it away, grabbed my backpack and headed for the stairs. "Frankie, Babe... listen."

"No."

One word and it whip cracked through the silence of the room. I had one foot on the bottom step and I glanced at all of them, but focused on

Archie.

"No, I don't want to listen. Not when you had months to tell me you were going to do this. That you wanted to give yourself some peace of mind to not worry about me, even if I've been spending months worried about all of you and what she might do, if this was her. I went around all of you to find out more from the detective and to look for my mother. But I also came clean with you. You could have told me then. You didn't."

"To be fair," Archie countered, meeting my gaze unflinchingly. "I didn't think you'd agree to it. I didn't want that fight with you. I just wanted to know you were safe."

"While you were what? A human target? It's okay for you to be in danger as long as you know someone is watching my back?"

"Yes." Not an ounce of hesitation. "Given the same set of circumstances, you'd do the same damn thing."

"I guess I should have," I admitted. "Bad on me for not thinking of hiring bodyguards for all of you without your knowledge so that they could keep tabs on your every movement and report back."

"Frankie, they weren't spying on you."

"Technically," Coop began but Jake cut him off.

"Stay out of this. Archie was right to do this. Frankie gets stubborn and she hates to feel hovered over. This was the best way to do it," he continued and at least he had the courtesy to glance from Coop to me. "Seriously, Baby Girl, you were safe and you didn't have the feeling of being smothered. Maybe he should have told you, but if you'd never noticed the guy, it would still provide you with security and I'm okay with that."

"Cool, make sure Archie hires some for you, too. In fact, why not someone permanent who walks us from door to door, they can all wear little ear pieces and keep in touch. When we want to talk I can have my bodyguard call yours. Who knows—maybe I'll get someone cute and they can really piss you off by pretending to flirt with me in public so it's not obvious they're a bodyguard."

I was so fucking mad at them.

"Okay, now you're being unreasonable," Archie said and Ian sighed.

"Arch, stop."

"What?"

"Just—stop."

"Let him, Ian. He thinks he's right, he might even be right. But there's one thing you forgot in all of this. It wasn't just your decision or your peace of mind. You should have told me. You should have taken steps for yourselves, too. Like I said, I don't want to talk about this anymore." Not when that guy's presence had scared me enough to have Jake come running. When I'd really thought it had something to do with Maddy.

What made it worse was Jake seemed to be okay with it. I made it all the way to my room before Coop caught up to me, but I shook my head.

"I don't want to talk right now," I admitted. "I'm so angry, but more than that—" I was hurt. Because once again, they didn't trust me with me. Enough to at least talk to me about it. I hated secrets. I hated deception even more.

"I know," Coop said, but he wrapped his hand around my nape and dragged me into a hug. "I even get why they did it and I know why you're mad. They're idiots, but they're idiots who love you."

"And that makes it okay?" I was trying very hard not to cry, but a part of me wanted to scream. Yes, having a security detail made sense. But a secret one? Non-negotiable while they ran around free as birds for Maddy to come at them?

"No," Coop said slowly. "It doesn't. Pretty sure, Bubba just ripped into him when you walked up here."

Great, now Ian and Archie were going to be fighting. "I just need some time."

"Okay. I'll get the coffee and the snacks and bring them up. Then bring up any dinner, okay? You don't even have to entertain. I'll bring it in, leave it and go."

He was offering to be my buffer and I managed a weak smile. "Is that my BFF or my boyfriend offering?"

"Both of us. I'd offer to kick their asses for you, but I think there's been enough physical fights and those hard heads are gonna have to learn to see around that kneejerk reaction to put you before everything."

"You do it,' I pointed out as I walked into my room and dropped my bag on the bed.

"No," Coop said as he folded his arms. "I can see around doing it. But I'm always going to put you first. Sometimes, that means backing off cause you need us to not get in the way of your independence. Doesn't make me any less of a neanderthal who wants to protect his woman. As much as I think he was wrong about not telling you what he was doing—I don't disagree with him getting you security. We were all trying to juggle our schedules to be with you as much as possible."

I nodded slowly. "Okay."

He sighed. "I'm sorry, Frankie. He loves you. You're more important to him than anything else."

I knew that. Like I said, I got it. Didn't mean I had to like being excluded. Coop lingered for another few minutes, but when I didn't say anything, he went down for the coffee and the snacks, then brought them back up.

True to his word, he brought up my dinner later.

Archie and Jake both came up and knocked on the door. I was childish, I put my headphones on and didn't answer. Hey, maybe they'd repair the rest of their relationship by being on the same side. I was alone when I went to sleep, but try as I might, I couldn't drift off. I pretended to be asleep when Coop crept in and curled up around me. I was out seconds later.

He was already gone when I woke up in the morning. Ian was waiting downstairs with coffee to go and a bag of pastries from Jeremy. If we left now, we'd miss Jake and Archie altogether and I took him up on the offer.

I couldn't avoid them forever, but I didn't really know what to say to them. They weren't sorry about their choices. For the rest of the week, I just skipped going to boxing with them. I made arrangements to work with Anton later in the day. I was sure my babysitters would let them know. I didn't *keep* it from them. I told them straight out, I needed a break from them and I would continue training.

It pissed them both off. Archie stopped trying to talk to me by the third day because I kept cutting him off. I couldn't let him talk his way out of this one. Not until he admitted what he'd done wrong in handling this.

By the end of the second week, the tension in the brownstone was at a breaking point. Ian seemed to understand more than Jake did, though like Coop, he appreciated the fact I'd been safer. He would have preferred to be in on the decision-making—imagine that—but he also believed Archie when he said they all thought I'd have fought having personal security.

Maybe I would have. Maybe I wouldn't. We would never know. I spent a couple of night's at Rachel's dorm and she didn't ask any questions, though there were a dozen in her eyes. When Archie came by to see me there, she turned him away and said I'd call when I wanted to talk. The longer we went, the more I didn't know how to get my point across. Especially if I was too angry to even talk to them about it.

Or how stupid it was for Archie to risk himself. Didn't he get it? If Maddy hurt him it would kill me.

Finally, I told Jeremy I wanted to go up to see my dad and he made arrangements for a train ticket. I texted the guys right after I finished packing. I'd be back for classes the next week, we had a four-day weekend, I was going to take advantage of it. I rather expected Archie's security would be following me, so they might need the heads up.

Jeremy also got me to the station, and I called Hank to let him know I was coming.

"Miss Frankie," Jeremy told me as he stepped up to me with my bag. He'd had a car bring us round and it would be taking him back. "Would you be opposed to a piece of advice?"

"Not at all," I told him.

"Mr. Archie's heart was in the right place. Sometimes, he rushes, but you are very important to him. More important than anything else in his life. I believe you feel the same way about all four of those young men, including Mr. Archie. He needs to respect those feelings as much as you need to respect his."

"Are you chastising me or telling me I'm doing the right thing?"

He smiled. "Perhaps a bit of both. You're very good for Mr. Archie, but he needs someone to push back. And if you wish to arrange for security for them, I'll contact your Mr. Walsh and Mr. Wittaker and get it taken care of."

It would serve them right.

"I don't know that I could do that without telling them. It would be as bad as what he did."

"Then tell them," Jeremy said. "As soon as arrangements are made, I'll let them know you have set up their security."

I almost laughed. "I'll think about it." Rising on my tiptoes, I pressed a kiss to his cheek. "Thank you."

"You're welcome. Please do let me know you've arrived safely, yes?"

"I promise."

I glanced around and found Mr. Shay waiting not far from the entrance to the station. I guess they'd gotten that message. Once inside the station, I made my way to the platform for the train going north to Boston. It wasn't until I was in my seat with my overnight case stored that I sent a message to the guys.

I considered it for a moment then added.

That was the truth.

I didn't care about the money or the family connections or even the idea of a rock star career. I'd loved these guys when it was just us in that two-bedroom apartment getting on each other's nerves and taking care of each other. We'd kind of forgotten that here, or maybe we'd let ourselves forget.

Shutting my screen off, I leaned my head back and closed my eyes. I was running home to Daddy. Hank hadn't missed a beat when I said I needed to get away and could I come up. No questions asked. All he wanted to know was when my train got in.

My phone buzzed in succession.

Each message was a variation on the same. They loved me. They would give me the time and wait to see me when I got back.

Chapter Thirty-One

YOU CAN'T HELP YOURSELF

Archie

From the minute I got the panicked message about someone following her, I'd known the jig was up. I'd hired a private security team and gotten Pax's people in particular because they were usually discreet. To be fair, they had been until now. The look in her eyes and the hurt aimed at me, but I'd do it again. A hundred times over if it meant she stayed safe.

What I hadn't expected, though I guess I should have, was how much she would shut me out after the reveal. Coop and Bubba were both pissed at me and Jake, of all of them, was on my side. I was there the morning Jeremy took her to the train, I heard them talking from where I sat at the top of the stairs. She never looked back as they went out the door.

My phone buzzed and I barely even glanced at the message. It was just a note that security was following her. Coop and Bubba might be mad, but neither had said to pull the security, and Jake's only complaint was that I should have mentioned it to him. Except, when I set this all up, he was still riding the pissy train.

An hour later, Jeremy returned and met my gaze. The guys weren't up yet or if they were, they hadn't come down. He had taken off his coat and gloves and stepped into the kitchen. I'd finished the coffee in the pot that he'd made for Frankie. Without a word, Jeremy started another one brewing. Once it was ready, he brought me a fresh mug and set it in front of me without a word.

Right.

He returned to the kitchen and began preparing breakfast. The sizzle of bacon which would usually make my mouth water did nothing for me. I sat there as the cats trundled in and out getting more attention from Jeremy than I did. Tiddles actually came over to rub against my legs. I scratched his head absently and when he went to get in my lap, I made room. He settled down, purring while I stroked him.

At least he still liked me.

When breakfast was ready, Jeremy set the plate in front of me before he checked his watch and then eyed the hall that led to the stairs before he pulled out a chair and took a seat with his own cup of coffee.

Oh, that didn't bode well. Jeremy only sat down with me when I was in deep shit.

"I don't think I can emphasize enough how much you have hurt her." There was no need to define her.

"I needed to protect her."

"I understand that," Jeremy said in the most solemn of voices. "I even endorse it. Miss Frankie is family. You care about her deeply. You think I wasn't aware of your feelings all these years or how much you wanted her?"

With a sigh, I shook my head. "Maddy's insane, Jere. A certifiable psychopath, in my opinion. She threatened Frankie before. She's hurt her before."

"The car she sabotaged, allegedly, was yours." Jeremy tacked that word on as though it were distasteful. I couldn't blame them. There was what we damn well *knew* and what we could prove. The fact we couldn't prove it made me sick.

"I'm aware," I reminded him. "But Frankie was driving it and even if she hadn't been, she would have been in the car with me."

"Yes," Jeremy said, agreeing with me. "Now put yourself in her shoes. What if she arranged security for you but left herself in the open so her mother could come to her at any time."

What little appetite I had fled. "She did go after her mother alone."

"Actually, she hired a law firm using the connections through Wittaker, and other legal services you encouraged her to learn about in order to manage her inheritance. Then she took a friend with her, one we're both well aware has a nature as suspicious as your own, to accompany her while she spoke to the police. Her efforts to locate her mother were passive in terms of her personal involvement."

"She still kept the fact she thought it was Maddy to herself."

"As did you." The prim note of reprimand stung. It didn't matter that I was nineteen. It didn't matter that he technically worked for me. He was more family than my own father, and his opinion fucking mattered.

Fuck me. I hated when Jere called me on my shit. "Because...I didn't want to upset her. If I was wrong, then I was wrong. But I don't trust that woman. The day Frankie severed her parental rights was one of the best days of my life. Particularly after she tried to destroy us with that lie about Frankie being my sister."

"I understand that. I believe Miss Frankie understands it as well. She loves you very much, Mr. Archie. She will forgive you, eventually. She always does."

Ouch.

"The question is, do you understand why you need to be forgiven."

"Because I kept it from her," I said slowly.

"And...?" Jeremy raised his brows.

"And I didn't get us security too, but—we can take care of ourselves."

"I will remind you, Mr. Archie, if you had been driving the Ferrari, you both would have been in that accident. Exactly how do you plan to protect yourself from that without security?"

He gave me a pointed look and then rose at the sound of steps on the stairs.

"Eat your breakfast." Then he retreated to the kitchen like he'd never sat down to scold me. Bubba appeared around the corner and I had to hold back a sigh. The look on his face said he had more to say to me, too.

Fine. I might as well get all my bruises in at one time.

Ian

Archie stared at me warily as I headed into the kitchen. Jeremy was already pouring me a cup of coffee and I grabbed the juice out of the fridge. I usually had both and he didn't typically mind when I helped.

"Breakfast, Mr. Bubba?" Jeremy inquired.

"Yes please," I said. "Thank you. I need to carb up before my run."

It would take a while for me to cool off the fact Frankie had needed to *run away* from us to deal with the latest problem. Not that I faulted her. She had a safe haven in Hank. For once, I could appreciate that with a parent who genuinely cared, she didn't need us as much. Though I hated not being able to fix this for her.

At the table, I took a seat and my phone buzzed with a message at the same time Archie's did.

Frankie

I love you all. I am coming back. I just need some time to stop being so angry.

Frankie

I need you to understand and respect why I am angry. Please be safe and don't risk yourselves. I love you way more than I need Maddy caught.

The heavy sigh Archie released echoed the one in my heart. I switched from the group message to a private one.

The little message flagged as read and I nodded. If what she needed was time, then we could give that to her.

Jeremy brought out a plate for me. Archie basically pushed the food around on his plate rather than eat. I dug into my own food in silence, it wasn't until I drained the orange juice that Archie finally spoke.

"So, give me hell," he said, his tone terse but his expression resigned. "It's my fault she's basically taken off on us for the weekend and doesn't want to talk to us."

Rather than reply, I considered my response while I took another bite.

"None of you disagreed with the idea she needs someone watching her back at least until Maddy is caught. Though if I had my way, she'd always have security."

It was hard to argue that point. We'd all experienced her hurts in different ways. I'd actually lost her for a time, though she'd still been in my life. I understood the driving need to protect her.

"Well?" Archie demanded. "You were pissed at me enough the other night."

"I know," I told him. "You don't need me to repeat it. Clearly you get what the problem is, so, what are you going to do to fix it?"

His eyes narrowed. "I thought you guys didn't want me to just arbitrarily fix things anymore."

"Don't be an ass." I tried to keep my tone patient, but some irritation escaped. "You want a fight so you can prove you were right in your choice and don't have to feel guilty. Unfortunately, I'm not going to give you that fight."

At that, his mouth fell open. "What?"

"I'm not going to fight you on this. You did what was necessary, but you did it in a way that hurt her. You also underestimated the depth of her feelings, and some might say that's a sign of disrespect."

I took another bite while he chewed on that.

"In the end, the only person who can forgive you is Frankie. I want her safe every bit as much as you do. If I could wrap her up in cotton and keep her with me at all times so nothing could ever touch her again, I would. But that's not living and it's not a life she would choose."

"So, you think I should have put security on all of us too." It wasn't a question. "And that I should have told her what I was doing so we could all have this argument then and when she was too stubborn to agree, I could have just done it anyway."

"No," I told him simply. "I think you shouldn't assume what her response would be. I think she deserved the right to be a part of that conversation. We all did." I'd almost finished my food and he still hadn't touched his. This was going to drive him mad until he could resolve things with Frankie. That, I understood deeply. I just hoped he gave her the weekend and the opportunity to come back to us rather than chased after her. "I wish I had known," I added almost as an afterthought. "I worried every time she was away from us. I couldn't relax until I got the text that said she'd arrived somewhere or she was with one of you. Knowing she had security would have helped that."

Plate emptied, I drained my coffee and then stood.

"I'm going to run. Do you want to go with?"

More surprise flickered across his expression. He glanced at his food then at me.

"I can wait."

Maybe he didn't see that he needed looking after, too. Frankie was right about his thick skull. He didn't quite see that he deserved the same considerations. We were a family. This was what families did.

"Thanks," Archie said slowly and I nodded. Jeremy took my plate and I went ahead and refilled my coffee before joining Archie again.

Then again, Archie and Frankie both grew up in what I would call horrifically dysfunctional families. They both needed to learn to give a little and to take a little, but mostly to talk and to listen.

Fine, we'd teach them what it meant to not be alone.

Jake

Coop waited until we were at the gym to talk. Of course, I was rather trapped when he was spotting my chest presses. "We have to fix this," he said, like I didn't know that.

"Except I don't think Archie was wrong. Crazy as it may seem to you, Frankie never puts herself first. We have to."

"Not crazy and don't be a jackass." He kept his hands in place as I pressed upwards. I'd added ten pounds to my normal bench press. I wanted the burn. "You always want to get in the way of whatever is coming after her."

"And so do you." I glared at him. We'd known each other too long to pretend otherwise. "You're just mad he didn't tell us."

"You're not mad about that for some fucked in the head reason, because you would have done the same thing if you could have thought of it."

My grip slid a little and he braced the weight, eyebrows raised until I nodded that I had it. "I'm not mad because it made sense," I told him as I pushed myself a little further. "I'm not mad because—because he was right and I hate saying that. I blamed him for the accident. Why the hell would he tell me anything? At least this way, he's got eyes on her at all times and we can avoid her getting hurt."

"Except, he hurt her by not telling her."

"Yeah, I know." I sighed as we set the bar back into the rack and I sat up. "Could have done that better. But she might have said no and then it would be twice as bad if he went against her wishes."

Coop rolled his eyes. "So, you'd be fine if he stuck security on you to follow you everywhere without telling you."

"Why would he?" I shook my head. "I can take care of myself. Besides, I'm not the one her crazy ass mother is gunning for."

"For fuck's sake, Jake," Coop growled. "That's part of the point. Her mother wants to hurt her or at least hurt Archie. You don't think if she hurt you or me or Bubba, it wouldn't hurt Frankie too?"

I grabbed the towel and swiped it over my face as he took some of the weights down to what he benched. Then took my place while I spotted him. "I know it would hurt her, but she's always been her mother's target."

"She has been," Coop said quietly, staring at me. "For far too long. I guarantee you the first thought that went through her head when she thought it might be Maddy was that Maddy wants to hurt Archie. Frankie would have been collateral damage, but she sabotaged his car to hurt him."

"Fine, but Archie wasn't in the accident," I pointed out. I shouldn't have to, it had been the thing pissing me off and granted, I felt stupid wishing he had been. I didn't even mean it that way. But at least we were getting that behind us.

"Nope, pure dumb luck saved him." Coop's presses were smooth and clean. They also weren't a hell of a lot of effort. But then he wasn't building. "The thing about it, let's say he hadn't left. That he'd been in the car driving Frankie back when it all went wrong."

My gut churned. Frankie in the passenger seat that had been crushed. She'd been hurt enough in the driver's side. I clenched my jaw.

"There you go," Coop said smoothly as he finished his reps and sat up. He wasn't even sweating. "Now you get it. Frankie knows that she wants to hurt Archie or any of us. Protecting Frankie is something I agree with, but if Frankie gets hurt because she comes after *us*, then what?"

"Son of a bitch," I swore.

"Yep. As her boyfriend, I'm right there. I will do anything to protect her but as her best friend? She has to have a say in it. We have to make sure all the ways that could hurt her are covered. If that means we get our own babysitters, then we get our own babysitters. What's good for the goose is good for the gander."

It was my turn to roll my eyes. "I'd feel stupid knowing I had a bodyguard following me around."

"But," Coop said, clapping me on the shoulders as he headed for the next set of weights. "You'd be alive to feel stupid and so would she."

In some ways, it was surreal to be even having this discussion. "Did you ever think..." I mean I couldn't even finish the sentence.

"That we'd ever have to contemplate something like this?" Coop shook his head. "No, I always thought something was off about the woman. That there was a streak of cruelty in her that I hadn't been able to define. Not then. Maybe not now. Honestly, I think she's mentally ill. She should probably be committed somewhere, but without evidence..."

Or a clear diagnosis.

Fuck. Frankie's message that morning had left my heart bruised. I'd understood in part why she was upset but the ends justified the means. Except, not if she was that hurt. Crap. "I need to apologize to her." The words didn't even taste like ash. "I didn't think about the rest of it."

"Good," Coop said. "Can't ask for more than that. Besides, I think after she spends a couple of days with her dad and his family, she'll be less bruised when she comes back."

"Why are you so calm about this?"

"Practice," Coop told me as he set the weights and then sat down to do the leg press. The first push he gave had a lot of aggression in it. "I don't want to be calm. I want to be pissed. I want to slug Archie for being a cocky overbearing asshole who made decisions without talking to any of us. At the same time, I want to thank him for putting her first. I am sorry her feelings were hurt, but I'm grateful as hell that there was something we could do. She deserves better. We all do. So, it's not just one of us that has to make the effort, it's all of us. She did—she told us about the investigation."

I sighed. She had.

"We'll do better."

"Agreed," Coop said. "Because if we have to start kicking our own asses it's gonna get real uncomfortable."

I laughed.

He wasn't wrong.

Coop

Longest weekend in history. Thankfully, Frankie didn't shut us out. She messaged each day. Sometimes to the group. Sometimes to each of us. I got the feeling that she was talking to Hank and I was good with that. If she needed me to be an ear, I'd be an ear. Or maybe she was talking to Rachel. The one time I checked with Rachel, she told me to get fucked.

That was usually best friend code for she was mad on Frankie's behalf. Fair enough. Jeremy, however, made his displeasure with all of us known in the most subtle of ways. Largely in his looks and his lack of verbal acknowledgements. He'd taken polite to an extreme level.

I didn't even know polite could be cutting. Learned something new every day. The gloom in the brownstone settled like a pall. The cats had started ignoring us. Apparently, even they knew we were in the doghouse.

The brownstone was pretty quiet, so I was in the game room getting caught up on my reading when a whoop carried down the stairs. I looked up in time to see Bubba jog down this level. "Are the guys still here?"

"Probably," I told him, but he was already leaning up the stairs and bellowing their names. "Something wrong?"

"No," Bubba said, but he had his phone out and he was calling it even as Jake and Archie descended wearing the same puzzled look that I had to have. "Hey, Angel, sorry to bother you at your dad's, but I needed you to hear this. The guys are all here so I'm putting you on speaker."

That snagged all of us.

He hit speaker just as she said, "Okay. Everything is all right? No one's hurt?"

"No one's hurt," he assured her, and I don't think I was the only one ready to thump him if he didn't hurry his ass up to the point. "I just got mail from Roll City Records asking to set up a time to discuss contracts and a possible tour. They're making a full offer for the demo with the caveat that we do a second album."

Wait...

"What?" Jake asked.

"Holy..." Archie started.

"...shit," Frankie finished on a squeak.

"I know," Bubba agreed in a breathless voice like he'd just run a mile. "I talked to the attorneys. It's a legitimate offer. We'd be contracted for the demo as our first album with some minor changes. Then they'd like a second one within the year. In the meanwhile, they'd arrange a series of local appearances for a tour over the course of the summer and maybe into the autumn. We'd have to figure that out with school. I told them we needed time to go over everything and to compare the offers...which was the attorney's idea. So they upped the figure."

A record contract.

Archie raked a hand through his hair and Jake blew out a breath.

A tour.

A tour would mean traveling.

They would be on the road.

But they would also release an album.

"Angel?" Bubba said when there was nothing but silence on the phone.

"I don't even know what to say," she answered in a voice filled with tears. "They really want the demo?"

"They really want *us*, Angel," Bubba stressed. "They want what we sent them, and they want more. You don't have to decide anything right now and I'll get the hell off the phone so you can go back to your time to yourself—but I needed to tell you. I needed you to know."

"Thank you," she said slowly. "Oh my god—Ian, they want you—us. It's real."

"Yeah, Angel, it is."

She let out a little scream and I wasn't the only one who was grinning.

Holy shit.

A record deal.

It was really happening.

Chapter Thirty-Two

WHY?

Frankie

The weekend with Hank, Kelly, and the kids had helped, a lot. Talking it out with Hank had given me some clarity. He didn't approve of Archie not telling me, but he couldn't fault Archie's choices in putting me first. At the same time, he also understood why I was angry they weren't protecting themselves.

"Frankie," he'd said while we sat together in the living room late one evening after the kids had gone to bed and Kelly left us to talk. "You're more afraid for them than you are mad. That's why you came here. You're worried about what they will do to protect you and what it might cost."

I sighed. "I just want to have a normal life."

"Sweetheart, there's no such thing as a normal life," Hank said as he sat forward, hands clasped. The indulgent smile on his face held an element of apology. "We all act like there's one because we see it on television or in books. We're told there are expectations. When my parents were your age, it was all about the nuclear family. Women got married to husbands and their husbands got jobs and then they had two or more children. They became all about their kids."

"*Leave it to Beaver.*"

"Right," he said with a grin. "But that was a show, and not every home or family looked like that. Growing up, that picture changed, single moms, single dads, mixed families—but it was still the idea that even these 'outside-the-norm' could be 'almost normal.'" Exhaling, he spread his hands. "Normal is a concept that we develop through to day-to-day life. Your normal, when you were growing up—it was your normal. The normal you have now? The one you're building with your boys? That's also going to be your normal."

"But they're very different."

"That's called growing up," Hank said. "We aren't our pasts. Our pasts may shape us. They may inform us. They may even help us grow. But we aren't our pasts. The girl you were growing up, she's still in there. She's how you measure your happiness. How you give your trust. Why your heart is so open and why fear in the new normal scares you even more. Because when you were little and afraid, no one was there."

"I had Coop."

"When you were five, you met him and I'm glad he became such a great friend and more. But right now, if Chloe were to have a nightmare, she'd run out of her bedroom and right into the room with Kelly, or come down here. She might even yell until one of us came to her. But she'd know we were coming and that she could find safety with us."

I sighed.

"You don't have to tell me you didn't have that with Maddy."

"It doesn't matter anymore."

"As your dad, it really does matter to me that you didn't have that—because you got scared and you came straight here. To me." There were tears in his voice and I blinked really hard. "So you do have a place to go, to be safe while you figure things out. You'll always have a place. That's your normal now, too. And mine."

I swiped away at the tears on my cheek. "Well, that sounds a lot better than I ran away because we had a fight."

"Well, you had a fight too, but sometimes, sometimes it's better to take the space to really think it out and avoid saying things you can't take back."

Fair.

That conversation replayed in my head after he dropped me at the train. I'd told him about the recording contract offer and his expression had been delighted and proud. Then he made me promise to send him some of the music so he could listen to it. Kelly and Hank hadn't hesitated when I'd called and said I was coming. They'd even fixed up the room I'd had with Coop the last time I was there. It had more things in my color and it finally hit me, they were fixing it up to be my room.

One night, Chloe even snuck in to sleep with me because she'd gotten scared. That little girl had this big trusting heart in a sister she barely knew. Didn't matter, I was her sister. That was all she cared about. The train I'd taken wasn't an express. It stopped at several towns along the way. I hadn't really paid attention when I'd booked the tickets.

Until the name of the little hamlet where my grandparents lived came up. We weren't that far from Boston. I glanced back to find Mr. Shay sitting a couple of rows away and then rose to move to him. "Mr. Shay?"

"Ma'am?" He started to stand but I waved him back down.

"We're about to stop somewhere and I'm going to get off and take a cab to my grandparents' house. They're supposed to be back...but there's a chance my mother will be there."

He nodded once. "I take it since you're telling me, you want me to go with you?"

"Well, it would probably work better if I wasn't playing hide and seek with the bodyguard and it may be for nothing, then we'll be stuck here until the next commuter train comes through."

The man made a faint huffing sound that I assumed was a laugh. Up close, he really wasn't that much older than us. He just seemed so fierce. With a glance at his watch, he nodded. "Commuters run every hour. We'll be a bit delayed getting in, but I'll cover that for now if you want."

Translation, he wouldn't rat me out to Archie. "I'll tell them. You won't get in trouble."

"Not worried about me at all, ma'am," he said.

I winced. "Um, could you maybe just call me Frankie?"

"Sorry, Miss Curtis. It's better to not get too informal. If you don't like ma'am, how about Miss?"

Sure. Fine.

At the next stop, we got off the train and I carried my overnight bag while he took his own. There were plenty of taxis available, so I just took one and gave them the address for my grandparents' estate and Mr. Shay rode with us. I supposed if I had to be Miss Curtis, then he could be Mr. Shay.

It was the longest twenty-minute ride of my life. We weren't that far from Blue Ivy. Any other time, I'd go see KC but not right now. I did need to check on her. Ten minutes out, I debated sending my grandparents a text.

Debated and discarded. I didn't want to warn them. I had the cab driver wait at the end of the drive, and I paid him extra to stay for at least an hour. The guy parked and pulled out a book. Said he'd give us until fifteen minutes after that hour. Not that I thought we'd need that long.

I had one question.

The walk up the drive gave me time to collect my thoughts. It was still cold up here and snow decorated the grounds, but they'd cleared the driveway. As the house came into view, I thought about the day Archie brought me here *last* spring. The first time I'd seen my grandmother in years and the first time I'd ever met my grandfather.

That visit had been illuminating. Over the last several months, I'd been trying to get to know them. They showered me with gifts and a trust. I wasn't sure if they thought they needed to purchase my affection as they had with Maddy, or if it was the only way they knew how to express their caring.

Sometimes, I'd catch my grandfather in a rare bit of humor and he'd relax. Like he had about the formal dress code over the long weekend in the Hamptons.

Patience, though, she never really relaxed. Always moving, always planning, and always on the edge of a fret.

When we got to the front doors, I stared at them with Mr. Shay standing just a couple of feet behind me. I was pretty sure if I went back to the cab and got in it, he'd follow without comment. Pulling my phone out of my pocket, I opened it to the text message I shared with the guys.

> Me
>
> Took a detour on the way home. Mr. Shay is with me. I'm going to ask my grandparents in person if Maddy was there that weekend. Probably be an hour later on the train. I'll touch base after I talk to them. Love you.

I shut the screen without waiting for their responses and rang the bell. I had to ring it a second time before the door opened. A woman I didn't know stood there. "Yes?"

"I'm Frankie Curtis," I told her. "Patience and Eugene's granddaughter. Are they in?"

"Oh," she murmured.

"Who is it, Linda?" Patience's voice carried and the woman standing at the door turned.

"Your granddaughter, ma'am."

If I hadn't been paying attention, I might have missed the faint hitch in her steps. The faint shuffle click of her shoes against the tiled entry way.

"And a friend."

"Well, let them in," Patience said after a pause that would have made me suspicious if I hadn't been already. Linda stepped aside and I carefully wiped my boots before stepping in with Mr. Shay in my wake.

My grandmother stood near the stairs. Her age hit me all at once. The lines in her face seemed deeper, her eyes just a tad more sunken and her hair duller. It was like someone had drained all the color out of her.

"Frankie-darling," she said as though finding herself and moving forward to embrace me. I took it and the quick kisses she gave me to each cheek. "I wish you'd let me know you were coming, we're wholly unprepared for guests and who is this young man?"

"It's all right, Patience," I said slowly. "I'm not staying." I didn't bother to answer about Mr. Shay. "Is Grandpa out in the solarium?"

"No, he's resting," she said, her lips tightening. "He does that a lot these days. The doctor wants him to get more sunshine, we might take a place down in Florida for a few months."

I scanned the foyer, and up the stairs. The house was—quiet. Not the quiet it had when Archie and I came here before, it was almost a pall. Linda had made herself scarce leaving just the three of us there and Patience didn't invite me deeper into the house.

"I should have made more time to come and see him," I told her. "Please give him my regards and tell him I'll be calling."

"Of course." She glanced from me to Mr. Shay then back again. "I would love to have you come and have some tea, but we're just getting settled back in. We've only just returned from Paris."

Right.

"That's fine, like I said, we have a car waiting."

Patience flicked a look to a set of closed doors and I followed her gaze. Five bucks said if I opened those doors, I'd find Maddy. A part of me wanted to charge over there and bust them in. But the rest of me just went ice-cold.

"And I haven't really seen you since the weekend in the Hamptons. I'm sorry about that. I don't know if Grandpa Ted let you know that I was in a bit of an accident on the way home."

A distracted look crossed her face as she glanced at the doors again then jerked her attention to me. "An accident? Ted didn't say anything about an accident. What happened?"

"The brakes went out on the Ferrari. Wrecked the whole thing. Pretty awful. I was in the hospital for a day or so, but I'm fine. The car wasn't salvageable. There's been an entire investigation."

Her frown deepened.

"You've been pretty quiet all these months, too. Fewer and fewer calls. A card here or there—and then the trips overseas."

I swore she grew paler.

"I just have one question then I'll leave you be." I locked my stare on her. "Was Maddy at the house in the Hamptons that weekend when Archie and I were there?"

A halting, hitched breath. "Frankie..."

"Yes or no, Grandmother. That's all I need to know."

"She was struggling after everything that happened at the graduation. Eddie left her again and she's been trying to put her life back together. I know you've had your own issues, so we had her stay in the other wing and keep her distance..."

I was going to throw up.

"Why?" It was all I wanted to know. "Why would you let her after everything she did to you?"

"She's my daughter," Patience said with a weary sigh.

"The police want to question her—about the car. And the brakes."

"Maddy would never..."

"Threaten you?" I asked. "Or threaten to kill me if you tried to take me away?"

Her expression went ashen and I felt almost cruel. I glanced over at those closed doors. Maddy was there. I could feel it. Like she was glaring out at me.

"I'll let the police know she's back in the country. You might want to hire her a lawyer." Then I really looked at Patience and lowered my voice. "If you need help, show me a sign and I'll make sure you get it."

"Frankie, your mother may be troubled, but she wouldn't have tried to harm you or Eddie's son."

Delusion it was.

I took two steps forward and pressed a kiss to her cheek. "Thank you for telling me the truth at least." Then I pivoted and headed straight for the door.

"Frankie..." Patience called, but I didn't stop, I didn't even bother closing the door as I headed down the driveway to where we'd left the cab.

Not even thirty minutes.

No one chased after us. Or if they did, I didn't see them. As soon as we were back in the cab, Mr. Shay told him to take us back to the train station. We'd likely make it just in time to get on the next commuter. I dug my phone out and saw the messages from the guys.

They were all encouraging.

Me

Maddy was at the house in the Hamptons that weekend. She's most likely at their house right now. Patience made excuses. Someone should probably let the cops know. Getting on train.

Archie

Come home, Babe.

Jake

Baby Girl, Arch is right. Come home.

Coop and Ian said the same things.

Home. Going home to them. Patience defended her. Even after everything Maddy had done, she wanted to defend her. Thankfully, Mr. Shay had it more together than I did. He got us through the station and back onto the train. He didn't sit with me, choosing to sit one away and over where he could keep an eye on me.

I smiled at the words.

I laughed and blinked back some of the tears.

It was the least confident I'd ever seen one of his messages. Always, he had a cocky kind of self-assurance that he could fix anything. I relied on that, too.

They were my normal. Hank had been right about that. Maybe my normal didn't look like others and that was okay. I liked mine just fine.

Archie followed it with a message that said the same. Just tell them what to do. I said I would.

Later.

After I was home.

For now, I needed to think.

Chapter Thirty-Three

MAKING UP

Frankie

The guys met me at the train. They were literally the first people I saw as I came outside and they were all holding roses. Considering Ian and Coop hadn't been in trouble, I thought it was sweet they had them. As it was, Archie opened his arms and I walked right into them for a hug. Eyes closed, I clung to him and he whispered, "I am sorry," in my ear. "For not telling you and for not understanding you'd want us safe too."

I leaned away and touched his cheek then just kissed him. One by one I went to them and got a hug from each before we climbed into the car they'd hired. We'd been in Manhattan for a few months and I'd gotten almost used to the cars being hired for us constantly. Archie used a service, I needed to ask him about it at some point.

My hand found its way into Coop's and he interlaced our fingers. I'd told them about Maddy in the text, but no one asked. I'd sent an email to

Dominic with the information and the address. The police still wanted to question Maddy. Patience could lie to them, she could say Maddy wasn't there. Honestly, she could do whatever she wanted. But I had Mr. Shay as a witness. He heard the admission the same as I did.

Maybe it would lead to nothing. It was a step forward in some ways and several steps back in others. I was worried about my grandfather, too. Maybe I should call Grandpa Ted. They were friends, maybe he could do something. Then again, what was possible if Patience kept covering for her? It stung a little.

At home, Jake carried my bag in and upstairs, before coming back down to join us. Jeremy had a whole meal laid out for us. Lasagna. Garlic bread. Wine. All my favorites.

"Thanks, Jeremy."

"Of course, Miss Frankie. It's good to have you home again." He gave the boys a significant look and I raised a hand.

"It's fine, we're all good now."

"Good. Very well. I'll leave you to talk. Please leave the dishes when you're done, I'll take care of them." Then he fixed me with a look. "It is Monday, after all."

"Duly noted." And duly chastised. As it was, we all sat there for a minute after Jeremy left.

Coop bumped his knee against mine. "Let's start with the light stuff first," he suggested. "Tell us about Hank and the kids. And whether or not we should sleep with one eye open the next time we're there?"

I laughed. Hank and the kids were a good place to start. "Well, he thinks Archie was right to do what he did, and he was grateful for it."

"Ha," Archie said with only a bit of a smirk as he poured wine for me.

"But that you should have told me and should have considered how I would feel if something happened to any of you."

"And that means your negatives canceled out your positives, so you're still scoring a zero with her dad." Coop winked and that just sent real laughter around the table and some of the unease left.

"Look, before we go any further, I need to apologize for leaving." This time I focused on Jake. "I said we should always fight things out and that we should stick to it and then I got angry and hurt and confused and I didn't want to be any of those things, but I couldn't see my way around it, so I ran to my dad."

My dad.

That would never get old.

"I didn't look at what you did as running away," Jake said. "First, you told us you were going and where. You also told us how long. That's not running away."

"That's taking a break," Ian continued the same thought. "You needed a breath. Honestly, I'm surprised you don't need more of them with all of us. You handle the balance of the four of us and your own needs pretty damn well, in my opinion."

"Seconded," Coop said. "It's healthy to be selfish. I'm pretty sure we've talked about that before, too. You needed time to not be mad. To work through the hurt. The feelings. I think your dad was a great choice. I'm actually pretty damn happy you have him."

"Me too," I said with a laugh. "It's still weird to think of him as anything but Hank, but he didn't hesitate, and he let me dump all over him and even seemed to enjoy that part."

Archie reached across the table and caught my fingers. "Because maybe he couldn't fix it, but he could be there for you. I know I get mono focused. I want to fix *everything* and sometimes I forget you need me to be there, too."

Squeezing his fingers, I smiled at him. Four days away hadn't been enough and yet had been forever. I missed them when they weren't there. It was the safest way to know that, yes I would forgive and would get over the hurt. I just needed to lick my wounds for a bit. "It's safe to say we all could have handled that better."

"Hey," Coop said. "I was a damn rock star. I think I handled it perfectly."

I burst out laughing as Jake flung a bit of garlic bread and it hit Coop squarely in the face. "Yes, Saint Cooper, the confessor."

Okay, that was funny. "Be nice boys," I said still giggling. Glancing at Ian, I raised my wine glass. "And cheers to you Mr. Other Half of Bound Hearts. Do we celebrate the offer yet or are we still thinking about it?"

"Oh, we definitely celebrate the offer," Jake said even as Archie commented, "Damn right we celebrate that."

Ian hooked his ankle around mine. "We definitely celebrate it. According to our lawyer, we should also let them marinate, because that's a first offer."

"And first offers," I said slowly, "are to open negotiations, not finalize them. We have room to make a better deal. Any deal they offer will initially benefit them more than it does us."

Archie swooned. "I love it when she talks my language."

More laughter followed, but that was part of the microeconomics course I was taking this semester. How the individual pieces came together. Contracts and negotiations were two separate stages. That shattered what was left of the tension. Ian and Archie talked about the offer and the fact that we'd have to record a *second* album, which Ian would have to write and that seemed like a lot.

"Then there's the tour," Jake pointed out. "That didn't seem to be specific, but you'd be hitting a lot of music festivals and clubs, I guess to kind of get your name out there, but they're talking a few months on the road."

I grimaced. A few months? Ian and I would be out there, but what about the guys?

"Look," Archie said. "We can figure anything out. It's just a bullet point right now, yeah?"

Ian nodded. "Exactly. I'm also thinking maybe we put some miles on flying back and forth, cause I don't want to pull Frankie out of school if she doesn't want to be out, or we limit it to the summers."

"But June is supposed to be all of us," I argued.

"It still can be." Jake's certainty helped. "You think any of us want you two to go on your first tour alone? I gotta be there to keep all the guys from trying to steal your attention."

I rolled my eyes.

"You might need to be there to keep Frankie from strangling the ladies trying to throw their panties at me." Ian deadpanned that so well, I cracked up.

"I'll do it, too."

Still, that helped. That night when we went to bed, I had a little lighter heart. In the pit of my stomach though, dread continued to build. The guys and I were still dancing around each other a little. While I had Mr. Shay down, I wasn't sure who the others were watching us. Archie promised that he'd added security for all of them, including Jeremy, and that made me feel better.

It wasn't until the end of that first week back that I got a call from Dominic. He kept the update brief. Long Island police had reached out to the local police in Connecticut. They had gone by to question my grandparents, my grandmother claimed Maddy wasn't there, and that she hadn't seen her in months. Now their attorneys were getting involved.

My heart sank. I knew it would go that way, but it didn't change the crush of disappointment.

"I know it's a setback," Dominic told me. "But our investigators are also watching. We'll track her down."

"I appreciate it," I said slowly, even as I glanced around to figure out who my babysitter was today. Mr. Shay wasn't present. I should probably stop trying to figure it out, but it was weird to be followed.

"Frankie," Dominic said gently. "There are a lot of people working on this and you've given us our biggest tip yet. You said your grandparents were in Paris. We're checking to see if she was with them. There are records, even with private planes, for people leaving and re-entering the country. If she has nothing to hide, she wouldn't be hiding."

"So just be patient?" I couldn't keep the skepticism from my voice.

"No, you can be frustrated, infuriated, and even pissed off. Our job is to be patient and methodical."

Okay, that made me laugh. "I appreciate that."

"You know her better than anyone," he said. "What do you *think* she is going to do?"

I hesitated.

"First thought that went through your mind when I said that," he urged. "What do you think she will do?"

"Blame me, blame us—because things aren't going her way." It was always someone else's fault.

"So, you think because you went there and the police followed up, she'll see it as an attack?" The speculation in his voice gave me a chill.

"Probably."

"Then don't take her calls."

"What?"

"If she calls you—hang up on her."

I pulled the phone away from my ear and stared at it a moment then put it back to my ear again. "That will piss her off."

"Exactly," Dominic said. "If she wants to talk to you, she needs to do it face to face. You have security, so does everyone else. We've assigned someone to Rachel as well."

They had.

"Thank you."

"My pleasure," he said. "I know she's important to you and while I don't think she'd be a target, I'd rather she didn't get hurt."

The corner of my mouth kicked up. It was the first time he'd brought up Rachel since I caught them in the middle of a fight.

"While we're on the subject..." he began.

"No," I told him with a bit of regret. "You're on your own with Rachel. She's a one of a kind and worth every ounce of aggravation. But I can't help you solve whatever puzzle you're trying to figure out."

He let out a sigh. "You're a good friend."

"So is she. The best. Don't hurt her. I like you, Dominic. I'd hate to have to sic my guys on you."

"Noted," he said with a chuckle. "I'll be in touch. And remember what I said. Don't take her calls. Don't respond to her messages."

Right.

"Well, she hasn't tried to talk to me in almost a year." Wow it had been almost a year since graduation. We were halfway through our second semester at college. "I don't expect that to change any time soon."

He didn't have much else to comment on that, but really what was there to say. A part of me wanted to wish him luck with Rachel. But Rachel deserved the best and if he couldn't figure it out on his own then maybe he didn't deserve her.

I was supposed to meet Archie and Jake at the gym for another boxing lesson, but I wasn't feeling up for it, so I just texted them that I was going home. They'd both been working hard to prove they were getting along and for that much I was grateful. Even if one of the ways they'd proven it had been that Jake had backed Archie's arbitrary decision.

They texted me back that they were just leaving their class, so I waited for them at the coffee shop and then we took the subway together. Coop and Ian both had later classes for the day. We'd almost made it back to the brownstone when it started raining. Since none of us had thought to bring an umbrella, it was a mad dash to get inside without getting soaked.

While it was definitely chilly rain, I couldn't help laughing. It was probably one of the silliest things we'd done in a while. Especially when Archie started bellowing *Singing in the Rain* as we ran. He might not be Gene Kelly, but he was adorable. Inside, we were a dripping sopping mess.

We had to deactivate the alarm, which told me Jeremy wasn't home.

"Strip," Jake ordered since we were all leaving a puddle, and I laughed. Not a hard order to follow. Shoes, pants, jackets, and shirts hit the floor. I used part of a shirt that hadn't been totally soaked to squeeze some of the water from my hair.

More than half of Jake's tattoo had been finished and the colorful flash of his dragon on his chest made me grin. They were going to start on his back soon.

Archie teased a finger against the corner of my mouth. "You're drooling a little."

I laughed and elbowed him lightly. "Get a sexy dragon tattoo and I'll drool over you, too."

"Ha," Jake snarked, sliding an arm around my middle and pulling me back against him. His skin seemed to not be quite as chilly as mine. "My dragon. He can get something else." We both looked at Archie who just raised his brows.

"Now we're claiming animals?"

"Hmm," I murmured then traced my gaze over his chest. Archie had always been on the lean side, but he had been bulking up some with all the boxing they'd been doing. "Wolf."

His grin turned positively wicked. "All the better to eat you with, Babe."

Laughter bubbled up through me. But I was wet, and half-frozen in the downstairs hall wearing nothing but my red lace bra and panties. The guys were in boxers and the chill didn't seem to be affecting them in the slightest.

"Shower," I ordered and ran for the stairs, but Jake hauled me up against him before I made it two steps and then it was dash between them all the way to the top. I had to admit. Four levels meant we got a lot of cardio in. Archie slid into the shower a half-step before Jake did and grinned in triumph.

"I win," he said.

I tsked as Jake started to set me down. "No," I scolded him. "I win." That got their attention. I leaned back against Jake and tilted my head up to find him watching me then I glanced at Archie. "Did you guys mean it when you said you were getting over this fight?"

"Yes," Archie said without hesitation, but his gaze went from mine to Jake's. "I think we've settled a lot of our differences."

Jake didn't respond immediately. I appreciated that he took his time. I didn't want lies or for them to just tell me what they thought I wanted to hear. "Sometimes I think Archie acts like he's the head of, instead of part of the family. He makes decisions for all of us when he should discuss it first." Archie's expression tightened a little. "But," Jake continued. "He also means well every single time and his focus is always protecting you, Baby Girl and by extension, he's protected us, too."

"The family thing is new," Archie admitted. "We've always been friends and I'm competitive as hell."

"No shit," Jake stated as he loosened his grip on me.

"Yeah and you're Mr. Team Player all the time," Archie countered. I moved over to the shower and flipped on the water to start heating it up. The thing was more than big enough for all of us.

"I'm more of a team player than you are," Jake retorted. "I'm the hothead. I get that. I get pissed off really easily and I don't like losing."

"Who does?" Archie said. "But I don't think any of us have lost in this relationship."

"No," I said slowly. "We haven't...but there's one thing I really can't handle right now. With everything else that's going on—I need you guys to be on each other's sides."

"You didn't like it as much when I took Archie's side over the bodyguard," Jake pointed out.

"No, I didn't like it that I hadn't been consulted, I kind of liked that you were looking after each other. I never want to be the thing that drives you guys apart." It had been the one fear I had way back when we first started this dating experiment. "I can't imagine my life without all of you in it. I missed you from the moment I got on that train and went to my dad's."

They were both staring at me.

"I miss you when we're all busy. I hate it when one of you won't come in the room because the other one is there. I need you to take care of each other as much as you look after me." Taking a deep breath, I unhooked my bra and let it slide down my arms. "I need you to let me take care of you, too."

"Babe," Archie said, eyes already hot on me. "You take care of us just by breathing. You're the first person in my life who's ever really just seen me and not my money. I told you once, five minutes after I met you, I knew you were the girl for me."

I smiled.

"You've always been my girl," Jake pointed out. "Even when I didn't get it and you didn't see it. There's only ever been you."

Anticipation quivered in my stomach. "Then will you both do something for me?"

"Anything," Archie said.

"Name it," Jake agreed.

I hooked my fingers into the sides of my panties and stripped them down and let them land with my bra. Straightening, I had both of their attention. Goosebumps still prickled over my skin, but it wasn't from the cold anymore. The bathroom was filling with steam. "I want you to share me...right now."

Jake had shared me plenty of times with Coop. They loved doing it. Archie had with Ian twice and more recently with Coop once, but those had been special occasions. The only other time had been my birthday.

Archie wasn't a big fan of sharing. Nor was Ian for that matter. But they'd made adjustments. We'd all made adjustments.

These two hotheads, so much alike that it made me ache when they fought. I wanted all that passion and intensity focused on me.

I stepped back into the shower and let the hot water cascade over my skin. They were still staring at me and then they looked at each other.

Always the competition with them. Always who could win.

Whether it was points in a game, the better project they built, or fuck me, how many orgasms they could get me to have. Everything was a competition.

"I'm game if you are," Jake said and there was no mistaking the challenge in his voice. "If you can't handle it, I'm sure we can work something out."

"If I can't handle it," Archie snarked right back. "You're forgetting who has given her the most orgasms."

"Ian's not here," I teased them both and that got their attention. Mentally, I blew Ian a kiss as I turned my back on them and my face up to the shower. Hot hands landed on my hips and pulled me around and then Archie kissed me like his next breath depended on it. The thrust of his tongue demanded entrance and the weight of his cock pressed against my stomach.

I wanted to laugh, but he barely released me when Jake slid a hand around my throat and tilted my head back so he could kiss me. I was sandwiched firmly between them. Oh hell. Maybe I should have thought about what challenge I was throwing down. The fleeting thought couldn't find any purchase as Jake palmed one of my breasts and Archie slid his fingers right between my legs.

No patience in them at all as they teased me right to the first orgasm that left my legs shaking and me gasping for breath. The water pounded all around us as I sucked in a deep breath of air, and then Archie captured my lips for another kiss. Jake kissed a path down between my shoulder blades and then to my ass. He squeezed and kissed each cheek once before he bit down right where it curved against my thigh and nudged my legs farther apart.

Archie caught my knee, lifted it until my foot was on the stone bench and then Jake's tongue replaced Archie's fingers as he began to lick, nip and suck at my pussy. The teasing strokes eddied around my clit, enough to make me squirm but not with the pressure I wanted.

A whimper tore from my throat and I fisted Archie's cock with one hand and he groaned against my lips as I pumped him. I couldn't reach Jake and when I tried to shift away from his tongue, his hand landed against my ass with a wet slap that made me jump. Archie pulled away and kissed his way to my breasts and the only thing keeping me up between them was the two of them.

The rake of his teeth over my nipple both stung and sent another hot pull bouncing between my pussy and my breasts. I braced a hand on the wall and then moved, twisting between them. I grabbed their hair one at a time and tugged. That got them to look up and I slid to my knees.

"Oh shit," Jake murmured as I fisted his cock with one hand and then turned to swallow Archie's between my lips. They both swore and Jake rose when I released Archie to turn my head and pull Jake's cock against my lips. They were both so different. Where Archie was curved, Jake was thicker and straighter. Where Jake's vein pulsed along the underside, Archie's heat filled the crown. They both tasted of hot skin and musk, but more they tasted like themselves, and it was my favorite mixed treat.

"Fuck," Archie let out on an explosive breath when I switched to take him deep again. "Your mouth is like fire and silk, I fucking love feeling you swallowing me."

They were both staring down at me and then Jake let out a growl when I went to take him in my lips again, he pulled me up and kissed me instead and backed me right up to the wall. Archie dragged my mouth from Jake's and then he was kissing me, and they had me caged between them.

I was on fire and when they weren't kissing me, I was stroking and biting them wherever I could reach. Jake's beard tickled and Archie's smooth cheeks left me aching.

It was as much a wrestling match as it was lovemaking. Who knew the push and pull between them would leave me aching for more. I kissed Jake's chest and bit gently at one of his nipples.

"I need one of you to fuck me, dammit," I finally cried because it wasn't enough. Not when they both had fingers teasing against my pussy, one stretching me while the other massaged my clit. "I need both of you."

"Where?" Archie demanded and then Jake let out a groan.

It was like they couldn't decide. Fuck this. "Pick a number," I demanded. "Between one and ten." Because if I didn't get one of them or both of them inside me soon, I was going to lose my fucking mind.

There was lube on one of the shelves. The boys had started stocking it in pretty much every room.

"Three," Jake said with a laugh.

"Five," Archie countered. "That's how many orgasms you need before you get both of us."

Oh. Hell. No. "Not making the rules this time, Standish," I challenged as I twisted and looked at Jake. "The number I had was two, so where do you want to fuck me, Jake?"

"Give me that ass, Baby Girl." That was an order I would gladly follow. Archie didn't offer an ounce of complaint as I turned to him and he backed up to the bench and sat down, between them they maneuvered me onto his lap, and I sank down on his cock with a groan and a sigh.

There. Oh fuck. That was what I needed. Jake had two fingers up my ass already stretching me as I started rolling my hips. Archie devoured my cries as he pushed up to meet every downward tilt of my hips. As much as I was into the care he took with the prep, I needed Jake now.

"I know, Baby Girl," he told me. "You're going to get me. Brace." It was the only warning he gave me before he replaced his fingers with his dick and the first push burned and the combination of pain and pleasure pushed me over the edge.

He fisted my hair and pulled my head back as he thrust inside me and kissed me. Archie let out his own series of groans. "Fuck, that's hot. Come for us, Babe, just like that. Keep fucking coming." He had two fingers against my clit and massaged me from one orgasm right to the next. I couldn't keep up a rhythm, but they managed it.

Every hard thrust from one drove me into the other and I swore they were battling it out to see who lasted longer and I was the rope in the sexiest battle of tug of war ever.

"Holy shit, that's hot," Coop said from somewhere behind us and I glanced back to find him watching the three of us with his dick in his hand and I lost it. Laughter swelled up from within me and this orgasm had me seeing white and I might have blacked out, but the guys shouted as they came and then we were just clinging to each other. Archie was keeping Jake on his feet as much as he was bracing me between them.

Eventually, we disentangled and I ached everywhere. The kisses turned lazier and so did the strokes. Coop invited himself right into the shower and since he still had a hard cock, I went down and sucked him off until he came. When I found Jake and Archie watching me with hot eyes after, I grinned.

"Tonight—" I suggested.

"Oh yeah," Archie said without me even finishing the thought. "Someone call Bubba. We need food, drinks, and condoms."

"You're gonna be too sore for school tomorrow," Jake warned.

"Mental health day," I declared. "For all of us."

Fuck knew we needed it.

Chapter Thirty-Four

MARCH WINDS AND APRIL SHOWERS

Archie

Spring break, I put my foot down and the five of us left New York for Florida. Sure, it was crowded as fuck, but I didn't care. We found a great spot, with good ocean views and a house right on the beach. Frankie brought homework with her, but we negotiated a deal. We could work on that in the mornings, but afternoons and evenings were for the five of us or for dates.

She and Bubba were working on their music and the attorneys had sent over reams of legal paperwork to look through. In addition to Roll City Records, two other producers had expressed interest. One was an independent and relatively new label. They offered fewer benefits but a lot more control. The other was a well-established label and they wanted a hell of a lot more control, including deciding what songs they would record and not necessarily what Bubba wrote.

There were pros and cons to all of them and it about killed me to stay out of it unless Frankie or Bubba asked me for my opinion. It wasn't my decision, in fact, I'd floated the idea we start our own label. Frankie and I could both afford it or conversely, Standish could stand to diversify, but she hadn't been as keen on the idea.

Bubba, on the other hand, said no flat out. "It's one thing to fund ourselves when we know we can do it. This is about proving we can and... Arch, it means a hell of a lot that you believe in us that much."

"But you still want to do it on your own." I got it. I did. I mean I had an entire corporation waiting for me to grow up, graduate, and take over. It was being handed down to me on a silver platter. Bubba wanted to earn that silver platter himself. They had the talent for it. I'd back them every step of the way.

It just *sucked* that I couldn't fix it. Jake gave me no end of shit over it, too. But I needed the reminders every time Bubba or Frankie looked exhausted after reading through the paperwork. The attorneys had given them some sound advice. To keep their options open. Contracts benefited the person who wrote them, especially if there was any kind of vague language.

Add to that the tour requirements, the fact they would be starting out as relative unknowns—granted unknowns who had also been given some major buzz from Torched at one of their final concerts—and it was a lot of work ahead for them. How much time would they be splitting between that and school? Bubba might be willing to walk away from his degree for a time or apply the music he wrote for some kind of credits.

Frankie? Not so much.

"Just let them figure it out," Coop advised one night while we sat out on the deck. The sunset had been spectacular, and we'd been grilling burgers and drinking beer and just relaxing. Frankie and Bubba were down by the water, chasing each other around. I had to admit the jogging on the beach every morning had been a good way to work off the stress.

"I am," I told him.

"Yeah, but you're practically vibrating with the need to fix it," Jake pointed out and I flipped him off. Yes, I was, but I wasn't going to interfere. "Just let us know if we have to tie you down at some point."

"Frankie would enjoy that," Coop said with a laugh, and I snorted.

Then again, it might be worth an experiment or three. Bubba had been working on his rope technique and he'd actually let us see a couple of photos the other day and I had to admit, Frankie all bound up in red rope was definitely sexy as fuck.

She was still laughing as she and Bubba made their way back up to the deck. I couldn't even remember what started them chasing each other. Only that she'd ended up getting dunked in the water. But the relaxed smile and laughing eyes were worth whatever it was. Her phone was on the table along with ours.

Rachel was also staying at the house with us, which kept some of our sex play to a minimum. Not that I minded. It was kind of funny to send her text messages that said, "better turn up your music." The fact she asked if we ever gave Frankie's cunt a break two days ago over breakfast was pretty fucking funny, too.

She wasn't eating with us tonight, in fact, she'd gone out with the specific goal of getting laid. Frankie offered to go with her, hell, we all had. No sense in Rachel running alone and she said no thank you. We were like a walking advertisement for domesticity, and she wanted wild and crazy.

Yeah, I left that alone.

When Frankie's phone rang, she picked it up. We had a car rental so we were ready to go get Rachel if necessary, but Frankie stared at her phone for a beat then clicked the side twice, declining the call before putting the phone down again.

"I'm starving, Jake," she said as she flopped into my lap. She was soaking wet. I was not. Not that I minded, I just pulled her legs up so she could sit sideways and handed over my beer when she reached for it.

"They're almost ready," Jake said. "Coop go grab the buns and stuff."

"On it."

"Don't turn them into charcoal," Bubba advised as he snagged a cold beer and pulled up a chair.

"If you want to cook them," Jake snarked. "Feel free to take over."

Frankie's phone rang again and she picked it up. This time I could see the screen. It said Grayson.

That had to be her grandparents.

She declined the call and put it down again.

I wasn't a fan of this plan. I wasn't a real fan of Dominic either, but the guy seemed to know his stuff. This time her phone chimed like a voicemail had been left. She flipped to the voicemail screen and tapped the number. It gave a broken version of a transcript.

"....Frankie, this your Mom calling. You need to answer like a responsible adult. Call me back at this number. We need to talk."

She just deleted the message without listening to it.

"You sure that's wise, Babe?" The message and the number were proof that Maddy was somewhere with her grandparents. Not that we didn't already know that. Grandpa Ted hadn't even been able to get through to them. Patience and Eugene were putting him off.

"Sooner or later, she will get tired of me ignoring her. I'm not allowed to do that. She can ignore me, but not the other way around. That means she'll show up. You've got security on us so when she shows up, they can snag her and turn her over to the cops." Despite the confidence in her voice, there was no mistaking the faint tremble.

I caught Bubba's eye. He shared my concerns, but he just gave a small shake of his head. Frankie knew her mother better than any of us. Still not a fan of anything that forced Maddy to come looking for her, but at the same time, Frankie was right. We did have security and I'd fucking double it when we got back.

The next morning, I'd just gotten back from a run and was drinking cold water when Rachel made her way in on her walk of shame. Well, more like her saunter of satisfaction. She smirked at me. "You stink."

"And you smell like sex," I retorted and she grinned.

"I do, don't I?" She reached into the fridge and pulled out a soda, I'm going to go up and shower then maybe take a nap.

"Uh huh."

"What?" She glanced at me.

"Tell me something," I said. "You were there with Dominic when she went to talk to the police."

Rachel's expression cooled. "Yes."

"He's advised Frankie to not take her mother's calls. They discussed the fact she might try to reach out and he wants Frankie to play hard to get." I took another long swallow of water as Rachel narrowed her eyes.

"Playing hard to get. That'll piss off someone like her mom."

"Without a doubt. But he wants her to force her hand. See if she'll come out from whatever rock she's hiding under to confront her."

Leaning back against the fridge, Rachel raked a hand through her disheveled hair. She really did smell like sex, and there were definitely hickeys on her neck that weren't there the day before. The urge to ask was on the tip of my tongue, but I strained for some discretion.

"That's playing with fire," Rachel said. "As much as I hate to admit it, he's probably right. We just need to make sure one of us is always with Frankie. Between us and your guard dogs, that will keep her safe. Physically, at least."

Which hit the nail on the head of the thing I worried about most of all. "She can hurt Frankie a lot of other ways."

"Yes, she can." Rachel said as she stretched and then popped open her soda. "It just means we don't let her."

I chuckled and raised my water glass to her in a toast she returned with the can of soda.

"Look," Rachel continued as she headed to the door and glanced up the hall to the stairs before looking back at me. "Dominic Walsh is an arrogant prick who thinks really fucking highly of himself. But he's smart. He's also pretty cold-blooded. If he thinks this will work, he's probably putting pressure somewhere else to make sure it works."

Good to know.

That was the last discussion we had on that topic.

Twice a day, sometimes three times, for the rest of Spring Break, Frankie's phone would ring or get a text message. Sometimes both.

Maddy's language grew more insistent with each message she was forced to leave. Frankie didn't answer or respond to a single message. She actually turned her phone off at one point and that told me more than anything this was getting to her.

"I can send someone around to check on your grandparents," I offered and the worry in her eyes cut at me. "Whatever they've done for her, they chose to do, but if you're worried about them. We can check on them."

"But will we know if they're really alright or if it's a lie?"

That was a good question. For the first time in a long time, I debated calling my father. Despite Muriel's invitation to Frankie, we'd never taken her up on it. I'd asked her point blank if she knew anything and she admitted it was mostly just old stories and hearsay. That was all I needed to know.

Edward...

Fuck, the last day of Spring Break, while everyone else was packing I took a walk on the beach and called him.

"This is a surprise," he said when he answered.

"Yeah, me too," I told him. "Maddy has been trying to reach out to Frankie."

Silence greeted that statement, then he said, "Has she?"

"Frankie is pretty sure Patience and Eugene are hiding her or were helping her. She's also worried about her grandparents."

Edward let out a long sigh. "What do you want me to do?"

"You're still not seeing her?"

"No. I've also not taken her calls at the office or anywhere else since

I changed my private numbers. I meant what I said, Archie. Even if it turns out that she had nothing to do with the accident, I can't condone her behavior or her choices. Not anymore."

I almost felt sorry for him. There was a broken note in his voice that had never been there before.

"Do you have a way of checking on Patience and Eugene? Of making sure they're all right?"

"Perhaps. Senior would probably have better connections. But I can have someone go and check on them."

"I'd appreciate that. She's worried and while Maddy might be their kid, I don't want Frankie to blame herself if Maddy is taking advantage of the situation."

He was quiet for a moment then said, "I'll take care of it. You are all returning to Manhattan today?"

"Yep," I said not even surprised he knew we weren't there. "Should be in by dinnertime."

"Have lunch with me later this week?"

Sure. Why not. "Text me where and when."

"Bring Frankie if you want a buffer. It would be good to see her regardless, but I would like to see you."

"I'll think about it." Then because there wasn't much else I could say, I added, "Thanks, Edward."

"You're very welcome."

That was that.

An hour before we were due to board the plane, Frankie's phone vibrated with a message from Maddy.

Instead of deleting it, Frankie screen-shotted it and then sent it in an email to Dominic, before turning her phone off and leaning her head against my shoulder.

Fuck, I hated that woman.

"It's going to be okay, Babe," I promised her. "It's going to be okay."

Chapter Thirty-Five

IT ALL COMES DOWN TO CHOICES

Frankie

The calls didn't stop after we were back in the city. I put a block on the number she called from, but then she'd use a different one. I finally just had my phone silence any numbers not in my contacts. Her messages ranged from coaxing and pleading to belligerent and hateful. They all had the same theme though, I didn't understand. I needed to stop listening to *that* boy. Archie, I presumed, but then again, maybe she meant any of them.

Twice, twice she'd pissed me off so much I'd almost called her back, but then fought the urge because the point was to ignore her and force her to come to us. Force her to come out of hiding, because no matter what excuse she might have—she wouldn't be hiding if she wasn't guilty of something.

She'd hidden her relationship with Eddie. She'd hidden my parentage. She'd hidden my grandparents. Everything she'd hidden from me before including herself had been to suit her own purposes. So no, hopefully this plan would work.

Archie's dad had wanted to have lunch with us after spring break, but I hadn't wanted to intrude. Besides, we were also closing in on the last few weeks of the semester and that meant I had a ton of finals and projects to prep. I wasn't quite as crazed as I'd been at the end of the fall semester, but there was still so much to do.

Ian and I were still discussing what we wanted to do about the deals we'd been offered. We could only put them off so much longer before we needed to commit. It seemed surreal. They seriously wanted us. When Ian first got me to sing with him, it had been to keep him company and to have something we enjoyed together. I never envisioned this.

Apparently, he had. But he was also happy to wait until we were done with college. How was that fair to him? What if the offers weren't there after school was done? Look how much work he'd put into this.

"It doesn't work without both of us," Ian maintained firmly as he had with every single discussion we'd had on the subject. "We can tell them we'll only tour in the summer, maybe do some weekend gigs in the fall, but..." He held up a single finger to stop my argument. "But, your degree is important to you. You worked your ass off to get into school, to get the scholarships and I don't care that your grandparents turned out to have money or that Archie would pay our bills forever...our dreams are compatible. You're not giving up yours for me and I'm not going to surrender mine for you."

"You make it sound so easy." He really did. "I want this so much for you."

"And I want you with me and I want your degree so much for you. See," he said with a smile. "Compatible."

I flopped back on his bed and stared at the ceiling. The guys had thrown in their thoughts here and there but for the most part, they were leaving it to me and Ian. Bless Archie, it was killing him not to step in, but he wasn't.

"Of the deals we've been offered," I said slowly. "What's the one that appeals to you the most? Just kneejerk reaction."

"The one that gives us the control," Ian said without hesitation. "It's not a guarantee, we'll have to work twice as hard, but I don't want them to take songs I write and give them to someone else while they have us record someone else's work."

I wrinkled my nose. Absolutely not.

"And I want the ability to have more say in *where* we tour. KC's warned me there's a lot of backroom bars on this path, I don't want you anywhere they have to put a cage up around the performers to keep them from getting hit by stuff."

"That's only in the movies," I said. "Right?"

Ian dropped to lay on the bed next to me. "Anything is possible," he said, propping his fist on his hand. "And I need the academic year to be respected."

"What if we do some online courses?" Some of my classes would allow for that. Not all of them. Archie and Jake definitely needed in person, so that might not work.

"That's a possibility, too," Ian said. "But at the end of the day, we have the rest of our lives to build our dreams. If we do it right, we get it all."

I grinned up at him. There was one thing I really wanted to do, but I hadn't figured out yet. I'd thought about it last summer, but everything since school started had kind of chased it away. That idea tickled at the edges of my mind again.

"Talk to our attorney, have them reach out to Roll City Records with the counteroffer. We'll still give them a second album but in two years, not one. We'll do a summer festivals tour and a select number of cities, but we get final approval on their list." I chewed my lower lip. "And June is supposed to be all of us. That's our month."

A thoughtful look crossed his face and he nodded slowly. "It's a starting point," he agreed. "I like building more time into it." Cupping my cheek, he focused on me and held my gaze. "Are you sure?"

"Yes," I told him. "It scares the hell out of me and at the same time, I think about how it feels when we sing together and it all comes to life—and I want that for both of us. But not at the cost of our family."

"Agreed." Then he kissed me and rested his forehead against mine. "Angel, believe me when I say, I could end up being a music teacher who coaches football on the side, while you run a fortune five hundred corporation and I'd be just as happy."

I squinted at him. "I wouldn't."

Surprise flickered across his face.

"Ian, then I'd have to go to all those football games." I deadpanned it as best I could, but the corners of my lips twitched, and he got his revenge by tickling me. *And* he made me watch one of the football games on television while I did homework.

To say I'd almost forgotten about my birthday was an understatement. I'd actually been up most of the night finishing a paper on how investments in individuals and individual ideas could have long term benefits not only for a corporate economy but for the longevity of the overall economy. It was three in the morning before I gave it a final proofread and then crawled into bed. Coop rolled over and wrapped around me like he'd just been waiting for me to come to bed.

It was adorable and I closed my eyes. I swore it was just a blink and then the guys were all there with a breakfast tray loaded with french toast and coffee and chocolate covered strawberries. I wanted to blame the paper for my bleary-eyed stare, but Jake laughed at me as he snapped a picture with his phone. The next shot he got was me flipping him off and they were all laughing.

"Happy birthday, Angel," Ian said as he settled the tray over my lap while I sat up in bed. Coop reached for my coffee and nearly got stabbed with my fork.

"Don't worry," Archie said and nodded over to my desk. "We brought up more for everyone."

Unfortunately, we couldn't spend our weekend in bed this year, though never say never. We still had classes.

"But," Archie said. "We have reservations tonight at that new fondue place in the Village. Terrace seating because it's supposed to be a gorgeous evening. Grandpa Ted and Edward may stop by because they wanted to drop off presents for you, but they aren't staying. Rachel will be there. I told her she could bring a date or two. Your dad wanted to come down, but they couldn't swing it with stuff both for his classes and for the kids, but wants us to come up once finals are over to do a birthday weekend there."

I grinned at Archie. "You've been busy."

"Of course, I have. We all have. Did you really think we'd forget your birthday?" He gave me a look that just said c'mon. "I even picked up this." He held out a charm of the Statue of Liberty. "We did all the graduation and school ones, but we hadn't done New York yet."

Scrambling out from under the tray I gave him a kiss and then a hug. My charm bracelet had turned into a charm bracelet and necklace. So many memories and he was always adding to it. I'd bet money he had a record charm for me when Ian and I were officially signed.

"My present next," Jake said, giving Archie a gentle shove. I sat back and reclaimed my coffee cup as Jake tugged his shirt off.

"Um, Jake, I'm pretty sure there's not enough time for that this morning, even if the body is definitely willing."

That earned a round of laughter and he just gave me a wink. "Hold that thought, Baby Girl. That's for tonight *after* dinner. For now..." He turned so I could see his back and my jaw fell.

It was done. The whole tattoo was done. "When did you...?"

"Last couple of weeks," he said. "You've been busy, and I wanted this done in time for your birthday." The very tip of one of the dragon's wings touched the infinity knot with my name on it. The dragon was done in blue and reds with hints of purple. It was magnificent. I got up on my knees to get a better look at it. You could tell the skin was still raw and healing so I didn't touch but...

"Jake," I whispered.

"You found it?" he asked, glancing over his shoulder at me.

Right in the midst of the dragon's wing was a butterfly that matched the one behind my ear.

I let out a little squeal. "I want to hug you, but I don't want to hurt you."

"Fuck that," he said turning fully and half picking me up for a kiss.

"Put her french toast back, Coop," Ian ordered.

"Aww, man, so mean. I was gonna tease her."

"Ha. Not on her birthday." Archie shook his head. "Birthday girl gets what she wants."

And I had it all right here.

"My birthday present for you is late," Coop said, almost mournfully, but then kissed me. "But I promise you'll love it."

I didn't need presents.

But Ian sat down and held out a sheet of paper. "This isn't really a present, but I think you'll like it."

I opened it up and stared. It was a Bound Hearts logo, gloriously rendered. "Oh my god," I said, glancing up from the paper. "They took the deal?"

"They took the deal," he murmured. "If we want it, we get everything we asked for and they get one extra year out of us, but that was it."

I swore I was gonna cry. Tears burned in my eyes and I looked from the sheet to the guys and back again. "Holy crap. Best birthday ever."

"Um..." Coop raised a hand. "Point of order. That was last year. We haven't topped that."

"Yet," Jake, Archie, and Ian all said at the same time, and I laughed. It was ridiculous and sweet and the best. Even if we had to start getting ready not long after I finished breakfast.

I kind of floated through the day at school. Rachel picked on me, but she also promised she'd be there for dinner later and was majorly evasive when I asked about her date. I left it alone.

For now.

I was still riding high when I got home to change before dinner. Jake and Coop were already there. "Bubba and Archie went ahead to get the table. Rachel's meeting us there. We tried to talk Jeremy into coming along, but he declined graciously."

"Next year, we have the party here so he has to show up," I decided and the guys chuckled. As it was, they were dressed nicely, but it wasn't a fancy dress place. I pulled out a dark green dress and held it up then reached for one of the red ones. Finally, I just went with black. As Rachel would say, the little black dress went with everything.

The guys hung out while I did very light cosmetics and picked out a pair of heels I wouldn't kill myself in. But I wasn't putting them on until we were downstairs. Thank fuck I'd gotten a pedicure and a wax the weekend before, so I didn't have to worry about the rest of that. It was one of the first things Rachel found when she got to the city, so naturally, we went together.

"Come on, Baby Girl, you're going to get hangry any minute and you're already stunning." Jake had my shoes for me, and I grabbed a shawl in case it got cold on the terrace though it had been really nice today. Considering how cold the city got, I never thought I'd miss eighty degree nights, but you could actually miss them. Who knew?

The car ride to the restaurant was pretty swift despite the evening traffic and it was a really nice looking place. The maitre'd showed us upstairs and out onto their terrace. The building wasn't particularly tall, but the terrace was lovely and there were fire pits and seated lounge areas as well as tables.

The fondue stations in the center were ready to go and torches were lit around to give it a kind of romantic if island atmosphere. It was a weird combination of flavors that worked together. Archie's grandfather and father were already there with Ian and Archie. Music played from somewhere, but it was too soft to make out.

Rachel was late, but then so was I. I accepted the hug and the kiss on the cheek from Grandpa Ted. He also held out two envelopes. "One is from me of course, and the other from Eugene. Tonight's a festive occasion, so we'll save this talk for another day, but your grandparents are doing well."

Okay. "Thank you. You really didn't have to."

"Of course, I did. Happy birthday, young lady."

Edward offered me an envelope and I eyed it then him. "Really? Please tell me it's not more stock."

That actually got a laugh from him, Grandpa *and* Archie. "Not at all," Edward said primly. "It's just a little something you can put forward to a gift of your choice. I'm afraid I've never been particularly good at picking out presents. I am," he continued with a glance at Archie, "working on that. So, if you don't mind, I may call you later this year when it gets closer to a certain someone's birthday."

"Wait a minute," Archie said, but he was smiling and I laughed. Maybe something good really did come out of Maddy losing her mind. I'd never seen that much warmth between Eddie and Archie before, and I liked it.

Rachel came, but she didn't stay for the whole meal. In fact, I had a feeling she was trying to leave as fast as possible. When I asked her, she said, "Just something came up and I'd rather celebrate privately. Don't be mad?"

"Never going to be mad. But if you're in trouble or something is up that you need my help with, like a certain pushy attorney, tell me, okay?"

"Deal." Then she brushed a kiss to my cheek before she left.

Because of that, I insisted Archie's grandfather and father stay at least for part of the meal and the guys backed me up. The conversation was a little stilted to begin with, but they gradually relaxed into it as Grandpa told embarrassing stories about Edward, who in turn actually offered up one or two about Archie. The food was excellent and I swore I ate so much steak there wouldn't be room left for the fruits and treats that came with the chocolate fondue at the end.

Ian and I talked more about the tour dates that had been proposed and Archie got his phone out. Jake mentioned applying for an internship that if he got meant he wouldn't be able to do the whole tour with us, but he would fly out to meet us every chance he got. June was still ours though. The first tour date was supposed to be the Fourth of July weekend and we'd have to do studio time before then, but we could do that here in the city.

"You kids want to borrow that island again?" Grandpa asked and I almost choked on the food when the guys said, "hell yes." Then again, I'd loved that island too.

I needed to use the restroom before dessert came and Archie offered to go with me.

"No hanky panky down there, Sprout," Grandpa said, and I swore my face turned beet red even as Edward said, "Senior." in the same tone that Archie said, "Grandpa."

"What?" Jovial as ever, Grandpa Ted grinned. "She's a beautiful young lady."

"And on that note," I said, letting Archie take my hand and all but fleeing the table.

"Sorry about that," he said, chuckling. "He's had a couple of drinks tonight and it's been a long time since I've seen him this relaxed."

"It's been a long time—if ever—that I've seen you this relaxed with Edward being here."

He blew out a breath as we stepped to the side to let patrons pass us before we made it around to the stairs leading down to the next level. "It's weird. I almost—like him now. It's still awkward, but he's been trying you know, and I don't know what we'll ever be close..."

"But it's so much better than it was."

He nodded and raised my hand to kiss it. "Thanks for asking them to stay, you didn't have to."

"They're your family," I reminded him. "You're mine." The restrooms were down a little hallway, secluded and classy. He walked me to the door of mine and said he'd meet back out there in a minute. It didn't take me long and I washed up. My cosmetics had held up and there was a smile on my face so wide that my cheeks ached.

The last person in the world I expected to see stepping into the little bathroom behind me was Maddy. My gaze met hers in the mirror and I turned to face her.

"Happy birthday, sweetheart," she told me. The gun she pointed at me said something else entirely. "You didn't think I'd miss it, did you?"

My heart stalled. "You've missed just about everything else," I said. "You were definitely not invited."

"Well, that's an oversight. After all, you didn't do the work on your birthday," she said. "I did. I was alone and it was just you and me and fourteen and a half hours of labor before you tore your way out of my body."

"Nice, Maddy. This isn't *Aliens*." I seriously couldn't believe she was standing there with a gun. And no bodyguards. They didn't stay when we were all together. Why should we need them at my birthday? "So, you came to celebrate with a weapon?"

"This?" She held the little pistol up as though she'd forgotten she had it before she pointed it at me again. "No, this I brought for someone else. You've been ignoring me. You know how I feel about that."

"You tried to kill me before," I told her.

"I didn't. You weren't supposed to be driving the car. But that boy never does anything he's supposed to."

Fuck, it hurt so much more than I could ever have imagined having her confirm that.

"You know I knocked Muriel down a flight of stairs once at a party. A little oops," she said. "Worked on television. No more baby, no more reason for Eddie to have to marry the slut."

Bile burned in my throat.

"But it doesn't work that way in real life, apparently. She was fine. They got married, they had him and that was it. My life was over."

"Gee, thanks, Maddy."

"What? You were mine. But no, along comes that boy and once again takes away what's mine."

She was insane.

"But Eddie still loved me," she continued. "*Me*. He would have been a *wonderful* father for you. He *wanted* to be your father. He wanted us to be a family. But no—just like before, that boy gets in the way and takes you and *Eddie* both."

"You're psychotic," I said.

Maddy laughed. "No, I'm desperate. This is what he's pushed me to. If not for him, you wouldn't have been in that accident."

"If not for *him*?" I couldn't help it, I shouted. "You're the crazy bitch you damaged his car."

"Yes...to hurt him. He drives too fast. It would have been tragic, but then he would have been out of the way."

"And if I'd been in the car with him?" Horror upon horror. "Well oops, so much for wanting me around?"

"No, you would have been fine and if not, then it would have been his fault. His foolishness. If he didn't exist *none* of this would have happened."

"If he didn't exist, you delusional bitch," I told her as I stalked forward. "I wouldn't exist either."

I was right in front of her when the quiet knock hit the door. "Frankie?"

Maddy's eyes lit up with a manic light. She half-turned to the door and I body slammed her as hard as I could to knock her away from it and then jerked the door open. "Archie go..."

His head jerked up and he looked past me. "Fuck..."

I turned because I hadn't hit Maddy near hard enough, she was looking right at us. "Get out of the way, Francesca."

"No." I locked my legs even as I felt Archie's fingers bite into my hips. "You're not going to hurt him."

"Get out of the way...this is his fault," she told me as she stalked forward. The whole world slowed down to this classy, isolated little hallway next to the bathrooms of this classy restaurant where we were celebrating my birthday. "Once he's gone, it will be you and me and Eddie again...it will be perfect."

"No," I said again, leaning into Archie.

"Babe," he said in a low voice. "Please move."

"No," I refused again, and she focused all of her attention on me as she pointed the gun.

"Well," she whispered. "I tried."

The echo of the shot in the hallway was deafening. I squeezed my eyes shut even as something warm and hot sprayed my face. Somewhere, someone was screaming. I was pretty sure it was me. The fingers biting into my hips dragged me backwards and arms tightened like bands around me.

I couldn't hear anything, the rush of noise was too intense. But despite the warmth on my face, nothing hurt and the arms around me were strong. I glanced down to see Archie's hands and then up as he whirled me around. He was running his hands all over me as the world rushed back to full speed.

He was fine. I checked him. No blood. But the warmth on my face...

I turned, even when Archie tried to stop me and I saw her lying there on the floor of the bathroom, half in and out of the hall. Her dress had shredded where a bullet had hit and blood stained it darker and spilled crimson onto the floor. Her eyes were open and glassy. Her chest wasn't moving.

Shouting came from somewhere else and it wasn't until Archie pulled me back again that I saw Edward. He had a gun in his hand and tears in his eyes. His mouth moved, but I couldn't make out any of the words.

I glanced back to the bathroom.

My mother tried to kill my boyfriend.

Three times.

And now she was dead.

Maddy Curtis was dead.

Happy birthday to me?

Frankie and the boys will return in
Songs and Sweethearts.
To keep up with Heather and all her series as well as enjoy bonus
scenes and other content join her reader's group on Facebook:
https://www.facebook.com/groups/HeathersPack/

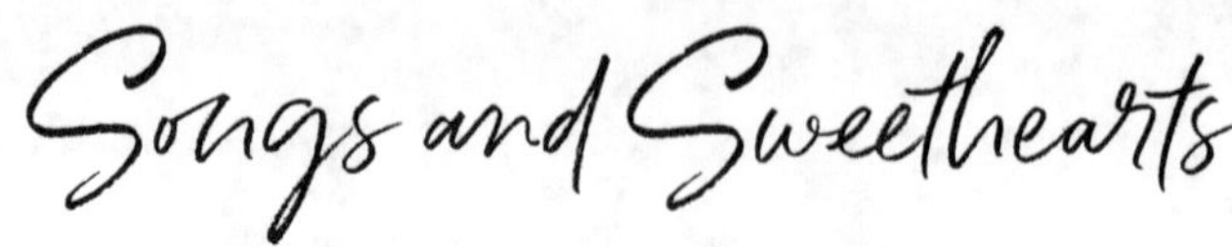

Everything begins.

Everything ends.

Sometimes, it has to end before it begins.

In the course of a year, I have had my heart broken, reforged, only
to be shattered again. The tears won't come. Not anymore. No more
looking back. No more asking *what if.*

Coop wants me to let myself feel it. Jake wants to distract me. Archie
wants to put the world at my feet. Ian wants me to not make choices
until I'm ready. I've got family ready to catch me, but I refuse to fall.

No more waiting.

No more holding my breath.

The future is now.

We have a chance to forge the path we want and I'm all in.

So why does it feel like I'm running away?

*Please note this is a reverse harem and the author suggests you
always read the forward in her books. Contains some bullying
elements, mature situations, violence, and is recommended for 17+.
This is the tenth in a series and the story will continue through future
books.*

Afterword

How are you? How is your phone? Your kindle? Do you need a minute to take a breath? I did. As I am often asked, did I know that ending was coming?

The short answer is yes.

The longer answer is a little more complicated. I will have so many stories to tell you when this series is over, but know that the decisions reached in this book were not always easy nor were they taken on lightly.

Frankie and the boys are growing up. No matter how mature they've always been, there's a lot more to adulthood than just maturity. To be honest, I don't know why we are all in such a hurry to get there.

Yet, here we are and I stand by what I said in the foreword, this was probably the most difficult book I've written in the whole series and ultimately, extremely rewarding. It's also the beginning of their real "life together" as opposed to just their love relationship.

Don't worry, we still have three more books to go. We have a lot of time left together.

xoxo

Heather

About Heather Long

USA Today bestselling author, Heather Long, likes long walks in the park, science fiction, superheroes, Marines, and men who aren't douche bags. Her books are filled with heroes and heroines tangled in romance as hot as Texas summertime. From paranormal historical westerns to contemporary military romance, Heather might switch genres, but one thing is true in all of her stories—her characters drive the books. When she's not wrangling her menagerie of animals, she devotes her time to family and friends she considers family. She believes if you like your heroes so real you could lick the grit off their chest, and your heroines so likable, you're sure you've been friends with women just like them, you'll enjoy her worlds as much as she does.

Follow Heather & Sign up for her newsletter:
www.heatherlong.net

Also by Heather Long

<u>82nd Street Vandals</u>

Savage Vandal

Vicious Rebel

Ruthless Traitor

<u>Always a Marine Series</u>

Once Her Man, Always Her Man

Retreat Hell! She Just Got Here

Tell It to the Marine

Proud to Serve Her

Her Marine

No Regrets, No Surrender

The Marine Cowboy

The Two and the Proud

A Marine and a Gentleman

Combat Barbie

Whiskey Tango Foxtrot

What Part of Marine Don't You Understand?

A Marine Affair

Marine Ever After

Marine in the Wind

Marine with Benefits

A Marine of Plenty

A Candle for a Marine

Marine under the Mistletoe

Have Yourself a Marine Christmas

Lest Old Marines Be Forgot

Her Marine Bodyguard

Smoke & Marines

<u>**Bravo Team Wolf**</u>

When Danger Bites

Bitten Under Fire

<u>**Boomers**</u>

The Judas Contact

Deadly Genesis

Unstoppable

<u>**Cardinal Sins**</u>

Kill Song

Chance Monroe

Earth Witches Aren't Easy

Plan Witch from Out of Town

Bad Witch Rising

Her Elite Assets

Featuring:

Pure Copper

Target: Tungsten

Asset: Arsenic

Fevered Hearts

Marshal of Hel Dorado

Brave are the Lonely

Micah & Mrs. Miller

A Fistful of Dreams

Raising Kane

Wanted: Fevered or Alive

Wild and Fevered

The Quick & The Fevered

A Man Called Wyatt

Going Royal

Some Like It Royal

Some Like It Scandalous

Some Like It Deadly

Some Like it Secret

Some Like it Easy

Her Marine Prince

Blocked

Heart of the Nebula

Queenmaker

Deal Breaker

Throne Taker

Lone Star Leathernecks

Semper Fi Cowboy

As You Were, Cowboy

Madison, The Witch Hunter

Every Witch Way But Floosey's

Magic & Mayhem

The Witch Singer

Bridget's Witch's Diary

The Witched Away Bride

Mongrels

Mongrels, Mischief & Mayhem

<u>**Shackled Souls**</u>

Succubus Chained

Succubus Unchained

Succubus Blessed

<u>**Sinners Keepers**</u>

Kiss of Fate

Taste of Karma

<u>**Space Cowboy**</u>

Space Cowboy Survival Guide

<u>**Untouchable**</u>

Rules and Roses

Changes and Chocolates

Keys and Kisses

Whispers and Wishes

Hangovers and Holidays

Brazen and Breathless

Trials and Tiaras

Graduation and Gifts

Defiance and Dedication

<u>**Wolves of Willow Bend**</u>

Wolf at Law

Wolf Bite

Caged Wolf

Wolf Claim

Wolf Next Door

Rogue Wolf

Bayou Wolf

Untamed Wolf

Wolf with Benefits

River Wolf

Single Wicked Wolf

Desert Wolf

Snow Wolf

Wolf on Board

Holly Jolly Wolf

Shadow Wolf

His Moonstruck Wolf

Thunder Wolf

Ghost Wolf

Outlaw Wolves

Wolf Unleashed